Blood Web

by Tessa Dawn

A Blood Curse Novel
Book Ten
In the Blood Curse Series

Published by Ghost Pines Publishing, LLC
Volume X of the Blood Curse Series by Tessa Dawn
First Edition Trade Paperback Published July 30, 2018 10 9 8 7 6 5 4 3 2 1
First Edition eBook Published July 30, 2018 10 9 8 7 6 5 4 3 2 1

Ghost Pines Publishing, LLC

CREDITS AND ACKNOWLEDGMENTS

Credits

Ghost Pines Publishing, LLC, *Publishing*
    Damonza, *Cover Art*
    Lidia Bircea, *Romanian Translations*
    Reba Hilbert, *Editing*

Passing Mentions

The Flintstones – An American animated sitcom, produced by Hanna-Barbera. Original broadcast: September 1960.

The Clan of the Cave Bear – A novel about prehistoric times by Jean M. Auel (*Earth's Children* book series). Original publication: May 1980.

For Wendy Lovetiggi

"In Ever-Loving Memory"

THE BLOOD CURSE

In 800 BC, Prince Jadon and Prince Jaegar Demir were banished from their Romanian homeland after being cursed by a ghostly apparition: the reincarnated Blood of their numerous female victims. The princes belonged to an ancient society that sacrificed its females to the point of extinction, and the punishment was severe.

They were forced to roam the earth in darkness as creatures of the night. They were condemned to feed on the blood of the innocent and stripped of their ability to produce female offspring. They were damned to father twin sons by human hosts who would die wretchedly upon giving birth; and the firstborn of the first set would forever be required as a sacrifice of atonement for the sins of their forefathers.

Staggered by the enormity of the Curse, Prince Jadon, whose own hands had never shed blood, begged his accuser for leniency and received four small mercies—four exceptions to the Curse that would apply to his house and his descendants, alone.

Ψ Though still creatures of the night, they would be allowed to walk in the sun.

Ψ Though still required to live on blood, they would not be forced to take the lives of the innocent.

Ψ While still incapable of producing female offspring, they would be given one opportunity and thirty days to obtain a mate —a human *destiny* chosen by the gods—following a sign that appeared in the heavens.

Ψ While they were still required to sacrifice a firstborn son, their twins would be born as one child of darkness and one child of light, allowing them to sacrifice the former while keeping the latter to carry on their race.

And so...forever banished from their homeland in the Transylvanian mountains of Eastern Europe, the descendants of Jaegar and the descendants of Jadon became the Vampyr of legend: roaming the earth, ruling the elements, living on the blood of others...forever bound by an ancient curse. They were brothers of the same species, separated only by degrees of light and shadow.

PROLOGUE

Natalia Giovanni sank deep into the cushions of the ten-thousand-dollar, custom-made sofa in her fit-for-a-palace bedroom, studying the intricate gold-and-red embroidery in the pillows as she powered up her laptop.

The World Wide Web was the only true escape she ever got from her life in a gilded cage.

She braided a thick band of her waist-length, dark-brown hair and folded it into a knot, just above her neck, to keep it off her shoulders—the luxurious, loosely waved tresses were compliments of a Tanzanian beauty queen for a mother and an Italian billionaire for a father, the former being gunned down in a business deal gone wrong when Natalia was only ten years old.

Ah, but then her father's business was sketchy at best.

Natalia didn't know if Luca Giovanni trafficked in illegal arms or drugs, along with the prostitution, but one thing she knew for sure: The women he kept housed in *The Fortress*, the name his henchman used for the enormous 25,000-square-foot building, surrounded by a ten-foot-high wall on their private 500-acre estate in Morrison, Colorado, were not there of their own free will. The fortress was divided by wings, or quadrants—north, south, east, and west—and from what Natalia had managed to discern over the years, her father kept his high-end call girls in the northern wing, his low-end prostitutes in the east, and the least fortunate of all in the south. Women he sold to be slaughtered.

She bit down on the rubber tip of a pencil, trying to dispel the thoughts.

It was inconceivable to Natalia that her once-beloved papa could traffic in a business so abhorrent. Who the hell purchased beautiful, innocent women for the sole purpose of taking their lives—in ways Natalia didn't dare to even imagine—and what kind of monster would kidnap, raise, or house such victims for years and years, only to sell them for top dollar, knowing their ultimate fate?

As for who he kept in the west, Natalia didn't care to speculate. She knew the southern wing brought $150,000 a head in trade, in *individual* sales. The sex slaves in the west brought $100,000 a head, so they must have been a very rare commodity —special, in their own right. And, ultimately, Natalia could do nothing about it.

Not any of it!

Her father had made one thing clear: Somewhere in the world, scattered amongst four separate countries, there were four ruthless mercenaries just waiting to receive their marching orders —five million dollars each to eliminate every living soul in The Fortress should the Giovanni compound ever be raided. Should Natalia Giovanni ever significantly disobey her father, leave the compound, or try to escape her life.

Should Natalia ever disappear.

Yes, Luca Giovanni had placed the lives of hundreds of helpless women squarely on Natalia's young shoulders. She held all their fates in her slender, elegant hands. She was Luca Giovanni's only child, and her father would rather see the world burn than live a day without Natalia present. In fact, his diabolical plan had gone further than that: Luca had placed the lethal contracts through his late attorney, Max Brazilian, and Max was the only one who knew the identities of the mercenaries—he was the only one who could call off the contracts.

And he'd taken that option with him to the grave.

Natalia sighed, staring at the bright-blue screen of her laptop as her programs came online, wondering for the millionth time if there wasn't some way around it. At only twenty-five years old, Natalia was a whiz with computers—hell, she was a virtual cyber-pirate—and there wasn't a website, firewall, or government security system Natalia couldn't hack. All it would take was a carefully placed email—or an anonymous letter sent to a dozen news organizations—to turn her father in and set the women free. But therein lay the rub: Could the FBI, CIA, or DEA move that quickly or efficiently? Could they get the women out in a matter of a few short hours—could they move them to safety before Max's mercenaries could strike?

Five million dollars was *a lot* of money.

Still, Natalia might have risked it if it weren't for the girl with the faery-princess eyes, the beautiful, innocent child with silver-blue irises that sparkled like finely spun glass, the four-year-old girl Natalia had seen on that terrifying, ill-fated night: the night Natalia had hidden in the back of a bodyguard's jeep in order to slip into The Fortress. The night her father had caught her and whipped her within an inch of her life.

Luca had never spanked Natalia before...or after.

And she had never forgotten those eyes: the eyes of a child growing up in captivity, a child only five years younger than Natalia...

She shook her head briskly to dismiss the thought.

There was no point to all the morbidity: It didn't free a single soul, and it didn't serve Natalia. Like the women in Luca's "*employ*," she was just trying to survive the hand that fate had dealt her.

Turning her attention to her cyber daydreams—her infinite need to escape—Natalia opened an elite social website and felt her stomach twitter with butterflies.

Where was he tonight?

And where had he gone?

Santos Olaru.

The dark, handsome stranger with crystal-blue eyes; unusual black-and-blond hair, with an occasional highlight of white; and teeth so perfect, so pearly white, they gleamed like a string of jewels: Natalia's strikingly handsome, cut-like-a-statue, imaginary cyber-boyfriend.

She had spied on him, cyberstalked him, and hacked into the places he'd hacked, eventually acquiring his first and last name, while watching the way he worked, just because he'd so impressed—and intrigued—her.

Hell, the man moved like a ghost in the machine.

In and out of secured, encrypted systems, without leaving the barest footprint.

Planting documents, or uploading information, without the host ever knowing he was there.

He was like a virtual magician, and Natalia had been watching him for years...

From a distance...

From the Web.

But it was only last year, on December 31st, that she'd managed to finally see a picture of the otherwise secretive and elusive hacker: a photo of the tall, stunning Adonis standing next to two other men at a New Year's Eve party in Dark Moon Vale.

At the Dark Moon Vale Casino, to be exact.

He looked like he might have been on security detail, at least from the way he was dressed, and for whatever reasons, perhaps to set the guests at ease, all three men in the photo were wearing nametags: Santos, Saxson, and Ramsey.

A guest of the casino had snapped the picture and uploaded it onto her social media page. And who could blame her? The men were pure, unadulterated eye-candy! Still, it was the only photo, the only ID of any kind Natalia had ever managed to find of Santos.

He had removed the photo within one hour, but Natalia already had it.

She logged into iChat Platinum with her fictitious name, ArabianNight500, and immediately scanned the page for his avatar: Sentinel2000. Clever. He had to be searching for something...or someone... Santos didn't chat with mere mortals. She chuckled at the silly thought. Of course she pretended he was a god; why not? In Natalia's eyes, Santos Olaru was far more handsome, brilliant, and slick than any man she'd ever met. And she'd managed to grab his attention, if only for a second, using a clever end-around technique where she'd bypassed his log-in, without knowing his password, and placed a pop-up chat box of her own making directly on his page.

He had hesitated for the space of two heartbeats before typing: *Who are you? How did you get in?* And that's when Natalia had logged off and added five layers of encryption. She didn't want Santos Olaru tracking her... The trail he would find would go back for years.

Twirling her pencil through her fingers, she inhaled sharply when she saw his bright-blue icon light up. So, he was there... online. She took a slow, deep breath, trying to muster her courage, and reopened the end-around chat.

What the hell.

It was now or never.

Natalia had just turned twenty-five earlier that month, and her father was determined to see her married before she turned twenty-six. He was planning to give her away to an imposing brute of a man, Oskar Vadovsky, with long, dark hair that seemed naturally black and red, and eyes the color of used charcoals: slate gray and black. Without conscience, clemency, or pity, Luca Giovanni intended to toss Natalia out of the Giovanni compound like so much expendable garbage, for one compelling reason and one reason only: to secure the business relationship between Giovanni, Inc. and its most lucrative, longest-standing client.

Natalia had pleaded with her father, on more than one occasion, not to do it, not to give her to Oskar. She had even dropped to her knees and begged. But Oskar Vadovsky made Luca Giovanni millions and millions of dollars each year, purchasing the southern-wing women.

Natalia was not supposed to know this.

She was not supposed to know that her future husband was a stone-cold killer.

The marriage was supposed to be a blood-bond contract between the Giovannis and the Vadovskys, a joining of their two powerful houses, and her father swore that Oskar would treat Natalia like a princess and provide her with the life she was accustomed to. After all, the man was supposed to be highly invested in their "ongoing joint ventures"—he wouldn't dare cross Luca Giovanni.

No one would.

Still, Natalia would rather die than marry the dark, tainted brute.

The man did not possess a soul.

Unfortunately—and for whatever reason—Oskar really wanted Natalia.

And that was the beginning, middle, and end of the subject.

Turning her attention back to her screen—and the fabricated, open iChat box—she stared at her keyboard and vacillated: Natalia would never know love. She would never know what it felt like to want something...or touch someone...from the truest depths of her soul. Reaching out from across the Internet to her imaginary, fantasy lover, Santos, was the closest she might ever come. And time was running out—she may as well do it.

Are you there? She typed the words in lowercase letters, literally holding her breath.

No answer.

She would have to be bolder.

Santos? Now this should get his attention. His name was supposed to be Sentinel2000.

I'm here, he shot back. *What is your real name?*

Holy cow!

Natalia slammed the laptop shut.

Santos Olaru had responded to her!

She jumped up from the couch, paced around the bedroom, and shook out her hands to dispel the nervous energy.

Holy hell!

He had spoken to her!

Squeezing her braid and squealing with delight, she hurried back to the sofa and reopened the screen. *ArabianNight500,* she typed, biting her lower lip so hard it left an indentation.

Ah. He typed fast. *ArabianNight500...I see. So you aren't going to tell me?*

I just did, she typed. *I'm afraid that has to be good enough.*

She felt her heart sink into her stomach—would he be annoyed? Or worse, disappointed? Would he think she was playing games?

She wasn't!

It was just...

It was just that she had to be careful.

Extremely, *extremely* careful...

Her father was a dangerous man, and her life was strictly off-limits. Her true identity could never be known. Still, she wanted this connection more than she wanted water, more than she wanted her next breath.

But what if she had already turned him off?

The laptop fan began to hum beneath her, even as the soft, pastel glow illuminated the couch. Natalia bit her nails. "C'mon, Santos," she whispered beneath her breath. "Say something...*anything*." When her eyes misted with tears, she knew she was a foolish little girl.

She was an idiot.

A child.

A twenty-five-year-old virgin who had been born into a criminal empire.

An expert hacker who was toying with the very best—her superior.

And she had just tainted the only pure, untouched fantasy— the only potential coveted friendship—she had ever hoped to contrive.

The daydream that kept her sane.

One minute turned into five, then five turned into ten, and Natalia felt sick to her stomach. Wiping her eyes with the back of her hand, she reached for the screen to close it: "*Stupid, stupid, stupid,*" she whispered.

He was too smart to play silly games with a child.

And then her screen lit up with a message from Santos.

Natalia...

Giovanni...

Where are you?

Can we meet?

* * *

Santos Olaru leaned back in his leather recliner, staring at the wall of monitors in his modern glass-and-steel domicile beside a private lake on the northwest end of Dark Moon Vale. The moonlight was shimmering like a spotlight on the serene, crystal water below, and it merged with the glow of his monitors, creating a peaceful halo effect.

She was at it again.

The human female.

Playing her coy cyber-games and following Santos all over the Web.

From what he could tell, she had followed him for years.

At first, he had found it cute...entertaining...something to cut through the boredom on his house of Jadon days off, but now, it was no longer amusing. The woman was an expert hacker, and for a moment, she had gotten the best of him, with her multiple layers of diversion and encryption.

But this time, the vampire had been ready.

Ready to follow her, ready to slip into her machine, ready to trace her expertly disguised, hidden address...the moment she reopened the chat box.

Only what he'd found was chilling.

The IP address led back to Luca Giovanni, the reclusive billionaire. And the human female's administrative credentials led back to several expensive software purchases, all under the name of Natalia. A quick scan of vital records, and Santos Olaru knew, at least with 95 percent certainty, that he was being followed...through cyberspace...by Giovanni's daughter.

What. The. Hell.

Human concerns—even human crimes—were off-limits to the house of Jadon.

Napolean's law was inviolable!

But this?

This was something altogether different.

Jocelyn Levi had come to Dark Moon Vale as an agent of ICE, investigating a human-trafficking ring, one she believed was run by Luca Giovanni, but she had never had a chance to follow up. It was no longer her concern: no longer her job...no longer within her legal purview.

Not to mention, she got derailed by Shelby and Dalia's tragic story.

By her and Nathaniel's Blood Moon.

But then Xavier Matista, a lycan enemy from the land of Mhier, had interfered with Saxson's *Blood Destiny*, holding the woman hostage for nearly a week while he'd kept another human sex slave in the Swingle-Duplex Suites: a pair of lavish Denver penthouses owned by Giovanni, Inc.

According to Nachari Silivasi, Zayda Patrone—Keitaro's wild, feral guest who just happened to be Xavier's biological daughter—was the offspring of one of Luca's human prostitutes, born in some nefarious brick structure where she grew up as a slave.

It was all supposed to be a coincidence.

Until now...

Luca Giovanni's daughter, following Santos on the Web...

For years?

This was no accident.

It couldn't be.

ArabianNight500—*my ass!*

He hit a button to activate voice dictation and spoke each word, including punctuation, clearly: *Natalia,* ellipsis. *Giovanni,* ellipsis. *Where are you,* question mark. *Can we meet,* question mark.

It didn't matter if she answered in the affirmative...

He was already looking up her physical address from an incredibly reliable source: her most recent bank statement.

CHAPTER ONE

S antos Olaru enlarged the screen in the upper left quadrant of a series of monitors, zeroing in on Natalia's bank statement, specifically, the paragraph at the top: Pine Ridge Credit Union; Giovanni, Inc.; Natalia Giovanni; 231 Upper Mill Creek Road; Morrison, Colorado...

He had it.

Her address.

He leaned forward in the soft, comfortable recliner and fixed both crystal-blue peepers on the center screen, once again worrying his full bottom lip with his upper teeth. "C'mon, sweetheart," he drawled beneath his breath. "Answer the question, Natalia girl. *Can. We. Meet?*"

Thanks to his heightened vampiric senses, what might have been a low, audible hum, buzzing from the base of his PC unit, was rapidly approaching a steady, high-pitched drone: His heartbeat quickened, his mind on high alert, and he began to tap his fingers on the edge of his desk, rolling them in quick succession like a highly skilled drum major.

"Speak to me, baby," he murmured beneath his breath.

Time stood still.

And then the iChat box began to glow with a pulsing, incandescent light, which informed Santos that Natalia was typing.

Not possible, she shot back.

Why not? he asked.

No answer.

Returning to the upper left screen, he maneuvered the mouse, entered some code, and slipped effortlessly into the Department of Motor Vehicles' main frame, where he entered Natalia's full name and address. While he waited for a photo ID or a driver's license to pop up, he dictated another line in the center screen's chat box: *You've been following me for years.* He was no longer playing games. *I know you're intrigued, baby girl. And so am I. Why not meet?*

He might have been flirting too hard, but he didn't think so—something about this woman struck him as unusually lonely, perhaps even isolated...an island unto herself.

If hesitation, nervousness, and fear could have shown up on a screen, then Santos' monitor would have been pulsing to the rhythm of a frantic heartbeat—Natalia's discomfort was just that palpable, her chaotic energy mixing with the signals in the Wi-Fi.

Just what *was* her game? he wondered.

So she knew she'd been caught—cyberstalking, that is—but so what?

Santos played his own fair share of virtual hide-and-seek. If anything, she should have been proud, perhaps even arrogant, about how deftly she had matched his cyber prowess.

Natalia???

She didn't respond.

Speak to me, angel, he tried again. *We're hardly strangers...right?*

Her driver's license popped up in the upper left quadrant,

and Santos had to catch his breath. *Whoa.* Typically, state IDs resembled hideous, nondescript mugshots, but there was nothing typical—or nondescript—about Natalia *Antoinette* Giovanni. He studied her photo in earnest: long, luxurious hair, falling all the way to her waist; perfectly sculpted brows framing dark, mesmerizing eyes; a nose that could have been painted by Michelangelo, such was the structural perfection; and lips—holy hell, that bottom lip—Santos could almost taste it.

He turned his attention to a light-green bar expanding slowly...horizontally...across the top left screen. Eighty percent. He was almost there. He was *this close* to being logged into Natalia's computer: *this close* to accessing her files; *this close* to downloading her calendar; and *this close* to viewing her photo library. "C'mon, cyber-magic; you're workin' with a powerful CPU. Just a little bit more."

A pale glint of moonlight streamed through the floor-to-ceiling windows towering above the crystal lake, and as if interacting with a prism, the moonbeams cast a subtle red halo against the living room wall, causing the hairs on Santos' arms to prickle and a corner of his heart to soften.

Like all the sentinels in the house of Jadon, Santos Olaru was merciless when it came to protecting the Vampyr's interest or hacking a human's computer, especially the daughter of Luca Giovanni's—Natalia was no exception—however, something told him he might want to approach this with a softer touch...

No sooner had the thought crossed his mind than Natalia's reply popped up: *SANTOS.* She typed each letter in caps on a single line—was she angry? *I have to go!*

Santos leaned forward in his chair, deciding to push harder, faster, stronger.

He had to keep her attention.

You live at 231 Upper Mill Creek Road, he shot back, hoping to startle her with the information. *Don't go, Natalia.* The vintage clock, sitting on a sleek, high-gloss steel shelf just above his desk, ticked ten times, the seconds advancing like hours, as Santos waited for Natalia's reply. He stared at the dual, old-fashioned hands adorning the Roman numerals; he unwittingly rocked to the timepiece's rhythm; and he twirled the end of a number-two pencil.

You know where I reside? she asked.

He smiled reflexively. *I do.*

Stay away!!! she shot back, the outburst catching Santos off guard.

I'm not going to hurt you, Natalia. He chose his words very carefully. *As I said before, I'm deeply intrigued. You've followed me, and now you've found me—why not bring the cat-and-mouse game to a close? I could come to your front door, but I imagine your father would frown on that. Giovanni, correct? You're Luca's daughter. Meet me, Natalia girl. I want to see the eyes and the smile behind all those brains.* He sat back and waited, wondering if he hadn't gone too far this time, pushed a bit too hard, whether flirting might have been the wrong approach.

Still...

Something in his gut, something in his instincts, was screaming: *Dangle a romantic carrot! This woman is savvy. She's smart.* And she may even be cunning or dangerous, but all she had done—following Santos for *years,* creating layers upon layers of encryption between them, just to fashion her own end-around chat box—was all in order to meet him. No, Natalia Giovanni was more than just curious...and industrious. The female was lonely, and she was equally intrigued by Santos. She wanted something...intimate...a connection with another soul, even if the connection was through the safety of a computer.

Please, she wrote cryptically. *I—*

She skipped a line and tried a different word. *You—*

Yet another line and another entry: *If you really do know who I am—*

I know who you are, he interrupted.

Then you know that us...that we...that meeting is virtually impossible.

Santos stared at that last sentence like it was written in Greek, but before he could fashion a shrewd reply, the light-green horizontal bar in the upper left screen reached 100 percent.

He was inside Natalia's computer!

He toggled through her programs first, using vampiric speed and alacrity to store them in his photographic memory, and once he had the programs stored, his analytical mind began to race: What to view first? What to save first? He might only have a couple of minutes. He stopped at her calendar, opened the month of June, and began to take a series of screenshots, just as a flashing red warning popped up on his monitor.

Incoming Virus!

EXIT NOW!

The program you have accessed may be harmful to your computer!

Son of a jackal, Natalia had caught him—that quick—and if he didn't act fast, she was going to infect his entire system.

Growling in frustration, Santos closed all the open windows, backed out of Natalia's machine, and shut down his PC—he would reboot it in a couple of minutes, check for any damage, and see if he had managed to grab the screenshots of her calendar...or any other data.

Rising from his anxious perch in the familiar leather recliner, he paced across the white-oak floors to the glistening wall of windows and stared down at the placid lake below, drawing from its tranquil energy. He brushed an absent hand through his black-and-blond locks, and then he smiled wolfishly...

Natalia Antoinette Giovanni...

Coy, beautiful, and smart as a whip.

Now that was a human woman he could pass some time with. He sighed...

But then again, she was Luca Giovanni's daughter, and he had to keep that fact in mind.

Luca had imprisoned a half-human, half-Lycan sex slave in a brick fortress on his property, and more than likely, Giovanni, Inc. had been supplying the Dark Ones with human sacrifices—women to procreate with and dispose of—for years, if not decades. Natalia may or may not be innocent of her father's crimes. She may or may not be involved. And beyond that troubling information, there was the matter of General Xavier Matista: a degenerate lycan from Mhier who had used that same sex slave—his very own daughter, Zayda—to incite and bait Keitaro Silivasi, the day Keitaro and his son Nachari had found her in the Swingle-Duplex penthouse.

Too many enemies.

Too many coincidences.

Too many overlapping layers.

If Santos had managed to save a legible copy of Natalia's schedule, then absolutely, the two of them would meet.

And soon.

But not for a romantic liaison.

In the meantime, Santos would pull some satellite images of the Giovanni compound, try to get the blueprints for Luca's (and Natalia's) residence. He would pay a visit to Keitaro at the old Silivasi homestead, on the northeastern end of the vale, and see what the Ancient Master Warrior had discovered. Keitaro had been nursing Zayda back to health for the past four months; perhaps after all this time, he had managed to make a breakthrough.

Perhaps Zayda had revealed something useful.

Regarding the moon's reflection on the crystal lake below,

Santos thought about the house of Jadon and his duty as one of its four sentinels. Both Ramsey and Saxson were mated now, and maybe that was why he felt so restless, so solitary...why a part of him could relate to Natalia. He didn't yet know how the pieces of this puzzle would intersect, but he was definitely up to the challenge...and the distraction.

CHAPTER TWO

I n the corner of her bedroom, Natalia stuffed her laptop
inside the elegant Louis XIV walnut armoire, slammed the
ornate panel doors shut, and leaned against the antique
wood as if she could simply shut out the distress of all that had
happened—lock Santos Olaru out of her life and her mind—by
turning her back on the related equipment.

Lord have mercy...

*You've been following me for years...I know you're intrigued,
and so am I.*

The man was so direct.

Why not meet?

He couldn't be serious!

We're hardly strangers...right?

Oh, they were definitely strangers, and it needed to stay
that way.

I know who you are...Luca Giovanni's daughter.

How much did Santos know about her father?

*Meet me, Natalia girl. I want to see the eyes and the smile
behind all those brains.*

The man was the devil in blue jeans, and if his smooth, sexy banter hadn't been enough to underscore that point, he had hacked into her computer and begun to sort through her files! How in the world had he done that?

Natalia braced one hand on her lower belly and drew in a deep breath of air, trying to quiet her racing mind: A fantasy was one thing—imagining the exquisite, crystal-eyed stranger as some kind of friend, an imaginary lover, and a make-believe escape— but meeting him, speaking to him, actually standing in the same space and time as the powerful, gorgeous, flesh-and-blood man? That was quite another matter.

No way.

No how.

Natalia's heart would give out, and her knees would buckle beneath her.

She wrung her hands together, then shook them out to relieve some tension.

I'm not going to hurt you, Natalia, he had said, but hurt her, he had...already.

He knew where she lived. He had her full address. And he had stepped into her room, burrowed into her laptop, and entered her sacred space as easily—and eerily—as mist traveled through fog.

Her father would kill him.

Oskar would kill him.

Hell, knowing Natalia would be Santos' demise...

And even if he made it out of the encounter alive, could she really withstand his presence, dare to meet him in person, give in to a singular flight of fancy, even for one evening? Or would she be just like Eve in the garden of Eden, staring at that damnable apple, contemplating the repercussions of taking just one little bite...

Hell, Natalia wasn't stupid.

She might be ignorant, naive, and even pathetic, but she wasn't entirely brainless.

Her life was owned by her father, and it was soon to be owned by Oskar Vadovsky—her future was sealed and prescribed. Not to mention, there were dozens of women living in a stronghold less than seven miles away on the Giovanni property, and each and every one of their lives depended upon Natalia's obedience.

She could never be that selfish.

Romeo and Juliet...Marc Antony and Cleopatra...Prince Paris and Helen of Troy—all romantic stories that came to tragic ends.

Love was not a game.

Lust was not a low-cost wager.

And Natalia was not a fool.

She had no doubt that Santos had blocked the virus—and if not, he could easily reverse the damage—but that was the beginning and the end of their short, interactive dalliance...such as it had been. Once Natalia had taken a long, hot shower, cleared her mind, and slipped into a comfortable pair of familiar pajamas, she would retrieve her laptop and do the unthinkable: She would remove every trace of Santos Olaru from her life, her world, and her hard drive. From her memory and her imagination. She would delete iChat Platinum from her machine and erase the end-around chat box, once and for all.

She would wash her hands—forever—of Sentinel2000.

He was a childhood fantasy she could no longer afford.

CHAPTER THREE

The Next Morning

S ettled in an easy divan, Santos Olaru stretched out his legs on the top tier of the polished, stamped-concrete deck, which sat on four massive stone pillars atop a second, lower tier, each overlooking the serene private lake. He shuffled through several satellite images of Upper Mill Creek Road in Morrison, Colorado, studying the unique topography in each of the frames.

From what he could garner from the aerial views—as well as a set of blueprints he had studied the night before—the Giovanni compound was nestled in a well-fortified valley, bookended by two lofty canyons and erected parallel to the Winding Mill Creek River, which flanked the entire property. Depending on the season, the gulch might be filled with flowing water or dry as a bone. Either way, the enormous family residence sat forward on the southwest corner of the property, almost abutting the road, and a massive white-brick building—hell, it was more like a modern castle, a fortress of sorts—sat farther back on the property in the distal northeast, about six or seven miles from the family home. The river ran behind both structures, a few acres back, and several well-worn roads snaked between the two prominent structures, the second one—the one that looked like a castle—surrounded by an ominous, ten-foot-high wall.

There were also several outbuildings: perhaps huts, housing guards, or cottages for servants; maybe guest houses or supply stores...who knew. One way or another, it was a fortified complex, as opulent and luxurious as it was naturally defended. Natalia had grown up in the lap of luxury, but for all intents and purposes, she existed in a corrupt, gilded cage.

Santos turned his attention to another set of images—screenshots of Natalia Giovanni's personal calendar. Yep, he had managed to snap three good images of the female's schedule before she had launched a counterattacking virus, one that he had managed to avoid just in the nick of time.

Mondays, Wednesdays, and Fridays, she went to the gym. Apparently, she liked to swim, take Pilates, and jog around an indoor track. Tuesdays and Thursdays, she alternated between the salon—hair, nails, or massage—and some sort of outing: shopping, a lunch date, some charitable or public event. It was obvious at a glance that Natalia was Luca Giovanni's public persona, like a mascot or a pet. He paraded her around like a pretty, prized pony for all the world to see, and he invested in her outward appearance—her looks, her body, her attire—like one might invest in stocks. No doubt, she was lucrative to his image, pivotal in selling Giovanni, Inc. as an upstanding and oh-so-attractive community-focused corporation.

What a crock of shit.

Question was: Did Natalia participate in the public circus with full knowledge of her father's crimes? Was she a major player in the human-trafficking ring, or was she being used like all of Giovanni's unfortunate girls? Just how long had Giovanni, Inc.

been providing human women to the Dark Ones, most likely unknowingly, and how the hell did the lycans fit in? When the hell did Xavier Matista find out about the compound and the sex slaves—based on Zayda's age, he'd known for at least twenty-one-years—and how was it that the two mortal enemies, the Lycanthrope and the Vampyr, had never crossed paths? The result would have been major bloodshed.

Santos zeroed in on today's date: Thursday, June 16th.

Natalia would be at the salon: a two-hour, deep-tissue massage at 8:00 PM.

Much later than her usual appointment, but the time would work.

In fact, being that the sun generally set around 8:30, this early in summer, the timing would actually be optimal—it would provide the HOJ sentinel with the cover of darkness, providing a nocturnal creature's playground. After all, the night belonged to the Vampyr...

To Santos' way of thinking, men like Luca often used legitimate commercial businesses to clean their dirty money, and a quick search of public records had confirmed what Santos suspected: Giovanni, Inc. owned both the Max Fitness Gym and the Serenity Salon & Spa. More than likely, anyone working at such a late hour was under Luca's *special* employ, and that just meant Santos had to be careful. He needed to slip in undetected and scrub the female's memories before he made his way back home.

Easy peasy.

Piece of cake.

Humans were no match for vampires.

Dismissing all concern, he turned his attention to the next string of items on his agenda: stopping by Saxson and Kiera's cliffside estate, letting his brother know what was up—what Santos was into—and making sure Saxson brought Saber into the loop. The king had already given the sentinels the thumbs-up to investigate the compound to the fullest, and as for Keitaro Silivasi? Well, the Ancient Master Warrior wanted Blood Vengeance on Xavier Matista worse than Saxson did. Yes, Xavier had held Kiera hostage, given her to a band of nut-job vampire-hunters, and put Saxson's *destiny* through pure, unadulterated hell—but Keitaro's grievance was far more severe: The Alpha General of the Western District Pack in the Lycan world of Mhier was one cruel, brutal, son of a bitch, quite literally, and as one of the late King Thane's inner circle, Xavier had reveled in torturing Keitaro in the slave camps for centuries before the Ancient Master Warrior's sons had brought him home. If anyone was going to have the pleasure of ripping out the general's throat, it was going to be Keitaro Silivasi.

Rising from his languid repose on the divan, Santos headed inside the glass-and-steel house.

First stop: Saxson's estate.

Second stop: Keitaro's homestead.

Third stop, later that evening, the Serenity Salon & Spa.

It was time to meet Natalia Giovanni in person.

Deep in the underbelly of the Dark Ones' Colony, Oskar Vadovsky sat at the head of the council table and glared at the remaining subordinate council members: Milano Marandici, Demitri Zeclos, Sergei Gervasi, and Salvatore Nistor, the idiotic but invaluable sorcerer for the house of Jaegar.

If one of these bastards questioned him again, he was going to lose his shit.

Yes, he understood their concerns, and he had answered their incessant questions with undue patience. But at the end of the day, *Oskar* was the chairman of the council—no one else—and as leader, his word was inviolable. Hadn't he proved that point, beyond question, just two short years ago when he had violated Salvatore on this very table, with all eyes watching? When he had removed Milano's eye and Demitri's right testicle as punishment for insubordination—hell, insurrection and treason—refusing to allow the powerful vampires to heal their wounds?

He glanced at Milano, making note of the gruesome scar running from the lateral side of the male's left temple to the corner of his insolent mouth, and he knew he had made his point. The fact that Salvatore could no longer look Oskar in the eyes for more than a fleeting second spoke volumes, in and of itself: Indeed, Oskar had made himself crystal clear to Salvatore as well. Vadovsky chuckled inwardly, eyeing Sergei Gervasi, who was sitting at the opposite end of the table. The male had no freakin' idea that his father, the previous Council Chair, Stefano Gervasi, had been murdered by Sergei's fellow council members.

He had no idea that Milano, Demitri, and Salvatore had butchered Stefano like a lamb cornered in a slaughterhouse, in order to appeal to the Dark Lords for favor—that the trio had hoped to purchase victory against Napolean Mondragon, and the price had been Stefano's blood.

That shit hadn't worked.

But the guilt and the shame—such as it was—had compelled the threesome to decorate Sergei with his father's honors *and* to install him on the Dark Ones' Council. To this day, the lie remained: Stefano, in all his fury, had gone after Napolean himself, and the venerable Chief of Council had died in the ensuing one-to-one battle.

Hogwash.

This council was filled with mutinous traitors, which was why Oskar kept one Master at Arms to his left and another on his right; it was why two members of the Colony Guard remained outside the chamber doors.

It was why Oskar was not about to take any shit from these bloodthirsty cocksuckers.

The tips of his fingers began to glow as he punctuated his words with animated gestures. "For the last time," he groaned, "I get it. Our own Nistor brothers, along with the house of Jadon's Silivasi jackasses, more or less destroyed the ancient cavern, the secret chamber in the belly of the Red Canyons where we brought our human captives to birth our beloved sons...where we watched them die in agony and sacrificed our firstborn to the Blood. Yet we are still beholden to the Curse. *I get it*," he reiterated with a guttural growl. "And Luca Giovanni has provided a valuable alternative; he has given us a convenient and easy substitution. We have always purchased his female slaves for our sacrifices—Nathaniel Silivasi's stupid mate was wise enough to figure that out, for all the good it did her—but now, we do more than purchase the piteous, doomed females. We use Luca's underground chamber, the basement beneath The Fortress, to carry out our sacrificial ceremonies, and the humans are none the wiser. A one-stop shop. Yes!" he thundered. "I get it." He clasped his hands behind his back and continued, dropping his voice to a lethal purr. "So why fuck it up?"

Milano leaned forward in his chair, his one good green eye practically glowing with anticipation...and hope.

"Because Natalia Giovanni is simply exquisite. Her body is perfection; her face is a work of art; and her mind—her intelligence—is damn near flawless. Is there any other human woman worthy of bearing my offspring, bringing my firstborn son into this world? Is there any other host whose death would be more glorious; whose suffering would be more orgasmic; whose body I would rather desecrate and ravage?"

The council chamber fell silent, and Demitri turned away.

"Makes your ball itch, boy, doesn't it?" Oskar chuckled. He knew Sergei wouldn't catch the singular reference to only one gonad, but the other council members would, and it was worth the timely reminder. "Who is Luca to question me?" Oskar continued. "He may be a dangerous criminal; he may be a notorious thug; he may even be a human monster—but to me, to us, to the immortal Vampyr, he is a bug to be squashed beneath our feet. Luca will do as I bid him. He will believe whatever I tell him to believe. He will think the thoughts I give him and offer the gifts I demand from him. He will continue to provide his slaves and his fortress for as long as I see fit. Taking Natalia. Killing Natalia. Using Luca's daughter to spawn my seed will not affect our arrangement, and frankly, I've grown tired of the discussion. No, I will not choose another woman. It is time for me to fulfill the demands of the Curse and secure my immortality." Standing to his full six-feet, two-inch height and flexing all two hundred pounds of hard-steel muscle, Oskar brushed his long, twisted black-and-red locks behind his shoulder and glided backward in the slink of a panther. "Does anyone...have anything...else to say?" The pauses were laced with vitriol, and the words were drenched in sarcasm.

Salvatore Nistor suppressed a smirk and cocked his brows upward, a gesture that accentuated his stark widow's peak. "Your Excellency," he drawled in a fake, arrogant tone, "your reasoning has assuaged our concerns. If you would like to go through the machinations of pursuing a human courtship...continuing to attend dinners you can't even eat at the Giovannis' compound...if you wish to continue dating Luca's daughter in order to garner her father's favor, as opposed to, oh, I don't know"—he shrugged a haughty shoulder—"simply placing a compulsion in the bastard's head, shagging the girl on the dining room table, and getting the whole sordid game over with, once and for all, then by all means, we support your need to play with your toys. We only ask that you keep us in the loop and let us know when the recreation grows tiresome."

Oskar licked his bottom lip.

One of these days, he was going to kill that insolent bastard.

He stepped forward and stared at the council table. "Shag the girl on top of the table?" he mocked. "Interesting suggestion—tabletops and sex." He let the words linger for all but Sergei to consider. "Do you think she would enjoy that, Salvatore?"

The ancient sorcerer gulped, his pupils shifting between black and red.

Oskar licked his lips again, and on a private, telepathic bandwidth, he added, *Did you enjoy it, vampire? The tabletop, that is?*

Salvatore's long, urbane fingers curled into fists even as his expression hardened to stone.

Oskar smiled amiably. He could be as fake as the next vampire. "For the record, it is my intention to compel Giovanni to continue our lucrative arrangement even after Natalia is gone. I would rather not have to control the minds, behaviors, and memories of all Giovanni's henchmen, the entire fortress full of guards, his family, his business associates, and every other Tom, Dick, and Lackey that gets wind of Natalia's death. However, I shall take Salvatore's sage advice into consideration and let everyone know when I am finished...playing with my toy." He swept his hand in a graceful yet demeaning arc. "Alas, I have lived a long time. Sometimes games are a welcome distraction. Does anyone else have something to add?"

Demitri shifted uncomfortably in his seat.

Milano scratched his scarred temple.

And Sergei glanced around the room, obviously clueless, like he had missed the first course of a delicious meal or failed to grasp the punch line of an inside joke...which, in truth, he had.

"Very well," Oskar intoned. "Now that Natalia Giovanni is no longer an issue, let us move to more important council business."

CHAPTER FOUR

The original Silivasi Homestead

Keitaro Silivasi sauntered languidly across the wide wraparound front porch, luxuriating in the mid-afternoon scent of juniper and pine as a balmy summer breeze flowed through the valley. In the past four months, he had managed to finish the new rustic portico which encircled the entire house; add two spare bedrooms to the existing master—one for his grandchildren so he could keep them overnight, and another for Zayda so she didn't have to come near Keitaro's Valencia canopy bed; the four large posts were far too reminiscent of stakes and chains to expect the girl to sleep in it—and he had finished the kitchen by necessity. Unlike Keitaro's species, the Vampyr, a half-human, half-Lycan female did have to fuel her body with protein, fiber, fat, and carbohydrates.

Human fare.

Lycan fare.

Zayda couldn't exist on blood.

While he was still working on the front sitting room and the foyer, he was pleased with the ever-expanding progress. To Keitaro's way of thinking, the sitting room was welcoming enough with its floor-to-ceiling, smoothed-stone fireplace; a row of skylights that welcomed the morning sun—as well as the nocturnal moonlight—and the comfortable, overstuffed furniture that Zayda had taken to like a cat to a cozy basket. He arched to stretch his back and considered Zayda's progress: She was quiet, like a mouse, incredibly withdrawn and wholly reserved, and she no longer acted feral. She didn't swipe at his face, try to destroy the furniture, hurl construction objects across the wide-planked floors, or scream at the top of her lungs for no apparent reason.

And she no longer reached for his groin—*thank the celestial gods and goddesses.*

Over the past five or six weeks, she had dropped the X-rated lingo, quit trying to seduce him, and she was no longer overtly sexual. More or less, she had ceased her constant weeping and trembling. In short, Keitaro had managed to gain her trust—well, some trust...a little trust. Zayda was still wary at best, but she no longer expected him to violate her, and she no longer sought to appease his base masculine appetites, assuming as she had before that all males were driven by their primal, carnal longings, however sick or twisted.

He blinked several times, and a low, nearly inaudible growl escaped his throat.

It was abhorrent what the female had been through.

Nachari had been correct—she had been born into sexual slavery, and she had been traded her entire life, like so much garbage, beginning at an age that made Keitaro want to murder an entire village. But at least she had not been sold for torture...

Until Xavier...

And lords knew the bastard had made up for missing time.

He had abused the hell out of his own flesh and blood—his

biological daughter—though he likely had no idea who she was when he bought her.

Strolling to the edge of the deck, Keitaro surveyed his property, admiring the acres upon acres of wild land and appreciating all the varied, rough-hewn boulders, the towering pines, and the swaying aspens. He regarded the numerous bushels of wildflowers and scattered pine cones, the randomly placed native shrubs and grasses that dotted the ancient homestead, and he zeroed in with absolute precision, one by one, on all the Lycan wards, the wolf traps that surrounded the homestead like a field of land mines.

Sooner or later, Xavier would come.

That is, if the general had any balls.

And just in case he didn't, the vampires were doing their best to egg him on.

Week after week, Keitaro and Nachari left cryptic notes at the lavish Swingle penthouse, sometimes taped to the door, sometimes shoved beneath it, sometimes attached to a rock that just happened to fly through an expensive window. Xavier may have already vacated the premises, but if any lycan visited the building...even once...his wolf would catch the scent: Zayda's blood, strained and diluted with Xavier's DNA accentuated by a Master Wizard, enhanced via Nachari's magic.

The missives stank like the werewolf.

They had Xavier's fingerprints all over them.

Vampires—one and all—whoever finds this missive; salutations from the land of Mhier! I trust you have found my pet. Please feel free to use her (she's like a wildcat: hungry, savage, and oh so responsive). Don't bother to track me all over this city; I've returned to my world, beyond the portal.

But do not fret; we'll meet again...

When you least fucking expect it!

General Matista

That was the missive Xavier had left.

Canines, lykos, loup-garou—but especially Xavier Matista—salutations from Dark Moon Vale!

We welcome you to the valley: any day, any time of your choosing...

We hope you have the courage to see your threats through.

Come out from the portal and play!

Curious as to why—how—we have your DNA? What else do we know about the so-called general, besides the fact that he's impotent, afraid, and weak?

By all means, stop by whenever you get the urge; we don't even require an RSVP.

These were the missives Keitaro and Nachari left...week after week...after week.

And each note, without exception, had Keitaro Silivasi's address stamped on the bottom, lest the general get lost or forget where to go...where to show up...who it was that was dying to see him.

In truth, there was no way—absolutely none—that a band of lycans were going to come through the portal and wage a war with the Vampyr in Dark Moon Vale. Been there. Done that. They'd all bought the bloody T-shirts. And the Silivasis had left the lycans' world—their government and hierarchy—in virtual ruin. The werewolves no longer possessed the organization, strength, or numbers to contend with their mortal enemies, at least not in a full-scale war.

But General Matista?

He was one arrogant son of a canis.

Eventually, his pride would get the best of him, and his temper would snap.

When it did, Keitaro hoped to confront him man to man—vampire to lycan. But just in case, and at his king's and sons' insistence, the wolf traps, the lycan wards, were wired to go off at each

Silivasi household simultaneously. Every member of the Silivasi family would hear the alarms the moment Xavier tripped the magical wires. And for added protection, Keitaro had cached a hoard of weapons beneath the planks of his remodeled front porch in an easily accessible trunk. There was a spiked cestus awaiting Marquis; an M4 carbine, cleaned and oiled, with Nathaniel's name all over it; a set of rusty scalpels, too antiquated and bizarre to contemplate, placed *just so* for Kagen; and a sickle, plus a sword, polished to a shimmering gleam, tucked safely away for Nachari—as if the wizard or the panther needed either one.

Just the same, the *destinies* had also insisted: If the grandchildren were going to stay overnight, then Keitaro's sons—the Silivasi brothers—could be no more than a heartbeat away: weapons ready, strategy prepared, able to defend the homestead and the grandkids in an instant. Naturally, Keitaro had acquiesced to all his daughters' requests—he wouldn't have had it any other way.

"Car." Zayda Patrone stepped out on the porch and looked off into the distance, her voice as monotone as it was hushed. "Someone's coming."

Keitaro's muscles tightened; he closed his eyes and listened for the sound of tires kicking up gravel in the distance. Next, he scented the air for the odor of flesh versus fur, and then he slowly nodded. Zayda was right—maybe three miles away, a vehicle was approaching the homestead. "If Xavier comes...*when* Xavier comes," Keitaro spoke evenly as to not alarm her, "he won't be driving a car."

Zayda Patrone lowered her head even as she lowered her thick, curly lashes, shielding her luminous faery-princess eyes from Keitaro's ever-keen, watchful examination. "Don't like visitors," she murmured, the sound coming out as a hiss.

Keitaro took a cautious step toward her, and she instinctively stepped back. She wasn't afraid; it was just a reflex, one she hadn't managed to quell in all this time. "Go inside," he instructed, gesturing toward the door with a gentle yet commanding hand.

Zayda held up two fingers, as if drawing a microscopic symbol in the air, an odd tic Keitaro had noticed on more than one occasion—she did it whenever she was deep in thought—and her nose twitched at the tip, several times in quick succession. Her wolf was sniffing the valley, trying to identify the stranger's scent, yet her human mind didn't even register the instinct, the fact that she was doing it.

Weeks ago, Keitaro had sat the girl down and cautiously explained the reality of the situation: the fact that he was a vampire, the cold, hard truth of her biological origins. Xavier Matista was both her father and a lycan, which meant Zayda belonged, at least halfway, to a race of prehistoric, vampire-hunting creatures. Yet and still, the female had no idea, no conscious awareness, of her primordial behavior or her inbred lykos instincts, whereas Keitaro saw them in everything she did.

She raised her chin and met Keitaro's stare head-on, causing his heart to skip a beat in his chest. Those eyes. Those damn, mysterious, enigmatic eyes. Silver blue. Spun from glass. Too large to be real; too exotic to be human. "If Xavier comes," she said. "*When* he comes," she corrected, pausing to lift her eyes upward and to the right as if retrieving a mental image from her subconscious, "can you remove his heart and save it for me?"

Keitaro furrowed his brow.

Could he remove Xavier's heart and save it for Zayda?

Why?

"Excuse me?" he said.

"I'd like to eat it," she murmured, and then she giggled like a little child. "Just kidding." She turned on her heel and strolled back inside, and Keitaro took a deep, steadying breath.

Blessed Sagittarius!

Okay...

So perhaps he had overestimated Zayda's progress, and her improvement needed to be measured in miles, not steps—this was a marathon, not a sprint. And perhaps Kagen had been right about seeking traditional human therapy for Keitaro's beleaguered guest.

Zayda would like to *eat* Xavier's heart...

Just kidding?

Before he could ponder her words any further, a smoky gray Porsche Cayenne SUV pulled into the drive and snaked its way toward the house.

Keitaro shook off Zayda's odd behavior and bounded down the steps, waiting patiently as the six-foot-three sentinel climbed out of the driver's-side door and slammed the panel behind him. "Greetings, Master Warrior," Keitaro called to Santos Olaru.

* * *

Santos Olaru unfolded his lithe, muscular body from the SUV and nodded in reply to Keitaro Silivasi. He strolled across the uneven ground and met the approaching vampire halfway, falling seamlessly into a formal greeting: "It is with great joy that I greet you this day, my celestial brother; a fellow descendant of Jadon; an Ancient Master Warrior; father to two noble warriors, a healer and a wizard; and son of Lord Sagittarius, who makes his home around the Trifid Nebula."

Keitaro clasped Santos' hand, then drew back in surprise. "Damn. Mighty formal, sentinel. So this isn't a casual visit?"

Santos declined his head in both respect and affirmation. "No, it's not."

"The king? Is everything well with Napolean?" Keitaro asked, his brows shooting up.

Santos smiled then, relaxing a bit. "The king is well...as usual.

Thank you for asking. This is more of a personal visit. Business, yes, but of the private variety."

Keitaro held up one hand, ostensibly to slow the vampire down. "Okay." He looked off into the distance, took a deep, measured breath, and flashed an amiable smile of his own. "First things first: How's the family? How are your nephews?"

Santos felt a spark of warmth alight in his chest. It radiated outward—then upward—until it settled in his eyes, and he could feel the creases, the corners beneath his eyelids, deepen from the joy. "Ramsey's good. Real good. And Saxson is still on cloud nine —in fact, I just came from his house—and Roman and Legend; they're growing like weeds. Roman will be six months the beginning of next week, and Legend will be four months, one week later."

Keitaro chuckled softly. "Good. Good...they're going to grow up close in age. And Tiffany? Kiera? How are the *destinies* doing?"

Santos shook his head from side to side, a sly, mischievous grin curling along the edges of his mouth. "Tiffany is still giving Ramsey fits, but if you ask me, they're two peas in a pod, which is why they bump heads when they're not...well...tearing each other's clothes off." His humor lessened. "And Kiera...she's adjusting. She and Saxson were definitely made for each other, so I think their lives are far more complete, but it's gonna take time... all the drama with her sister, Kyla...that kind of thing doesn't heal overnight. It isn't easily forgotten."

The house of Jadon was a close-knit community, and even those who weren't as intimately involved in Saxson Olaru's Blood Moon as Santos and Ramsey knew all about Kyla Sparrow's betrayal of her twin sister, how she had tried to take Kiera's place and pass herself off as Saxson's *destiny* with only one end goal in sight: to murder as many vampires as she could. She'd been a member of a secret vampire-hunting society, and the whole plot had hit way too close to home. After all, Santos and his two younger brothers had lost their mother to a stake through the heart...

But that had been many centuries ago.

And it had made Saxson uniquely qualified to comfort his mate.

Ultimately, Kyla had lost her life to vampiric justice, so Saxson and Kiera were embracing both a beautiful beginning... and a tragic ending...together.

"Those two are strong," Keitaro said, drawing Santos from his internal thoughts. "Both separately and together. Your sister-in-law is a welcome addition to the house of Jadon."

Santos nodded, and he allowed a bit of silence to settle between them before pressing onward. "Speaking of recent additions to the house of Jadon... It's why I stopped by Saxson's clifftop estate, and it's why I'm standing here now."

Keitaro angled his head toward the house. "This is about Zayda?"

"Yes. Zayda. Luca Giovanni. Xavier Matista. The whole sordid affair." The sentinel felt his features harden and his jaw slightly stiffen as he fell into a more businesslike protocol. "I stopped by Saxson's before I came here because I wanted to bring the warrior up to speed on the same thing I'm about to tell you. I wanted him to pass it on to Ramsey and Saber, which sort of speaks for itself: There's enough cross-over between players, enough concern to the whole house of Jadon, to make all of this official sentinel business, and I figured, since you've been watching over Zayda and goading General Matista, you need to be brought into the loop."

Keitaro's features were as placid as the lake below Santos' house, which meant his emotions were running just as deep and murky. "Okay."

"And there's something else," Santos added. "I'd like you to speak with Zayda—to allow *me* to speak with Zayda—assuming she's stable enough...lucid enough...to answer some difficult questions. I wouldn't ask if it wasn't important."

Keitaro nodded slowly, a lock of his thick black hair falling forward into his eyes, the hue of his mane so deep and dark it nearly gleamed purple in the afternoon sunlight. True to his cunning warrior's nature, he cut to the chase right along with Santos. "Give me the gist of it, Santos: the executive summary. A few paragraphs or less."

Appreciating the vampire's brevity, Santos tried to rise to the challenge. "Over the last few years, give or take a month here and there, I've been...followed...in cyberspace by a human hacker, a sort of cat-and-mouse game between computer aficionados." When Keitaro's brows immediately dipped down into a frown, Santos decided to take another approach—hell, the male had been held captive in a prehistoric world, reminiscent of the *Flint-stones* or *Clan of the Cave Bear*—he could do without the technological jargon. "Let's just say someone was watching me closely, and that someone happened to be Luca Giovanni's only offspring: his daughter, Natalia." He paused for the space of several heartbeats to let the significance sink in. "I made contact with her last night, and while I intend to follow up, try to meet her in person, I have more questions than answers. I'd rather not go in blind if Zayda can fill in some holes."

There.

That was short, sweet, and to the point.

Now it was just a matter of awaiting the vampire's answer. Zayda was Keitaro's charge, and the formidable patriarch was nothing if not fiercely protective over his ward. No one knew exactly why, and no one, save Napolean, had the rank or right to question the Ancient Master Warrior—Keitaro would either say yes...or no.

Keitaro glanced at the house, looked out across the acreage, and drew his shoulders back. "You think this Natalia might know something about Xavier or whatever goes on in that compound? Zayda's plight and her upbringing? You think Zayda might be able to connect some dots?"

Santos shrugged. "Don't know, but it's possible. If nothing else, she can fill in the blanks with regard to the compound's blueprints, and she may have heard a thing or two, growing up. Regardless of circumstances, people gossip."

Keitaro bit down on his lower lip, and a stern, almost imperceptible hint of warning flashed in his deep, espresso-brown eyes. "You can speak to her as long as I'm present. But if she starts to degenerate, if she gets too agitated, the conversation is over. We understand each other?"

Santos let out a breath he hadn't realized he was holding. "Understood. And since I don't know her as well as you do, just signal me if something goes awry."

At this, Keitaro smirked. "I highly doubt you'll need a signal, not with Zayda, but we'll play it by ear." He gestured toward the front door. "Please, come in. I'll go get Zayda, and we can talk in the living room."

CHAPTER FIVE

Z ayda Patrone stood in front of the full-length, oval mirror, staring at her wild, unruly hair. She had tried to plait it into a smooth, even braid, just like Deanna had shown her, but there were tresses sticking out everywhere: thick, golden red, and rebellious. For a moment, she wondered, *What would Keitaro think?* But the thought was quickly replaced by another: *Who cares!*

She stared at the plain white T-shirt hanging down to her knees over a boring pair of gray yoga pants and winced, not so much because she didn't like the outfit—again, who cared—but because she didn't like the constant noise in her head, the opening and closing of separate compartments Zayda could no longer control.

Growing up in The Fortress, she had learned how to shut those doors, to literally force her mind to be blank, like a cold, empty room without windows or doors. Nothing but dark gray silence. And when she'd been forced to meet with a John, she'd crawled inside that compartment while her body remained outside of it. Basically, Zayda could go in and out of nothing-ness...at will.

Until Xavier Matista.

Until The Fortress guards had moved her from the eastern wing to the south...

She knew.

Of course, she knew!

Everyone did.

She had just gone from a $200-per-night prostitute to a deranged hunter's prey. The next time she was purchased, she wasn't coming back.

And when Xavier had chained her inside that duplex, her walls had broken down...like they had crumbled or cracked. She had tried to slip inside the gray ramparts, but they wouldn't hold. *They wouldn't hold.* And so, it was kind of like she created a whole new set of compartments...of rooms...places she could go. As odd as it sounded—especially to her—those partitions split apart as well. She could be in several compartments at once or moving in and out. She could be nowhere—or everywhere—depending on the event. Sometimes, the calm, cool call-girl she had learned to perfect strolled in and out of the compartments with ease. This was the girl who still doubted Keitaro Silivasi, wondered what he wanted, when his mask would break. Still other times, she felt like a little girl, lost in her imagination, running in and out of the rooms, pretending: wishing on a rainbow, making things up, wanting Keitaro to love her. Yet other times, she was just Zayda, too old for her years. Cynical. Bitter. Maybe broken. And this was the girl inside the compartment who thought, *Who cares!*

A brisk knock on the door startled her out of her musings, and then she heard Keitaro's deep, commanding voice: "Zayda, can you come out for a minute? There's someone here who would like to see you."

Her throat immediately constricted.

Someone there who wanted to see Zayda?

Who?

Why?

Maybe Deanna or one of Keitaro's other daughters—maybe that nice one, Arielle—or was it a man...a predator... Had Keitaro Silivasi's mask broken after all?

She shuffled slowly to the heavy, six-panel door and spoke through the partition. "Who is it?" Her voice sounded feeble, and she hated that.

"His name is Santos Olaru," Keitaro said evenly. Why was he controlling his voice?

So it *was* a man...

A John? she wondered.

"Zayda..." This time, Keitaro's voice held something almost magical in it, something soothing and gentle and warm. And Zayda felt her anxiety let go, release, as if she'd just taken a wonderful drug. How the hell did he do that with his voice? "There's nothing to fear. I'll be right beside you. Santos is like... he's sort of a police officer, but you aren't in trouble." He rushed the last five words. "And neither am I. He wants to ask you some questions about your life, before we found you. I know it's not a pleasant topic, but it won't take too long. And if at any point, you wish to stop, just say the word. Zayda, I wouldn't ask if it weren't important. Will you do this for me, wild one?"

Zayda shut her eyes.

Wild one...

She loved when Keitaro called her that.

It didn't feel like an insult; it just felt...true.

"You know him. And trust him?" she asked, her voice a little stronger.

"I do."

She took a long, measured breath, in through her nose and out through her mouth, prolonging the exhale through slightly parted lips, and then she opened the door and followed her protector—no, her keeper—into the newly remodeled living room.

A tall, handsome man stood up at once, and his smile was actually jarring.

Spectacular.

Well, it would have been if Zayda didn't inherently distrust all men, which she did.

Still, the guy was stunning to the eyes and intimidating as hell. He camouflaged all that raw, barely leashed power beneath a slow, gentle smile, and unless Zayda was mistaken, the kindness reached his eyes. Eyes were amazing crystal balls. They usually—but not always—told everything. And kindness was sort of a glow, like a light behind the pupils that radiated outward, and those little lines in the corners became smooth instead of tight.

"Zayda," the handsome guy said, "it's nice to finally meet you. I'm Santos Olaru. I'm in charge...I work with a security detail here in Dark Moon Vale, and I'm hoping you can answer a few questions for me." He extended his arm and offered his hand in greeting.

Zayda didn't take it.

Rather, she padded to the edge of the sofa and curled against the arm, relieved when Keitaro Silivasi remained standing, yet leaned against it, almost like he was hovering above her.

Protecting her.

Keeping her...

At least she was safe for the moment.

Santos seemed unfazed. He strolled back to the oversized armchair, situated cater-cornered to the couch, and sat down lazily, like a big, sleepy cat, flashing that million-dollar smile once more at Zayda.

"Go ahead," Keitaro prompted, placing the pads of three fingers on Zayda's shoulder as if to give her courage. "Ask your first question, Santos."

The guy spoke carefully, like he was weighing every single word way too carefully, like Zayda was prone to break. "I understand you grew up in a large, brick building in Morrison, Colorado. A building surrounded by a ten-foot wall. You were born there...raised there...and not treated kindly. I'm sorry for that." His eyelids lowered, and the crystal-blue prisms beneath his thick lashes faded a bit, not like the light was going out, but like the kindness was sort of deepening.

Zayda held her chin steady. "Yeah, I grew up in The Fortress."

One of Santos' eyebrows shot upward like he was zeroing in on a detail. "The building is like a fortress—how so?"

Zayda shrugged. "It's not *like* a fortress. It's *called* The Fortress. And yeah, it's pretty solidly built, I guess."

Santos nodded. "I've spoken with Keitaro's son Nachari, and I've also looked at some early blueprints, building permits, and aerial satellite images. Would it be correct to say The Fortress is divided into wings...or quadrants?"

"Yeah," Zayda answered, "but it's more like...if you've ever been to a hotel, not a cheap one like in a strip mall, but the nice kind where rich people go; every wing is like its own floor, even though it's not. But they're separate like that—you can't just go from one to another."

Santos' eyebrows creased, like he was thinking it over, picturing what Zayda had described in his mind. If he was anything like Keitaro, he was probably really smart—not like a lot of Luca's Johns... "That makes sense." He paused, once again, carefully selecting his words. "Zayda, do you know how many guards are in The Fortress—just a ballpark guess?"

She narrowed her eyes in concentration and tried to count from memory. "Maybe twenty. Twenty-five. Somewhere around four or five to a wing and then a few who patrol the halls."

Her shoulders curled inward, and Keitaro placed his remaining two fingers on her shoulder, stroking the curve by her neck with his entire hand. She had to resist the urge to lean into his touch. "Take your time, Zayda," her keeper said. "We're not in any hurry."

She nodded faintly.

"Do you remember any of their names?" Santos asked.

Zayda stiffened, but she tried to recall the guards. "In the eastern wing, where I used to live, there was a guard named Roberto and another named Danny—I didn't know the others. And in the southern wing, where they moved me to, I think his name was Domenico, the head guard, but everyone called him The Reaper." A low, gravelly sound reverberated in the room, and if Zayda hadn't known better, she would have turned and looked for a growling dog, but she'd heard Keitaro make that noise before. It meant he would like to kill somebody, only the person wasn't there.

If it were possible to be even more gentle, Santos softened his voice. "Any last names?" he asked.

"No," she said quickly. "I never heard any full names."

He nodded with approval. "So...what about Luca Giovanni? Did you ever see him in The Fortress?"

The walls in the empty gray room—in the compartment Zayda was using—seemed to close in on her, and she suddenly felt her emotions splinter, different pieces of her cornered soul scattering into different compartments. "King Giovanni came sometimes; he wasn't always in the castle." Her mind went blank, and that was all she could remember.

Santos bit his bottom lip. "What about King Giovanni's

daughter, Natalia? Did you ever see or meet her? Hear anyone speak about her?"

Zayda's heart lit up, and she smiled. "Princess Natalia is going to marry Prince Oskar. That's all anyone knows."

A curious look—maybe anger or disgust—swept over Santos' striking features, but then he looked handsome again. "I see. Does Prince Oskar have a last name?"

Zayda frowned. "Oskar is his last name. His first name is Prince."

Santos exchanged a curious glance with Keitaro, and if Zayda hadn't known better, she would have sworn the two were talking to each other—only without using words. The subtle expressions on the security guard's face registered like fine ripples in an otherwise still pond, and when Zayda glanced over her shoulder, Keitaro's pupils narrowed. After a few awkward moments, Santos spoke again. "So you never met Natalia—you never saw her in The Fortress?"

Zayda licked her bottom lip. "Once, when I was just a little girl, I think the princess snuck into The Fortress. I don't remember much, except...she got caught...her father caught her, and the king was really, really angry. He said so many bad words, I couldn't even count them, and then he snatched her by her arm and dragged her away. But...but there was like this moment when everything stopped, and she stared right at me. Her eyes locked with mine, only hers were so incredibly beautiful. She looked like a big kid, maybe nine or ten, and she just couldn't stop staring... into my eyes. She was crying then. She was so, so sad, but I don't think it was because the king had caught her; I think it was because she was looking at me. And I remember knowing for the very first time that I must be in a really bad place. She never came back again. At least I never saw her after that day."

Keitaro Silivasi was leaning over Zayda then, brushing his thumbs across her cheeks.

She thought she heard him say something to Santos like "that's enough" or "she's not ready to do this," but the words seemed far away.

Keitaro swiped her cheeks again, and his thumbs were really wet, like he had just washed them under the faucet, or like her face was covered in tears.

But that wasn't what had happened.

Princess Natalia had been the one who'd cried.

* * *

Santos Olaru climbed into the front seat of his Porsche Cayenne, slammed the door shut, and laid his head on the leather steering wheel, trying to collect his thoughts.

Shit.

Just shit.

He'd never seen anything like that.

Zayda had gone from twenty-one years old—according to Keitaro, she'd just had a birthday a few months back—to three or four years old in a matter of minutes. She'd simply regressed right before their eyes. Santos had left a handful of documents with Keitaro in hopes that Zayda could fill in the blanks—satellite images of the compound, as well as a black-and-white duplicate of The Fortress blueprints. Maybe Zayda could mark X's for the guards; estimate the number of female prisoners; and recall some of their names. Perhaps she could describe a few of the captives... the Johns...or Giovanni's associates.

It was probably a long shot at best.

Still, Keitaro had said he would work on it, depending on how Zayda felt.

How Zayda felt...

Holy hell.

Santos could not stop considering how Natalia must have felt at only nine or ten years old. Assuming Zayda's story was accurate, he wondered what Luca's daughter had seen, what she'd heard, what she'd witnessed. For some reason, the thought of that beautiful, intelligent woman being dragged away by her father, weeping at the sight of a baby Zayda, made Santos want to rip out someone's throat with his teeth.

He clutched the steering wheel and tried to get a handle on his irrational emotions.

None of this made any sense.

Growing up in Dark Moon Vale, Santos had seen everything under the sun: every cruelty, every devious plot, every size, shape, and type of enemy. And being one of Napolean's sentinels, a warrior inside the king's inner circle, Santos understood the law. He got the delicate interplay between vampires and humans: The former were predators; the latter were prey. They lived in different worlds and worshipped different deities; hell, they came from completely separate origins, and never the twain shall meet.

Yeah, he got it...

The celestial gods had not created the ancestors to act as superhero crusaders, interfering in human madness. They were a separate species, distinct and independent, and outside of their chosen *destinies*, they lived a life apart.

It wasn't Santos' job to police Luca Giovanni, despite the fact that the human's crimes were unconscionable, and his sins were numerous. The Dark Ones, the Lycans, Napolean Mondragon's enemies were more than enough to contend with.

But this shit was foul.

The Fortress...

A human slave-trade that made sport of little girls, and one that was coming just a little too close to home.

Zayda was half Lycan.

Xavier was the house of Jadon's enemy.

And Natalia had followed an HOJ sentinel around the World Wide Web...for years.

To Santos' way of thinking, that was enough to warrant crossing some lines: enough of a coincidence, enough of a threat, enough of a reason to continue digging deeper. And should the gods be merciful, it would be enough of an excuse to burn that insidious fortress to the ground and murder every living soul involved in the trafficking and the prostitution.

Enough of a reason to set the females free and punish Giovanni for putting his hands on Natalia...enough of a reason to rip out his heart.

"What the hell, Santos?" he murmured beneath his breath.

He sat upright, rolled his shoulders in a few loose circles, and tilted his head back and forth to each side, releasing some stress from his neck.

He would have to run this whole thing by his brothers and Saber, perhaps bring Julien on board since they often worked side by side with the tracker, but he needed more information first. The more dots he could connect the better. The more likely Napolean would be to approve the destruction of The Fortress—to give the sentinels carte blanche to ruin Giovanni, Inc.

The one thing that needled him—because it made no damn sense—was how Luca had pulled it off all these years. Hundreds of women, housed in broad daylight: kidnapped, kept, and sold. Where the hell was the FBI or Homeland Security? Hell, Johnny-fucking-lawman from the local county jail? How had Giovanni pulled this shit off without ever getting caught? Without mind-control, the ability to alter records...and memories...the talent to compel neighbors, officers, even Luca's enemies to never speak a word, the feat was damn near supernatural.

And having seen Zayda...

He pinched the bridge of his nose and glanced out the windshield to observe the sun. Santos rarely wore a watch, but as a descendant of celestial beings and humans, he didn't need one to tell the time—he had three more hours before he met Natalia.

Before he showed up, uninvited, at her massage...

Hopefully, the meeting would be fruitful, because he needed something...*anything*...to compel his king to allow the house of Jadon to annihilate Luca Giovanni, once and for all.

CHAPTER SIX

Later that evening

Natalia Giovanni snuggled beneath the lightweight sheet on the padded massage table and rested her head in the pillowed cradle, luxuriating in the warmth of the heated blanket beneath her. She hadn't enjoyed a two-hour massage in almost six months, and she could really use the relaxation, the inevitable release of pent-up tension. She relished getting lost in the pleasant sensations as her taut, tense muscles gave way to the therapist's gentle manipulation, if only for one evening.

When the door to the dimly lit room creaked open, she took a slow, deep breath and tuned into the soothing sounds of nature—wood pipes and trickling water—streaming through the surround-sound speakers. Hopefully, this therapist was a good one, and he could work magic on Natalia's uptight body. "Full body rub," she murmured, familiar with the routine. "Medium pressure is fine, but not too deep. Oh, and light on the thighs—they're always kind of sensitive. If you don't mind, I would also appreciate a little extra attention on my neck and shoulders; I'm unusually tense tonight."

"And why is that?"

The deep, dark tenor that reverberated through the room played across Natalia's skin like silken, icy fingers reaching through a winter's wind, and Natalia shivered all the way to her bones.

Why is that?

It was none of his business.

She chose not to answer his question, waiting anxiously instead as he sauntered to the head of the table, lowered himself onto the stool, and placed two strong hands on the elegant curve between her shoulders and her neck. A current of pure heat and electricity surged from his fingertips and flowed into her body, as two firm, commanding hands began to work her muscles. Surprised by the strength and the surge of the energy, Natalia arched her neck and tried to raise her head, but he met the subtle lift with counter pressure, gently pressing her back into the cradle.

"Shh," he whispered, languorously. "Just relax, and tune into my voice."

Her heart nearly leaped from her chest.

Something wasn't right.

But before she could struggle in earnest or protest more emphatically, the mysterious therapist continued: "You will not struggle or try to leave this room. You will not scream or call out for help. Be at ease; I am not going to harm you. When I give you the command, you will sit up on the table, wrap yourself in the sheet or the blanket, and answer all my questions truthfully. Do you understand me, Natalia Antoinette?"

She gulped, every instinct inside her wanting to rebel and protest.

Hell no, she didn't understand him!

And hell no, she wasn't going to sit up and answer all his questions, truthfully or otherwise.

But something involuntary, something stronger than her will —something deep inside her subconscious mind, like an invisible thread connected to her soul—felt like it was tethered to a wire, and this therapist was a puppeteer. Her resistance turned liquid and malleable: clear, obeisant, and calm. "I understand," she whispered.

"Very well." He removed his hands from her shoulders and slowly rose to his feet. "Sit up, Natalia." He sauntered to the other side of the dimly lit room and sank leisurely, once again, into a waiting, empty chair, the paltry piece of furniture far too small for his large, muscular frame. As Natalia rolled into a seated position, he crossed one leg over his knee at a ninety-degree angle and leaned back like he owned the entire universe.

Dazed and confused, Natalia gathered the sheet above her breasts and dangled her legs over the side of the table. She was acutely aware of her nudity, the fact that she was wearing nothing beneath the thin cotton barrier other than a pair of white lace panties. She tightened her fist around the bunched material and raised her chin to stare at the stranger—and that's when she gasped in both alarm and recognition.

She would know those perfect features anywhere.

That divine, sculpted nose; those haunting, crystal-blue eyes; those full, perfect lips; and that unusual black-and-blond hair, with scatterings of snow white, mussed at the front above the slightest widow's peak.

Holy Mother of Mercy, Natalia was staring at Santos Olaru.

The ghost from her machine.

"Hello, Natalia," he drawled lazily, and there was something almost primal in the sound. "It's a pleasure to finally meet you."

She gulped again. "Santos..." It was all she could push from her throat.

He smiled, and God bless the sun and the moon, because his radiance outshined them both.

The man was positively decadent.

Divine.

Dangerous.

And he was staring at Natalia like a wolf gazing at a helpless sheep.

She pursed her lips together and let out a slow, reedy exhale of air. "W...w...where is the therapist?" This man didn't give massages for a living. Maybe he hunted dangerous prey; maybe he dispatched enemies for some foreign government; or maybe he was a sniper—or an undercover agent—but he sure as hell wasn't anyone's massage therapist.

He raised one shoulder in a dismissive shrug, his head tilting ever so slightly to one side. "He's taking a break for a while, nothing to worry about. I wanted the two of us to have sufficient time to get acquainted...and to talk." He glanced upward at the plain, sterile clock affixed to an otherwise blank wall, and Natalia's stomach clenched in wariness: *Oh lord, she'd booked a two-hour massage.* No one was going to enter this room before ten o'clock.

Her lips felt suddenly dry, and she swiped them with her tongue.

And true to that palpable, animal nature, Santos' discriminating eyes followed the movement like a hawk's. He stirred restlessly in his chair. "You're beautiful," he said softly. "Exquisite, actually." He uncrossed his leg, leaned forward in the chair, and braced his forearms on his thighs, studying Natalia more intently.

And heaven help her, she wanted to run: to get up from the table, dash to the door, and sprint through the salon, screaming bloody murder. This man was dangerous in a way she'd never known—raw, intense, and innately sensual, unlike anything she had ever encountered.

More powerful than her father.

More dominant than Oskar.

And she didn't know how she knew, but she was absolutely certain...

Natalia was staring into the eyes of a timeless predator.

* * *

Santos didn't know what was up.

Blessed Delphinus, he was a seasoned sentinel, and this was a clear, clean-cut mission: slip into Natalia's massage room, take control of her mind, and regulate her reactions. Ask a dozen or so questions, then scrub her memory and get the hell outta the room.

Get the hell outta Dodge!

So why were his fangs throbbing in his gums?

Why was his heart racing in his chest?

And why couldn't he take his gaze off her exquisite body or her stunning face?

The female was positively striking.

She was incomparable, to be sure: that regal bone structure; those dark, exotic eyes; the perfection of her smooth, flawless skin. Every plane, every slope, every gentle angle on her face was absolutely transcendent. And that was to say nothing of that body, those gorgeous feminine curves, barely concealed beneath a thin cotton sheet. Her skin was a pure copper hue—rich, hazelnut coffee swirled with vanilla cream—and her hair was as dark as the night and ten times more enchanting: thick, softly textured, and full of subtle waves, even as it was loosely pinned to the crown of her head.

And when he'd touched her—*oh gods, he should not have touched her*—those thin, elegant shoulders leading to that long, enticing neck; every instinct in his vampiric body had wanted to bend over and taste her. *Bite her.* Pierce her carotid artery and drink to his heart's content. He couldn't cross the room, put enough much-needed space between them, plant his ass in the silly little chair fast enough. And now, instead of peppering her with questions, he was staring at the female like a hungry, wild beast.

He needed to get a grip.

And fast.

Tearing his eyes away from her face, he stared at a plain white clock hanging on the wall. There was nothing else in the room to distract him. "Tell me, Natalia"—his voice sounded ragged—"what do you know of your father's business?"

She jerked in surprise, and her dark eyes narrowed. "Is that why you're here?" she asked, sounding oddly disappointed. "To inquire about my father?"

Santos furrowed his brows. "Your father, and you. What do you know about your father's business?" He regarded her eyes, yet again, and all traces of emotion had been replaced with a mask of indifference.

"Who are you?" Her voice grew suddenly cold.

Interesting.

Very interesting...

He deepened his tenor and increased the coercion. "Answer me now, Natalia: What do you know about your father's business?"

Helpless to defy the vampire's compulsion, she closed her eyes instead. "Everything."

He swept his hand through his hair while the disturbing word sank in: *everything.*

Natalia Giovanni knew everything about Luca's criminal empire?

Damn.

"You know about the human trafficking, the prostitution, and the slavery, not just the real estate and the legitimate holdings? You know about his entire corrupt enterprise?"

Natalia didn't flinch. "Of course."

Now this set Santos' teeth on edge. "Of course," he mimicked sardonically, "how could you not? What role do you play in Giovanni, Inc., *Princess* Natalia?"

To his surprise, this elicited a laugh: snarky, low, and defiant. She opened her eyes and stared right through him. "What *role* do I play?" She nodded her head. "I'm Luca's only child, his daughter, and his heir. I play whatever role he gives me." She started to whisper something beneath her breath, but quickly pulled it back. "No, Mr. Olaru, I'm not a corporate executive for Giovanni, Inc. I don't keep—or cook—the books. I don't run around with my father's henchmen, and my hands are relatively clean. Well, as clean as hands can be when one lives in a sewer. I attend public functions, participate in charitable events, and entertain his wealthy friends—not as a whore, but as a representative of our *wonderful* company. Soon, I will marry one of his more despicable business associates, an international partner whom I've never met and likely will not meet before the future arranged wedding; and I imagine I'll take orders from him as well. Does that answer all your questions, Santos? Have I given you a sufficient dossier on my father?" She tilted her head to the side and smirked. "I'm not sure if he's hiring right now, but he always has room for another...predator. However, you might fare better if you approach him directly. I don't handle his... intimate...personnel."

Santos nodded slowly—wow, he had really pissed her off— and by the strength of her emotion, the hurt just beneath the surface, he knew there was more to Natalia Giovanni than immediately meets the eye. And there was more to her knee-jerk, glib answer, the assertion that she knew everything about Luca's shady business, than her snarky reply revealed. "Does your father traffic in illegal arms?" he asked bluntly.

She shifted nervously on the table. "Um, I'm not entirely sure, but it wouldn't surprise me."

"Does he sell drugs?"

She shrugged. "I don't know."

"Hmm. I see. So you don't know everything. Is Luca involved in illegal gambling?"

At this, Natalia rolled her eyes. "I know about the human trafficking, the prostitution, and the slavery, Mr. Olaru. Isn't that more than enough?"

Santos crossed his arms over his chest, studying Natalia intently. She was right on the edge of either rage...or tears...and there was one sure way to get at her culpability, to discover just how deeply she was involved in Luca's illegal activities—and that was to push her over the precipice. He stroked his chin with his thumb and his forefinger in a purposeful, cocky gesture. "How do you live with yourself?" His voice was intentionally harsh. "The women. The Fortress. The sexual abuse. Why don't you just call the fucking police?"

At this, her eyes filled up with tears, and she bit down hard on her lip to hold them back. She was struggling mightily not to answer, actually resisting his compulsion.

"How can you let them suffer?" he persisted.

She tightened her jaw and stared daggers, straight through him.

"Answer me, Natalia." He laced his voice with undiluted power, and her body began to tremble, but she didn't utter a word.

Damn, this woman had an iron will.

He rose from the chair, strode directly to her, and cupped her jaw in his hand, locking their gazes together and boring his crystal-blue orbs into her dark, troubled pupils. "How can you let them suffer?" he repeated.

She slapped at his wrist, but it didn't budge.

He tightened his fingers on her chin, and she dug her nails into his forearm.

Staring up at him through tear-stained lashes, she grit her teeth and nearly snarled: "I am my father's trip-wire, the pin in his grenade. My darling dad has placed a contract on the head of every woman, girl, and child housed within that hellhole, *The Fortress*. Should I disappear...should I disobey...should I pick up the phone and call the *fucking* police..." Her voice trailed off and she glanced at the plain white clock, now looming above them both like a ghostly specter. "Should I fail to return home at exactly 10:40 tonight, they all die. They all get slaughtered. That's how I live with myself, Santos. I live exactly as my father instructs me, so all those women stay alive."

Santos relaxed his grip and took a cautious step backward. "I don't understand," he murmured. "Explain."

She smiled then, and it was the saddest smile Santos had ever seen. "Somewhere in the world, scattered across four unknown countries, there are four hired killers—mercenaries, thugs—and they've each been paid a handsome price to eliminate every living soul in that compound, should my father give the word. Oh, and he has backup, upon backup, upon backup. Killing him won't kill the contracts. And the only man who knows the identity of the assassins is dead—my father can reach them, but he cannot name them. No one can. So you tell me, Santos Olaru: How fast can our police department act? How quickly can the FBI marshal its forces? Can the CIA or the DEA—hell, the National Guard—assemble faster than four hardened criminals can murder a host of women and children? And would our country even care? Is The Fortress booby-trapped? Will the chambers explode; will the walls collapse;

or is there gas or some other deadly poison hidden in the pipes and walls? Maybe there are cannons in the basement. I honestly don't know; I never go in there. I can't bear to see my father's atrocities up close. But I do know that everything I do, everyone I know, and everything I touch is monitored—my phone, my tablet, my beautiful room." She laughed half-heartedly, and her sad, beautiful eyes became vacant. "Why do you think I'm such an expert hacker... why I've learned to move through cyberspace like a ghost? I don't just follow—and hide—from strangers like you; I maneuver around my father and his goons. It is the only world I exist in where the trip-wire isn't live, and the pin cannot be pulled."

Santos blinked several times, trying to make sense of everything Natalia had just told him.

Trying to digest the full breadth of what she was saying.

It seemed too outlandish to be real, but her emotion—that wasn't fake.

The female had an incredibly strong constitution—she was stubborn, defiant, and brave—but she was also this close to falling apart, coming unglued right on that table, despite her carefully constructed masks.

He held his compulsion, but he gentled his voice. "Have you ever heard of a man named Xavier Matista?" It was best to change the subject, get a little more out of her while she was still talking freely...while she was still emotionally raw. "General Xavier Matista."

She blinked several times, like someone coming out of a trance. "No. I...I don't recognize that name."

He nodded, turning his attention to Jocelyn Levi-Silivasi's long-ago suspicion that the Dark Ones might be involved in Giovanni's human-trafficking ring, and the Swingle-Duplex penthouses. "Do any of these surnames ring a bell? Just tell me if you've ever heard any of them spoken: Nistor, Gervasi, Zeclos, Marandici, Zahora, Zvara..." He studied her expression carefully as he rattled off each name: families and lineages from the house of Jaegar. He was just about to say *Vadovsky*—head of the Dark Ones Council—when Natalia dropped her head, clutched her left wrist, and squeezed her forearm until her knuckles became mottled.

"What's wrong?" he asked, following the peculiar motion.

"My wrist is on fire!" She gasped.

He glared at her wrist and frowned. "What do you mean, *on fire?*"

He reached for her hand to pry it free from her arm, but she immediately drew it back. "I don't know, but don't touch me!"

The sheet she had been clutching slid down her chest, exposing the full curves of her breasts, just short of...exposing everything...and Santos inhaled sharply. "Let me see your wrist, Natalia, while you fix that sheet."

She glanced at the top of her breasts and grimaced, then slowly extended her arm. "It feels like a freakin' branding iron, like there's lava inside my veins."

Alarmed by her words, he took her hand more forcefully than he would have liked to and rotated her wrist to examine her arm. He had already fashioned an ice-cold breath, and he was holding it inside his lungs, ready to cool her blistering skin, in the event it was truly burning. As he bent to study her wrist more closely, an electric bolt shot up his spine, and he drew back with a start, stunned by the phenomenon he was witnessing: There was an oblong rectangle, with four distinct, jutting quadrants, etched into the flesh of her arm. And raised, like a scar, inside the uneven lines were several idiosyncratic dots and patterns, all as familiar to Santos as the nose on his face.

A tail.

Two fins.

And a head better known as Job's Coffin: a distinctive,

diamond-shaped cluster of stars, denoting Alpha, Beta, Gamma, and Delta.

Santos was staring at an original Greek constellation.

Delphinus, his own ruling lord...

A dolphin, leaping from waves.

Natalia appeared dumbstruck—rattled and afraid—as she gawked at her wrist in fright. "I must be allergic to this sheet or something in the parlor," she complained, struggling to get up without releasing her covering.

Santos released the compulsion.

He would not delve that deeply into this female's mind, not if she truly was his *destiny*.

He backed away from Natalia and began to pace around the room, scanning the top of each wall for a window.

Nothing.

The parlors were designed to be private and dark.

He chose to reach out to his brothers instead.

Telepathy would have to take the place of sight.

Besides, he didn't have time to make his way outside, and he wasn't about to leave Natalia unattended. *Ramsey...Saxson...are you near a window? Are either of you outside?*

Ramsey's guttural, no-nonsense brogue burrowed into Santos' mind. *Brother, where the hell are you?*

I'm looking right out my back window, Saxson chimed in.

Santos struggled to remain as calm as possible, if only for Natalia's sake. His feral instincts were riding a razor's edge. *No time for Q and A, Ramsey; just answer the question—can either of you describe the sky?*

Delphinus, Ramsey bit out. *Delphini!* He named each of the celestial god's designations.

The moon? Santos asked.

Red as scarlet, Saxson replied. *The sky is pitch-black, and every last cluster is shining as bright as the noonday sun.*

Before Santos could reply, Ramsey rushed a string of questions: *Who is she, Santos? Are you with her? Do you need some help?*

Santos let out a low, drawn-out hiss.

Holy.

Hell.

He still couldn't quite grasp what was happening.

Speak up, brother, Ramsey insisted. *Or in another two seconds, we're gonna track your blood and show up, whether we're wanted there or not.*

Not advised, Santos shot back, still collecting his wits. *I'll get back to you both; I just needed confirmation—I'm not someplace where I can see the sky, but I've got her. She's with me. Hang tight for a bit.* With that, he closed the connection and spun around to regard Natalia.

His destiny.

She was no longer standing in front of the table.

Rather, she was huddled on the floor, trying to crawl beneath the obstruction, one hand clutching the sheet in a death-grip, the other held up and out in a piteous gesture, like she was pleading with Santos not to harm her.

He was just about to squat down when it hit him: Despite his best efforts, he had lost his composure...his civilized, human mask: His fangs were fully extended. His eyes were undoubtedly glowing red. And that distant, inhuman rumble echoing throughout the parlor was not the wind or an airplane flying overhead—it was a primordial vampiric snarl.

Shit.

Just shit.

CHAPTER SEVEN

Natalia cowered beneath the massage table.

Well, as far beneath the table as she could shimmy and manage.

Santos Olaru was like a creature from a dream—a nightmare, that is.

His unique black-and-blond locks were practically electric with energy; his stunning crystal-blue eyes had long since turned red—yes, deep sanguine, pulsing red—and that gorgeous mouth, that beautiful smile, those perfectly aligned white teeth? They were sharpening. Lengthening. Jutting down from his gums in two razor-sharp, thin points.

The man had fangs!

And now he was squatting down in front of her, those otherworldly eyes seeking hers.

Why oh why had she lied about Oskar—angry, yet still wanting Santos to think she was available—when she'd told him she was promised to a man she'd never met, an international business associate of her father's? At least if she had pretended to have an intimate companion, a significant other in her life right now, Santos might have expected her fiancé to show up. He might not be so confident that the two of them were all alone... that they would *remain* alone for hours.

Natalia tried to back up, but she was tangled in the sheet, and heaven knew, she didn't dare release it. The man was a savage —*was he even a man?* What the hell was he going to do to her? "Santos," she whimpered, her voice sounding raw. "Please...*please*...whatever I said...or did...I'm sorry."

He closed his eyes.

He regulated his breathing.

In fact, he became so still—so quiet—that Natalia could hear her own heart beating, trembling like a tambourine in her chest. And while his fangs did not recede, his entire countenance softened. "Natalia...Antoinette...my angel. Please do not fear me." His voice was a hushed, ragged whisper. "I would never, ever harm you. In truth, I would protect you with my life. I am not angry, my love—I am a slave at this moment to my primitive nature and to you."

Natalia drew back in surprise, trying to make sense of his words: I am a slave to my primitive nature...and to you?

What the heck did that mean?

And why had he called her *my love?*

He extended his hand and crooked his fingers, beckoning her forward. "Come out from beneath the table, Natalia. Please, sit down. We need to talk."

She stared at his hand like he was brandishing a loaded pistol, and as insane as the questions sounded in her mind, they spilled out of her mouth in quick succession: "Who are you? What are you? *Why do you have fangs?* What do you want with me, Santos?"

He sighed, and he truly sounded weary. Concerned. "I am Santos Andrei Olaru, firstborn of a curse to Santiago and Ruth; brother to Ramsey and Saxson; warrior in the house of Jadon; and sentinel to our king, Napolean. I am Vampyr, Natalia. Nosferatu. A creature of the night. The distant progeny of celestial gods and humans, and I am also your eternal mate."

Natalia opened her mouth to speak—or protest—to pepper him with further questions, or maybe just to make sure she wasn't dreaming, but nothing other than a squeak came out. She tried again. "You're a warrior...in what? Some house or club? You're the offspring of celestial...who? What's Vampyr—you...you don't mean *vampire*, do you?" Even as she asked the question, and her mind shouted, *Foul play; this is bullshit*, she already knew the answer. His eyes. His teeth. That animal nature. *Yes.* Santos Olaru was a vampire.

And Natalia Giovanni had finally lost her mind.

She was having a psychotic break.

Hallucinating.

And any moment now, she would either come back to lucid awareness or slip away for good.

Maybe recalling the memories, her once-beloved father's betrayal, the noose he kept tethered around her neck—all those years living with such a heavy weight on her shoulders had finally caused her to snap.

Santos braced her arm by the elbow, tugged her forward from beneath the table, and lifted her to her feet, even as he rose like a preternatural gust of wind, hauling her upright with him. His touch was exquisitely gentle. His manner was eerily calm. "The house of Jadon is a clan, a brotherhood; it is a faction of Vampyr from a specific line of paternity: from Prince Jadon's royal lineage. The celestial gods are real, but they do not oversee human affairs. They are ancient beings, powerful deities who long ago mated with humans and created supernatural offspring. And yes, I am a vampire, but not like anything you have been taught in your human mythology and films. I am not undead. I was not made—I was born. And while I do drink blood, I do not kill my prey, at least not innocent humans. I can walk just fine in the sun."

Natalia felt like she was going to puke.

Her stomach was doing summersaults in her abdomen.

Bracing the same with her hand, she fought against the nausea and tried to back up...to somehow shuffle away... This wasn't happening. It. Just. Wasn't. Real. "What is the Curse?" she murmured, unsure of where her courage came from. She just somehow felt it was important.

Santos licked his bottom lip, as if he didn't even know he was doing it, and the gesture conjured images of animals...and bites... and trickles of blood flowing down a ravaged throat. "My people...my ancestors...the celestial and human offspring, they committed a horrible crime long ago, and they were cursed as punishment. It was then we were turned Vampyr; it was then we were told of our mates; it was then we were promised the moon and the stars as a sign that we had found our *destinies...*" Even as his voice trailed off, he reached out to take her left hand in his, turned her wrist over, and ran his thumb over the strange, enigmatic marks—the allergic reaction imprinted on her skin. "This isn't an allergy," he explained softly. "This is a constellation, a celestial deity: Delphinus, the Dolphin." He traced one line after another with his forefinger, explaining something about quadrants and clusters of stars, naming their places in the cosmos. "If we were to go outside right now, the moon would be as red as blood, the sky would be dark as pitch, and this very constellation —my ruling lord—would be highlighted in the sky, all around it. It is a sign, Natalia, a sign for me...a way to recognize you."

She gulped.

She had heard enough.

Her eyes misting with tears, she jerked her arm, yanking it free, and held both palms forward in front of her. "No. Not another word. I know I asked for an explanation, but...no more."

"Natalia…"

"No."

"Listen to me—"

"No!"

He closed his eyes, pinched the bridge of his nose, and waited for several anxious seconds before trying again. "Listen to me, angel—"

"I want to go home." She sidestepped around him, spun on her heel, and made a beeline for the door, knowing full well he wasn't going to let her walk out of that room.

He was suddenly behind her, his fingers brushing over her jaw, trailing the length of her neck down to the crook of her shoulder, and circling her jugular vein.

No!

He wouldn't dare.

He couldn't!

No. No. No. No.

But yes, he pressed his hard, unyielding chest against her back, encircled her waist from behind, and drew her snugly against him. And then he lowered his mouth to her throat, swirled his tongue over the exact same area, and bit her—just like that.

She started to gasp…from pain and shock… Her legs started to tremble.

But then a glorious warmth and an unearthly calm enveloped her, and she fell back against him. Every nerve ending in her body came alive. Her breasts tightened, and her stomach clenched. The hairs on her arms stood up, and she bit down on her lip to suppress a moan.

She felt his canines retract, leaving her bereft, even as he relaxed his grasp on her waist. And then he spun her around with the palms of his hands, cupped her jaw…ever so gently…and sealed his mouth to hers.

Santos Olaru kissed Natalia like he was moments away from drowning and she was his last gasp for air.

He bewitched Natalia.

He worshipped Natalia.

And he sealed his soul to hers—she felt it on a cellular level.

Whatever the vampire was doing, he was no longer relying on words...

And as his tongue swept seductively into her mouth, and her knees nearly buckled, she felt a stream of consciousness—like an internal film playing on her cerebral cortex—and her questions were all at once answered: A king. A castle. Two beautiful princes. A land far away in Romania.

Women, young girls, females being slaughtered...

One tragic sacrifice after another...

Until the blood of the victims, their celestial cry, rose up from the ether and cursed their tormenters: "*You shall be made immortal. Condemned to roam the earth in darkness as reviled creatures of the night. Forever forced to feed on the blood of the innocent to survive... You shall never know the love or companionship of a female, nor shall you be capable of producing female offspring. Your sons will be born in sets of twins—two children of darkness, the spawn of human hosts who will die wretchedly upon giving birth—even as the firstborn of the first set will be demanded as a sacrifice of atonement...*"

And then the righteous brother—the noble soul—Prince Jadon Demir fell to his knees. He begged the Blood for forgiveness, and he received four mercies: "*You will walk in the sun...you will not be forced to take the lives of the innocent...you will be given one opportunity to claim a mate, and the sign of her arrival shall be heralded in the heavens... Your twin sons shall be born as one child of darkness and one child of light, and you shall be allowed to sacrifice the former while keeping the purer soul to carry on our noble race.*"

Natalia pulled away from the enchanted kiss and stared into the vampire's feral eyes. She had done more than process all she had seen, heard, and felt—she had gotten it on a primordial level.

She knew it.

She believed it.

She felt the certainty of the history, deep in her bones.

Santos was telling the truth.

He was a vampire, and she was his *destiny*—an enigmatic pantheon of ancient deities had chosen it long before their births. It was beyond comprehension, but it was simply and indelibly true.

Nonetheless, that didn't make it palatable.

Natalia Giovanni felt flustered, overwhelmed, intrigued...and trapped.

And everything in her soul wanted to weep. She had led the vampire right to her door with all her artful hacking and her childish flirting. She had danced with a ghost inside her machine, and the ghost had come out of the shadows to claim her.

CHAPTER EIGHT

T he private line in Luca Giovanni's study began to ring just as he sat back in his favorite fireside armchair, relaxed against the luxurious burgundy leather, and raised a crystal glass of scotch to his lips.

Who the hell was calling him at ten o'clock at night?

He set the scotch down on the rich cherry end table, leaned forward in the seat, and glanced at the display: Oskar Vadovsky.

Not again.

The man was insufferably arrogant, a roguish bully, and he didn't afford Luca half the respect and obsequience the billionaire had become accustomed to. He didn't show Luca the appropriate amount of fear.

Just the same, Luca could not deny that Oskar was likely his most crucial and irreplaceable ally, the one business associate he could not stand to lose. Not ever. Oskar must have spent upward of three million dollars each year, purchasing women from the southern wing of The Fortress at $150,000 a head. Well, he didn't necessarily acquire them all personally, but when the peculiar, terrifying males showed up, every last damn one of them with some form of black-and-red banded hair, regardless of the style or cut (it must have been some sort of secret fraternity), all they had to say was *Oskar sent me*, and Luca knew their money was good. They had never failed to come up with the cash, not even once. And whatever they did with the women, they never left a trace of their dalliances.

Or their crimes.

They were virtually zero risk.

Beyond that, Oskar Vadovsky was charmed. While it was true that Luca had more nefarious associations and powerful men in his hip pocket than one corrupt man had a right to—judges, senators, CEOs—his power and influence paled in comparison to Oskar's. Oskar Vadovsky did not show up in any public records; he virtually lacked a vital-statistic footprint. Yet the tall, imposing cutthroat could make unprecedented miracles happen: bodies disappear, district attorneys change their minds, legal cases vanish into thin air. If Oskar wanted someone to do something, they did it. If he wanted someone to change their mind or course of action, it was a foregone conclusion. If he wanted to hide something, it vanished. And if he needed a resource, a weapon—hell, a supernatural intervention—the assassin conjured it out of thin air.

It was positively uncanny.

Yes, Oskar Vadovsky was a force to be reckoned with, and as long as Luca and the "Chief of Council"—whatever the hell that meant—remained aligned, business was more than just smooth sailing. It was charmed. And that's why Luca had agreed to turn over his most valuable and cherished possession to the six-foot-two extortionist: his exquisite daughter, Natalia.

Hell, *in for a penny, in for a pound.*

"*No*" was simply not a word Luca could use with Mr. Vadovsky.

Reaching for the base of the phone, which was still ringing off the hook, Luca pressed the speaker-button and tried to infuse some animation into his voice. "Mr. Vadovsky, so nice of you to call."

"The phone rang fifteen times, Luca. Next time, pick it up on the first fucking ring."

Luca sucked in air. He wanted to say something commanding to set the bastard straight, something like, *You do understand who I am, do you not? I respect you, Oskar, but you need to watch your step...and your tone.* He chose silence instead.

Oskar cleared his throat. "It's late, Luca, and this isn't a social call." Blunt and to the point as usual.

Luca reached for the crystal glass of scotch, slammed it down in one gulp, and thrummed his fingers along the arm of the chair. "Very well. What can I do for you at this late hour, Oskar?" He wished he'd never given the bastard his private line.

"Natalia," Oskar bit out.

"Natalia?" What the hell did that mean? Luca had already promised his daughter to Oskar in marriage; what more did the overbearing tyrant want?

"Dinner at the country club; a night at the theater; supervised visits in your private limousine," Oskar ranted, "enough of the dog-and-pony show. You promised to give me your daughter when she was yet a child, and I waited for her to grow up. At this point, I have courted the full-grown woman for the last several months. You have agreed that the two of us will be married this year and Natalia is aware of the arrangement. She's mine, Luca. All that's left is for the ink to dry on a certificate. Fine. You want pomp and circumstance; you desire a traditional ceremony—I'll play ball to appease your Catholic sensibilities, but I'm done waiting for what's been promised."

Luca wrinkled his nose in confusion. What the heck was Oskar saying? "You'd like to move up the wedding? August isn't soon enough?"

At this, Oskar chuckled, and the sound raised the hairs on Luca's neck. It was downright creepy, maniacal. Luca would have almost called it evil if he believed in such a thing, but he didn't. There were only wolves and sheep, Darwin's law in full effect. The wolves ruled by sheer strength and dominance, and the sheep got slaughtered. There was no good or evil—only power.

"No, Luca. The date is fine," Oskar scoffed. "It's the seventeenth-century chastity bullshit that I have a problem with. If you would like me to continue the public performances...the incessant dating ritual...then so be it. I can keep it up until August 5th, but between now and then, I desire Natalia's private company, her intimate attention and personal loyalty, and I refuse to wait any longer."

A period of silence lingered on the line as Luca swallowed his revulsion. "Oskar, please, do try to understand. We are a traditional family, as you mentioned, Catholic, old fashioned. It is important that Natalia walk down the aisle wearing white, both symbolically and literally, if you get my meaning."

At this, Oskar nearly growled. "You're a cold-blooded killer, Luca Giovanni. You worship no other god than yourself. You enslave little girls and sell them for slaughter, and you order the death of men like some order take-out. Can we please dispense with the bullshit? And really, here's the thing: I'm not asking. I'm demanding." A tangible spark of electricity shot through the phone, and it literally hummed with malevolent energy. "Tomorrow is Friday night, and I intend to send a limousine of my own for Natalia...at eight. I would like her groomed and dressed for the evening, the same as she would if we were attending the orchestra. I will pick her up, alone, and I will return her in the morning. All you need to tell her is that Oskar is taking her somewhere special. Do we understand each other, Luca?"

Luca held his breath, his blood beginning to boil, and then his inner anarchist came out. "Oskar, you know that I have the deepest regard for you, our business relationship, and our long-term friendship. You know that I am deeply committed to a mutually prosperous future, and that includes seeing you married to my only daughter. My beloved only child. But with God as my witness, if you hurt her, Oskar, if you defile Natalia or treat her like one of the insignificant whores you purchase—"

"Shh..." Oskar cautioned, sounding more like a snake than a man, "no need to get testy or paternal, Luca. I will take great care of my future wife, as I am equally committed to the future. But do know this: We have never been friends, and the only warning that matters is mine. There is no god—in heaven or on earth—that could bear witness to what will happen to you, Luca, if you ever dare to threaten me again. Have Natalia ready at eight. I will return her in one piece when I am done with her."

He didn't wait for Luca's answer.

He simply hung up the phone.

* * *

Oskar Vadovsky paced around his private lair, avoiding several of the natural stalagmites rising from the cavern floor. The room was dimly lit with torchlight—he often preferred fire to modern illumination—and the heavy, antique furnishings loomed like medieval statues, scattered about the expansive grotto.

Perhaps Salvatore Nistor was correct: Humans were no more than diminutive bugs to be squashed beneath a vampire's feet, and their petty, Homo sapien games grew tiresome at best. Perhaps Oskar should just take Natalia tomorrow, breed his sons once and for all, then scrub Luca's mind spotless of the memory that he'd ever had a child to begin with.

Perhaps it was time to be finished with the whole sordid mess.

But then...

He would also have to scrub the minds of all Luca's guards and companions, his servants and associates...blah, blah, blah. He would have to destroy vital records, clean out Natalia's room, and remove every trace of her existence from the opulent mansion: quite a laborious task just to tap an exquisite piece of ass.

And besides, Oskar was not ready to relinquish the thrill and the pleasure the whole distraction gave him. He stared at a box full of gold-foiled condoms—magnum, extra-large—resting on a fifth-century, black-and-gold commode, and he cringed. He'd never used the damnable things before—he simply killed his humps before they could swell with child—so this would be a new adventure in its own right. And while he was trying to embrace it wholeheartedly, the necessity of using a condom rankled his gut.

In truth, the Dark Lord Ademordna was quite capable of producing an infertility serum, one he had once given Salvatore Nistor in a small blue vial. The serum rendered a male vampire infertile for at least thirty days, and possibly up to sixty. In short, it made the guy shoot blanks. Salvatore had pleaded with Ademordna to provide the house of Jaegar with just such a weapon for years, and the Dark Lord had finally gifted the sorcerer with the powerful elixir following Saber Alexiares' capture by the house of Jadon. As the plan went, the elixir was to be ingested by Dane Alexiares, Saber's baby brother, and infused into Saber during the sacred rite of *feeding*—the eldest son taking sustenance from the youngest—during a clandestine midnight meeting between the house of Jaegar and the house of Jadon deep in the communal Red Canyons. If all had gone according to plan,

Saber would have been rendered infertile, unable to fulfill the demands of the Curse, and the child stolen by the house of Jaegar, only to be returned to his rightful tribe, would have died in the sacrificial chamber...

Regrettably, the plan had not worked out.

Unfortunately, Ramsey Olaru—that pit bull guardian—had interfered just in time, and Saber had never ingested a drop. Beyond that debacle, Lord Ademordna had forbidden the elixir's use as anything other than a weapon, wielded against the house of Jadon. To the dark deity's way of thinking, blocking procreation was sacrilege—a mortal sin. He wanted his progeny and his servants to procreate, prolifically, not to practice birth control.

Alas, Oskar had thought about the elixir so many times...

He had thought about the high cost of obtaining it—two hundred female virgins, slaughtered on a makeshift altar, their hearts carved out while still beating, their bodies offered in smoke and fire—and yes, he had thought about just how difficult it had been for Salvatore to procure two hundred female virgins of child-bearing age in such a wicked, immoral world. Yet and still, Oskar would have gladly hunted the earth and collected two hundred virginal girls in order to buy extra time with Natalia Giovanni: to brutalize...then heal her...time and again.

To screw her blind, so to speak, until she lost her fragile sanity.

And then rinse and repeat...

Rinse and repeat.

Was that so wrong?

Such an unreasonable dream?

Oskar was weary. He had lived so many years. Hell, he was bored to tears half the time, and all he wanted was to enjoy a beautiful woman for as long as he could before his demonic offspring clawed their way out of her nubile body, decimated her ribs, and left a lifeless corpse in their wake.

Surely, that wasn't too much to ask.

But as it stood, Oskar was a noble leader, a cut and caste above the rest. Sure, he was willing to manipulate the rules when necessary, to call upon the Dark Lords for the good of the Colony, but he had never petitioned the lords for his own selfish gain... asked for something as self-indulgent as the serum for his private, carnal use. And he was pretty damn sure Ademordna would slay him where he stood for defying the Dark Lord's edict: The serum was meant to be used as a weapon; indeed, no one outside of the council even knew it existed.

Sighing, Oskar resigned himself to the use of the gold-foiled condoms.

He shrugged off his longings and smiled.

He might not have forever, but he had today.

He had tomorrow night.

And he would pick Natalia up at eight o'clock sharp, take her to a dark, secluded hideaway where the moonlight shone bright, and finally consummate their union with the assistance of a blasted rubber.

He picked up a golden wrapper and turned it over in his hand, thumbing the brittle edges of the foil. Yes, indeed, Oskar would adapt.

So be it.

This time tomorrow, he would *adapt* inside Natalia.

CHAPTER NINE

Still dazed and overwhelmed, Natalia Giovanni sat cross-legged on her gold-and-lavender coverlet, staring at the sleek silver burner phone that Santos had provided her, trying to make sense of all that had transpired over the past few hours.

Nothing seemed real.

In the blink of an eye, her life had become a dreamscape—or a nightmare, depending on one's perspective—and Natalia was having a very hard time making even the smallest adjustment, let alone agreeing to the insanity that was Santos' universe. "Be careful what you ask for," her personal maid, Sylvia, had always told her. "You just might get it." Truer words had never been spoken, but Natalia hadn't asked for this.

She had not asked to be claimed by a vampire.

She had not asked to be some immortal warrior's pre-fated *destiny*.

And she had not asked to change her existence, give up her life, and adopt a new identity at that immortal vampire's insistence. Good lord, Santos had spoken of so many incomprehensible things like conversion, sacrifice, a forty-eight-hour pregnancy. He had given her three days to process the whole of it, to somehow come to terms with it, and to move to Dark Moon Vale...as if she could just pick up and relocate without batting an eyelash.

Beyond the absurdity of moving, he believed he could do the impossible.

Something no one had ever attempted before...

Should his vampire-king allow it, Santos believed he could lay waste to The Fortress this Sunday—in under fifteen minutes. He could set the female captives free, without suffering a single casualty, and unshackle Natalia from Luca's control, perhaps even spare her from Oskar Vadovsky.

Well, truth be told, she hadn't uttered a word to Santos about her detestable fiancé, other than the pitiful lie she had told, claiming that Oskar lived abroad, and she had never even met him. Of course, before the night had ended, Santos had asked about her engagement—somehow, he had even known Oskar's first name, not all that surprising for such an expert hacker—but Natalia had decided to leave well enough alone...to let sleeping dogs lie. Santos had not been the least bit concerned about some human male on the other side of the world, a man, he assumed, Natalia was never going to meet. The vampire was determined to bring Natalia to Dark Moon Vale as quickly as possible, and he was equally confident in his celestial gods...in the inherent power of this surreal Blood Moon.

Natalia didn't dare tell him otherwise at this point.

There was no reason to give him Oskar's full name.

Besides, she didn't want to complicate matters by provoking a supernatural creature's territorial instincts, waving a red flag in front of a paranormal bull, especially since Natalia didn't know what she planned to do. What if fate had a wicked sense of humor, and this Blood Curse was the worst fate imaginable? What if she needed Oskar, after all, to save her from Santos?

A stone-cold human killer to protect her from a vampire...

She was so damned confused.

Relying on Oskar Vadovsky?

What the hell was she thinking!

Natalia didn't want any of this.

None of it was copasetic—or doable.

Every last bit of it was certifiably insane.

Natalia did not belong to Santos Olaru, Delphinus, the goddess, or some ancient Blood Moon. She couldn't possibly leave her life in an instant and just take up house with a complete stranger, let alone a preternatural being.

She clasped her right hand over her left wrist, unable to bear the sight of the enigmatic markings a moment longer, simultaneously trying to ignore the subtle tingling in her neck, the place where Santos had bit her on the throat.

"Argh," she groaned, freaked out by the very thought of it, even as the memory of those lips, that tongue...his warm, talented mouth...left her clammy and unsettled.

The man had siphoned her blood.

No, the *vampire* had savored her blood.

He had said something about being able to track her, knowing where she was at all times, at least until Sunday, but there was far more to it than that—his bite had been dominant as well as sensual, as possessive as it had been erotic. He had meant to stake his claim, capture her heart, and consume her soul, all three in one; and he had used a primitive...seductive...bestial rite of *feeding* to do so. She shivered, feeling as if she'd never be warm again, and as if on cue, her burner phone lit up with a six-word text, set apart on three separate lines:

Natalia girl...

You there?

You good?

The shiver deepened in response to his casual, friendly words —it was almost as if the two were already intimate, as if they had known each other for years. Her hand rose absently to the vein in her neck, and her throat tingled with latent, erotic energy.

You there?

She knew she had to answer, or he might just show up in her bedroom.

You good?

What the heck kind of question was that?

No, Natalia was anything but good.

She picked up the phone and texted a candid reply: *Alone in my bedroom. Still processing everything. As good as can be expected.* She pressed send, and then she remembered her manners—not that she owed the vampire anything, but until she decided what she intended to do, it would be better to appease him than oppose him. *And you? How are you doing?* Her throat constricted as she typed the last four words—every cell in her body resented this surreal encounter.

A moment of silence passed with no reply; then Santos typed: *I miss you.*

Natalia gulped.

She wasn't going to touch that with a ten-foot pole.

Do you have details ready for me yet? he asked next.

Natalia sighed. In addition to already knowing her itinerary for the month of June—he had stolen her schedule when he slipped inside her computer—Santos wanted to know every fine detail, spanning the next three days: who was in the house— guards, servants, visitors, you name it—every time she planned to step foot outside the mansion, whether going to the salon, the grocery store, or just to take a dip in the hot tub. He wanted her to stay home, in her room if possible, until the raid on The Fortress was over on Sunday, but he understood that her family—

and her father—would likely become suspicious if her routine changed too dramatically. He had also indicated a desire to tail her, but the work involved in planning the raid, in mobilizing and attacking in such a short span of time, required the vampire's full attention. He needed to devote his time and energy to devising strategy and marshalling his fellow warriors, whomever they might be.

Natalia bit down hard on her lower lip.

Undoubtedly, they were an entire coven of blood-suckers...

She couldn't believe she was *thinking* such words, let alone considering them as if they were real. Ah, but real they were, and she had the mark of Delphinus on her wrist to prove it.

Before she could reply, there was a gentle knock on her bedroom door, and Sylvia's soft, lyrical voice drifted through the panel. "Miss Talia, it's Sylvie; may I come in? I have a message from your papa, and we need to select a dress for tomorrow evening. I'm sorry to interrupt you so late at night, but I'd like to steam and press it before I head home. I have several personal errands to run tomorrow."

Natalia furrowed her brow.

What in the world?

Who needed to pick out a dress at eleven o'clock at night—and what was happening tomorrow? Natalia had nothing on her schedule for Friday evening. She palmed her burner phone, tapped on the screen to reopen Santos' last message, and rapidly *tap-tap-tapped* on the keyboard:

Maid is here.

Just knocked on door.

Needs to tell me something.

BRB.

For the space of several heartbeats, Natalia felt the oddest sensation, like a cool winter's breeze wafting through her chest and swirling around her throat as if emanating from her blood.

The cool, icy draft shifted to warmth and then just as swiftly retreated.

Was Santos...

Was Santos what?

Seeking information from her blood?

She glanced around her bedroom in a quick, furtive peek, almost prepared to see a ghostly apparition floating through the air: a ghostly apparition with crystal-blue eyes, pearly white teeth, and stunning black-and-blond hair.

Could vampires do that?

Did Santos have some extrasensory radar connected to her blood?

She shuddered.

She would have to be so very careful, if and when she told him half-truths—when she wanted to hide her feelings or maintain some modicum of privacy...of dignity; when there were things she simply wasn't ready for the vampire to know. She didn't fully understand what their blood-bond meant, but it had definitely given him access to something more than she was ready to relinquish...

Natalia would be the one to decide what Santos did—or did not—know.

No one—and nothing—else.

"Come in," she said to Sylvia, stuffing the phone beneath a gold-and-red embroidered pillow and tugging on the sleeve of her nightgown to make sure the markings on her wrist were well and truly hidden.

The five-foot-two spitfire quickly wrenched the knob and shot into the bedroom. Sylvia never moved slowly—she darted around like a hummingbird, always intent on her duties and full of boundless energy, even this close to midnight. She was as thin as she was short, and she kept her midnight-black hair cropped short, but there was something timeless in her keen, smoky gray eyes, something that reminded Natalia of the dark side of the moon: deep, wise, and ripe with hidden secrets. "Did I wake you?" Sylvia asked, eyeing Natalia sideways before stopping dead in her tracks.

She saw something.

She always saw something.

"You were already up, weren't you? Your bed is still made." She answered her own question. "Are you having trouble sleeping, Miss Talia?" She planted both hands on her hips. "And why are you wearing a long-sleeve nightgown in June? Are you feeling well, Tesoro?"

Natalia laughed, trying desperately to act as natural as possible. "Sylvia, I'm feeling fine. And yes, I was still up—I took a late shower."

Sylvia wrinkled her nose and stepped closer to the bed, her wise eyes narrowing to slits. "Where is your laptop?" She eyed the armoire, then turned her attention to Natalia's dresser. "And the TV isn't on. So what? You're just sitting on the bed, staring into space?"

"*Sylvia,*" Natalia groaned, drawing out her name. "I'm fine. I was just—"

"What's wrong, Miss Talia?"

Natalia drew a slow, deep breath, searching for a way to appease the insightful housekeeper. "Sylvia, I was saying my prayers."

The maid cocked her head to the side.

"What?" Natalia said. "I can't pray? I had a...a very relaxing massage earlier. And I just felt like...you know...spending some quiet time in prayer."

"Hmm," Sylvia murmured. "I see."

Oh lord, Natalia thought, *the woman saw too much!* "At any rate, what's this business about a dress? I don't have anything on my schedule for tomorrow evening." Praying, for real this time, that the not-so-subtle shift in subjects would work, Natalia held up both hands. "And you said something about a message from my father—what is it? What's going on?" She practically held her breath.

Sylvia's smoky gray eyes deepened to charcoal as she strolled to a nearby chest of drawers, swiped at a nonexistent smattering of dust with two fingers, then turned around, leaned back, and crossed her skinny arms over her ample chest. She sighed, long and hollow. "I'm afraid you have a date tomorrow night."

Natalia leaned forward and furrowed her brows. "You mean an *appointment*? With whom?"

Sylvia shook her head slowly. "No, Miss Talia, not an appointment. I mean you have a date."

Natalia struggled to keep up.

A date?

Natalia didn't date.

She was promised to be married to—*oh, shit.*

Her mouth dropped open and she sank back on the bed. "A date with Oskar? He's coming to the house?" That was the last thing she wanted—or needed: to see her creepy fiancé tomorrow night, especially with everything that was going on. Not only did the man give her the willies, but Santos was practically embedded in her head—or her blood—whatever the case may be, and she had lied about the fact that Oskar was in her life...that he lived in the United States.

How in the world was she going to get through a long, drawn-out dinner with Oskar Vadovsky, Luca Giovanni, and heaven-knew who else, without sending out a ton of distressing signals to a territorial vampire?

She would think about that later.

"So why the fancy dress?" she asked. "Who else is coming to the house?"

Sylvia shook her head again, far more adamantly now. "Miss

Talia; you're not hearing what I'm telling you. You have a formal date with Oskar Vadovsky. He is sending a car for you at eight o'clock sharp. Your father finally gave him permission to see you... alone...and he is taking you out for the night."

Natalia frowned, feeling suddenly sick to her stomach.

She had always known this day would come. She was going to have to spend private time with Oskar at some point, and that point was likely sooner than later—but her father was very traditional when it came to Natalia's honor and her reputation. Until now, her time with the terrifying brute had always been chaperoned. The two of them had never been alone, and frankly, she hadn't expected it to happen prior to their wedding night. "You're kidding..." The words were merely a whisper.

Sylvia bit her lip, then forced a tight, pitiful smile. "It would seem he is taking you somewhere special, so we need a formal—or at least an elegant—gown. Oskar's request."

This time, it was Natalia who shook her head, and then she rolled her eyes. "No." She sounded like a two-year-old, and if she had been standing, she might have even stomped her foot. "Just...no."

Sylvia didn't try to fake any more good humor. "I know," she acquiesced, "it's...it's soon...it's unexpected...it's got to be a little awkward."

"It's gross," Natalia clarified, cutting to the chase.

"Well, okay, perhaps...but he is your intended, and you have to be alone with him at some point."

Natalia's shoulders drooped. "I'd rather be alone with an alligator in a swamp or stuck in a cage at the zoo with a bear." Forgetting about the burner phone behind her, she snatched the lacy, embroidered pillow and hugged it to her chest like a child, clinging desperately to the inanimate object for reassurance. Fortunately, her adult neurons began firing; she remembered the hidden burner phone; and she leaned back against the padded white satin headboard before Sylvia noticed the device.

Not that the maid would have asked any questions.

And she certainly would not have told Luca!

But Natalia was more than just a little bit paranoid...

"I'll never get used to him, Sylvie," she groaned.

Sylvia wrung her dainty hands together until at last her expression brightened. "Well, there is one bright spot in this... unlikely engagement: Oskar is rather handsome, Natalia. Very handsome, actually. And he's very well off. Plus, he does seem to care for you. He can give you the kind of life you deserve; take you to all kinds of wonderful places; and fill your future home with gorgeous bambini. Perhaps, if you—"

"Stop," Natalia interrupted. "Just stop." She gave Sylvia a sympathetic nod, understanding that the kindly woman was only trying to cheer her up, but honestly, they both knew how creepy Oskar was. "He's incredibly handsome," she admitted, "if you're into the overbearing, Lord of the Flies, Jack the Ripper type. Oh, and if you don't mind the whole possessed by an evil spirit thing, then yeah, he's quite the catch."

Sylvia crossed herself and stared at the ground. "Sì, Miss Talia." She whispered something pious in Italian. "I'm sorry, Tesoro—you deserve better than him."

Natalia stiffened her lip and steeled her resolve. "Well," she muttered, determined to let it go, "we may as well get on with it." She gestured toward the closet and forced a half-hearted smile, trying to lighten the mood—after all, it wasn't Sylvia's fault, and it was only one night. Natalia could endure a single date with Oskar. "Maybe we can find an all-black ensemble with a stiff collar and tails, something that comes with a similar pointed hat and broom. At least that way, Oskar and I will match."

The maid giggled, conspiratorially. "I think you should make him take you somewhere fancy, Miss Talia, definitely a five-star restaurant. Then order something really, *really* spicy and burp a lot. Hell, pass gas...break wind...just fart and fart and fart. Then pick your nose between courses—maybe he'll bring you home early. Better yet, maybe he'll call off the engagement." Even as she laughed, her keen, watchful eyes swept over Natalia's empty fourth finger, and they both arrived at the same conclusion: *a ring.*

Natalia nodded. "Shit. You think my father finally picked a date? Maybe Oskar's taking me out to give me a ring? If so, he should be on his best behavior. Despite his arrangement with Papa, he'll still want me to say yes to a proposal."

Sylvia wrinkled her pert little nose and shrugged. "Possibly. At least that would make sense—why the sudden need for a private date." She hung her head in sympathy, regathered her composure, and switched her attention back to the closet. "Come. Let's look through your wardrobe and find a dress." As she pranced in the direction of the enormous walk-in cabinet, she glanced over her shoulder and turned up her lip. "Just remember: spicy. Something really, *really* spicy, Miss Talia!"

Giggling, because she couldn't help it, Natalia set the pillow aside. "I'll be right there," she called after Sylvia, waiting to reach for the silver phone until the maid had completely disappeared behind the panel.

You still there? she texted Santos.

Always, cara mia. ALWAYS.

Whoa...he was calling her darling—my dear, to be exact—in Italian, and he wrote the last word in caps—her heart skipped a funny beat. *Maid is still here. I have to go. We have to find a dress for tomorrow night.* She backtracked and inserted the words *for an event tomorrow night,* before hitting the send button.

As expected, Santos shot a question right back: *What kind of event?*

Natalia sighed.

Blessed Mother of Mercy, she had to be careful.

Very, very careful.

Just dinner, she typed, *here at the house with some family friends, discussing some charity business, nothing criminal or too eventful.* She grimaced at the lie, but it had to be told. *The entire affair should last two to three hours,* she added, hoping she hadn't just made a misstep by going out of her way to downplay it.

That wasn't on your schedule, he quickly shot back.

Natalia chewed on her fingernail, thinking... *True,* she finally texted. *Last-minute change of plans, nothing too unusual.* She held her breath and waited.

What time do the guests arrive?

She sighed. *Eight.* Then she quickly hit the backspace button, typed in *nine* instead, and pressed send.

If she knew Santos, which she obviously did not—but she had certainly garnered a feel for his possessive, protective nature: the license and entitlement he took with Natalia that she wasn't so sure she appreciated—she could imagine him popping in at exactly eight o'clock, catching a glimpse of Oskar's limo, and ripping the doors off the hinges.

Hell, flying through the air and chasing the vehicle, disguised as a vampire bat.

Could Santos actually do that?

Did vampires shift into bats?

Natalia had no idea, and she didn't care to find out. As far as she was concerned, she only knew that Oskar Vadovsky and Santos Olaru were a disaster waiting to happen: two primal, alpha males, one with the soul of the devil, and one being fueled by an ancient curse, which had to make him feel somewhat desperate. In her mind's eye, she could picture Oskar brandishing a gun or saying something vile to Santos, and then the vampire would twist Oskar's head off his neck, put his body in the trunk, and cart Natalia away before Sunday. Or worse: Oskar might unload his weapon into Santos, eliminating all hope and possibility for the women being held in The Fortress. Either way, it was a lose-lose proposition.

And always—absolutely always—Natalia could see those stunning, otherworldly, faery-princess eyes, the ones that belonged to that four-year-old girl, and she was reminded of the high-stakes game she was forced to play, every day of her life.

She could see her father overreacting to his livelihood being threatened, to the imminent risk of incarceration, or to Natalia having been disobedient—and what would be a greater disobedience than the challenge, attention, and confrontation of another man? How would she ever explain Santos' presence?

She could see The Fortress burning.

She could hear bullets explode in rapid fire.

She could picture those eyes, the ones that always haunted her, closing for a final time.

And she could never, ever live with the guilt.

At least this way, if Santos decided to check up on her, he would be an hour late.

Please shoot me a list of first and last names—the guests who are coming to dinner, Santos texted. *Then text me again, tomorrow night, both when the guests arrive and when they depart. If plans change again, I'd like to hear about it.*

Natalia stared at the commanding message, chills running up and down her spine.

The vampire-sentinel was not playing games.

He was giving her three days before he claimed her because he understood her predicament, but he wasn't about to back off. And challenging him now would only be foolish.

At least he hadn't questioned her story.

Will do, she texted, keeping it short and sweet—she could come up with a list of plausible names, and she could also tread water until Sunday, continue to play her father's game...

She could even endure Oskar Vadovsky for another three days, and then, if Santos and his fellow warriors were truly capable of doing all he'd claimed, she would at least be free to choose, going forward: free of her overwhelming responsibility to the women in The Fortress; free to run, to hide, or to try to resist. Free for the first time in as long as she could remember—her choices would finally be her own.

Well, not exactly...

She would have a whole new nightmare to contend with because, as sexy and alluring as Santos was, she had no intentions of trading one prison for another, becoming the bride of a vampire. But she would cross that bridge when she came to it.

One day.

One hour.

One minute at a time.

Right now, she needed to join Sylvia in the closet and find a dress she could wear with elbow-length gloves—something that would hide the enigmatic markings on her inner left wrist, the brand of ownership affixed by the gods, the stamp of her latest would-be captor.

CHAPTER TEN

2:00 AM

"Explain this shit again," Ramsey Olaru groused, standing in the center of Santos' living room like a menacing giant, his heavily muscled arms crossed over his iron chest. "Why that female...your *destiny*...Natalia Giovanni, isn't already here in this lake house?"

Santos regarded Ramsey circumspectly, aware of Saxson's demeanor as well—the second twin was sitting on the edge of Santos' sofa, cracking his knuckles and popping his neck. Both males were clearly amped up and loaded for bear. "You have all the details, Ramsey," Santos said, a hint of exasperation in his voice, "but in a nutshell, and if I must repeat it: The entire fortress is like one enormous grenade, and Natalia's body is the safety pin. Her obedience is all that's securing the fuse. If I pull her from the Giovanni compound, that metaphorical grenade goes boom, and everyone in it disintegrates. Clear enough?"

Ramsey harrumphed. "So it's a metaphor, not an actual bomb?"

Santos chuckled. "Yes, brother; it's a metaphor. No idea how Giovanni worked out the potential annihilation of the women. I only know we have to get in and out, real quick. And that means removing what could be a hundred or more women in under fifteen minutes; preparing to take out Giovanni's goons; avoiding or neutralizing any local law enforcement or meddling humans; and getting everyone transported to someplace safe. There are a lot of unknown variables, but it should be doable—just so long as Napolean gives the thumbs-up."

Saxson shifted nervously on the sofa and exchanged a knowing glance with Ramsey, an unspoken understanding passing between the twins, before Saxson locked his hazel peepers on Santos. "Yeah, well, we just came from Napolean's manse, and the king was explicitly clear: You are his sentinel. Natalia is your *destiny*. Giovanni's business is no longer a human affair—or off limits. We have permission to take the slave trade down, to demolish that building, and to free all the women: to get your female—and your future—the hell out of that compound. As in yesterday." Settling a bit, Saxson shrugged one shoulder. "Well, *yesterday* is also a metaphor, but you get the gist: Napolean agreed to our tentative plan. He believes we can get this orchestrated and ready in three days' time. And we have the go-ahead to pull the trigger, Sunday at midnight, when most reasonable humans are sleeping. If all goes as planned, you should have your *destiny* home where she belongs no later than Monday morning."

Santos didn't realize how worried he had actually been —*would the king say yes; would the king say no?*—until a wave of relief swept over him. He literally felt his shoulders loosen. "Who is the king giving us for the operation?"

Saxson stood up and sauntered to Ramsey's side in a spontaneous, if not unconscious, show of solidarity. "Saber and Julien are a no-go," he said, his hand slicing back and forth, left and right, beneath his chin in a familiar *not gonna happen* gesture. "With all the shit going down between Keitaro, Zayda, and Xavier Matista—the fact that the Ancient Master Warrior has recently upped the ante, trying to bait the son of a jackal into a confrontation—the king wants at least one sentinel, as well as the tracker, close to home. You know: just in case a wild pack of mangy wolves shows up in Dark Moon Vale."

Ramsey snickered, a hint of longing in his eyes. There was nothing the warrior loved more than a brutal, bloody, fist-to-fist—or trident-to-torso—battle, and Santos genuinely hoped nothing would go down while the warrior was stuck at the Giovanni compound.

His thoughts shifted seamlessly to Xavier Matista and the probability that something might happen before Sunday: A few hours after interviewing Zayda, before he had headed to the Serenity Salon & Spa to meet Natalia, Santos had called Keitaro Silivasi back on his cell phone to follow up on a few more questions...get a little more information, without Zayda present. His first inquiry had been fairly straightforward: Whatever happened to Zayda's mother? Was there a significant likelihood that she was still at the compound? In other words, at some juncture, could the lycans get to Xia and use her as leverage against Zayda and Keitaro?

According to Keitaro, the female was presumed to be dead.

Like Zayda, Xia Patrone had started out in the eastern wing as a low-end prostitute, before she had been moved to what Zayda called "Death Row," the southern quadrant where the women were sold to be slaughtered. Unlike Zayda, who had also begun in the east and been moved to the south, there hadn't been anyone to rescue her, and she had never returned to The Fortress.

Satisfied with the answer, Santos had asked the next question: What did Keitaro plan to do if Xavier never took the bait, if the lycan never responded to the provocative missives?

This time, Keitaro had expressed a high degree of confidence —just so long as Xavier was getting the messages, the plan was going to work. He'd explained that Deanna Dubois-Silivasi, Nachari's mate, had recently drawn an incredibly detailed sketch of Xia Patrone, using a photographic snapshot from Zayda's early memories—Nachari had retrieved the information from Zayda's mind so effortlessly, she had never known he was in her head— and Keitaro was just itching to send the drawing, along with his next missive, to Xavier.

The father and son duo were through with leaving hints.

They had grown weary of trying to goad the lycan out of hiding with superficial taunts and innuendos—they were going to tell Xavier exactly who Zayda really was: his biological daughter.

So yeah, there was a high likelihood that Xavier would take the bait and something would happen, sooner than later. In light of the fact that Keitaro had also apprised Napolean of this new information, the king's judgment made a lot of sense. Of course he would want at least one sentinel, as well as Julien, to stay close to home.

"By the same token"—Saxson's voice pierced the silence, interrupting Santos' musings— "Keitaro obviously stays in the vale, but so does Marquis Silivasi. Again, the king wants to make sure Keitaro has some family close by to watch his six. He did give us Nathaniel and Nachari—never know when a wizard or a panther might come in handy—and he also gave us Kagen. So at least there's that."

"Since we're only dealing with humans," Ramsey chimed in, "Napolean also thought it would be a good opportunity to bring in the younger generation, allow a couple neophytes to get their feet wet on the operation. Braden Bratianu and his friend Blade

Rynich will be riding shotgun, just in case we need the extra hands...or fangs." He chuckled, deep in his throat, and the sound was far more menacing than humorous. "All in all, the king figures the eight of us can handle it: you, me, Saxson, Nathaniel, Nachari, Kagen, and the two fledglings."

Santos did the math in his head.

Assuming Zayda was correct—there were between twenty and twenty-five guards patrolling the halls of The Fortress—that would leave around three humans for each vampire. Assuming Luca's personal entourage of bodyguards jumped into the fray, the moment the shit got real, that might add another five to ten humans to the mix. Say a few cops made an appearance, and a couple of nosy neighbors reared their heads, each vampire might have to contend with four to five Homo sapiens, not too hard for a supernatural species. Worst case scenario: The women might panic, try to struggle or resist their rescuers—place themselves in danger during the height of the confrontation. Then things could get a little hairy, but that would be a good assignment for Braden and Blade, control and contain the captives.

"Ramsey," Santos said, "I may need you to run point on this in terms of devising specific strategy, assigning individual roles, and finalizing the execution." He sauntered over to the glass-and-steel coffee table, dropped into a squat, and pointed toward a half-dozen scattered papers, all blueprints of Luca's compound and The Fortress. "I'm feeling the need to go back and forth as often as possible between now and Sunday, to keep an eye on Natalia. She's gotta be freaking out, and her energy is all over the map: She's curious, terrified, and skittish as hell, vacillating between fight and flight, but her father has her so trained to be obedient that I can't completely trust what she says and does. At least not yet. The attraction is there, and the pull between our souls is strong—but the female lives in survival mode, looking out for number one. And frankly, texting via a burner phone is not a solid enough connection. I would prefer to be hands-on. Not to mention, having the hidden phone leaves her exposed to her father and his henchmen. What if she gets caught?" He sighed, turning his attention to more concrete matters—there were always a host of *what-ifs,* and worry for the sake of worry was never helpful or constructive.

"Tomorrow night," Santos continued, "she has to entertain some guests at the compound around nine o'clock. It's supposed to be a routine dinner, some friends of the Giovanni family, but something's not right with the vibe." He shrugged to indicate he had no idea what was off. "So I'll definitely be MIA at some point after sundown, and likely a few times each day, between now and Sunday. Point is: I'm all in on the rescue of the women and taking down The Fortress. The sooner we get this shit handled, the better—the sooner I can bring my *destiny* home. But I don't want to run point on the operation; I need to be free to come and go."

Ramsey retrieved a small monogramed silver case from his right hip pocket, opened the thin container, and stuffed a toothpick between his lips. Rather than balancing it between his teeth or adjusting it here and there with his tongue, he chewed on the end out of nervous energy. After a minute or two had passed, he grunted in agreement and flicked the toothpick into the trash. "Not a problem, Santos. Do what you need to do. Honestly, I prefer it that way, anyhow."

"As do I," Saxson agreed. "The next twenty-nine days are going to be one crazy ride—a topsy-turvy, supernatural roller coaster—and you can't foresee the twists and turns, no matter how hard you try. You're just gonna have to play it by ear." He smoothed his hand through his light ash hair, running it all the way down the back of his neck. "Claiming your *destiny*; converting her to vampire, and bringing her into the house of Jadon is a monumental task, all on its own. If you can make inroads with Natalia, begin to win her trust, then that's where you need to focus your attention. Just so long as you have a chance to meet up with the team before Sunday and go over the final details of the mission, I say handle your business, however you please."

Santos felt a sudden surge of emotion swell in his chest, and it honestly surprised him how much he appreciated his brothers in that moment.

Of course, they understood...

Why wouldn't they?

They had both claimed *destinies* of their own.

But it was more than the understanding that caused his chest to constrict; it was the unspoken current running beneath the whole conversation: In addition to understanding what a dangerous, high-stakes game a Blood Moon really was, Ramsey and Saxson were stepping up to the plate, trying to stand in the gap for their older brother.

And while that shouldn't have come as a surprise—the Olarus had always been an unbreakable triad—it was just that Santos was seeing the twins in a whole new light, like their roles had suddenly been reversed. For centuries, Santos had taken care of his family—he had looked after his "baby brothers" and stepped into the role of guardian, following their parents' tragic deaths. As the firstborn son of Santiago Olaru—and a twin to a dark soul who had been sacrificed at birth—Santos was already a solitary figure, so it had just seemed natural for the vampire to step up and take the mantle, move into the role of protector-provider.

He had been a father figure, a disciplinarian, a watchdog, and a mentor.

And truth be told, he had made the shit up for centuries, flying by the seat of his pants, with only one clear compass to guide him: his unshakable love for two hazel-eyed troublemakers. And now, for some bizarre reason, it just sort of hit him—he wasn't accustomed to being on the receiving end of the nurturing, and he wasn't quite sure how to take it.

Eyeing each warrior in turn, he blinked both eyelids in quick succession, removing the moisture that was threatening his corneas.

Damn.

Where were these emotions coming from?

"You all right?" Saxson asked, eyeing Santos attentively.

"Yeah, I'm good," Santos muttered, "just thinking about the past." He meandered toward the floor-to-ceiling windows and looked out over the lake. "I appreciate you guys having my back."

Now this made Ramsey snarl. "You know," the warrior said brusquely, "we've always had your back, even when we were younger. You may have stepped up like a Viking, and there's no question, you made a helluva difference—but we all played a role in our family's survival." He softened his delivery just a bit. "You think we didn't know...you think we never talked about it...how much you also needed us, how much you needed to *be needed*?"

Ramsey's words struck Santos' heart like a hammer striking an anvil, and he couldn't turn around and look at him. "Saxson?" he asked, the unspoken question implied.

The youngest twin cleared his throat, his discomfort as obvious as the others'. "We needed you to be like a sire, Santos—it gave us a sense of control...predictability...heck, *sanity*—but you needed us to be like your sons. It's how you kept Mom and Dad alive...for all of us."

Santos bent his head toward the window and rubbed his forehead with his hand.

They were right.

As the odd son out, a vampire without a twin, Santos had almost been destroyed by Santiago's death, and knowing how much he was needed by his brothers had pulled him back from the brink.

Ramsey lumbered forward, his heavy footsteps echoing off the white oak floors. "Look," he grunted, his voice thick with intensity and unusual emotion, "none of us are babes in the woods anymore. We're all Master Warriors. Hell, we're the house of Jadon's sentinels, and we did more than survive—we grew up to become the king's protectors. We secure the vale, and we vanquish our enemies, but we've never stopped being a family, *first*." He let the declaration linger for a couple of seconds before pressing forward. "Point is," he barked, "Saxson and I aren't about to let anything happen to you, Santos—not on account of some ancient, evil omen. The Curse isn't going to harm you, and The Blood isn't coming near you. No matter what goes down...no matter how this month plays out...nothing is going to touch you, big brother, not while we draw breath."

Silence permeated the lake house like darkness permeated night, until Santos finally turned around, leaned back against the window, and rested the heel of one foot against the glass, his head falling backward.

He couldn't respond to Ramsey's declaration.

Not with words.

They were far too inadequate.

Besides, he knew if he tried, he might just fall apart.

So he curled his hand into a fist, placed it over his heart, and thumped it two times: one tap for each brother.

Saxson nodded and returned the gesture, placing his fist over his heart, and his luminous eyes spoke volumes: *We would kill for you; we would die for you; and the three of us are in this together.*

In his own rugged fashion, Ramsey stared Santos down for the space of several intense heartbeats before he finally reached for another toothpick. "Just so long as you feel us," the brutal warrior grunted, speaking around the obstruction.

"I feel you, Ramsey," Santos said earnestly, "both of you, and it's mutual."

So there it was.

The long and short of it.

I love you was not something the Olaru brothers said often—they weren't very big on open emotion—but they had practically shouted the sentiment, this night in the lake house, without uttering a single word.

And all three sentinels had heard each other clearly.

* * *

Santos stepped outside, onto the top tier of his polished, stamped-concrete deck, needing to grab a breath of fresh air.

Needing a moment of solitude.

He needed to collect his thoughts, while his brothers continued to work on strategy. He needed to concentrate, for a moment, on Natalia Giovanni; the next few days of his Delphinus Blood Moon; and what it would take to get through them.

In truth, he knew he had a lot of headway to make up with the mysterious, beautiful female, and the burden was sitting squarely on his shoulders like a two-ton vest sewn from bricks.

The woman was a paradoxical, delicate, *defiant* enigma.

She was smart as a fox, and her self-protective instincts were powerful.

She was cunning, quick, and would not just fall into his arms—come into his world—like a joyful, energetic puppy bounding toward its beloved master.

No one was going to *master* Natalia.

And that was not what Santos wanted.

Yet and still, every instinct in his ancient, rational mind—his primordial, vampiric body—told him to take charge now: remove her from that compound, consequences be damned; let the chips fall where they may with regard to the innocent captive women; and convert Natalia *tonight*...make his female immortal.

Make her stronger.

Make her supernatural.

Try to make her invincible, or at least as close to invincible as possible.

But Santos was also a male of honor—he was Santiago and Ruth's true son—and beyond his duty to the Curse, he was honor-bound to that which was moral and correct. And he wanted to win Natalia's heart as well as her trust. Good, bad, or indifferent, that gorgeous female's soul—her pain, her duty, her very core—was twisted around that fortress like vines around a trellis. Natalia was virtually tethered to those helpless women...she always had been...which made the only path forward relatively clear-cut: Setting those women free was the only way to free Natalia.

And while it was almost certain, the moment the raid was over, Natalia's first instinct would likely be to run—as far and as fast as she could, from Santos—the sentinel had seen the longing and the hunger in her eyes. He had seen the *wanting*, the need, and the emptiness in her soul. And no one—not even the daughter of a corrupt, wicked man—was meant to live with that much loneliness. Not unlike the final phase of a lunar eclipse, a beacon of light transcended the darkness in Santos' thoughts; his mind meandered back to his brothers; and a smile creased the corners of his mouth.

Warmth filled his heart.

Peace infused his soul.

And everything settled into place, even as the moon shone brilliantly above him and reflected off the lake.

He chuckled softly, recalling fists over hearts—the way Saxson had returned Santos' gesture and Ramsey had declared his fealty: how he had stared Santos down and underscored his sentiment, spitting it out around a blasted toothpick. And it struck Santos as funny that in a strange, backward way, the three had played their own version of *rock-paper-scissors*.

Only all three vampires were rocks.

And together they formed an unbreachable canyon.

And *that* was the anchor, the ever-constant fortress that would see Santos Olaru through this transition.

CHAPTER ELEVEN

Gwen Hamilton etched another slash in the back wall of her cell.

Her dirty, confining, cement and iron cave.

She wished she could tell what time it was, but she had no idea—maybe two or three in the morning, maybe later. The only thing that came to mind was *thirty days...*

She had been in this abominable prison for exactly thirty days.

Ever since that tragic afternoon at the Aspen Ski Resort when her entire world had been turned upside down. When the life she had known, planned, and embraced—the life she had every right to live out—had been so cruelly changed at the whim of criminals.

She still remembered every detail leading up to her loss of freedom...

Months and months of planning a dream vacation to Aspen, Colorado, with her three besties from college; arriving at the ski resort and shredding fresh powder; feeling like they were on top of the world as they explored the scenic slopes and breathed the fresh mountain air. Surrounded by a world of juniper and pine, she had felt so reinvigorated as she packed away her skis on the last day of the trip and headed for the rustic lodge.

Gwen had never arrived.

She had never met up with her friends.

Somewhere between the parking lot and the heavy front doors of the lodge, she had made a single miscalculation in judgment—she had walked beside a parked blue van, and everything had changed in an instant.

It had happened so damn fast.

Even now, playing it back, she couldn't imagine what she might have done different, how she could have possibly thought—or fought—her way out of it.

The side door to the van swung open, and two husky, masked men leaped out. Before Gwen could scream or run, raise a fist to fight back, one had her arms wrenched behind her back, and the other stuffed a cloth over her mouth. Those seconds may have felt like hours, but they weren't. Her consciousness had faded fast, faster than what seemed possible within the laws of physics, faster than Gwen could react; then her legs had been lifted from the ground, and Gwen had been tossed into a van.

Just like that.

Just like that...

She had awakened in a small dirty cell, with a cement wall behind her and iron bars on either side, like a prison. She was terrified, screaming, nearly hyperventilating, desperate to find a way out, but her cries had fallen on deaf ears. And all the while, she'd just kept thinking: If she only had an eraser...if she could just turn back the hands of time...redo the past few hours of her life, then none of this would be real.

These things just didn't happen—they were only on TV. Gwen was way too smart, too aware, too alive...she had far too much life ahead of her.

But, of course, that had nothing to do with anything.

Gwendolyn Marie Hamilton had been in the wrong place at the wrong time.

That was it.

That was all.

And ever since that day, the world that didn't exist—that "thing that just didn't happen"—had come into full, panoramic view.

She was in The Fortress.

Not just *a fortress*, which it definitely was, but a dungeon known by that name, with dozens of other women, being held captive to be sold and used as a slave. There were isolated cells and numerous tunnels, several floors used for different things, and guards that patrolled on a regular basis who were as ruthless as they were heartless—especially the one they called The Reaper.

Fortunately, the guards weren't allowed to sample the merchandise.

Or at least that's what Gwen had been told.

And as the days turned to weeks, and the weeks turned to a month, the true horror and depravity of her situation had been made abundantly clear: Gwen was never getting out—no one ever escaped—and if she wasn't extremely careful, she might be moved from the northern quadrant, which housed the high-end call girls, to the south.

The women in the south did not come home, and it wasn't because they'd escaped.

She gulped, still shocked and revulsed by the truth of the hidden citadel: Young girls, barely adolescent, were housed in the west, in a wing they called "The Orphanage," and in the east, better known as "Street Walk Row," the women were sold so cheaply and so often...any manner of treatment or degradation was permissible with the low-end girls. And the two wings she had already mentioned—"Easy Street" and "Death Row"—sort of spoke for themselves.

So many women—sad, broken, resigned, or bitter women—had cautioned her to consider herself lucky, to think before she spoke, to weigh the cost of every word and action. Gwen was twenty-two years old and athletically built, with all the right curves in all the right places, and her shoulder-length blond hair was full and natural, her light green eyes unusually exotic.

They'd told her to count her looks as a blessing.

Had the other women wanted to escape?

Hell yes!

No one had ever bargained for slavery.

But they had learned over months, over years, and some, over decades, that it was easier to go along with their captors, that it was better to live...

To survive.

In a nutshell, if Gwen could live on Easy Street, keep her place in the northern wing, then she needed to fight like hell to stay there. Nothing happened in The Fortress that the guards didn't choose or allow, and the best a woman could do was try to elevate her station, make damn sure her skill and her body were worth the money—never disappoint a John.

Gwen swallowed the bile that rose in her gut.

She got it.

She really did.

And she deeply empathized with the handful of women she had managed to meet, the ones who took the time to speak to her: Some had been runaways; others had been homeless; several had been abducted from various school grounds—college campuses, elementary playgrounds, middle school gyms, and locker rooms. Still others had been taken from home or work—vacant halls, empty parking lots, late night lounges in hotels or airports. There were lawyers, nurses, and corporate employees. You name it;

Luca Giovanni did not discriminate. As long as a woman (or a girl) was beautiful, as long as she fit some pre-defined profile or some sick, perverted fantasy of a man who could afford to pay—young, old, heavy, thin, blonde, brunette, bald, *whatever*—she was fair game.

And even more chilling than the women being taken was the fact that others had been born there—some had been raised in The Fortress.

Gwen couldn't bear to think about it: spending a lifetime in this particular hell.

Becoming pregnant and giving birth to a new generation...of slaves.

She pressed her palm against the barren wall and stared fixedly at the thirty slashes.

So far, she had remained unmolested.

She had been given one month to lose ten pounds—*whatever the hell that was about*—to study the most vulgar, explicit videos in order to "learn the most requested techniques," and to take advantage of the other high-end class girls, to be tutored directly if she chose what was good for her. Short of actually—and fully—sampling the merchandise, the guards were more than willing to help the women out.

Gwen would rather take her chances.

The whole thing turned her stomach.

It assaulted her soul, and she had no intentions of remaining in The Fortress, even if her only way out was in a body bag.

Still, she wanted to live, to reclaim her life, and to that end, she had taken every opportunity to watch, listen, and learn. She had explored the communal restrooms and the vent above the shower stalls—and she'd found an interesting passage of duct-work. Every time she had been allowed go to the restroom—whether to relieve herself, to vomit, or to shower—Gwen had pried that vent open, shimmied through the hole in the ceiling, and explored the tunnel in the ductwork. Eventually, she had followed the narrow passageway to the cellar, where she'd hoped to escape—at least until last night, when she'd finally had a chance to explore the dark, dungeon-like space, and what she'd found had chilled her blood.

In the center of the bleak, clammy cellar, positioned in the middle of the floor, was a large stone slab with a smoothed, hollow surface, much like a bed made of granite. On either side of the stone, there were intricate carvings, some sort of ancient, cryptic symbols, and they were unlike anything Gwen had ever laid eyes on before...unlike anything she had ever seen in a history book. And the color of that stone, the stain in that bed of granite, it was an eerie, jarring, deep crimson red—the very pores of the rock had been soaked in blood...again and again...and again.

Women had been executed on that slab.

Gwen didn't know how she knew—she just did.

And once she'd been able to tear herself away from the horror of that killing room, she had managed to follow two long, narrow halls, each to their end, each to a heavy, iron, padlocked door.

And that's when she'd known her fate was truly sealed.

Not only were the doors locked and secured, but they were wired to a simple control pad, and the control pad was wired to both a cell phone and a timer, which looked a lot like a basic sprinkler-system box, regulating four separate zones. Each zone required a coded entry in order to "start running," and by the looks of the contraption, the code could be entered either manually or by remote control. And all that apparatus—whether triggered by an opened door; a phone call or a text; or a manual code entered by a guard—was connected to a row of four heavy metal cannisters, each tank marked *"Poison—Toxic Chemicals"* beneath a row of hanging gas masks.

What kind of nerve agent was inside those tanks, Gwen didn't know, but she really didn't need to speculate.

Because the type didn't matter.

She had already seen the intricate and excessive plumbing from inside the ductwork.

She had already noticed that every cell in The Fortress had a showerhead, but no shower: no water, no drains, and no apparent use.

And she could follow the pipes, the ones leading out of the cylinders, and see how they were linked to four corresponding main supply lines—and how those four supplies fed each wing in The Fortress. They were pumps, and it had all suddenly made sense.

The Fortress had been designed as an armed chemical weapon—a death trap—and depending on the lethality of that toxic agent, if the doors were ever opened, if a guard ever set it off, if someone from the outside made a call or sent a text—if they systematically entered all four codes—the women would be dead within minutes.

One by one—north, south, east, and west—victims of chemical warfare.

Luca Giovanni wasn't just a greedy racketeer—the man was diabolically insane, a true sociopath in every sense of the word.

He was as evil as evil came.

And Gwen Hamilton had been trapped in his web of darkness.

Come Monday, she would be taken to her very first John. Her one-month reprieve was over, and come hell or high water, she had to escape, even if it cost her her life.

Gwen closed her eyes, bowed her head, and said a short prayer for courage.

Kill or be killed—the law of the jungle.

She would escape, or she would die trying.

* * *

From his perch on a large gray rock, Xavier Matista crumpled the blasted missive in his fist, threw back his head, and howled at the timber wolf moon, his long, golden-brown mane twisting in the preternatural wind sweeping through the Mhieridian air.

Those vile, cursed vampires.

Keitaro and Nachari Silivasi.

They had been leaving daily missives at the Swingle-Duplex penthouse for months, and this last one, well, it had finally gone too far: It had stolen Xavier's breath and chilled his very soul.

Canines, lykos, loup-garou—but especially Xavier Matista— salutations from Dark Moon Vale!

As always, we welcome you to the valley: any day, any time of your choosing...

And this little tidbit of information (forgive the doggy-treat reference) might help sway your decision: Does the general know that twenty-one years ago, most likely at the beginning of summer, he purchased a slave named Xia from Luca Giovanni (her likeness has been drawn at the bottom of this dispatch just to refresh the memory), and that slave had a child, a half-lycan female, named Zayda Patrone. Yes, how ironic; the general has a daughter.

A daughter he also purchased twenty years later, chained inside a penthouse, and left to be found by the Vampyr.

A daughter he freely gave away to his enemy (thank you).

We understand that most lycan women are barren; human females are used to carry the mantle; yet children remain quite rare —and while they may not be valued, they are certainly kept close to home...

Perhaps Daddy would like to come out from the portal and play.

As usual, Keitaro Silivasi's address was stamped at the bottom of the missive.

The bastard!

Xavier stared at the tops of the trees, regarding the Wolverine Woods, just south of the Western Pack's villages, and once again, he recalled all the insult, all the damage, all the havoc the Silivasi brothers had left in their wake—all the bodies of dead werewolves that could not be replaced.

He snarled, curling his hands into angry, clawed fists.

Prior to this latest note, the vampires had always played fast and loose with the wording, some trifling bullshit couched in cryptic words: *Curious as to why—how—we have your DNA? What else do we know about the so-called general, besides the fact that he's impotent, afraid, and weak?*

And now Xavier knew why—how they got his DNA—what else they knew about the lycan general. The despicable vampires weren't lying. The drawing looked just like Xia Patrone. Xavier never forgot a face or a name—and now that he thought a little more about Zayda, the girl's mysterious eyes and that wild mane of hair, there wasn't a doubt in his mind.

Son of a bitch!

General Xavier Matista had a daughter, a child of his own flesh and blood—apparently, he was neither impotent, afraid, nor weak—yet he had virtually handed the girl over to his mortal enemies on a silver platter. He had invited *and watched* as other lycan males took the most gratuitous and carnal advantage of his own genetic offspring.

He sighed, trying to rein in his temper.

At least the last part didn't bother him...too much.

Had Zayda been born in Mhier, her fate would have been quite similar: He would have eventually bartered her away to a powerful male. However, he would have chosen someone worthy, someone deserving of Xavier's rank, someone meritorious of claiming, bedding, and mating a general's daughter. He would not have passed her around so casually. It was beneath his station. Yet what was done was done...

Rising from his perch on the uneven stone, he prowled into the dark, haunting night.

Yes, Keitaro Silivasi, your missive changes everything.

Wolves do not abandon their pups.

And I would rather see Zayda dead than let you have her.

Shifting effortlessly into his massive beast, Xavier loped toward the woods on all four paws.

For tonight, he would run it off.

Tomorrow, he would devise a plan.

And soon, he would come out from the portal...to play.

CHAPTER TWELVE

Natalia Giovanni exited the mansion through an exterior kitchen door. She traversed the narrow bridge across the Winding Mill Creek River and made her way along the unpaved path to the large wooden stables. As she pried the barn doors open, her heart began to ache. More than anything, she just wanted to saddle her favorite mare, or perhaps the proud blue-black stallion named Midnight that her father had recently purchased from a top, renowned breeder, and take him for a run.

She never felt freer than when she was riding Midnight.

Fifteen hands of power at her thighs; such grace, beauty, and stealth beneath the reins; the wind in her hair, and the world at her back. There was no feeling quite like it on earth, just Natalia and the horse, nothing and no one else—nobility, majesty, and absolute freedom, all at the courtesy of a resplendent beast.

She sighed, letting go of the longing and her reverie.

She couldn't ride.

Not today.

At least not far enough to run.

She would have to text Santos first, let him know where she was going, and didn't that just feel like—sound like—the script from a really bad movie, or perhaps a nonsensical dream, the kind where flowers were made out of candy, frogs hopped around on clouds, and the mailman was really a clown, recently escaped from the circus? And, of course, the whole damn thing made sense because, after all, it was only a dream. And dreams were notorious for existing within an altered, fantastical reality, not unlike what Natalia was living right now...ever since Santos had found her.

In a way, meeting the terrifying, handsome, elusive hacker after all these years was kind of like a living dreamscape: a crazy, bizarre, outrageous fantasy that wasn't supposed to intersect with real life. Yet, the etchings on her wrist; the memory of his fangs; the fact that he was a nocturnal creature from a dark, foreboding mythology—he was literally a separate species—was a waking nightmare to be sure.

And Natalia was caught in the spider's web.

It was as real as real could get.

No matter how badly she wished it were so—that Santos was only a dream, or even a hallucination—she couldn't deny the facts. And now, as she did her best to go about her daily routine, to move forward in the light of day, it all seemed so far away...so surreal...like it could have happened on a cloud...while she slept. Perhaps it was a dream after all...

She wound her way through the maze of stalls, searching for the new, prized stallion—she couldn't ride him, but she could stroke his mane, perhaps brush his coat for a while. She could at least begin the slow, intimate process of forming a bond with the magnificent animal; after all, horses didn't like to be alone, and Natalia could use the distraction. Besides, if she could establish a connection this early on, create a safe, inviting nexus for Midnight, the effort would go a long way toward cementing their burgeoning *horse-and-rider* relationship.

Yeah, right...

What the hell was she thinking?

"Get a grip, Natalia," she muttered beneath her breath, as the reality of her situation came rushing back, front and center. "You aren't going to have the time or the chance to get to know the beautiful stallion. One way or the other, your life is about to change irrevocably."

And that meant...forever.

She refused to give the subject any more thought.

She had this moment to herself, and she was determined to live in it.

Brushing some lint off her collar, she turned on her heel, strolled in the direction of the desired stall, then reached for a wooden mane-and-tail brush.

Damnit.

It was a good two feet out of her reach, hanging on a high metal hook beneath the rafters.

She climbed on a stack of nearby haybales and stretched her arm forward, teetering on the uneven surface.

She was so close now...

Just a few more inches...

If she could just lean forward a little further and flick it with her fingers...

She extended her hand as far as she could, leaned toward the brush, and just barely grazed it with the tip of one fingernail: *Damn, damn, damn!* She was still too far away. Realizing she either needed to add a stepping stool to the miniature haystack or use some sort of implement to knock the brush free, she climbed down from the haybale, headed across the center aisle of the barn, and ducked inside a tiny tack room.

There...

Right inside the doorway...

She found a small loop of rope hanging on the wall, one she could definitely use to dislodge the brush—it would work as well as anything else. Heading back toward Midnight's enclosure, she climbed on the bales a second time and flicked the rope at the brush.

What the actual hell?

She must have hit it five times.

Was the damn thing nailed to the wall?

"Allow me."

A deep masculine voice brushed against her ear, even as a strong, muscular chest molded to her back, and Natalia didn't have to turn around or glance over her shoulder to know who was pressed against her. She would recognize that sexy tenor—and that intoxicating scent—anywhere.

Santos Olaru.

Where the heck had he come from, and how long had he been watching?

Natalia dropped the rope on the ground and held her breath as Santos extended a divine, chiseled arm around her shoulder, then reached over her head and removed the brush with ease. *Show off,* she thought, but "Thank you," she said, waiting for him to step down off the haybale and give her some room to breathe.

The male didn't budge an inch.

He just stood there.

Holding the brush in one brawny hand and crowding against her, his chest glued to her back as if he were trying to absorb her warmth and infuse her with his. She cleared her throat to give him a hint, and he placed his free hand on the curve of her hip. She wrapped her arms around her waist to create a barrier between them, and he immediately tightened his grip. She decided to use her words instead...

"How long have you been here, *stalker?*" she asked.

He chuckled softly. "Not long at all, *cara mia.*"

She sucked in air through her teeth. "How did you know where to find me?" And then she held up two fingers to forestall his answer. "Never mind. Don't tell me. I'm sure it has something to do with blood."

If such a thing were possible, Santos leaned further into Natalia's body. He bent his head and nuzzled her neck, then softly inhaled her scent. "It has everything to do with blood, pretty lady," he drawled like a lazy jungle cat. "Yours has such a sweet, vanilla aroma, almost like a flask of cologne."

Natalia gulped. "Would you mind backing up?"

"I would mind," he murmured, "but I'll respect your wishes if it really bothers you."

Natalia's face felt hot.

Clammy.

Swollen.

And suddenly hot.

Like she was coming down with the flu.

"It bothers me a lot," she said. And then, afraid she might just pass out, she fanned herself with both hands.

Santos bent to her neck again, only this time, he blew an ice-cold frisson of air over her heated skin. "Better?" His right arm snaked around her waist, the brush resting loosely in his fingers. His free hand settled on her belly, and he tugged her back against him. "Don't lose your balance," he whispered. Then he hoisted her into his arms as if she were virtually weightless, stepped down from the haybale, still holding her close, and raised her up in the air—to shoulder height at least—before setting her down gently atop the railing. Her legs dangled over the edge, falling naturally to either side of his hips, and he didn't hesitate to settle his hips between them.

"Are you crazy?" she panted, feeling both trapped and flustered. Her mouth was unusually dry. *What the hell did he think he was doing?* "You can't just touch me whenever you want. You can't just pick me up and move me around. And for that matter, you can't just show up in the barn. Do you have any idea how many armed guards patrol this compound?"

The corner of Santos' mouth quirked up in a devilish grin. "I can't?" he asked. "I think I just did." He flashed those pearly whites, his smile like a strand of jewels, before winking like a mischievous kid, and his crystal-blue peepers lightened. "Apologies, Natalia girl." He took a respectful step back, and Natalia exhaled with gratitude. "How are you today?" he asked, in a moderately normal tone. "I see you came to the barn to get away... a lot weighing on your mind?"

She blanched.

What was with him?

And more important, who did he think he was?

Yes, there was a lot weighing on her mind.

Not the least of which was his boldness, his confidence, the license he took with her body, and the games he played with her head. She thought better of voicing her protest, lest he think he had the upper hand. "Yes, I came to the barn to get away from the mansion and to be *alone*." She placed undue emphasis on that final word; then she snatched the brush from his hand and shimmied down from the railing, careful to avoid making any more physical contact. She took three purposeful steps toward the gorgeous stallion, who was prancing a bit nervously in place, perhaps reacting to the presence of a dangerous predator, stroked his neck, and whispered a gentle greeting. Midnight immediately settled down, and she began to softly brush his mane—anything to keep from looking at or dealing with Santos Olaru.

The presumptuous vampire...

"He's gorgeous," Santos said, appraising the stallion with

appreciation, and there was nothing in his voice but sincerity. "How long have you had him? What's his name?"

Natalia exhaled a sigh of relief. "Midnight. He's fairly new. My father..." Her voice trailed off, and she lowered the brush. Luca was a sensitive subject, the fact that she was the daughter of a wicked and dangerous man. And as if her emotions weren't conflicted enough, she had no idea what would become of her papa after Sunday, whether Santos would ever let her see Luca Giovanni again.

She wasn't sure that she wanted to see him...

"Your father?" he prompted.

His tone was absent of judgment, so Natalia swallowed her shame and tried again. "My father purchased him from a prominent breeder about three months ago for thirty thousand dollars. I absolutely adore him...riding him... I think he might be my favorite *anything* in all the world." She cringed at the stupidity of her words, and why had she told him Midnight's price?

It was just...

It was just that she was so accustomed to playing her role, maneuvering in haughty and nefarious circles, entertaining millionaires on behalf of Giovanni, Inc.'s shell corporations, seemingly innocuous charities, trying to make her family...and their wealth...more legitimate.

But in truth she sounded like a spoiled child.

My favorite anything in all the world...

My father purchased him for thirty thousand dollars...

Santos must think she was a brainless prima donna—he couldn't possibly understand what she meant, or what she lived: the fact that Midnight's presence—his feel and his smell, his powerful spirit, and his indomitable will—was more enticing to her than all the wealth on the planet, than all the servants, expensive clothes, or trips to the salon. He couldn't possibly know that if Natalia had her way, she would throw a time-worn saddle on

Midnight's back, fill two saddlebags with a week's worth of provisions, and head up to the hills where she could get lost in nature: listen to the sound of the wind, revel in the warmth of the sun, and meditate to the rustle of leaves all around her. Yes, this beautiful, unpretentious, wholly magnificent animal was her most favorite anything in all the world. When she wasn't exploring her laptop or hacking into databases for the challenge, she was usually in the barn.

She raised the brush, returning to Midnight's mane—she wasn't going to try to explain it.

Santos grew enigmatically quiet.

He reached for her wrist, halting her motion, then gently removed the brush from her hand. Once he had balanced the brush atop Midnight's railing, he rotated Natalia softly by the waist, turning her around to face him, and then he cupped her face in his hands. "Look at me, *cuore mio*."

He called her *my heart* in *her* second language, and despite herself, she looked into his eyes, and her heart fluttered wildly in her chest.

"How long have you done that, Natalia girl?" he asked.

She frowned, not understanding. "How long have I done what?"

"Apologized for being Luca's daughter?" he said. "Carried your father's guilt? Wrestled with shame because of your very existence? We don't get to choose our parents, Natalia. We play the hand life deals us."

Natalia blanched at his words. He was prying much too deeply. "Are you reading my thoughts?" she asked, feeling utterly exposed and appalled.

"No," he said emphatically, "but then, I don't need to. Your eyes, your body language, your energy is quite expressive." He placed both hands on the railing behind her, boxing her in with both his body and his scrutiny. "You are so incredibly beautiful,

Natalia Antoinette. So regal. So smart. So capable. But you wrestle with demons that are not your own. I felt that footprint, even on the web."

Natalia raised her chin in defiance, ignoring the arms that fenced her in. "You don't know me, Santos Olaru. You have no idea who I am or what kind of life I have lived."

He nodded. "That's true." His eyes turned molten, and his voice softened into a caressing purr. "But I'd like to, Natalia girl. I'd like to know everything about you: your life, your secrets, your dreams, and your hidden longings. I find you so enchanting and mysterious." He released the railing and took a generous step back, allowing her room to breathe. "Perhaps one day you will tell me."

If Natalia could have laughed aloud, she would have, but the seriousness of the situation prevented it: who he was, *what* he was, why he was standing there in the barn watching her, pressing her, still treating her like...his possession.

Staking his claim and his ownership.

It was all too damn...familiar.

Her father. Oskar. Her entire life...

It hit way too close to home.

Hell, Natalia didn't care to talk about who she was, what she wanted, what she dreamed about or longed for. It was all so wholly irrelevant—it always had been: Natalia Antoinette Giovanni was a virtual, sheltered child; an inexperienced, pampered virgin; a caged bird who couldn't fly; and her daddy's favorite showpiece. She was kept in a gilded cage, and she could sing on cue as commanded. She just had no intention of singing for Santos Olaru.

Not ever.

"Mysterious? Enchanting?" she mocked, surprised by the strength of her anger and equally flummoxed by the potential source. "I know exactly what you see, Santos Olaru: a precocious little girl who played with you online. A spoiled child who lives her life in hiding, safe and protected inside a gated compound. And I also know why you're here right now—why you're standing in this barn and speaking such endearing words—because you literally have no choice. You didn't seek me out because you wanted to solve some enchanting mystery; you were compelled by an ancient curse. A moon. A dictate. A primitive vampire rite. You might look at me and see many things; you might even find me beautiful—do you have any idea how many powerful men have lusted after Luca Giovanni's daughter?—but we both know you wouldn't be here if it wasn't for your celestial gods. And you would never choose a woman like me if you had another option… if your name and your ownership weren't virtually branded on my arm. So, I'll save you some time and some trouble. There's only one thing you need to know: Despite what it looks like, I am not that gullible, and I'm not a child. I cannot be flattered or cajoled or seduced. I don't melt at the sound of a sexy man's voice, and I don't simper at every touch. I'm not your *Natalia girl*, Santos; we're just caught in the same damn web. And right now, in this moment, I'm biding my time and processing the facts, hoping you can make a difference on Sunday. But if you think for one moment you can corner me in a barn, whisper sweet nothings in my ear, and get me to prance like one of my father's prized ponies, then you do have a lot to learn about who I am. I am not such an easy mark."

Santos appraised her thoughtfully.

He linked his rugged hands together, narrowed his stunning gaze, and studied her from head to toe as if he were appraising her with X-ray vision. As if he were measuring her very soul.

Natalia wet her lips in a nervous swipe of the tongue and fought valiantly not to tremble. Needing something to do with her hands, she reached for Midnight's brush, lifted it from the railing, and started to turn on her heel—

The vampire reached out so swiftly, she never saw him move.

He flicked the infernal brush out of her hand and sent it spiraling to the ground. "Good," he snarled in a primal rasp. "Then don't hide behind your circumstances or that horse."

Midnight whinnied and pranced to the other end of the stall, leaving Natalia without her armor. "Excuse me?" she snapped.

Santos ran his tongue over his fangs in a curious, animalistic gesture before settling back into his natural stance. "You wish to speak frankly? Honestly? To put aside the childish games? Then I'm relieved...and eager...to do the same. But face me when I speak to you. Do not give me your back. I've listened to every word you said to me; now show me the same respect."

She lowered her lashes and nodded, startled by his direct reproach, but she didn't dare utter another word, not until she had heard him out. Up until now, he had been so gentle and flirtatious, so accommodating and kind, she had almost forgotten what he truly was—perhaps it had been careless to confront him.

"Precocious little girls," he began, "don't hack into intricate computer systems. And *children* are usually afraid of monsters— they don't learn that vampires are real and still maintain their composure. The fact that you have been sheltered, that you live in a gated compound, surrounded by daily exploitation and your father's lascivious henchmen, yet you manage to survive and even function, to meet cruelty with kindness, brutality with compassion, tells me volumes about who you are, Natalia Antoinette." His voice dropped to a lethal purr. "And as for all these other men—those who have desired to seduce you, those who wish to own or possess Luca Giovanni's daughter—take care, sweet Natalia, when mentioning other males. You are in fact speaking to a savage creature, a vampire, not a human. And I don't give two fucks about your powerful father, but on one count, you are absolutely spot-on: The Curse; the Blood Moon, our pre-destined connection; it is the reason I am standing in this barn, trying to get to know you, to see beyond all that well-placed armor, to learn more about you...if I can." He stepped forward and leaned into her, his sensual, otherworldly power practically swirling around him, and the tips of his fangs crept down from the tops of his gums, even as his crystal-blue eyes flashed red, illuminating the silhouette of veins in his corded, muscular throat.

"And trust me, *Natalia girl*," he continued, "when I look at you, I do not see a spoiled child. I see eyes so deep, dark, and haunting that I want to know what they look like when they're hooded with lust and drunk with passion. I see a throat so slender, elegant, and sensual that I just want to sink my teeth into it...again and again...and again. I see a body so expertly fashioned—every slope, every curve, every contour—that I can hardly restrain myself from undressing you just to answer the questions: Are her legs really that long? Is her skin really that smooth? Are her breasts really that full, that soft...as perfect as they look? Will her nipples harden when I tease them with my tongue? You are stunning, Natalia Giovanni, the most striking and desirable woman I have ever laid eyes on, and if you were not my *destiny*, I would have still sought you out. But yes, with one critical difference—I would have already taken you to my bed. We wouldn't be standing here talking in a barn because you would be lying beneath me. I would have already crawled inside of you." He wet his full bottom lip with his tongue, and Natalia nearly fainted. "But you're right. I want more. So much more. And I do see both your beauty and your innocence, sweet woman. But unlike the men you have known until now, I also value your mind and your individuality." He reached out to twirl a lock of her hair and caressed it with his thumb. Then he traced her lips with his middle finger before touching the pad to his tongue. "All that said, don't ever get it twisted: My desire for you is overwhelming. I do not see you as a child, and I trust that the celestial gods would give me nothing less than an enchanting, mysterious, formidable *woman* to spend the rest of my life with."

Natalia began to tremble.

She couldn't help it.

For all intents and purposes, Santos had just undressed her, and she felt naked and exposed before him.

She turned around, giving him her back, just as he had instructed her not to.

But heaven help her, she couldn't face him.

She fisted her hands in her hair and just stood there, praying he wouldn't touch her, try to kiss her, ask anything of her.

If he compelled her now, she'd scream.

Or she'd melt.

Perhaps she'd curl up on the floor of the barn and whimper. She was in so far above her head, and Santos had seen right through her. "Please go," she whispered, hugging her arms to her chest. "Please, Santos. I need to be alone."

"Shh," he intoned, answering her plea with a whisper. Then just like he'd done when he'd first entered the barn, he pressed his chest up against her—only this time, he also wrapped his arms around her, splayed the fingers of one hand open, and laid them gently over her throat.

It was the oddest sensation, the strangest gesture, the most erotic touch she had ever felt.

"Shh," he repeated, "don't run away. Sometimes being real is hard." He kissed her gently, where the slope of her neck met her shoulder, and then slowly worked his way up to her ear. "Your body burns for mine, Natalia," he murmured, tightening the hand on her throat. "It's why you tremble; it's the source of your terror, but you don't need to be afraid. I promise to be exquisitely gentle." He massaged her larynx, stroked her jugular, and her stomach began to clench. The vampire was literally commanding her body with his every touch and whisper.

A single tear escaped her eye, and she fought for air—she was about to panic. "I can't...I don't...you don't understand. Even if I could reconcile this whole Blood Curse thing—which I cannot, at least not yet—Santos, I don't know what I'm doing."

Santos froze for the space of two heartbeats, and then he moved his hand from her throat to her shoulder, slid it down her arm, and gently massaged her wrist, his fingers curling around the celestial tattoo. "Natalia..." He whispered her name like a prayer. "Are you saying...you have never known passion, have you? No man has ever touched you?" He bent his head and nuzzled her hair in a tender, nonsexual gesture, and his next words were more like internal musings than intimate, disrobing questions: "Your father has kept you under lock and key, undoubtedly, so he could one day barter your honor, offer you to the highest bidder..." His voice grew thick with conviction. "Apologies, sweet angel. I didn't realize..."

Mortification settled on her shoulders like dew on the morning grass, and Natalia grimaced.

She wanted to crawl into a hole and die.

Here she was, this beautiful, exotic woman who made men mad with desire, yet she didn't even know how to touch one. Not that her first, second, or even third choice would have ever been an immortal vampire—but still, she felt so inexperienced...so exposed....so awkward.

"Turn around, angel. Look at me."

"Please just go," she whispered.

"Not until you turn around."

Natalia covered her face in her hands, gathered her courage, and slowly turned around.

"Beautiful," he breathed, removing her hands from her face. "Absolutely stunning." He tunneled his fingers in her luxurious hair, caressed her jaw with his thumbs, and then gently pulled her forward until she was forced to arch her back. Then he dipped down slowly to taste her, and the moment he brushed her lips with his, he groaned from the purity of the contact. "Beautiful, stunning, and exquisite." He pulled away and held her burnished gaze. "We have forever, *cara mia*, and for whatever it's worth, I prefer things this way. I prefer you this way. When I finally take you, when you finally let me, our pairing will be perfect. Erotic. Sensual. Passionate. Divine. You couldn't be more perfect."

* * *

Santos knew he had pushed too hard.

Moved too quickly.

Been too direct.

But it wasn't about seduction or foreplay.

It was about Natalia's hunger and her need...and her pain.

Just as he had suspected, Natalia Giovanni was lonely. Hell, she was starving—and it wasn't for some casual sex play. She needed to be held, to be heard, and to be seen. But most of all, she needed to be validated as a woman, not someone's child, not someone's prize, not Luca Giovanni's best asset.

Natalia needed to feel alive.

And Santos had read that hunger like a journalist reads the news.

Yes, he had come on a bit strong, early on—he had pushed her beyond her boundaries and flirted with her fear, but at the end of the day, it had been an intuitive calculation.

He had pressed his body against hers, because she was desperate for the physical contact.

He had been bold, to the point of being obnoxious, so she would feel empowered to push back with sarcasm.

And when she'd finally shown her hand—used a wall of

words to disarm him—he had ramrodded his way past her defenses because it was precisely where she'd wanted him.

And yes, he had undressed her: mentally, emotionally, and spiritually.

But he had also gotten undressed.

And now, wherever the pairing led them, they could at least go forward together—male and female, vampire and *destiny*—not Luca's daughter and another self-serving master.

Squatting down, he reached for Midnight's brush and scooped it up for Natalia. "Here," he said softly, placing it in her palm. "Go back to what you were doing and forgive my interruption, though I make no apologies for wanting to see you...check up on you...make sure you're okay. That said, I do have to meet with the warriors about the raid, discuss our plans for Sunday, but I'll be back tonight, once you're finished with your guests and your dinner." He flashed a gratuitous smile and winked. "Perhaps I'll slip into your bedroom if you'll let me." Before she could panic, he added, "And I'll bring a deck of cards."

She accepted the brush with a tentative hand, then furrowed her brow. "A deck of cards?"

"Yep," he said. "You do play poker, don't you?"

She smiled, and for the first time that morning, it was genuine and unguarded. "Yes," she answered cautiously.

"Texas Hold 'Em?"

She nodded her head. "Yes, Santos, but why—"

He pressed a finger to her lips. "That whole virus thing," he teased, "when I hacked into your computer... I'm still trying to figure out if you're smarter than I am. I think Texas Hold 'Em will answer the question, once and for all, or at least give me a chance to settle the score."

Despite herself, Natalia giggled, and the sound was pure, unadulterated magic. "But what about my father's guards? They would shoot you on sight."

"They'll never see me," he answered.

"The security system is state-of-the-art," she insisted.

"Oh, so now I'm an inferior hacker? Don't you know me better than that? Your system will be child's play for me."

"Texas Hold 'Em?"

"Texas Hold 'Em," he said, "and we're playing for real money, so don't try to be cute. I'm not going to go easy on you just because you're a girl."

She rolled her bewitching eyes. "I would so kick your ass, vampire," she mused.

"You *would* kick my ass?" he asked.

"I will kick your ass," she asserted.

At this, Santos chuckled. "Then consider it a date. Oh, but don't get too confident, Natalia Antoinette. You do know, that virus you concocted—it never took."

"Mm," she countered, "but if I recall, it did force you to back out of my computer."

"That it did," he said, and then he leaned in and whispered, "but I only came back stronger." He stepped back and winked. "See you tonight, *Natalia girl.*"

CHAPTER THIRTEEN

I n a secluded ravine in eastern Dark Moon Vale, Keitaro
Silivasi leaped from a twenty-foot-high ledge, beneath the
roaring apex of a waterfall, and dove gracefully into a cool,
deep pond below.

It had been months since he'd gone swimming at the falls
behind his property, and now, more than ever, he needed the
release. Just a chance to clear his mind and recharge his body. A
moment without thinking about Zayda, Xavier, or those centuries
in Mhier. As it stood, Marquis was at the old homestead, keeping
close and careful watch over Zayda, while Nathaniel, Nachari,
and Kagen were meeting up with the sentinels. The boys would
be assisting with the Giovanni raid on Sunday.

No sooner had he embraced the invigorating feel of the water
than he heard a branch snap beneath a foot, no less than fifteen or
twenty yards away.

He shot to the surface of the pond, his senses heightening, his
muscles tensing, his keen, alert eyes scanning the ravine and
immediately locking in on the twigs that had crackled. And then
his formidable, eldest son, Marquis, stepped out from behind a

tree. And wouldn't you just know it—he had Zayda in tow, shuffling right behind him.

Keitaro felt instantly fatigued. "Everything all right?" he asked, his eyes shifting back and forth between the massive vampire and the diminutive girl.

Zayda smiled, unusually relaxed. "Oh, yeah, everything's good. We just decided to go for a walk, and then I told Marquis I wanted to come find you."

Keitaro didn't buy that for a minute. No one, save maybe Ciopori, wanted to go on a leisurely walk with Marquis, and it definitely wasn't the warrior's style.

Marquis harrumphed, his phantom-blue eyes narrowing in annoyance. "This crazy female could not sit still. I must've put her on the couch five times and told her to stay. I finally gave up, and we left the house—I figured I could walk it out of her. The restlessness."

Keitaro winced.

Oh, lord, Marquis...

It was true: Zayda could sometimes be a handful. She was a bit wild at the core—after all, she was half-Lycan—but hell, that didn't make her a dog.

Damn, Marquis...

For a moment, Keitaro was actually surprised his son hadn't tethered her to a leash or thought to bring a Frisbee.

Zayda rolled her eyes. "I was a little bit restless." She tugged at her wild, unruly hair, the golden-red tresses concealing her shoulders, and tried to push it away from her face. "I guess I'm just not accustomed to being in the house without you. I may have gotten a little...upset."

At this revelation, Keitaro turned his full attention to Marquis and switched to a private, telepathic bandwidth. *Warrior?* he asked. *Did something happen?*

"Yeah," Marquis grumbled, not bothering to answer telepathically. "The female is batshit crazy—that's what happened. The entire ordeal was very upsetting. *She refused to stay on the couch.*"

"Marquis!" Keitaro bellowed, censuring him with a glare. "Have a care, son."

The vampire held up both hands and frowned. "Father, you need to speak to me in English...or Romanian...the language doesn't matter—I know at least twenty-one—but whatever you're saying, you need to make sense." He snatched Zayda by the hand and began to half lead, half drag her forward toward the pond, clearly anxious to be rid of her. All the while he mumbled beneath his breath: "What does that even mean...*have a care.* Take better care of yourself, son? Take better care of Zayda? Be more careful. Try to be more caring. Or don't be so carefree? Shit —I have never been carefree."

Keitaro's censuring glare became a piercing, paternal warning. "It means one more ignorant word, and I'm going to come out of this pond and kick your carefree ass. Have a care that it doesn't happen, Marquis."

Marquis blanched at the insult, his features growing hard. "You mad at me, Dad?" Before Keitaro could reply, he released Zayda's hand, bowed his head, and lowered his bulky mass down on one knee. He crossed his right fist over his heart in the traditional gesture of a formal apology. "Apologies, Father." Only he didn't wait for Keitaro to give him permission to speak. He stood right back up, furrowed his brows, and grumbled, "Can I go now?"

What kind of half-ass apology was that?

Keitaro shook his head. "Yes, Marquis, you can—"

The warrior had already vanished.

Well, damn. Keitaro would have to have a word with his eldest son, later.

That boy was getting more unruly by the day...

Zayda shrugged her slender shoulders, drawing attention to the narrow straps of her bright yellow summer top and the way it bunched up at the waistband of her shorts. "I don't think he likes me." She didn't sound concerned. She padded to the edge of the pond, kicked off her shoes, and sat down leisurely, staring at Keitaro, while dangling her feet in the water.

Reluctantly, Keitaro swam forward to meet her, stopping a few feet shy of the bank and treading water. "Is everything okay, Zayda? Did something spook you? Did Marquis upset you? Was there some reason you didn't wish to wait at the house?"

To his surprise, she laughed aloud. "He was right when he said I was batshit crazy, although who puts a human being on the couch and tells her to sit and stay?" She smirked. "I'm surprised he didn't toss a blanket over my head and command me to roll over. Toss a handful of bacon bits on the cushions."

Keitaro winced and glanced away.

When he finally looked back, she had linked her hands in her lap and she was kicking her feet playfully in the water. "I am sorry that I interrupted you, Keitaro, but *sheesh!* One more minute with Marquis, and I really would have turned into a fruit-cake, not just played one all afternoon to try to get off the sofa." She scrunched her features into a severe, brawny cast and drew back her soft, feline lips, trying to make them taut. "Zayda, *stay!*" She did her best Marquis imitation, shaking her finger in the air and pointing. "Do not get up from this couch. Sit down, Zayda. *Silence!* Stay." She switched back to her normal voice. "You would be batshit crazy, too."

Keitaro stared at his wild ward like she had just morphed into a unicorn and grown a horn on her head.

Wow...

Okay...

So Zayda actually had a sense of humor.

Damn...who knew?

She really had come a long way.

Not only was she conversing in a somewhat normal fashion, but she was also displaying appropriate wit and commensurate affect. Maybe he hadn't seen the transformation because he was always in her company, but this—this playful, easy nature, and even calculating how to get out of the house—it was progress to be sure, albeit a bit strange. But then, Zayda was always a bit strange. "Marquis can be a bit brusque," he offered. "His social skills are a little...rusty. You can't take it personally."

She batted her faery-princess eyes playfully, the obscenely long, dark lashes fluttering in the sunshine. "Marquis can be an ass."

Keitaro barked in laughter. "That too."

Silence settled all around them, the moment being strange and unfamiliar.

And as the sun beat down on Keitaro's brow, and the waterfall pumped ambient white noise behind him, he wasn't sure what he should do. Climb out of the pond, dry off, and take her back to the homestead, or ask her to join him? She didn't have a suit! Continue swimming while she sat there watching?

He was honestly caught off guard.

And Zayda must have sensed it because she began to study his face in earnest, those otherworldly eyes measuring each of his features, one at a time, before dropping down to survey his unclad chest, stare longingly at his broad shoulders, and examine the striations in his arms. She absently licked her lower lip, and her heart beat faster in her chest, the smooth, unmarred skin rising and falling in quick little pitter-patter motions.

Her eyes drifted lower, as if of their own accord, and even though she was looking through the prism of the water, they seemed to settle on his abs...and then his belly button...and then they drifted lower, still...

Okay...

That was quite enough.

This needed to stop.

Right now.

"Can I ask you something, Keitaro?" Her voice was absent of *crazy*...or guile.

He nodded hesitantly, feeling suddenly trapped.

"Why don't you ever touch me?"

And just like that, the light-hearted, companionable moment was gone.

Maybe she wasn't so healthy after all, Keitaro thought. He had a momentary flashback of those first two months: the day he had first brought her home from Xavier's high-rise prison, the way she had groped at his groin and her X-rated language, the vulgar way she had been trained to act—and he did not want to experience a repeat performance.

Calming his nerves, he deliberately chose not to read too much into it: Zayda was nothing if she wasn't direct. Yet, for having lived such a tainted life, she had maintained an uncommon honesty—her words, however disturbing, were almost innocent in their purity and truth. "I do touch you, Zayda." He spoke in a fatherly tone. "I've held your hand. I've given you a hug. I've even helped you put on your shoes."

I've even helped you put on your shoes?

He cringed inwardly.

What the bumbling hell, Keitaro?

Maybe she would just accept it and move on.

She smiled then, but her eyes looked sad. "Is it because I'm so broken and damaged? Because of my past? You must look at me and see the most disgusting girl..."

Keitaro felt his face flush in horror, and he had to bite down, hard, to stifle a gasp. "Where is this coming from, Zayda?" The look on her face was breaking his heart. "Sweeting...I didn't bring you to my home to use you."

"Why *did* you bring me?" she asked. "I mean, are you not still a man? A male vampire?"

Something inside him recoiled. "No, not that kind of male, Zayda."

"Ah," she said, "so you don't see me as a woman?"

Keitaro was well and truly flummoxed. "Zayda, I am well aware of your gender. However, I am also over twenty-three hundred years old, and you just turned twenty-one. I think there is a very wide gap between us."

Zayda appeared to be thinking that over. "I don't see why that should matter, Keitaro. Immortal is immortal, right? And while I'm not quite that...fully immortal...I am a somewhat rare find for your species. I mean, I will live much, much longer than a human, and I'm definitely infertile—the life I was forced to live has confirmed that—and isn't that the biggest threat to your kind? I mean, pregnancy, that is?" She gnawed on her bottom lip as if chewing the possibilities over. "One would think I'd be better than nothing."

Keitaro took a slow, deep breath. He wanted to dip under the water, sink to the bottom of the pond, and stay there for the next millennia –what the hell had gotten into Zayda?

She rose from her perch on the bank of the pond and began to pace rather nervously. "It's just...it's just...no one has ever treated me the way you do, or talked to me in such a nice, gentle voice. No one has ever taken care of me before, or even cared about my needs. You're so different from other men, Keitaro. You're loving. You really are. And I love you. I do. At least as much as I know how."

He gulped and swam a few feet back, putting some distance between them.

What. The. Devil.

Seemingly undaunted, or perhaps unaware of his distress, the girl pressed on. "See, the thing is this: I know that you're lonely, and you still miss your wife. But I don't want you to make me go away. I've seen the way other women look at you, other vampire women who have lost their mates, like Katia, Kagen's nurse, and even humans too, like Shelly Winters, that pretty blonde who's always offering to *feed* you."

Keitaro held up one hand. He had to make her stop rambling. "I prefer to hunt my prey," he countered. "It's an old-school thing, I guess." Okay, that was *random, disjointed, and totally irrelevant comeback number two*, but just like rejoinder number one, it would have to do.

She placed both hands on her hips, absently hooking her thumbs inside the loops of her stone-washed jean shorts. "You prefer to hunt your prey. You prefer to sleep alone. And you prefer to remain celibate for the rest of your life; either that, or I'm in your way." She twirled a finger around her unruly hair, tugging the loop in a nervous fidget. "I know I was crazy at first, Keitaro, and I know I'm damaged goods. But I think I could try, for you—well, maybe—I think, with you, it wouldn't be so bad." To her credit, she angled her shoulders toward him and faced the conversation directly. "I just...I just know that the day is coming, and probably soon—especially once the threat from Xavier is over —that you're going to want your life and your space back. You're going to want to live again as a man, and then what will happen to me? Where will I go? Who would even want me? I need to do a lot more to earn my keep."

Keitaro had heard more than enough.

He ran a tentative hand through his wet, thick black locks and concentrated on his answer. He could not just discard and deflect this time—he needed to hit the subject head-on. "Zayda, sex is not ever something you do to earn your keep. It isn't something you barter as a favor. It isn't something a male takes in exchange for giving you protection. It is something deeply personal and intimate. I brought you home because I have been in your shoes, at least in terms of the lycans and living in captivity. I brought you home because you needed a chance to heal, and no living being should ever suffer what you were enduring. But I did not—not ever—bring you home with the thought that I might one day take advantage of your body."

Zayda sighed, and her expression reflected her exasperation and angst. "I know that, Keitaro, and maybe my words came out all wrong." She padded to the edge of the pond, lowered herself onto the bank, and then she slid seamlessly into the water, gliding forward like a fish. She treaded water in front of him with her feet, placed both delicate hands on his cheeks, and leaned in brazenly to kiss him.

Keitaro froze.

He didn't push her away, and he didn't kiss her back.

He just froze for the space of three heartbeats, and then he shackled her wrists.

A gentle shove forward, and the water accepted her weight. As the wave propelled her backward, he sought her mortified gaze. "No, Zayda." The rebuke was too harsh, and he made a conscious effort to gentle his voice. "Just...no. This isn't going to happen."

She blinked several times, and her eyes—those beautiful, hypnotic, enchanting eyes—glassed over. "I see," she whispered, spinning in the water to swim back toward the bank. Being half-Lycan, it took very little effort to hoist herself onto dry ground, and careful to keep her back to Keitaro, she began to wring out her shirt. "That was then, Keitaro...when you first brought me home," Zayda whispered. "I wasn't in my right mind...then."

He angled his head to the side and glanced at her warily. "I'm afraid you're not in it now, Zayda. At least not all the time. What just happened here...that's still some old baggage."

"You might be right," she said coldly. "I'm childish, I'm broken, and I'm fifty degrees of fucked up. And I have no business trying to touch you, seduce you, or even talk to you about what I'm feeling...or wanting. If anything, I should just fall on my knees and thank you." She twisted around then, angling her body to face him. "Which I do, Keitaro; I really do thank you. The thing of it is: I also love you, even if it is just a stupid, broken girl's love." She searched for her shoes, took a seat in the grass, and swiftly slipped them on.

"Zayda..."

She didn't reply.

Keitaro nodded.

So, it had come to that...so soon.

He'd had his concerns—he wasn't stupid. He understood the impropriety and the issues that came along with bringing a young, sexually abused woman into his home and nursing her back to physical and emotional health.

Shit.

Just shit.

He still couldn't articulate why he'd done it.

He had just felt...so strongly compelled.

Now, as he swam to the bank in silence and joined Zayda in the clearing, he watched—and waited—until his ward stood up.

"Come here." He ushered her forward with the crook of his finger, and when she didn't oblige him, he went to her instead. Wrapping his arms loosely around her, he pressed a chaste kiss atop the crown of her head. "I want you to know that I care for you deeply, Zayda Patrone. I think you are an exceptional and singular young woman—not crazy or broken or fifty degrees of messed up. Just bruised and battered and deserving of a break." He pulled away and gestured toward the path that led out of the clearing, away from the waterfall and the crazy encounter. "Let's go. You need to get home and dry off." As she shuffled in front of him, her head held low, her eyes affixed to the ground, Keitaro cleared his throat. "Zayda..."

She glanced over her shoulder to look at him, her thick, dark lashes wet with tears.

Damn...

Just damn.

"This thing with Xavier, it isn't nothing," he said emphatically. "I have four sons, four daughters-in-law, an adopted child in Kristina, and four beautiful, precious grandchildren. I have a lot to live for and a lot to lose, yet I have picked a battle with a powerful mortal enemy, primarily *for you*. I will fight to protect you, Zayda, even unto my death. Trust me, sweeting, that is a form of love."

* * *

The wolf burrowed its snout into a pile of pine leaves, trying desperately to block out the scent of deer dung, which coated its massive fur. Rolling in the shit had been necessary if Xavier hoped to get anywhere near the valley and survey Keitaro's homestead.

The blasted Ancient Master Warrior and his detestable wizard-son, Nachari, had long ago placed wolf traps, some crazy, homemade brand of energetic wards, all over Dark Moon Vale, and the powerful deterrents repelled wolves like sunlight repelled the vamps from the house of Jaegar.

It wasn't even a choice.

The lycans could not go near them.

Still, the Silivasis couldn't cover every blasted inch of every stupid mountain, meadow, and hillside in Dark Moon Vale, and Xavier had come as close as he could get to the Silivasi homestead without setting off one of the traps. When he had heard the distant sound of footsteps and smelled his familiar enemy approaching a secluded waterfall, he had known the tide had finally turned in his favor. Lady Luck had smiled on Xavier at last.

Already covered in dung, and knowing he couldn't approach or attack, he had crawled beneath the lower ledge of a large gray boulder and turned up his supernatural hearing, projected it forward for all he was worth...

And damn, if he hadn't caught an earful.

Zayda Patrone—she was truly Zayda Matista, *General Xavier Matista's daughter*—was either falling in love with Keitaro Silivasi, or true to her lykos nature, the girl was just getting horny. Maybe she was coming into some latent genetic season.

No matter.

It curdled Xavier's gut.

Yet and still, all was not lost—Xavier's precarious trip through the portal had not been a complete waste of time. Although he now knew he could never successfully attack Keitaro's homestead, not with any number of soldiers—alpha, beta, or otherwise—his careful explorations through the minefield of wolf wards had exposed an opportune weakness: an outdoor shower beside a private herb garden, about one-quarter mile outside the southern cliffs, beyond a raging river and an isolated bridge.

About one-quarter mile behind Kagen Silivasi's clinic.

And wasn't that just poetic justice: ironic, hilarious, and divine...

The fact that the quaint little shower was part of Kagen Silivasi's herb garden, and the entire rugged outbuilding reeked of Arielle Nightsong: her body, her hair, and her skin. Her scent was all over the outdoor shower; she was likely using it daily. And there were no lycan wards in the direct vicinity, which was all the opportunity Xavier Matista would need.

Keitaro Silivasi would never know what hit him.

And neither would his arrogant son, the Ancient Master Healer.

A girl for a girl...a daughter for a daughter...a life for a life.

Yes, Keitaro Silivasi would make that trade: Arielle in exchange for Zayda.

Xavier was absolutely certain of it.

CHAPTER FOURTEEN

Later that night

Natalia Giovanni sank back into the plush leather chaise longue in the long, black-and-white limousine, gawking at the extraordinary opulence: garish purple lighting; a fully stocked bar with crystal decanters; and a decadent open moon roof. The surround-sound stereo system was playing soft, mellow jazz—*just how old was Oskar, anyway?*—and far more disturbing, the seat at the back of the limo extended forward into a bed.

Natalia stared fixedly out the dark tinted window.

She was unimpressed with the opulence; she was certainly unimpressed with Oskar; and the tight, black sleeveless dress she had managed to shimmy into was hugging her curves so tight, she could hardly manage to breathe. Her soft, satin gloves concealed Santos' mark on her left, inner wrist, but she couldn't think of anything else.

The vampire.

Their interaction in the barn earlier that morning.

The fact that he would be coming back later that night.

Natalia felt abominable for keeping the secret, for in truth, she and Santos had made a connection, however tentative—but she just couldn't risk the drama and the confrontation. She couldn't risk the lives of the women in The Fortress.

Sighing, she tried to close her eyes and go somewhere else in her head—perhaps a sandy beach in the Bahamas or a winter wonderland in the gorgeous Swiss Alps—anywhere but where she was. As far as Natalia was concerned, the sooner they arrived at the restaurant or the theater or some country club—wherever Oskar was taking her—the better.

She could get through this night.

She would get through this night.

Sunday was only two days away...

And even though it would usher in an entirely new set of challenges...fears...realities, it would also open the door to new opportunities.

The limousine turned on to a narrow, winding road, and Natalia leaned forward in her seat.

What the hay?

It was heading in the opposite direction of the city—of the majority of the metropolitan area's nightlife entertainment—onto a back, country road: a gravel drive lined with high, arching English oak trees and virtually absent of businesses or houses. Perhaps ten or fifteen minutes later, the vehicle slowed to a halt at the edge of a narrow creek, and a faint golden light began to glow outside the window.

Natalia pressed her nose to the glass, trying to see more clearly in the darkness.

The golden light was coming from a candelabra, set atop a white linen table erected beside the stream. There was a bottle of Champagne—or perhaps it was wine—chilling in a sterling silver bucket of ice next to a glorious centerpiece of exquisite flowers: coral roses, purple lilies, white orchids, and baby's breath.

Natalia gulped.

Less than five feet away from the table, someone had erected a platform, and for all intents and purposes, the first word that came to mind was *sultan*. The platform was bordered by four conical posts, not unlike a tent, and all four sides were draped in a pale lavender gossamer film, some sort of ethereal fabric, the front of the drapes drawn back. Good Lord in heaven, she had to catch her breath. There was a bed on top of the platform: a soft, plush white canvas lounge, covered in overstuffed pillows.

What the hell was Oskar planning?

As if she couldn't figure that out.

No sooner had the nausea-inducing thought crossed her mind than the door to the limo opened.

Natalia scooted away.

She reached for a nearby button to roll down the window between the backseat and the driver—to hell with this, she would ask him to take her home. Sure, Oskar would be angry, and it probably wasn't wise to provoke such a powerful man, to toy with a criminal she already knew to be a stone-cold killer, but she didn't believe he would hurt her. They weren't yet married, and he couldn't send her home bruised or battered.

Besides, Oskar needed Luca, and Luca needed Oskar...

And Natalia just needed to go home.

As she held the button, the window scrolled down, and Natalia's jaw dropped open.

What!

How?

Wh...wh...

No.

The driver wasn't there. The front seat was simply empty. And she'd never heard him open the door. Falling back against the plush leather seat, she searched her mind for a reasonable explanation: What the heck was going on? Limousine drivers didn't just disappear into thin air.

And then Oskar Vadovsky's cruel, deep voice pierced the summer night's air. "You look lovely this evening, Natalia. Please, come. Get out of the car."

She turned her head to the side in slow motion, terrified to meet his gaze.

Oskar was standing in the doorway like a titan of a man in a pair of black linen trousers and a blood-red silk shirt, the top five buttons undone, revealing a corded muscular chest and pecs made of steel. And didn't that just strike a demonic visage considering his long, straight, black-and-red hair. Hell, the man wore it halfway down his back.

She shivered, refused to move, and his charcoal-gray eyes receded to black. "Is there a problem?" he purred, his voice as dark as the looming sky. Moonlight reflected off his severe, chiseled features, alighting his gorgeous but ruthless face, and Natalia pressed her hand to her chest.

"I...I just need a minute to catch my breath." She forced cordiality into her voice. "I thought perhaps we were going to a restaurant, or maybe to see a show at the theater. I just...I'm surprised... Where are we, Oskar?"

A slow, raspy hum rumbled in the air, and for a moment, Natalia could have sworn it was coming from his throat. "I wanted a more private setting," he explained. "I wanted you all to myself."

She cringed inwardly. "Oskar..."

"Natalia, you have been promised to me for quite some time, yet I have only seen you in your father's presence, in the presence of his guards or your escorts. Enough is enough, sweet minx. There is no need to prolong the inevitable. You *belong* to me, Natalia. And I am not such a patient man." He extended his hand a few inches forward, glaring at her satin-gloved fingers. "Now then, come."

Natalia placed her hand in Oskar's—what else could she do?

She was no longer certain, not in the least, that the merciless thug wouldn't hurt her.

As he pulled her out of the car, his enormous, barely leashed strength evident in his grip, she reached for her handbag, containing the burner phone—it had to be close to 8:30 PM, and she had promised to text Santos around nine, whenever the make-believe guests arrived at the fabricated dinner party. If she didn't text in the next half hour, the male would certainly check in or call. She would have to find a way to steal a moment alone, even if she had to insist that Oskar take her to town to make use of a restroom, and she would have to find a way to avoid that bed, even if she had to feign a migraine headache.

"Leave it," Oskar growled, gesturing with his chin toward the purse. "There will be no distractions this evening, Natalia." His voice was more than commanding—it was laced with a latent threat.

Feeling real, tangible fear for the first time that evening, Natalia set her purse back down on the seat. *Why the hell had she lied to Santos...again?*

Oh, yes...

The Fortress...the women...the very high stakes.

Oskar and Santos together.

Her father's armed henchmen surrounding the house.

Natalia wasn't free to choose.

Natalia had never been free...

Wetting her bottom lip in a nervous gesture, she slowly climbed out of the limo, and that's when Oskar shut the door behind her, pressed her against the panel, and molded both of his powerful, unyielding hands to her slender, graceful hips. "I've chilled Champagne; I bought you flowers; I've arranged a more comfortable...repose...for our enjoyment; and your father does not expect you home before morning." He grasped her jaw in the palms of both hands and raised her chin to anchor her lips where he wanted them. "Do you have *any* idea how long I have waited to taste you?" With that, he covered her mouth with his, and his kiss was equal parts ravenous and savage.

Natalia had to force herself to kiss him back...just barely.

She had to force herself not to bite him.

As her stomach turned queasy and her palms began to sweat, she had to force herself not to puke in her mouth.

"Oskar...*Oskar*. Wait!" She weaved and bobbed, drawing back her chin, and then she quickly turned her head to the side. "Please, slow down..." She gentled her voice, trying to pretend like she didn't feel threatened. "I'd like to have a glass of Champagne, take a look at the flowers, perhaps we could talk for a bit—now that we're finally alone." She wrung her gloved hands together, twisted out of his reach, and strolled leisurely toward the table, trying to fake like she was still in control. "Come," she said sweetly, eyeing the opposite chair, "I've been eager to get to know you better."

He halted for a moment, and she tried to read his expression: It was leery, hungry, predatory. But to his credit, he nodded his head in an almost antiquated, old-world gesture, and then he took three long, noiseless strides in her direction and slid her chair back from the table.

Exhaling with relief, Natalia stepped sideways toward the proffered chair, and that's when Oskar sidled up behind her, wrapped an iron-clad arm around her stomach, and tugged her back against him. He pressed his harsh, thick lips against her throat, nipped her skin, and nuzzled the crook of her neck. And then he brazenly raised his hand to her chest and kneaded her breast through her gown. Flicking her nipple before he let go, he sauntered to the other side of the table, took a seat, and reached for the bottle. "Sit, Natalia. We will drink, and we will talk. And then, my dear tease, we will fuck."

* * *

Santos Olaru stood next to Ramsey and Saxson at his kitchen counter, glancing at the blueprints they had retrieved from Keitaro and Zayda. The female had done an adequate job, filling in various details that both illuminated The Fortress and brought the horror to life.

She'd placed X's next to each guard's station and O's to indicate captive women. She'd drawn lines along halls where the guards patrolled and drawn in any physical obstacles or barriers. She'd even listed shift changes and routes—which doors were used most often and which remained closed. Staring at the map of the complex, it was hard for Santos to reconcile the damaged girl he had seen in Keitaro's living room, the one who had so regressed so easily, with the one who had tackled this diagram.

Tuning his brothers out, he reached once again for his cell phone, skimmed his messages, and scanned the time—it was 8:45 PM, and he hadn't heard a word from Natalia, at least not yet. His stomach tightened with both apprehension and anticipation as he told himself for the umpteenth time to just be patient: The two of them had made definite inroads at the Giovanni compound earlier, and Santos had been looking forward all day to their playful game of poker, to a chance to get to know her even better, an opportunity to deepen their connection.

And that's why he couldn't go all stalker-hunter and blow up her burner phone with texts.

She'd said she'd text around nine, as soon as the guests arrived for the dinner party, and that meant she still had fifteen minutes to check in.

In truth, it was just counterintuitive for a vampire male to be apart from his *destiny* during the tenuous period that encompassed his Blood Moon, but Natalia's situation was different, and there were a lot of lives at stake. Hell, Zayda's marked-up blueprints had underscored that fact in bright, bold ink.

"Santos...*Santos!*" Ramsey's gruff voice interrupted his thoughts. "Where the hell are you, brother?"

He sniffed and redirected his attention to the vampire. "Where the hell do you think?"

Saxson chuckled then. "It's maddening, isn't it? All the shit you start to think and feel the second you meet your *destiny*..." It was more of a statement than a question.

"What time are you supposed to hook up?" Ramsey asked.

Santos shrugged a nonchalant shoulder. "No idea just yet. I'm hoping she'll be free by ten thirty or eleven. Dinner shouldn't take much longer than that."

Ramsey nodded, then eyed the cell phone sideways. "She checked in yet?"

"Nope," Santos answered, feeling curiously annoyed by the question.

"You gonna wait much past nine before you text her?" Saxson inquired.

"Nope," Santos said. There was no use in lying.

"And the moment you know the guests have arrived..." Ramsey's voice trailed off—it was a rhetorical question.

Santos smiled. "Then I'm out."

Saxson laughed. "Stalker Olaru, misting through the shadows, watching through a window across the street." All three brothers laughed, though no one really thought it was funny. A vampire could never be too careful...too trusting.

"Whatever it takes," Santos said, dryly.

Just then, Ramsey bent over the blueprints and pressed his finger over an "O" in the diagram. "You know," he rasped, "I get that we're going in blind, and we know that these females are facing some kind of imminent threat. According to Natalia, they can all be executed in less than fifteen minutes if something goes awry, and we don't know if we're dealing with explosives or what —just heavily armed sentries carrying automatic rifles. But look at all these O's. Presumably, these are all women in separate cells, right?" He hopped from one cell to the other, pointing several examples out. "Then look at each wing...the end of each hall... there's all these communal shower stalls. So why the hell does the plumbing snake into each individual cell? What the hell do you need a communal shower for if there's one in every cage?"

"Maybe restrooms...*toilets*," Saxson offered.

"Maybe," Ramsey grunted. "But that doesn't make much sense. Why put in that much plumbing, then place the latrines somewhere else?"

Santos nodded thoughtfully. "I noticed that myself—the first time I glanced at the blueprints."

"That's a helluva lot of pipe work," Ramsey offered.

"No doubt," Saxson said.

"And another thing that doesn't make sense," Ramsey said. "These four hired killers...Luca's mercenaries...*whatever*...they're somewhere in four different countries. So how the heck do they get the call and transport back to the ole U.S. of A. in less than fifteen minutes? I'm just not buying it."

"You don't think the threat is real?" Santos asked, feeling suddenly uneasy.

"Oh, I think it's very real," Ramsey said. "Luca's too smart to leave his shit that exposed. He definitely has a doomsday plan. I'm just saying: These hits that he's preordered, they were never meant to be up close and personal."

Santos stared harder at the drawing, this time focusing in on the electrical grid and what he could discern from the wiring. "Remote control," he said, speaking to no one in particular.

"Some kind of detonator?" Saxson chimed in.

Ramsey shrugged his massive shoulders. "Don't know. But whatever it is, we need to stay mindful of those pipes."

A cryptic silence settled over the kitchen as all three sentinels considered the same possibility: poison gas or a chemical nerve agent, something that could kill in less than five minutes.

No one had to speak a single word.

"Well, hell," Saxson finally said, "we designed our plan to get in and out in less than fifteen minutes—ten at the least, hopefully twelve, but we can't pull it off in less than five."

"Nope," Ramsey agreed. "We would need a whole new game plan."

Santos shook his head in frustration; unfortunately, he agreed with Ramsey. "What say you, brothers? Time to call Nathaniel, Kagen, and Nachari—see what the warriors and the wizard think?"

"Yeah," Saxson answered, without hesitating. "We need to draft a plan B."

Santos picked up his phone to pull up Nathaniel's number—telepathy wasn't always necessary, and depending on what a warrior was doing, it could sometimes be intrusive, if not rude—and he absently checked the time...and his messages...again.

What the hell? he thought, frowning.

It was 9:05 PM, and Natalia hadn't texted.

Maybe she got hung up, or there were too many eyeballs watching...

Whatever.

He was still free to reach out.

Tapping his message icon, he opened the screen and scrolled down to her name. Touching the phone once more, he opened the message platform and *tap-tap-tapped* three words: *Baby, what's up?*

CHAPTER FIFTEEN

The bottle of Champagne was empty.

The conversation had been stilted at best.

The moon was hanging low in the sky, casting dark, haunted shadows over the candelabra and the flowers, and the river had increased its pace. It was almost as if all of nature was reacting to the sick, perverse energy coiled in the meadow.

Natalia glanced over her shoulder at the limo and thought about her phone. "Oskar," she said, mildly slurring her words. She'd had way too much to drink, but it had been unavoidable. She had done everything she could to stall her fiancé, and if she were being honest, she had kind of been hoping he was a happy drunk. Hell, miracles sometimes happened, but no such luck. The alcohol hadn't even fazed him. "I really need to use the restroom...all that Champagne. Would you take me into town, just for a couple of minutes?" She waited with bated breath.

He jerked his chin in the direction of the limo, indicating the pasture just beyond it. "See those trees on the other side of the road." He tilted his chin again. "See that river right behind us?"

He snorted. "You can't be that spoiled, Natalia. Pull up your dress and go take a piss."

Natalia seethed with anger. "What is wrong with you tonight?" She slid back her chair, stood up defiantly, and planted her hands on her hips, deciding to take a different tack—clearly, kindness, subservience, and avoidance wasn't working. "You have never spoken to me like this before, Mr. Vadovsky. You have never treated me like a piece of meat. I am your *fiancée*—I am going to be your wife! But not if this is what the future looks like." She held up both hands in a pacifying gesture, hoping to give him an out. "Look, maybe you had a bad day; maybe this isn't a good night. I'm willing to let bygones be bygones—we can try it again another evening—but for now, I'm tired, I've had too much to drink, and I'd like to use the bathroom like a *lady*. Please, Oskar, just take me home."

* * *

Oskar Vadovsky stared at Natalia Giovanni like she had suddenly grown two heads.

What the hell did he care if she was tired, ticked off, and unwilling to play ball?

She was a human, and he was a vampire—he could do whatever the hell he wanted!

Any way...in any position...and with any amount of force.

And then he could just scrub her memory afterward.

True, if he returned her all battered and bruised, he would have to deal with Luca Giovanni, but even that would only be a momentary inconvenience. Luca's mind could be scrubbed like anyone else's. Hell, if the billionaire got too out of line, Oskar could break his cocky neck.

Of course, then the house of Jaegar wouldn't have continued and easy access to all the women they could breed with...defile...

and dispose of, without having to cover their trail and clean up their own mess, so maybe she should go home in one piece.

But that was the only prerequisite.

He had played her game; he had toyed with her mind; he had allowed her a brief indulgence, mainly because he'd been bored to tears, and anticipation almost always made sex better.

But this...

Now....

Her blatant defiance?

Pshaw.

He was done.

He stood up from the table, hooked his pointer finger under the lip of his chair, and tossed it nearly five hundred feet across the river. Natalia's face went pale, but he didn't give her time to react. He reached across the linen tablecloth, flicked the flowers into the dirt, and snatched her by her thick, flowing hair. And then he wrenched forward for all he was worth, careful to relax his grip at the last minute so he didn't accidentally scalp her before they could have some fun.

As if she weighed no more than a child, he hefted her feet off the ground, dragged her over the table, and then tossed her through the air onto the waiting platform and divan. "Piss on me, and I'll break your neck," he bellowed, allowing his full vampiric rage to echo through the pasture.

He stalked to the platform like a hungry lion, his manhood jerking angrily in his pants.

Natalia screamed for all she was worth, and Oskar flicked his fingers at her throat. "Silence!" he commanded, but the compulsion wasn't necessary; he had stolen the sound from her throat and extinguished her piteous voice. As he climbed up the platform, advancing stealthily and slowly—there was nothing more heady than fear—Natalia's eyes grew wide, she rolled to her side, and to her credit, she kicked off her shoes.

Kudos for that, Oskar thought. *Only a dimwit would try to run in those heels.*

Laughing, he marshalled his vampiric speed and headed her off at the pass. He grasped both of her elegant, slender shoulders in his powerful, brutal hands and pinned her back on the divan.

She kicked at his groin—no, she tried to stomp it into dust—and he caught her ankle with ease. "Resistance doesn't serve you, fiancée," he mocked. And then he braced both hands around her delicate ankle and twisted in opposite directions.

The tibia snapped, and he grimaced.

Damn...

That would be hard to explain to Luca—or to just scrub away—especially when the ankle was still broken tomorrow.

But oh well...

In for a penny, in for a pound.

He crawled over her trembling body, even as she writhed in unspeakable pain—her brow beginning to soak with sweat—and hooked a clawed fist beneath the top of her dress, ripping it all the way down her thrashing body.

And then he moaned.

Dark lords of the underworld, she was spectacular.

Perfect, unmarred skin; supple, voluptuous curves; and a quivering stomach—so flat, smooth, and taut, he could have bounced a quarter off it.

He cut the front of her bra with a talon and gorged on her pliant breasts.

And then he moved his hand lower, down to her panties, and slid two claws underneath.

She bucked like a wild bronco, and her gloved fists came right at his eyes, each desperate punch following the other in quick succession.

"Tsk, tsk, tsk," he reprimanded her. "What did I say about resisting?"

He caught the second fist in the palm of his hand, stared deep into her dark brown eyes, and watched her with pure, erotic pleasure as he slowly closed his fingers over her delicate bones.

All five of the digits collapsed beneath his inhuman strength, fracturing inside of the satin glove and undoubtedly leaving an unholy mess. Thank goodness the garments contained it.

"Now then," he drawled. "You still have one healthy hand and one working foot. This will be so much more exquisite if you just lie back and enjoy it." Her eyes nearly bulged out of her skull, and Oskar sighed, at last accepting the reality of the situation. Natalia was not going to go along with her seduction; things had gotten way out of hand; and any chance he'd had of bedding a willing, wild woman had flown out of the metaphorical window the moment he'd snatched her by the hair. "Why, Natalia?" he murmured in frustration.

When he had first procured the limousine, set up the tent, and staged the seduction, he had hoped to enjoy an eager slut: to seduce her, compel her—hell, direct her like a puppet if need be —but she had managed to short-circuit that possibility. Now, the only mutual pleasure available, the only entertainment left to be had, was sadism, pure and simple...

His dominance—her fear.

His brutality—her pain.

His release—her suffering.

She would be lucky if he had the self-control to still use the condoms.

Stradling her hips, he stared down at her delectable, albeit broken body and thought, *What a tragic turn of events*. Natalia Giovanni was not a piece of garbage, someone to simply use once and dispose of, and now he had no idea if he could piece her back together in order to use her more than once. "Be still," he snarled, still hoping to salvage some future use. "I do not wish to kill you, and I do not wish to end our pairing prematurely." He ran the backs of his fingers over her womb, languorously, and groaned. "And I do not wish to plant death in your belly—not yet, sweet Natalia. Not yet." He rose above her and grasped her by the jaw, simply intending to command her full attention. But blasted bad luck and supernatural strength, he felt the bones in her chin collapse.

Sighing, he made a mental note to try to be gentler, to at least hold back when he shoved his erection inside her—if he destroyed her womb, there would be no offspring. And of course, *if at first you don't succeed, try, try again...*

He would be better at this next time.

Wincing in apology, he slid down her torso and began to slowly...carefully...remove her panties.

CHAPTER SIXTEEN

S antos Olaru stepped onto his balcony, grateful to finally be alone.

Saxson and Ramsey had left the lake house to head to Nathaniel's estate, and Santos was struggling with a difficult call: Natalia had not texted him back, not even when he'd hit her up three more times, and while that didn't necessarily mean anything was wrong, he wasn't willing to take that chance.

He could play it conservative and just track the GPS on her burner, but that wouldn't tell him much of anything. What if she'd set it down? What if she'd had to turn it off? What if the battery had burned down, and she was waiting for it to recharge, right now? Locating Natalia's phone did not equate to locating Natalia, and it wouldn't give Santos any more information than he already had.

He supposed he could be a bit more aggressive and actually head to the house...

He could slip into the mansion, while remaining invisible, and if everything was as it should be, he could slip right back out —she'd never even know he'd been there.

Or he could just act like a sentinel and do the damn thing he really wanted to do: track her blood, locate her exact position in the mansion, and materialize into the room. He could eyeball the guests, make sure everything was satisfactory—that things were going smoothly, as planned—then transport right back to the lake house. In other words, he could more or less stalk her like some sort of control freak, hide what he was doing, and lie about it later.

To hell with boundaries, honor, or trust.

Besides, what did he intend to do when he got there?

Watch her eat dinner?

Eavesdrop on her conversations?

Follow her down the hall, if and when she excused herself to the restroom?

Damn.

Blood Moons really sucked.

Realizing that the war between his intellect and his gut was not going to cease—that trying to keep some modest distance between himself and Natalia until he could bring her home on Monday was just never going to fly with his primal instincts— Santos decided to call it a day.

So yeah, he would do the damn thing.

And he'd do it right now.

After all, he'd asked her to text, and she hadn't complied. Trust went two ways.

Closing his eyes, he focused his awareness while conjuring an image of her throat, recalling the scent of her skin, and evoking the feel of her blood as it had snaked down his throat.

His awareness deepened.

His heart quickened.

Until he could actually hear the faint pulse of foreign platelets thrumming in his veins.

Natalia's blood, Natalia's anima, Natalia's distinctive spiritual essence in the universe.

"Where are you, *cara mia?*" he whispered softly, sending all his senses outward in search of that pulse.

The night was filled with many vibrations—birds flying overhead, water rushing through rivers, vapor rising softly in the atmosphere, though it was much too warm for rain—but none of the pulses matched the one he had latched onto until he systematically narrowed the field.

And then—just like that—there it was.

Natalia's individual imprint.

Her pulse...

Moving from the foyer, down the cement steps, dipping into an unusually heavy car.

Traveling down the winding drive, passing through the gates of the compound, and ultimately heading down a dirt road—

Heading down a dirt road?

Son of a bitch!

Natalia had lied...

Santos channeled every ounce of intention he possessed, forcing the impressions to speed up. She was not supposed to leave that house. She'd said she was staying home.

A dirt road.

A river.

A secluded meadow...

He strained to see through Natalia's eyes, and the first image that popped up was that of a tall, imposing man—*with black-and-red banded hair*—pulling her out of the limousine.

Santos gasped in shock, and then he snarled like a feral beast.

Desperate to transport into that meadow, and cursing for all he was worth, he shredded his atoms into focused quantum energy and hurled them into the cosmos.

CHAPTER SEVENTEEN

Natalia groaned in inexpressible agony.

But she couldn't scream—her throat didn't work.

"I do not wish to kill you, and I do not wish to end our pairing prematurely." Oskar ran the backs of his fingers languorously over her womb, and in that instant, she wished for death. He mumbled something else, and then he slowly rose above her, grasped her by the jaw, and squeezed.

She felt her jawbone crack, and the breath left her body.

She could no longer reason; she could no longer struggle.

She couldn't even think.

The whole world was blackness, pain, and futility.

Oskar was truly a monster.

As he slid down her torso and gripped both edges of her panties, she no longer cared what he did—she just wanted the suffering to stop. Perhaps the demon would have mercy and just kill her when he was done defiling her body. Nothing in the world was what it once seemed.

Absently, and for some inexplicable reason, she thought

about Santos showing up in her room later that night with an innocent deck of cards...ready and eager to play poker.

Poker.

It was much too late for that.

Oskar Vadovsky, her father's most revered client—and a stone-cold savage—had already played the winning hand: He had wielded a royal flush, and Natalia had dealt him the cards. She had virtually given Oskar the ace, king, queen, jack, and ten of diamonds the moment she had lied to Santos.

* * *

Santos Olaru exploded into the meadow, homing in like a pigeon on Natalia's blood.

He gathered his atoms until they coalesced around him—within him, throughout him—until they became him, and he materialized at the foot of a bed: a garish, raised platform beside an icy, snaking river.

He narrowed his feral gaze on the atrocity before him, taking in every microscopic detail in an instant, and then he raised his chin and roared.

Natalia was lying at an unnatural angle, her sleeveless black dress ripped down the center, and one leg was twisted—her ankle was broken—and one arm hung limp at her side. Her hand was masked beneath a blood-soaked glove, and even beneath the tattered satin, it was obvious to the warrior that there was nothing but an indefinable mass of ligaments, bone, and tissue...in no particular order. The hand was virtually crushed. And her beautiful face, those regal features: They stood stark against a hollow jaw. The left side was broken, her jawbone disfigured, which meant her assailant was most likely right-handed...

He turned his attention to the devil on top of her, the Dark

One who was about to defile her body, and something inside of him snapped.

His crystal-blue wings shot out of his back, his fangs descended from the roof of his mouth, and his claws extended to lethal lengths as he descended upon the son of Jaegar, wrenched both arms around his shoulders, and flipped them both over backward, somersaulting off the bed.

His teeth sank deep into the Dark One's throat, and he ripped out a chunk of raw meat as they landed. While the Dark One struggled to regain his bearings, his silk black pants hanging down to his knees, Santos took advantage of the vulnerable moment and blasted him with a fisted, right uppercut. The Dark One's jaw exploded. "How do you like it, bastard!" Santos snarled, and then he immediately struck at the heart.

The son of Jaegar caught the sentinel's fist, his mind and his instincts coming back on board. He spit out a set of bloody teeth, released his fangs, and smiled. As their eyes remained locked in unspoken, mortal combat, the Dark One used his magic to elevate his pants; fasten the bottom two buttons with a dexterous twist of his fingers; and release Santos' hand, gliding backward, ever so slightly, out of the vampire's reach.

And that's when Santos recognized his face.

Oskar Vadovsky, Chair of the Dark Ones' Council, preeminent statesman in the house of Jaegar.

A pregnant moment settled between them, and then the two supernatural beings virtually exploded in anger and old-fashioned savagery: fist to fist; uppercut to jab; weaving, bobbing, punching and counter-punching; blood and spittle and flesh flying freely.

The supernatural boxing gave way to bloodthirsty combat: throat-punching, eye-gouging, elbow strikes to the back of the head. Santos nicked Oskar's jugular and broke his left arm. Oskar retaliated in kind by scoring Santos' carotid artery and gouging his left cornea with a razor-sharp claw. Each male applied venom to heal his own wounds even as he kept coming, attacking...striking...never ceasing.

The blood was copious.

The wounds were gory.

The snarls, grunts, and rumbles called down thunder, lightning, and hail on the clearing, but the two rage-filled vampires kept going. They were like a deadly, supernatural sand storm in the Egyptian portion of the Sahara Desert: frenzied, brutal, and unrelenting. And if they didn't stop soon, Mother Nature would eclipse the carnage with her own special brand of destruction.

Impervious to the violent weather all around him, Oskar leaped from the meadow, landed in the river, and hefted a heavy boulder, the size of a small car, at Santos Olaru's head. The sentinel ducked, fell to one knee, and crossed both forearms above his head, bracing for the impact. The boulder struck his radius, and both arms fractured, but Santos seemed impervious to the pain. He shook it off, darted sideways, and wrenched a twenty-foot ponderosa pine out of the ground like a mere flimsy tent stake. He hurled it at breakneck speed, aiming at the center of Oskar's face, and hissed in pleasure when the Dark One's regal nose imploded.

Oskar shook his head like a water-soaked canine, ran his tongue over his fangs, and stalked toward Santos, knees bent, feet shuffling sideways, his center of gravity low to the ground.

Santos fell into a defensive posture, both arms up, ready and waiting.

Oskar pounced, and the two traded snap kicks, roundhouses, and targeted strikes, utilizing the fronts and backs of their fists, the tips of their fingers, and the outside edges of closed—and clawed—hands. At last, Oskar Vadovsky retreated, once again. The head of the dark council was visibly winded, no match for the godlike sentinel's stamina.

Santos licked his lips and measured the bastard's labored breathing.

If he could just shut out the pain—and he would do more than that for Natalia—he could wear the Dark One down, wait for an opportune moment, and then snap Oskar's head off his thick, demonic shoulders. *May the celestial gods be merciful*—the battle had just turned in Santos' favor.

CHAPTER EIGHTEEN

O skar Vadovsky was well and truly stunned.

His head was splitting; his muscles ached; and every bone in his body, those that were broken and those that were only bruised, hurt down to his dark, malevolent marrow.

What. The. Hell. Was. Happening.

Oskar was an ancient vampire, and his powers were immense —legendary among the house of Jaegar. No one would dare take him on. They couldn't possibly win. Yet, Santos Olaru was getting the best of him. Oskar was tiring, weakening, running out of steam, and he had lost far, far too much blood.

He couldn't fend off the markedly stronger sentinel much longer.

The inglorious son of a hyena was like a battering ram—he just kept coming and coming...and coming.

His blows landed with the force of a freight train; his lightning-quick strikes were precise and exact. His skill, determination, and lethal intention were overwhelming, and ultimately, it would be Oskar's demise if something didn't give. If Oskar kept this up, if he continued to go toe-to-toe with this crazed, bestial bastard, this might very well be his last night of life.

The realization was stunning.

What the hell was going on?

And then it struck him: the Delphinus Blood Moon.

They had all seen it the night before, stark as a neon sign above a Vegas hotel, and it hadn't taken any deep psychic intuition or undue research to discern which vampire—which cocky, self-righteous, undeserving male in the detestable house of Jadon —the ominous moon belonged to.

Oskar had known it was Santos.

But up until this very second, he hadn't put two and two together, and Salvatore Nistor's blasted, worthless cube had been silent. There had been no leaks out of the house of Jadon, no leaks from any of the light vampire's human servants, nothing to give away the identity of the sentinel's *destiny*.

At least not until now.

Natalia's long, sleek, satin gloves...

She had worn them to cover her wrists.

She had donned the clever accessories to hide the truth from Oskar—she was Santos Olaru's preordained *destiny*. Well, no wonder the bastard was fighting like this night was Armageddon, he was the last angel standing, and all of humanity was threatened by the devil. The male was fighting for his soul, his *destiny*, and his eternal life.

To hell with the dumb shit.

Oskar had no intentions of going out like this...not now...not here, and not over a human woman. Not at the hands of Santos Olaru, Napolean Mondragon's sentinel. Oskar's death, defeat, and humiliation would be legendary.

Reaching out on a familiar dark bandwidth, he called to the Colony Guard, searing his SOS into the minds of Achilles Zahora, a brute of a bastard; Silas Slovinsky, a brain-dead mute with a ring in his nose who could fight like a drug-crazed maniac; Nuri Bolasek, the demonic-looking freak with albino skin; and Falcon Zvara, the jackal with a Mohawk: *I'm ten miles west of Morrison, being attacked by one of Napolean's sentinels. Follow my signal—get your asses here now!*

The four deadly slayers appeared beside the river in less than thirty seconds, their huge, straining biceps encircled with the familiar venomous black mamba tattoos, their ruthless fists wielding both modern and medieval weapons: hatchets, daggers, an AR-15...

Achilles stepped forward first, his pale, citrine gaze locked like a laser on Santos.

And wouldn't you know it—but just like that—the five-to-one odds equalized.

Ramsey Olaru, Saxson Olaru, Julien Lacusta, and Saber Alexiares—the traitorous bastard turned house of Jadon sentinel —appeared in the meadow, armed to the teeth and ready for whatever the Colony Guard desired.

Santos must have called them the moment he saw the Dark Ones.

"Pick your poison, you genetic mutant," Ramsey grunted to Achilles, raising his trident to obscure the Dark One's path to Santos. "Blood sport, iron, or just plain fists and knuckles—we don't really give a shit, but you're not getting anywhere near either one of them." He gestured with his chin toward Santos, Natalia, and the garish, raised platform. "This is vampire to vampire, soldier to warrior, Colony Guard to HOJ Sentinel. May the baddest bastards win." He snickered, and Oskar could almost taste the hunger on Ramsey's tongue. The sentinel was salivating like a wild animal, practically gnashing his teeth in anticipation.

Achilles Zahora sneered, and the chuckle in his chest rumbled like thunder, even as the lightning storm all around them began to pick up. And then the seven-foot-tall giant made an unexpected shift and turned his full attention on his council chair. "Oskar, my liege. What say you as our council chair? Blood, death, and war—or protection, security, and retreat?"

Oskar was momentarily baffled by the question: protection, security, and retreat?

Kill the worthless bastards! he wanted to shout, but Achilles was not a neophyte, a coward, nor an idiot—and the male must have had his reasons for posing the question the way that he had...choosing the alternatives he'd chosen.

True to Oskar's supposition, Achilles continued, his right hand tightening around his bola, his massive shoulders trembling from the primal, nearly overwhelming desire to strike. "The way I see it is this," he barked, hocking up a wad of phlegm and spitting it at Ramsey's feet. "We can give these cock-sucking, whore-loving, sycophant pieces of shit a run for their money, probably take a couple hearts and heads"—he shifted his murderous gaze to Saber Alexiares, scanning the ex-Dark One from head to toe, and there wasn't a vampire in the meadow who didn't catch his drift: If all four of us have to attack as a unit to make it happen, we can at least slay that particular bottom-feeding slime—"or we can work as a unit toward a singular purpose—to get Natalia Giovanni back underground—to take her to the Colony." He glared at Ramsey again. "Can't take on all five of us *and* protect that woman. At some point, something—or *someone*—has to give. There's always at least one casualty of war." He licked his bottom lip in a lascivious fashion, then shrugged it off with a snarl. "Or we can accept the inevitable, avoid the gamble, and return with what we came for: the irreplaceable head of our colony's council. Accept the fact that Napolean Mondragon is going to be here any moment, worried about his precious Homo sapiens, insisting on stopping the battle, and able to channel the sun, however weakened under the cloak of darkness."

Measuring Oskar directly, again, he added, "Frankly, I don't give five fucks about the storm or a thousand humans dying. It's a Friday night, and I've got nothin' better to do than kill an enemy or die while trying, but the final call is up to you: What is the woman worth? How far do you want us to take this?"

All eyes shot to both Oskar and Santos, but the question was summarily answered when Marquis and Nathaniel Silivasi shimmered into view at the head and the foot of the makeshift platform. The warriors in the house of Jadon must have been broadcasting the conversation, and the threat to Natalia was immediately answered.

Saber Alexiares' nose began to twitch; his lips curled back involuntarily; and he exposed his lethal fangs beneath a snarl. The male wanted to fight so badly, he looked like he was in pain.

Julien Lacusta shifted in place, the implacable mountain widening his stance, while running a brazenly defiant hand, the middle finger extended, through his short, mahogany trim. "Damn, you bitches can talk all night. I think we all agree—there isn't an actual fuck given by anyone here, so let's do the damn thing."

Oskar felt an icy shiver run from the top of his spine to the bottom of his toes. He wanted to teach these arrogant swamp dwellers a lesson more than he wanted to take his next breath. Yet and still, he wanted to live, and he wasn't sure a war with the house of Jadon this night was prudent...advisable...worth the reward of Natalia Giovanni.

He hadn't even had a chance to shag her.

Damn, this shit was jacked up.

Nevertheless...

He straightened his back, smoothed his collar, and finished fastening the last three buttons of his trousers.

Achilles was right.

This wasn't the night, the place, or the time.

A war with Napolean—with the entire Colony and the house

of Jadon—wasn't something to be initiated on the fly over a spoiled, recalcitrant slut. There would be other opportunities to get back at the enemy; after all, eternity was a very long time.

Resolved to return to the Colony *alive,* to live to fight another night, Oskar pressed one hand to his stomach and bent at the waist in an old-world mockery of a bow. "Alas, Achilles, you are as wise as you are strong. While I haven't any doubt we could best these sons of bitches, that whore on the platform isn't worth it. Besides, she's all broken and bloody, not half as sexy. I wouldn't want to soil my cock."

An orange-and-red flash exploded in the background as Santos launched his body at Oskar, detonating like a rocket. Fortunately for the council chairman, Marquis Silivasi was right on Santos' tail. He caught the sentinel in midair, and he wrenched his body back by the shoulders, even as Achilles dove in front of his liege to protect him.

Oskar figured enough was enough.

These sentinels were way too amped up.

And Achilles was ultimately correct: There was always at least one casualty of war, and Santos was gunning for Oskar. "Until we meet again," he snarled, knowing he was going to regret this decision, "may all those present from an inferior house rot in the Valley of Death and Shadows. One of these days, your king will fall, and we will all get our bloody battle, but for this night, we shall take our leave." With a wink and a nod, Oskar vanished from sight, confident that his kindred in darkness would follow.

CHAPTER NINETEEN

Santos Olaru somberly approached the obscene bed atop the makeshift platform. Now that Oskar, his minions, and the house of Jadon's warriors were gone—with the exception of Saxson and Ramsey, who were still standing watch in the meadow—Santos could place his entire focus where it needed to be: on Natalia and her injuries.

"Natalia girl," he whispered softly, kneeling beside her broken body. "Oh, my darling, I am so, so sorry..." His words trailed off. There would be plenty of time for apologies later. "Let me check your injuries."

She moaned in pain, and her eyelids fluttered weakly. She was in and out of consciousness and clearly in shock as she mumbled something incoherent: "Oskar...fiancé...the driver disappeared. I didn't know. I shouldn't have—"

"Shh," Santos intoned, cradling her head in his hands as he shuffled closer beside her on the bed. "Don't try to talk; just let me attend to you." He had already surveyed her ankle, her hand, and her jaw, and the damage was appalling. Not to mention, her blood pressure was low; her breathing was rapid and shallow; her skin was cold and clammy; and her pulse was growing weaker by the minute. Even if her injuries weren't life-threatening, the shock could certainly kill her. And yes, Santos could treat the condition. He could call Kagen Silivasi or Kagen's protégé, Navarro Dabronski, to come attend to Natalia's injuries. He could treat the same with his venom, but one disconcerting fact remained: In order to protect the women in The Fortress, he would still have to allow Natalia to stay at Luca's compound until Sunday, albeit with an invisible vampiric guard at all times, if not Santos himself standing sentry. As much as it sucked to consider the agonizing alternative—and as eerily as it reminded Santos of Saxson and Kiera, what had happened in Owen Green's urban warehouse apartment—Santos knew what he had to do.

What he should do.

What would give his *destiny* the best advantage.

And that unconscionable thing was conversion.

"We were supposed to be married," Natalia mumbled, cringing in pain and panting. "I...I thought I could just get through this date and—"

"Quiet, my love," Santos urged her, the muscles in his jaw tightening at the very thought of Oskar Vadovsky playing Luca Giovanni for a fool and claiming his only daughter. So this was the Prince Oskar Zayda had mentioned; the thought made Santos sick to his stomach. Just how long had this been going on? How many times had Oskar touched her? When was he planning to take her back to the Colony...and rape her...kill her...breed his dark, soulless spawn from her virtuous body? *Don't go there, vampire,* he told himself. *Concentrate on the task at hand.*

"Angel," he whispered, "you are very seriously injured. And while I could work to heal you, it is not the safest...the most advantageous option. I am going to do something you may not understand, and it is going to make your pain worse for a while..." Shit, now wasn't that just the understatement of the century.

What if Natalia never forgave him? "But it will give you an arsenal of defenses between now and Sunday; it will save your life and heal your injuries. It will allow you to return to your father's home in one piece and keep up the ruse until I can take you out of there." *Forgive me, love,* he added, but he couldn't speak the words out loud.

Natalia turned her battered face listlessly to the side, and her hypnotic eyes met his. And in that pure, suspended moment, they were so completely absent of cunning—so filled with need... and trust...and longing. The glance was both a plea and a prayer: *Save me. Make the pain go away. Take me away from this nightmare.*

Santos wanted to gather every warrior in the house of Jadon—past, present, and future—blast a black hole into the Dark Ones' Colony, and wage war until there was only one vampire left standing. If that just happened to be Napolean Mondragon, and the king had to rebuild the house of Jadon from inception, so be it: The world would be a better place for it.

He forced himself to dismiss the thoughts. They weren't going to help Natalia.

Without further ado or explanation—he didn't even reach out telepathically to inform his brothers; what was the point? They'd figure it out soon enough—he braced both palms on either side of Natalia's waist, drew her into his lap, and held her tightly against him. He hooked his legs over, and around, her thighs, then shackled her shoulders with his powerful arms, anchoring her frame to his...holding her close to his heart. "Try to breathe, sweet girl. I will make this as fast as I can."

Pain was pain.

Agony was agony.

And Natalia was about to descend into hell.

There was no point in prolonging the journey when the end goal was to emerge on the other side.

With that in mind, Santos released his incisors and sank them deep into Natalia's jugular. Taking a deep breath for courage and pausing to offer a short prayer, he began to pump his venom in earnest. She stiffened, and he tightened his hold. She groaned, and he tuned it out. She began to jerk and writhe and protest in earnest, and he concentrated on pumping more venom.

She screamed so loud, the garbled cries so full of angst and terror, that Santos felt a barrier go up in the meadow, and he knew—*he just did*—Saxson and Ramsey were containing the sound, blocking it from escaping the area. As the luminescent dome of a cloaking cell enveloped the platform all around him— once again, compliments of Saxson and Ramsey—Santos began to pray: *Dearest Delphinus, I beseech you to have mercy on Natalia. My destiny has already suffered enough. Please bring her comfort; take her mind somewhere else; and hold her close in your celestial arms. May mortal death come swiftly as you transform her human body. Resurrect this chosen female as Vampyr as painlessly as you are able.*

CHAPTER TWENTY

Twenty-four Hours Later ~ Saturday, 11:00 PM

"So, Oskar Vadovsky was a vampire too? And that's how his driver disappeared from the limo?"

"Yes, my love."

"They were both...dark spawns in the house of Jason?"

"Dark Ones in the house of Jaegar," Santos corrected.

Natalia nodded slowly. "Jaegar," she repeated, in a low, incredulous voice. "And you think the Dark Ones...they've purchased women from my father for decades...to breed. To violate. And to kill? You believe that's what Oskar ultimately wanted from me?" Santos looked away, and Natalia shivered. It was better that he didn't answer. She leaned against the soft, pillowed headboard in her private bedroom suite; wrapped her arms around her knees; and closed her eyes, trying to take it all in.

Santos had been by her side since late last night.

Ever since the unspeakably painful conversion: a grueling, unholy, seven-hour descent into hell, an assault against every human cell in Natalia's mortal body, one that had left her mindless with agony, cursing the day she had been born, and wishing death and damnation on Santos—as well as every vampire the Blood had created—a process that had left her whimpering and wasted, but ultimately perfect.

Healed.

Changed.

Forever immortal.

It had been child's play for Santos and his brothers—Saxson and Ramsey—to slip past her father's guards, take her back to her bedroom, and compel all the servants and henchmen in Luca's manse to stay away from her room: Do not knock on the door; do not ask any questions; do not disturb Natalia until further notice.

It still gave Natalia the willies to contemplate the enormous powers Santos' species possessed—*her* species possessed—and while Santos had helped her turn down the noise, moderate her now heightened senses, and acclimate, at least a little, to her far more powerful body, what he couldn't help her with was the mental adjustment.

In the past forty-eight hours, give or take a few, Natalia's entire world had been flipped on its axis: turned upside down and altered irrevocably. Until she'd come back to clear, lucid consciousness in that meadow—until Santos had explained all he had done and all that had happened—she had still held out some measure of hope that she could change the trajectory of her future. That once the women in The Fortress were freed on Sunday, she could find a way to avoid The Curse, avoid the vampire's clutches, and slip away into obscurity to live a solitary life of freedom.

That was never going to happen now.

No pun intended, but the nail was well and truly secured in her coffin.

Natalia Antoinette Giovanni was a vampire, and she belonged to a warrior-sentinel named Santos Andrei Olaru. And like it or not, this Blood Moon was happening, all of it, over the next twenty-seven days. Somehow—some way—she had to make sense of it, or least begin to accept it.

"You still with me, Natalia girl?" Santos' deep, alluring tenor caressed her ears, bringing her out of her contemplation.

She exhaled slowly and opened her eyes. "I'm here. Just... still...processing."

He nodded solemnly. "How are you feeling?"

Since six o'clock that morning, when the hellish conversion had finally ended, Natalia had rested, off and on all day, taking intermittent naps between Santos' patient tutorials; testing her new body and her heightened senses; then withdrawing into the solace of her mind. "I'm fine, as well as can be expected under the circumstances."

His gorgeous, crystal-blue eyes deepened with compassion. "I am sorry for the way I chose to proceed, Natalia. I hope you know that was never my intention...to force this new life on you the way that I did. I had hoped to bring you into my world more gently."

Natalia forced a paltry smile; it was the best she could do. Santos had already apologized a dozen times, and it was certainly too late to take it back. "I understand," she murmured, tightening her self-protective grasp around her knees and leaning into the cocoon for comfort.

His keen, watchful gaze followed the motion unerringly. He sighed, lifted his hand, and crooked two fingers in a beckoning motion. "Come to me, Natalia."

She shuddered. "No, not yet. I'm comfortable here."

His eyes swept over her bare feet; traced the upward contours of the pale-blue silk nightgown; paused to survey her hands, her quivering shoulders, and the vein in her neck that was surely convulsing from all the nervous swallowing; and finally settled on her uncertain features. He crooked his fingers again. "Come," he repeated.

She shook her head. "I can't."

"Natalia..." His commanding tone softened. "You cannot hide forever."

She chuckled then, the sound absent of humor. "Perhaps not, but I think I'll hide just a little longer."

He reached out and slid the palm of his hand along the underside of her once-broken ankle, up her calf, and along her hamstring, circling to the top of her thigh. "Let go of your legs and come to me."

The weight of his hand, resting someplace so intimate, was almost too much to bear.

Too close.

Too suggestive.

Too entitled and possessive.

"Santos—"

"Shh." He placed both hands over hers and pried them away from her body. And then he grasped the underside of both legs and tugged her gently forward. As her body slid toward him, he rested his palms on either side of her waist and hoisted her effortlessly onto his lap—her legs fell naturally around him, and her bottom settled against his pelvis.

Natalia gasped.

"Shh," he repeated, encircling her with his arms and holding her tightly against him. "Nothing sexual, Natalia. Just let me hold you...surround you...envelop you. Nestle into my heart, sweet girl. I'm here. Always here. We will get through this together."

Her heartbeat became a frantic rhythm...

Every atom in her body wanted to protest—and bolt.

Her thighs quivered. Her palms began to sweat. And she held her breath for several seconds, trying to detect any hint of arousal—there were only so many new experiences a girl could embrace in forty-eight hours! And while the thought of finally, eventually—*inevitably*—making love to Santos consumed the vast majority of Natalia's thoughts, she couldn't handle it right now.

"Trust me, Natalia," he whispered in her ear, his breath as warm as a summer breeze and just as gentle. "I am not a monster, nor am I that selfish. I only wish to hold you, to comfort you, if you'll let me."

Natalia felt the truth of his words even more than she heard them.

She felt it in his tender touch. She sensed it in his matching heartbeat. She felt the power of his spirit—and his aura—radiate all around her like the two of them were sharing one cosmic mind, one will, one soul. Like their union was already consummated, somewhere deeper than flesh and bone. And she allowed herself to sink into that feeling...that knowing...as she laid her head against his shoulder and unwittingly nuzzled his neck.

A deep, sultry, nearly inaudible purr rumbled in the vampire's throat, and Natalia settled into the sound like an ambient, tranquil vibration, lulling her to sleep. She didn't sleep, however; she just gave herself over to his warmth.

And true to his word, Santos Olaru held her...and held her... and held her, until there was nothing in the world—at least for now—than a tender, compassionate vampire and his cautious but compliant *destiny*.

* * *

Oskar Vadovsky seethed and seethed, pacing like a caged, wild animal in his dimly lit, underground quarters, deep in the bowels of the Dark Ones' Colony.

He was sexually frustrated.

He was deeply humiliated.

And every cell in his dark, vampiric body ached to lash out at someone...or something.

By all the dark lords, he had wasted so much time genu-
flecting to that pampered princess and generally kissing her ass,
all with the promise that he would one day have her—brutalize
her, enjoy her, make use of her body to spawn the Colony's most
perfect offspring—and now, all those plans had failed.

Crumbled to dust like a castle built from sand.

And Oskar demanded satisfaction—both for his aching groin
and his embittered heart.

Bottom line: Luca had promised something he couldn't
deliver—who cares if it wasn't the billionaire's fault—and Natalia
had been *this close* to receiving Oskar's most brutal attention,
taking every sadistic inch of his hate, enduring a pain and
savagery that would have satisfied Oskar's most depraved
appetite and black-hearted instincts for years, when a gods-
forsaken warrior in the house of Jadon had stepped in and interrupted the blissful act.

Fine.

What was done was done.

But Natalia also needed to pay: She needed to suffer—indefi-
nitely—for years and years. She needed to carry the weight of
anguish, guilt, and horror on her slender shoulders, as well as her
sexy back, compliments of her former fiancé.

And there was only one way to make that happen.

Oskar wasn't a fool, and he had no intentions of biting the
hand that fed him. Yet and still, he could still punish the
Giovanni pair without harming the Colony's self-interests. With
Achilles Zahora at his side, the vampires would enter The
Fortress and violate, mutilate, and creatively slay every living,
breathing female in the northern quadrant: Luca's high-end call
girls, living on "Easy Street."

There would be nothing *easy* about it.

He would leave "Death Row" alone—those females could

still be purchased by the house of Jaegar in the future, and simi-
larly, he wouldn't touch the eastern or western wings: Prepubes-
cent girls were just not his thing. They didn't put up a
worthwhile fight, and they broke too quickly and easily—while
the low-end prostitutes were beneath his ministrations: too ugly,
too fat, too skinny, too smelly, too polluted by the drug-tainted
seed of human men. Besides, they wouldn't cost Luca nearly
enough money.

The high-end bitches were the way to go.

Oh yes, the whores as well as Luca's beloved, badass guards—
wholesale slaughter was definitely on the menu. And when
Oskar left a note attached to the front door of The Fortress,
letting Luca know the reason for the massacre—his precious
Natalia had been a tainted disappointment; the engagement was
off; and this was Oskar's payback—there'd be nothing the slave-
trader could do but cry. Oh, he'd stew for a while, perhaps plot
some misguided revenge, but at the end of the day, he would
swallow his pride, accept the loss, and give Oskar a very wide
berth. He would bow down to the vampire, despite his ignorance
of Oskar's species, like the inferior, human trash he was.

And he would lose millions and millions of dollars in inventory and assets...

And as for Natalia?

She would be overcome with guilt.

All those deaths...all those bodies...she would carry the shame
in her heart forever.

And then, once Oskar was satisfied, both sexually and
emotionally, he could turn his attention back to life in the Colony
—he would eventually find another woman, an even more appropriate human sacrifice, and life, as it always did, would go on.

But for now, he needed to alert Achilles—*get ready for the
slaughter of a lifetime*—the time to strike was while the iron was
hot, and Oskar was hot right now.

CHAPTER TWENTY-ONE

Gwendolyn Hamilton awakened with a start, her shoulders aching from the hard, metal-framed cot, her senses becoming instantly alert.

Something wasn't right—she could feel it all the way to her bones.

Instincts kicking in, she rolled off the abrasive canvas onto the hard, dirt floor and crawled on her belly to the edge of her cell, peeking through the iron bars: There was a dense, glutinous fog—as dark as the night, as eerie as skeletal fingers—snaking along the row of cages. The word *snaking* came to mind because the fog moved like an electric eel through murky water: gliding, meandering, coasting down the hall. A lump formed in Gwen's throat, and her trachea constricted. But she didn't gasp or cry out—she didn't dare. Her cell was the last along the row, the furthest from the fog, and the closest to the communal restroom.

She needed to remain silent...and think.

Her heart began to beat a frantic cacophony in her chest, and that's when she heard the bone-chilling echo—*click, click, click*—all the cages unlocking at once: plug after plug rotating in sharp synchronization, tumbler after tumbler falling into place, lock after lock releasing.

Someone had just opened *all* the cages.

But why?

Who would do that?

The guards typically let one woman out at a time, whether to take her to a John or allow her to use the restroom. They never opened all the cages at the same time.

Gwen's first impulse was to get up and run, yet something in her mind screamed, *Stop!*

Don't do it.

It was almost as if the unlocked cages were intentional—a row of dangling carrots—and that unholy fog was just waiting to see who would reach out and grab one.

Gwen blinked several times, trying to get a grip on her wild imagination. Fog didn't think. It didn't hunt or plot. So why were the hairs on the back of her neck standing up? And why was she suddenly so cold?

Swallowing her terror, she strained her neck to peek further down the hall, toward the end of the row, and it took her a second to comprehend what she was seeing: The tail of the fog had entered Laura's cage; the head had snaked into Tia's. Laura's ankles jerked; Tia's hair stood on end; and Gwen's eyes shot back and forth in a panic. Something—or someone—was tugging on Laura's legs, snapping her ankles, and slithering between her thighs. Something just shredded her pajamas!

And Tia?

Holy shit!

This wasn't possible...

She was being raised in the air by her hair, dragged upward along the bars of her cell like a convict caught in a hangman's noose. Her neck began to bleed. Her chest and her thighs followed suit. Shuddering, Gwen thought about the human arteries—the carotid, the pulmonary, and the femoral—as Tia's blood spurted out, as if from a geyser, creating a crimson waterfall. Her back struck the wall of the cell, again and again...and again, her arms and legs flopping like a rag doll's.

And then Gwen saw the outline of a man, a monstrously tall slayer with chin-length, black-and-red banded hair, and a bare, bronzed, muscular back. He was cut like an inhuman statue, and his bulging upper right bicep was encircled by a horrifying tattoo. From this far away, Gwen might not have made out the Black Mamba, except the serpent's red eyes began to glow, and for a moment, it looked like it raised its head from the giant's body, snaked out its tongue, and flashed its fangs before retreating back into the bicep.

Back into the man.

Back into the fog.

Gwen pressed her palm over her mouth to stifle a scream. She back-crawled away from the bars, dug the nails of her free hand into the earthen floor, and trembled uncontrollably. Laura and Tia were being assaulted and murdered...mutilated and drained... by something inside of the fog.

Where the hell were the guards?

Where the hell was The Reaper?

Paralyzed with fear and unable to see what was happening, Gwen clenched her eyes shut and listened. Laura's inhuman groans. Tia's last gasp of breath. Women were coming awake now, and the entire northern wing was filling with terror: blood-curdling screams, cage doors opening, bodies being slammed back into their cells, bones cracking as they splintered against cement walls.

Gwen was running out of time.

If she didn't make a move right now, if she didn't shake off her fear and act, it would be too late—she was only six or seven cages away from dying a brutal death.

Forcing her eyes back open, she tuned into every conceivable sound, paying closest attention to the grunts and snarls rising out of that evil fog. Clawing at the dirt in her cell, she stripped out of her pajamas, then coated her hair and covered her back with the soil before crawling on her belly, as noiselessly as possible, to the door of her cage.

Several grunts—she tapped the iron, allowing the door to glide open an inch.

A prolonged moan—she pushed it further, holding her breath as the metal creaked.

Agonizing screams, two more women being assaulted—she shimmied through the open doorway and crawled like a lizard to the end of the hall.

The moment she rounded the corner, she shot to her feet and took off running: arms pumping, heart pounding, lungs burning like magma in her chest. *Don't look back!* she repeated like a mantra. *Run, Gwen, just run!*

She darted into the communal restroom, zigzagged between the dingy shower walls, and climbed atop a slippery ledge to reach up and remove the shower vent. Then somewhere in the distance, a fist barreled into a stomach; an open palm thundered against a captive's face; and a series of piteous, ear-piercing screams followed, causing Gwen to lose her balance.

Her bare feet teetered on the border of the ledge, and she tumbled to the ground.

The metal vent hit the shower floor with a clang, causing a large commotion, and she landed right on top of it at an unnatural, sideways angle, slicing her right hip against the rim of the metal. She pressed her palm to her mouth to stifle a scream, even as she moaned in pain. Then she dipped the pads of her fingers into the soiled blood, checked the size and depth of the gash, and grit her teeth as she got back up.

The ledge was even slicker now.

Her blood was coating the tiles.

And she scrambled wildly—slipping again and again—before she secured a steady perch.

Reaching up to grasp both sides of the opening in the shower ceiling, she struggled to hoist herself up, and that's when she saw the cover of the vent, still stained with blood, lying on the shower floor. "No, no, no-no-no!" she whimpered, staring helplessly at the metal cover.

They would find it.

It would find it.

Those things in the fog would see the blood beneath the opening in the ceiling, and they'd know exactly where she was.

Bitter tears stung her eyes, and her entire body shook as she glared at that *stupid, stupid* vent and tried to make up her mind: The man, the one she had seen in the fog—he would never fit into the vent. He could never crawl inside such narrow ductwork, but then, what the fuck was that misty shit anyway, and how were they moving in and out of it?

What the hell were those supernatural creatures?

And could they follow her as vapor?

"Impossible," she murmured, but something in her heart knew that it wasn't.

Choking back her sobs, she listened more attentively—the screams were coming closer; the carnage was growing louder; there were...there were...*footsteps* coming toward the bathroom stalls.

Oh god, oh god, oh god!

She released her grasp on the ceiling, jumped off the ledge, and cringed as a sharp, piercing pain shot through her ankles the moment her feet struck the tiles. The pain traveled upward, blasting her knees, and she fell forward, slamming her hands against the drain—but she didn't utter a whimper. She didn't have time for self-pity. She turned the valve on the shower, placed her hands beneath the spray, and feverishly pumped a dollop of soap out of a nearby dispenser, instinctively knowing she had to mask the scent: the scent of her sweat, the scent of her body, the scent of the dirt from her cell...but most of all, the scent of her blood.

Gwen used the palms of her hands to scrub the vent, the shower floor, and the ledge with the soap. She used the soles of her feet to whisk the grime down the drain, and then she snatched a thin white towel off a nearby hook and climbed back onto the ledge, wiping everything behind her as she backtracked. It wasn't completely dry, but it didn't scream "recently wet."

Last, but not least, she tossed the wet, soiled towel into the opening in the ceiling, patted the vent cover dry, and reached for a loop she had tied around the inside of the metal a couple of weeks before. She twisted the loop around her foot, careful to coil it twice: in and out, around her big toe, and over the ball of her foot. As she sped through the familiar motions, she thanked the angels in heaven that she had seen fit to rip a strip from her pajamas and create the vent loop earlier. Now, she could only pray that her next series of motions were embedded in her muscle memory.

The door to the restroom creaked open.

A swirl of fog began to snake along the tile floor...

And Gwen scrambled to get moving.

She hoisted herself into the ceiling, drawing everything inside except her anchored foot, and then she rotated her body, squeezed her shoulders together, and reached down through her legs to unloop her toes. She tugged on the vent, pulling it up just as the moist, dank scent of fog began to envelop the shower...

Holy shit.

Holy...shit...

Holding her breath, her body quaking, she held the vent in place by the loop.

And then there was a virtual explosion of gunfire, bullets ricocheting off the bathroom walls, and she heard a furious string of guttural curses as one of the guards entered the women's restroom.

Gwen took the chaos as her cue.

She tightened the vent, made sure it was secure, and began to shimmy backward through the ductwork until she reached the widest point in the opening—a tunnel she had dug for just this purpose—and flipped her body around in order to crawl the rest of the way, facing forward.

CHAPTER TWENTY-TWO

"Santos!" Natalia whispered. "Something's going on."

The Master Warrior opened his eyes and rested his hand on Natalia's hip. His *destiny* had been sleeping soundly beside him, their bodies in a spooning position, when her newfound, superior hearing had woken her up.

Santos had already heard the alarms. "I hear it, angel—where is it coming from?"

She shot up in bed, her eyes wide with terror. "My father's study and the central control room in the basement. Oh God, Santos, that's not the home security system. I've only heard it once or twice during carefully controlled tests, but I'd know that high-pitched shrill anywhere—it's the sound of my nightmares. That's the panic siren for The Fortress. The one that triggers... containment."

Santos cocked his brows. "Containment?" He reached over her shoulder, placed his hand on her jaw, and turned her gently to make eye contact. "Be very clear, Natalia: By *containment*, you mean what?"

She choked back a sob. "The Fortress has been breached. I

have no idea by what or whom—perhaps a federal raid, perhaps my father's enemies—but the mercenaries, the ones I told you about, the hired killers in other countries... Santos, they just got their marching orders. By *containment*, I mean they will kill them all. Tonight. Right now."

Santos shot off the bed like a rocket.

In the space of ten heartbeats, he shoved Natalia's armoire, desk, and chest of drawers against the only door to her bedroom. In the space of a fifteen heartbeats more, he wrenched several metal slats off the frame beneath her bed, bent them to fit snugly inside a five-by-seven frame, and secured them against her bedroom window. "Do not move the furniture or open this door to anyone but me or my brothers," he commanded, his tone brooking no argument. "Stay here, inside this room, until we come for you. Do you understand me, Natalia? Let no one in."

She nodded emphatically. "Yes. I understand, but what—"

He didn't have time to listen...or answer... He was already transporting through the bedroom wall. *Ramsey! Saxson!* he shouted on their common, family telepathic bandwidth. *Alert the other warriors—The Fortress has been breached! The clock is already ticking. We can't wait for Sunday night. The raid goes down right now.*

* * *

Santos, Saxson, and Ramsey Olaru; Nathaniel, Kagen, and Nachari Silivasi; Braden Bratianu and Blade Rynich all materialized in less than two minutes, appearing beneath a dense, shadowed grove of cottonwood trees a couple of feet behind the ten-foot-high wall that surrounded the enormous fortress.

The moonlight glistened against the silhouette of olive-green leaves.

The wind whispered secrets of duplicity and danger.

And the garish, white brick structure within the robust wall beckoned to the warriors like a lonely siren: dangerous, deceptive...and taunting.

Wordlessly, the vampires chambered, cocked, and checked their weapons: Ramsey handed Santos his familiar iron stake, although the sentinel was just as comfortable fighting with his hands, even as the hazel-eyed vampire rotated and fingered his own beloved trident. Saxson sheathed his medieval axe in a worn, leather belt loop, while Nathaniel shouldered his M4 carbine—one glance beneath the devious Ancient Master Warrior's cloak, and it was clear that he was also carrying his polished silver stiletto, the one with the custom handcrafted grip. Kagen, on the other hand, was wearing a peculiar makeshift holster, outfitted with every manner and size of wicked-looking surgical implements and scalpels, while true to form, Nachari brandished his beloved sword.

Braden was wearing a set of brass knuckles, and he had an Old West Colt 45 tucked in the back of his belt, while Blade appeared to be strapped with nun chucks and several Shuriken—throwing stars. He had studied Okinawan martial arts and Ninjutsu at the local academy this past semester, and he was clearly eager to try them out.

The circle of vampires lit up with a faint iridescent light, and a host of translucent colors danced through the air, narrowing into a stream of prisms that hovered before each HOJ male, save Braden and Blade—the fledglings were not yet adept with the creation of a communal hologram, something that took an inordinate amount of energy to sustain and project during a battle against lycans or other vampires, but would be easy enough to maintain against humans.

One by one, the Master Warriors projected their images, each one adding his individual imprint into the string of holograms until the impressions linked, and then they brought Braden and

Blade's individual auras into the common mix. From this moment forward, as the Vampyr entered The Fortress, they could call up the collective screen and see each and every vampire's individual position, opponent, and stage in the fight.

In other words, the eight were intrinsically connected.

No one was alone or blind.

And while Santos momentarily regretted the fact that they had not had time to bring two more warriors into the raid, they would just have to make do with what they had.

"Braden, Blade," Santos spoke with lethal purpose, "while you can't create your own holograms yet, can you hold this...can you call it up? You good with the communal projection?"

Braden Bratianu nodded, and his now six-foot-two iron frame tensed with electric energy and purpose. "Yeah, I'm good."

"And you, Blade?" Santos asked.

Blade Rynich opened his mouth to speak, and his taut lips curled back over his fangs so that his affirmation was no more than a guttural grunt.

Good enough, Santos thought. *Both of these fledglings are ready.* "Then let's do the damn thing," he barked with authority, and all eight warriors vanished from the shadows of the cotton-woods, scattering to take their predetermined positions.

CHAPTER TWENTY-THREE

The instant Santos materialized in the northern wing of The Fortress, he knew something was terribly wrong.

The stench of blood and death permeated the dark, dank structure.

What might have been an odorless chemical to humans assailed his hypersensitive nostrils.

And the wing was way too quiet.

Nothing was as the warriors had anticipated.

Switching his vision to infrared, he immediately began to search for heat signatures, even as he tuned into the cacophony of faint and fading heartbeats and pulled up the communal hologram.

Ramsey! he called out on a telepathic line. *What's happening in the southern quadrant?*

Damn, brother, Ramsey grumbled, *you need to take a look at this shit. Three guards dead, their limbs literally ripped off their bodies: one is missing a head; the other two are missing their hearts. The sons of bitches never knew what hit them.*

Santos zoomed in on the hologram, rapidly scanning

Ramsey's field of vision. "Damn," he whispered, and then, one by one, he zoomed in and out of all the other warriors' projections. Saxson had entered the facility in the west, and he had stumbled upon the same thing: six dead sentries, their disemboweled corpses stacked in a gruesome flesh-and-bone pile. Nathaniel Silivasi was patrolling the halls, and they were empty with the exception of three more dead bodies, all belonging to Giovanni's guards: one male was hanging from the ceiling by his intestines; one was slumped against a wall, his vacant eyes still open; and on the other end of the corridor, near the back of the building, the last guard in the hall had been impaled through the sternum by his own rifle. *These aren't human executions*, Santos murmured.

No shit, Ramsey replied, undoubtedly scanning the collective hologram as well.

Nachari was slinking through the eastern wing as a silent, graceful black panther, sniffing dead guards—looked like two— and searching for captive women, while Kagen stood as a sentry, stationed at the front door. The Ancient Master Healer's orders had been to head off and destroy any enemy stragglers or human guards trying to escape, while guiding panicked women out of the building—Blade had been given an identical mission at the rear door of the structure. Yet there were no rebel fighters, no enemy combatants trying to flee The Fortress. No guards to engage in combat. No desperate women, panicking. No screaming, no scrambling, no one trying to escape.

Just rivers of blood, dead guards, and the pungent odor of chemicals...

Further below, in the compound's basement, Braden Bratianu had stumbled upon five more dead henchmen. By the looks of things, they *had* been trying to escape the facility, but Santos didn't have time to inquire further—he needed to check his own post, survey the cages in the northern quadrant, and enumerate any remaining dead guards. More urgently, he needed to check all the northern women: Was anyone still conscious? How many were passed out? *Blessed Delphinus*, let somebody still be breathing...

He needed to shift into light speed now.

Wings punching out of his back, he raced in the direction of the ghastly cages, darting feverishly in and out of each cell, and his stomach twisted into sickening knots.

Indeed, there were five dead guards in total, spread out among the many cages, but these bastards had died trying to protect their chattel. They had died defending the northern women, who clearly hadn't stood a chance—the females had been cornered and decimated like pigs in a slaughterhouse, along with their worthless protectors. And judging by the telltale fang marks on their necks, the sharp indentations of claws gouged into their thighs, and the numerous pools of blood beneath them, clearly formed by arterial spray, there was no longer any question as to what had happened.

They're all dead, Santos reported, sending the observation across a communal, telepathic bandwidth, addressing no one in particular. *All the women in the northern quadrant are gone, but they didn't die from poison chemicals. They were brutalized... ruined...ripped apart. They were definitely slain by vampires. And to my way of thinking, this has Oskar Vadovsky written all over it —he didn't go quietly into the night.*

Mine are still breathing! Saxson thundered, interjecting a voice of hope into the mayhem. *At least thirty souls, still in their cages, all but three are unconscious. We can still get them out.*

It's the same in the south, Ramsey chimed in. *The guards are dead, but the women are still breathing. I'm counting twenty-five.*

Thirty-two girls. Nachari's calming voice. *All still alive, but barely.*

And that's when Ramsey Olaru took charge: *Santos, Nathaniel, Blade: Forget your previous assignments and posts—we* need to carry as many of these women as we can, as fast as we can, out of this toxic cesspool. Santos, join Saxson. Nathaniel, get over here with me, and Blade, hump your ass over to the eastern wing to help Nachari with the unconscious females. Kagen, you need to do your thing, Healer; try to keep these gods-forsaken women alive. We'll lay 'em on the ground as fast as we can fly them out, but you've gotta work some serious magic. And for what it's worth, Healer, you might want to make it rain!

Braden! Try to locate the pumps—if you can't stop the nerve agent, at least obstruct the flow in the pipes. And warriors, one and all, blast as many man-sized holes in these walls and the roof as you can. We need to get some fresh air and water into this bitch. Oh, and keep your eyes out for Luca and his henchmen; you never know when they might show up. Same goes for Oskar Vadovsky and our dark, soulless cousins—more than likely, the cowardly bastards went home, but just the same, watch your six. I doubt anyone in Giovanni's employ has called the human police—they probably have the compound locked down, tight—still, stay aware. There are innocent servants on this property as well as some really bad actors, so play it by ear. Scrub memories when you need to, snap necks if it's called for, and call out to another warrior if you need some backup. Now let's move like the dark hounds of hell, themselves, are breathing down our necks.

At Ramsey's telepathic command, Braden Bratianu began to survey the basement: scanning the corners for containers or drums; checking the ceiling for strange, exposed pipes; and generally avoiding the creepy-ass, bloodstained stone situated in the middle of the floor. No doubt, the Dark Ones had been birthing their children in this basement for years...using Luca's captives to spawn them.

Shit...just shit...the house of Jadon sure had some jacked-up enemies.

Trying to keep Nachari's earlier instructions in the back of his mind, he worked to reset his preternatural gas mask. "When we enter the structure, Braden," Nachari had told him, "you might encounter any number of threats: a hail of bullet fire, an explosion, or even toxic chemicals. You need to be prepared to deflect any oncoming bullets; to scatter your molecules and recollect them in the event of an explosion; and to block any lethal toxins. With regard to the latter, do not panic. Remember, the Vampyr race descended from humans and celestial gods—we are interconnected with the elements; they react to our emotions, but they also do our will. With that in mind, the moment you sense the presence of toxic vapor, reach out to the universe and call forth the base elements of charcoal—as you've learned at The Academy, these are carbon, hydrogen, oxygen, nitrogen, and sulfur. Break them down into the exact atomic structure of charcoal, then hold them in the back of your throat. Heat them with a stream of oxidizing gas—steam, CO_2, and air—to activate the compound. This will create a barrier like chicken wire, a filter of sorts, and any toxins you inhale will become bonded to the holes in the activated charcoal net before they can reach your lungs. Once you've set it in the back of your throat, leave it there—literally command the filter to hover if you need to. Once it's in place, you won't even notice it—it'll sit there until you remove it."

Thank the gods, Nachari had made Braden practice...

The filter was still holding strong.

Turning his attention to the first of two long, narrow halls, Braden eyed a series of four large cannisters, and sure as shit, they were wired to a simple control pad. The control pad was wired to both a cell phone and a timer, and it looked as if the timer had gone off—the apparatus had clearly been triggered. Drawing nearer to the barrels, he eyed them up close: Each tank was stamped with a skull-and-crossbones, and beneath each symbol were three bright red words—

POISON—TOXIC CHEMICALS.

Yeah, well, no shit, Sherlock, Braden thought. *It's not like this neat little row of hanging gas masks, right beneath the effin' control pad, doesn't give that obvious fact away.*

He followed the interconnecting pipes, those that snaked out of the cylinders, and it looked like they were linked to four main supply lines: to an obvious series of pumps. He dropped down into a squat, rubbed his chin thoughtfully, and tried to figure out how the system worked.

He didn't want to act too impulsively, to bend or crush the pipes prematurely—where would the toxic agent go if it was side-lined? Was there something in the chemical makeup that could explode under pressure, thus setting the whole damn building on fire? Same thing if he screwed with the actual pumps: For all he knew, he would blunder, screw something up, and end up streaming the poison out faster. He returned his attention to the four main supply lines: Yep, all the chemicals were funneling into those pipes before branching out into the various wings of The Fortress...

Nodding with decision, he sidled up to the first main supply and braced both hands around the iron, about four or five inches apart. Grunting with effort, he tightened his fists, flexed his muscles, and rotated both wrists outward. Sure enough, the pipe snapped in half, and toxic chemical agent began pouring into the basement. Remembering Nachari's words—*remembering not to panic*—he quickly sealed the outflow shut, then repeated the process three more times. The poison already in the pipelines would continue to flow to the upper floor, but no new vapors would join it. As for the open streams now flooding the basement, he would leave those alone to avoid the potential of an explosion

—better they pumped into the basement than the entire noxious structure.

He jumped to his feet in a dexterous bound and began to high-tail it to the other end of the basement, to the second, identical hall, in order to repeat the process. No doubt, he would find another set of cannisters linked to another set of main supply lines, but at least he knew how to disable them. And he wasn't going to lie—not to himself or the gods. He was chomping at the bit to get out of that poisonous basement.

Plus, he wanted to help the other warriors.

And that's when he heard a mousy scratch, an almost inaudible sound, coming from the center of the cellar, high above, in the ceiling's ductwork.

His heartbeat sped up; he dropped down into a crouch, rocking onto the balls of his feet; and he retrieved his Colt 45 from his waistband, silently cocking the trigger. Then he narrowed his gaze at the celling and listened intently, trying to discern the origin of the sound.

There it was again.

Scratch, scratch, scratch.

Then a frantic gasp for air, followed by muffled breathing—a woman's pitiful whimper.

Braden zoomed in on the faint, distant sounds until he was standing directly beneath them. Releasing the trigger, he rotated the Colt in his hand and gripped it by the barrel. With a strike as fast as lightning, he leaped from the ground and slammed the butt-end of the weapon into the ceiling. He ducked and shuffled backward as plaster, wood, and a sheet of galvanized steel rained down all around him. And then he flipped the weapon back into position, cocked the trigger a second time, and pointed the barrel toward the gaping hole—*just in case*—as he waited.

Nothing happened.

Just another desperate gasp for air, this time followed by a wheezing cough, then more muffled breathing.

He levitated off the floor, floated into the opening, and peered cautiously inside the decimated ceiling—and then he jolted: A filthy, yet beautiful blond-haired woman was huddled inside of the ductwork, her pale green eyes as wide as saucers. Her breasts were exposed; her hip was bleeding; and she was breathing into a wadded-up pair of panties. A quick glance—up and down, back and forth—made it clear where she had gotten the underwear.

Braden cringed in embarrassment and stretched out his hand. "Crawl forward." His voice sounded gravelly, too deep to be his own, and the woman practically hyperventilated, trying to shuffle backward. She was *this close* to passing out, maybe even dying. "Hold up," Braden commanded, instinctively lacing his voice with compulsion. Stunned when her body froze in mid-motion, he blew out a breath and softened his delivery. "Just hold up; stay right there. I'm not going to touch you. Let me go get you a gas mask, all right?"

Despite her panic, she slowly nodded, and her eyes were desperate with pleading.

Braden flew to the end of the hall in a heartbeat, snatched one of the gas masks off a plastic hook, and quickly zoomed back, setting the contraption inside of the duct where she could reach it. But she didn't reach out to take it. As desperate as she was to live—as close as she was to passing out—she dropped the panties, her jaw fell open, and her expression registered pure horror. Then two bloodcurdling words shot out of her mouth as she pointed a trembling finger behind him:

"The demons!"

CHAPTER TWENTY-FOUR

"Easy come, easy go." A dark, dissonant drawl.

"Ten points for the fledgling; one point for the ho." A deeper, more malevolent brogue.

Braden spun around just in time to see two lethal Dark Ones standing in the basement: one with slate-gray eyes and long, obsidian-and-red hair flowing halfway down his back, and another citrine-eyed monstrosity, at least seven feet tall, with the tattoo of the Colony Guard on his right bicep.

Braden tried to drop back into a defensive stance—*he needed to call out to the other warriors!*—but the Dark Ones struck like they shared one mind, one strategy, and one demonic purpose: In the blink of an eye, less than that really, the giant transported behind Braden, grasped both his arms, and wrenched them backward, shackling the vampire's wrists. Braden's chest bowed forward, exposing his heart, as the Colony Guard held him in an implacable, iron grip. At the same exact moment, the monster with slate-gray eyes drew back his right arm, released his claws, and thrust the wicked-sharp daggers forward.

The moment streamed in slow motion.

The inevitability of death was too sudden...too shocking...too surreal as Braden exhaled in defeat, braced both shoulders, and thought about Kristina Riley-Silivasi...

The fact that he would never get to mate her.

And that's when the panther slammed into Oskar, catching his homicidal talons in its wide, powerful jaw, and flinging his body sideways. Nathaniel Silivasi shimmered into view, less than two seconds later, and the Dark One behind Braden let go of his arms in order to face off with the Ancient Master Warrior.

Nathaniel twirled his stiletto in and out of his fingers, whistling low beneath his breath, and then the devious vampire from the house of Jadon chuckled, his dark black gaze alighting with both mischief and excitement. "You want to play with a grown-ass vampire?" He spat the words in a thick, Romanian accent. "*Atunci, hai sa dansam,* motherfucker. *Sunt aici.*" *Then let's dance,* motherfucker. *I'm right here.*

The seven-foot monster matched Nathaniel's arrogance, cynicism, and eagerness with a wicked echo of maniacal laughter, withdrawing a long, serrated dagger from his belt.

Nathaniel didn't wait for him to wield it—he lunged forward, caught the soldier off guard, and head-butted him so violently, Achilles' skull split open. The Dark One stumbled backward, drew his hand through the blood, and countered with a lightning-quick throat punch, bayonetting Nathaniel's trachea.

Nathaniel slathered his throat in venom, even as he swallowed the same—he feigned as if he were doubling over, trying to catch his breath, and rose like a Phoenix, with rocket-propelled wings, slamming his knee into the Dark One's groin...then driving it up through his gonads.

Achilles hit the deck.

He puked on Nathaniel's boots.

And his expression turned ashen and sallow.

But no sooner had he sunk to the ground than he grabbed the

Ancient Master Warrior's ankle, locked onto his flesh like a rabid animal, and began to tear at the tendons with his ungodly long fangs.

"Achilles!" A harsh, dominant bark from the other, angry Dark One, who had just wrenched free from the panther.

Achilles' massive arms twitched, and his entire body shuddered, but he continued to ravage Nathaniel's flesh.

"*Achilles...*" The second Dark One spoke his name again, this time in a quiet command.

The giant released his hold on the ankle, and just like that, the evil duo vanished.

A moment of silence—if not relief—filled the basement. Then Braden dropped his head in his hands and struggled to catch his breath. "Thank you," he panted, to no one in particular.

Nathaniel Silivasi smiled and shook out his wounded limb. "You two good?" he asked Nachari.

The panther, who had already shifted back into a formidable Master Wizard, strolled over to the hole in the ceiling, floated up to retrieve the girl, and then glanced over his shoulder to regard his older brother. "Yeah, we're good. Be outside in a minute."

Nathaniel bowed his head in a surprisingly noble nod and disappeared from the basement.

"Nachari," Braden said, watching as the wizard hoisted the naked woman, now wearing the gas mask, from the ceiling.

"You're welcome, son," Nachari answered.

Braden felt a hot, embarrassing tear well up in the corner of his eye. "No, really, Nachari." He swallowed a lump in his throat. "I thought I was a goner." If he kept on talking, he was going to start crying, and wouldn't that just be the most pansy-ass thing he had ever done in front of the other vampires. At this point in his development, his body had filled out, he had shot up to six feet, two inches, and his voice was as deep and resonant as any other male's in the house of Jadon. The last thing he needed to do was break down and sob like a little girl.

"You all right?" Nachari asked him.

Braden cleared his throat.

"We've all been there," Nachari said. "That's why we rely on a band of brothers." He smiled then, that notorious grin. "Shake it off, Braden. Things aren't always what they seem."

Now this caused Braden to cock his eyebrows and frown. "What do you mean?"

Nachari took off his coat and wrapped it around the female's slender shoulders—she looked like she was in shock.

"Your chest, vampire. Take a look."

Braden glanced down at his sternum, his eyes fixed just above his heart, and he blanched at the sight of a swirling, incandescent light, a million streams and prisms pulsing outward.

Nachari shook his head in wonder. "Don't know if that was some makeshift holding cell, adapted as body armor, or if you just made a psychic, energetic shield—but those claws weren't getting anywhere near your heart, at least not on the first strike. And that right there, my acolyte, was the feat of a Master Wizard."

Braden gulped.

Well, holy shit...

And then he heard it: the energy, the pulse, the heartbeat of the house of Jadon.

Thrum, thrum, thrum...

And he heard something else: a pure and absolute synchronicity pounding inside the human woman's chest. He sighed. "Nachari..." He focused, trying to find the right words. "Not sure how to say this, but we need to take her back to the brownstone. She belongs to the celestial gods—she belongs with the house of Jadon."

No sooner had he spoken the words than the terrified, disheveled blonde passed out, and Nachari caught her. Perhaps she'd been overcome by the vapors she'd already inhaled, or perhaps she'd been overcome by trauma.

Either way...

Didn't matter...

Nachari's expression grew exasperated. "Are you absolutely sure, son?"

Braden nodded. "Don't know why...or what...or even how I know, but I'm absolutely certain."

* * *

It was two o'clock in the morning when Santos Olaru slipped noiselessly through Natalia's bedroom wall, traversing the physical barrier with ease, and found her sitting on the hardwood floor, her back up against a fractured section of plaster, shivering beneath a throw blanket with red bloodshot eyes.

"Natalia...*cuore mio*..." he whispered, hurrying to her side. Squatting down in front of her, he eyed the gaping hole behind her and asked, "What happened? Why have you been crying?"

She shuddered and clutched the blanket tighter, her dark brown gaze seeking his and carefully studying his features. "Is it over?"

He exhaled slowly. "Mostly." He ran the backs of his fingers over her high, angular cheekbones and lowered his heavy body onto the floor in front of her. "I'll tell you everything, but first; tell me what happened."

She glanced over her shoulder, indicating the splintered wall. "Domenico, one of my father's most loyal henchmen—we often refer to him at The Reaper—tried to break through the plaster with an axe."

A feral snarl escaped Santos' lips, and he had to struggle to tone it down. "Why...when...how did you stop him?"

This time, it was Natalia who sighed. And then she simply

began reciting the facts in a cerebral, unemotional monotone, as if she had no emotions left. "I found out what—or rather who—tripped the alarm, the one alerting my father to trouble in The Fortress. Domenico showed up for his late-night shift and found a note stapled to The Fortress' front door. Santos, it was left by Oskar." She started to cringe at the sound of the dark vampire's name, but immediately pulled it back and returned to an even cadence. "I...I guess Oskar, and maybe some other vampires from the house of Jay—of Jaegar—broke into the building earlier, and they...they..."

"Shh, *cara mia*," Santos interrupted.

Her eyelashes fluttered, still wet from tears. "Then it's true?" she whispered. "They murdered—no, they massacred—dozens of the women?"

Santos nodded his head, feeling weary. "Yes, Natalia. It's true. Oskar and a soldier named Achilles Zahora attacked the northern wing of high-end call girls; they executed all but one before we got there."

Natalia's hands shot to her chest, and she gasped as her eyes fell shut. Her body began to tremble, but she quickly contained it, forced her eyes back open, and stared blankly, almost absently, at the bed in front of her. "I see. Then it's also true that they murdered the guards?"

Santos studied her carefully—she was hanging on by a thread. "Yes, it would appear, all but The Reaper." Taking her hand in his, he clasped it gently and sent a stream of warmth, a calming energy, flowing into her palm. It wasn't much, but it was better than nothing.

"Well, at least there's that," she murmured bitterly. "The fact that they executed all those worthless bastards." She raised her shoulders as if hefting an impossibly heavy load and pushed forward: "At any rate, Domenico insisted that my father flee the country, get out right away on his private jet—he didn't say where they were going, most likely Italy, but he informed Papa that he had initiated *doomsday*, that all the women would soon be gone." She shook her head in disbelief. "I still can't comprehend such wickedness—the fact that they were willing to kill every single woman in that building with nerve agents..." Her voice trailed off, and she had to take a moment to collect her thoughts. "You have to understand, the women were merely objects to Luca, monetary assets to be traded, sold...or disposed of. My father has billions in assets and dirty money, much of it stored in international banks. While destroying every soul in The Fortress would cost him millions, for him, it would barely put a dent in his holdings. Domenico was afraid of a federal raid, and he was also worried that Oskar Vadovsky and his hatchet men might attack the mansion as well...try to assassinate my father. They didn't know they were dealing with vampires, but they definitely got Oskar's message: He's a far more powerful enemy than my father ever suspected."

Santos licked his bottom lip, his brow creasing into a heavy furrow. He was anxious for Natalia to get on with the story, but he didn't want to push her. Still, he had some important questions. "Baby," he said, rubbing his thumb along the center of her palm in reassurance and calibrating her pulse to match his, "how do you know all this? Who gave you this information?"

She snickered then, a humorless sound. "My laptop of course," she answered. "A year ago, I gave my father a framed picture of the two of us for Father's Day. There was bug planted in the frame."

Santos nodded with appreciation—Natalia had never been a clueless, wilting violet. She had been trapped, but she had never been a victim. "So, Domenico insisted on getting Luca out of here, and if I'm guessing correctly, that trip included you."

"Yep," she said dryly. Then she pointed at the hole in the

wall. "When I refused to come out of my room to escape with my father, Domenico threatened to break down the wall."

Santos shook his head in frustration...and fury. "How did you fend him off?"

She smiled then. "At first, I tried to reason with him. You know, to lie. I told him someone had to stay behind to manage the family's image, deal with the staff and servants, that I'd meet them at whatever destination they chose in a couple of days."

Santos brushed a loose tendril of her hair behind her shoulder and away from her eyes. "And clearly they weren't having it."

"Nope. Not any of it." She sighed. "Finally, I told Domenico that I had a gun, which was true—I fired it into the ceiling to prove it—and that I'd blow his brains out if he came through that wall."

Santos snickered. "And that backed him off?"

"No, not entirely. He backed off when I threatened to call the police." She wrung her hands together. "If I recall, he called me a batshit crazy, traitorous, spoiled bitch, and then he dragged my father out of the house, kicking and screaming, because Luca refused to go without me."

Santos grew still...pensive...trying not to conjure the image in his head.

He had bigger fish to fry right now than hunting—and executing—a piece of trash named Domenico. "Natalia, I want you to go through the mansion and gather anything that has significant or sentimental value to you: photographs, jewelry, keepsakes, personal effects, any important electronics. Then pack enough clothes for about one week. If there's anything else you need, we can purchase it later. I'm taking you back to my lake house. We can sort everything else out later, but the bottom line is this: I'm not leaving you here any longer."

She shook her head sadly. "Santos, you don't understand. My

father will never let me go. If he doesn't come back for me personally, he'll send someone else to find me—but he'll never quit looking. He'll never give in to Domenico, and he'll never let you have me."

Santos snarled, not bothering to mute it. "Oh, but he will. Trust me on that one." He paused to temper his anger and muster his courage, unsure of how she would react to what he still had to tell her. "Natalia, right now, as we speak, there are a dozen more warriors descending upon the compound, including a tracker named Julien Lacusta. Before the sun rises in the morning, your father *and Domenico*"—now that Santos knew about him—"will be dealt with. By this time next week, those four mercenaries hiding in other countries, waiting to slaughter dozens of innocent women with a mere text and a code, will also be no more." Before she could react or protest, he pushed forward, needing to get out the rest of the information. "As for the remaining warriors, they've created a perimeter to head off human interlopers, to make sure no one sees, hears, or knows anything happening within this compound, and they've begun the process of scrubbing the grounds and eliminating any remnants of the toxin. That said, we are also transporting all the surviving women to shelters and hospitals in Morrison, Lakewood, and Denver." He softened his tone out of respect and compassion. "We're delivering the corpses to the county coroners; we want to make sure their families can bury them. Either way, reports about The Fortress and tales of the women's captivity are bound to get out—it'll be all over the national news by morning—but there won't be anything left for the human feds to find, at least not here in Morrison. The rainstorm notwithstanding, we're going to incinerate the entire compound tonight, and as far as anyone else involved with Giovanni, Inc. is concerned, Natalia Antoinette died in the fire." He tunneled his fingers in her hair, sensing her desperate and helpless energy. "Natalia Olaru, on the other hand, is just an immigrant from Romania." He tilted his head to the side, his eyes narrowing with sympathy. "You know me, angel; you know what I can do: vital statistics, coroner's records, pointing any humans who are meddling in a permanent, opposite direction—it's all child's play for me. Your staff, servants, and charity acquaintances will grieve the death of Luca's daughter, and your life as it existed before will be wiped from the annals of history. At least on paper, it will be as if Natalia Giovanni never existed."

Natalia let out a muffled sob. "*Santos...*"

"I'm sorry, love, but I have to protect you. And I'm sworn to protect the house of Jadon. Your father. The mercenaries. Destroying the compound and your history... These are all orders from Napolean Mondragon, the vampire-king, the male to whom I have sworn my eternal fealty. I can make no objections, and there can be no loose ends." He knew that his words sounded harsh, that his delivery had been swift, if not almost merciless, but it was what it was. Natalia was living in a whole new world; the gods had seen fit to usher her into it; and he could do no other than fulfill his duty to Napolean, while trusting the celestial deities had chosen his forever partner wisely.

That Natalia would somehow come through this...

She swayed to the side, and he reached out to catch her, tucking her lovingly beneath a strong arm. Holding her tightly and nuzzling her hair, he whispered. "*Cara...*angel...*Natalia girl*, I'm so sorry. I'm so very sorry for everything. What your father has done, the life that you've lived, the weight you have carried on your shoulders all these years. I am sorry for the Blood Curse and all it has initiated—the fact that you weren't given more time to make this transition...the fact that I couldn't ease you into this. But at some point—*at this point*—you are going to have to trust me, allow me to help you shoulder your burdens. All you once knew is gone now, sweet angel, and I know it has to be terrifying. But there is a whole new world of life, love, and freedom awaiting you, a world beyond your imagining, if you'll just take my hand and follow. You're already Vampyr. There's no going back. Baby, please; try to trust me. Give me a chance to win your heart and soothe your soul—I swear as a sentinel on the honor of my house, you will never live to regret it. I will live, exist, and breathe for your happiness."

Natalia clung to Santos' shoulders, perhaps more out of horror than hope.

But it was something...

For now.

And it would have to be enough.

However diminutive her trust, Santos would safeguard it, honor it, and eventually cultivate it until she knew it hadn't been misplaced.

She cried a river of silent tears while he held her, soaking his shirt and her delicate, long lashes. When at last, she had no tears left to cry, she raised her head and sniffled. "How many?" she asked, and he instinctively knew what she meant.

"Thirty innocent souls are dead. Eighty-eight survived."

Natalia drew back and massaged her temples, her expression unbearably tired. "Can I see the bodies...the women who passed?"

Santos sucked in a horrified breath. "Oh, baby...no. It's not... they're too...I'm sorry, Natalia." What else could he say? Oskar and Achilles had left a blood bath in their wake, and there was no way—absolutely none—that Santos was going to subject Natalia to those images. Besides, many of the bodies would already be gone. Vampires didn't play around or waste time.

Seeming to understand, she slowly nodded, but her tears welled up once more, threatening to rush out in a flood. "Can you see into my mind if you want to...if I let you? Can you glimpse my thoughts or my memories...if I show you?'

Santos nodded cautiously, wondering where this was going.

"With your permission, *cara mia?* Absolutely." He stroked her temple, smoothing her worried brow with his thumb. "Oh, Natalia..."

She sniffled—"I want you to do it now, Santos"—and then she closed her eyes and conjured a distant memory: a dark, moonless night; a little girl, hiding in the back of her bodyguard's jeep; a dark-haired child sneaking, unnoticed, into The Fortress, then crawling on her hands and knees through dirty halls in order to peer inside the cages...

Staring into the eyes of a four-year-old girl...

Eyes that sparkled like finely spun glass: beautiful, innocent, silver-blue irises.

The eyes of a faery princess.

"Can you see it?" she asked softly. "Can you see *her?*"

Santos continued to peer inside his *destiny's* mind, appalled by such tragic, haunting images. "I see what you see," he whispered.

"She was a child back then," Natalia explained. "She would be a young woman now. But her eyes are unmistakable...incomparable. Santos, was this girl among the dead?" Her entire body shook from emotion, and Santos had to blink back a tear, take care to contain his reaction.

He cupped Natalia's cheeks in his hands and pressed a tender kiss to her forehead. "Natalia girl; look at me."

Her eyes met his, and they were so filled with longing—with fear, hope, dread, and desperation—she was *this close* to coming unglued.

"Her name is Zayda. And she is very much alive. She is well, she is *free*, and she is living in Dark Moon Vale."

CHAPTER TWENTY-FIVE

Xavier Matista couldn't believe his good fortune.

The timber wolf moon had finally shined down upon the lycans, imparting inordinate good luck, particularly on the Alpha General of the Western District Pack, such as it was these days, following the devastation caused by the Silivasi brothers in Mhier.

No matter.

He wouldn't think of that.

Tonight, all was well for the werewolf.

About half past midnight, he had received a call from a human devotee, Bo Cooper, a nobody, really, in the hierarchy of the Council of Governing Nations. Considering that the overarching and elusive council of human vampire-hunters existed in several countries, each employing several operative Head-Hunters to work out of national offices—maintain regional militias—and those militias employed displaced, disgruntled, and generally confused ex-special forces, often in bands of seven, Bo was just one of many long-ago recruits the lycans used to do their dirty work. He wasn't even as significant as Owen Green, the charismatic leader of the Denver militia that had royally screwed up Kiera Sparrow's captivity—she was now safe and sound and living in Dark Moon Vale with Saxson Olaru.

But again, Xavier's mind was wandering...

The point was: Humans could go where werewolves could not, and since Bo rarely slept at night, he spent a lot of time in his secluded fifth-wheel, deep in the Roosevelt National Forest—far enough outside Dark Moon Vale to not provoke the suspicion of the vampires, yet close enough to the supernatural valley to keep an eye on the various happenings—monitoring his expensive satellite equipment.

And this night, Bo Cooper's insomnia had truly paid off.

For reasons the human could not fathom, the house of Jadon had come alive in an instant: warriors mobilizing, vampires assembling, and of singular importance, Kagen Silivasi had been one of them. Thinking quickly—and kudos to the human because his swift improvisation had been brilliant—Bo had thumbed through his registry of covert intelligence; scanned the roster of human servants, those who lived in or near the vale, serving the Vampyr for generations; and quickly come across Cole and Chrissy Bailey. The couple lived in a small log cabin just outside the outskirts of the Dark Moon Hot Springs, and Chrissy was eight months' pregnant. She wanted to have her baby at home, and Kagen had overseen her maternity care, visiting the cabin often, along with Arielle. Alas, Xavier would not need to stake out the outdoor shower beside the private herb garden...

Utilizing his satellite phone, Bo had called the Dark Moon Clinic, pretending to be Cole, both frantic and desperate: "Chrissy is in labor! The baby's coming early. We don't know what to do...please, please help us."

True to her healer's heart and her caring nature, Arielle Nightsong-Silivasi had left her son, Ryder, with the clinic's nurse,

Katia, and set out in the family's Jeep Rubicon to get to the young couple's cabin.

Only she hadn't quite made it.

The moment she had reached the fork in the road, the wolf-trap-free intersection that led to the couple's secluded cottage, Xavier Matista had pounced.

Now, as he sat by the fire on the other side of the portal, safely ensconced in Mhier, where Kagen could neither track his mate's blood, nor follow her through worlds, he stared at the beautiful copper-haired warrior before him, studying her familiar aquamarine eyes.

The female was terrified.

Good.

"Welcome home, Arielle." He growled the words, scanning the diamond-embedded cuffs on her wrists. Goldilocks wasn't just a girl anymore; he would have to take caution during her captivity. She grunted something vile beneath her leather gag, and Xavier laughed.

Her terror was positively orgasmic.

It was too bad he couldn't kill her...use her...have his way with her and deliver her body back to his enemy in a deerskin bag.

But restraint was the name of the game.

As much as Xavier wanted vengeance on the Silivasis, a chance to best his detestable enemies, he wanted his daughter, Zayda, even more. And assuring Keitaro that Arielle would remain safe and sound—undamaged and unmolested—was his only chance of getting Zayda back.

If Xavier killed Arielle, the Silivasis wouldn't sleep.

The warriors would never stop hunting.

The Master Wizard might do...*hell, who knew what!* Magick was an unpredictable variable.

And for all the general knew, Zayda might be returned in a

deerskin canteen, as a blasphemous mockery, her organs churned into liquid, her bones ground to powder through a blender. Nathaniel Silivasi had a wicked imagination and an even more devious sense of justice.

No.

Xavier would stick to the plan.

Besides, Bo had already delivered Xavier's note to Kagen's doorstep...

Tomorrow, Xavier would slip back through the portal and call Keitaro Silivasi on a basic human device—he would contact his enemy on a cell phone to schedule the exchange of their daughters.

Kagen Silivasi clenched his fists, rotated his neck on his shoulders, and cracked two upper vertebrae, inadvertently, trying to control his trembling.

Then he read the note a second time:

Vampires—one and all—just kidding! This note is for Keitaro Silivasi, but I'm certain it will be of interest to Kagen, too—salutations from the land of Mhier!

As you read this, I am sitting in my front room beside a blazing fire, admiring Arielle Nightsong's legendary beauty—yes, Kagen's beloved destiny and the daughter of Keitaro's heart (how quaint by the way).

Before you go off half-cocked, think it over: We both know you can no longer enter Mhier—isn't that why you have begged me for months to "come out and play" in Dark Moon Vale? Well, here's the thing: I no longer wish to play. I would rather forge a limited truce—at least long enough to exchange our women. A captive for a captive. A daughter for a daughter. Arielle Nightsong-Silivasi for Zayda Patrone-Matista.

It's a very simple offer, and I'll make it only once.

Kagen, do tell your father that I am not playing games with him over this, nor will I tolerate any treachery or attempts to get over... I will contact Keitaro tomorrow, so make sure he stays by his phone. In the meantime, take care of Zayda as I will take care of Arielle. Certainly, you understand, the reverse would also hold true.

Sincerely,

General Matista

Kagen knew he needed to head directly to the old family homestead, take the note straight to his father, but his soul demanded—and his very DNA raged—to make another stop first...

He had already searched the house, and Arielle wasn't there.

He had checked on Ryder, spoken to Katia, and called Cole and Chrissy Bailey—the female had not gone into labor, and Cole had not called the clinic.

Xavier had lured Kagen's *destiny* into a trap...

And that was the rage consuming Kagen's soul.

The note reeked of the mangy lycan's foul scent, but it also carried traces of a human male—likely the one who had called the clinic—and Kagen had turned that stench over in his nostrils like a human drug addict, suffering from withdrawal, snorting a line of cocaine. He had dissected every olfactory sensory neuron as it traveled through the odor receptors and made its way to the limbic system in his brain, until the fragrance was cemented for all time in Kagen's memory...

Forever a part of his primordial awareness.

And now that he had the scent banked in his very soul, there would be no peace until he tracked it.

Stepping onto the second-floor terrace, he released his dark brown wings, the moon's light catching the silver highlights as he shot into the air. What might have been a twenty-minute drive was traversed in under two minutes, and it only took that long because Kagen had to filter out an infinite number of competing odors.

At last, he descended in a thicket and approached a hidden camper, well concealed beneath a dozen towering pines, and then he blasted through the aluminum and steel and snatched the nearest occupant—a lone human male—by his scrawny, convulsing throat.

He had no intentions of toying with this prey.

The situation was too dire.

Still grasping the human by the neck, he flew through the hole in the camper; soared to the top of a towering tree; and impaled the piece of shit on a jutting, spindly branch, dissecting him through the sternum. And then he tunneled so violently into the fool's temporal lobe that a lobotomy would have been kinder.

Kagen absorbed every thought, emotion, and memory as the soon-to-be-dead Homo sapien screamed and convulsed, and then he released his fangs, pierced them deep into the bastard's jugular, and drank until *Bo Lee Cooper* expired from exsanguination.

Leaving the lifeless body hanging from the tree, Kagen made a mental note to contact Napolean's sentinels tomorrow, let them know about the human vampire-hunter and the covert fifth-wheel parked just outside the vale, and then he careened through the dark, ominous sky on his way to awaken Keitaro.

CHAPTER TWENTY-SIX

Later That Morning ~ The Lake House

Natalia wasn't sure why she had slept so deeply when her mind was so fitful, her heart was so troubled, and her spirit was still all but weeping.

So much loss.

So much change.

So much violence and confrontation...

Santos must have used his vampiric powers to impart some temporary measure of peace, so Natalia could get some sleep while alone in his bedroom, as he spent the night on the couch.

Now, as she crawled from beneath the luxurious sateen sheets in the soft, comfortable bed, which faced a wall-length panoramic window overlooking a hidden lake, she padded softly across the master bedroom and headed into the water closet.

She brushed her teeth, ran a comb through her hair, and slipped into her familiar cherry blossom, charmeuse satin robe before ambling her way out of the bedroom and heading toward the aroma of freshly brewed coffee. From what Santos had told her, the morning after conversion, vampires no longer needed human food, and few of the males in the house of Jadon partook of the same. However, *destinies* were renowned for clinging to their favorite cravings, and it wouldn't hurt their immortal bodies to do so, just so long as they primarily imbibed on blood...

Ew.

Just ew.

She didn't want to think about that now.

She would simply focus on a morning cup of coffee, grateful that Santos had been considerate enough to think ahead...to brew the java for Natalia.

Locating the elaborate stainless steel coffee and espresso machine, she began to rummage through several dark mahogany cabinets in search of a mug—and that's when she glanced absently out the floor-to-ceiling windows, and her breath hitched in her throat.

Santos Olaru was standing on the top tier of his expansive deck, wearing nothing but a pair of loose-fitting, knee-length gym shorts, and leaning over the rail.

His bronzed, muscular back was arched.

His strong, angular jaw revealed a masculine hint of a five o'clock shadow.

And the sun was gleaming off his broad, powerful shoulders like the rays were reaching down to caress his flawless skin.

Natalia gulped.

For all intents and purposes, he looked like a statue of a Greek god, posing atop the battlements of Mount Olympus: proud, regal, and chiseled from timeless granite.

He must have felt her presence because he turned his head to the side and rotated that magnificent body in a slow, almost feline glide: his shoulders rolling, his hamstrings flexing, and one of the globes on that faultless backside contracting.

His eyes met hers, and he smiled.

Natalia almost fainted.

And then he indicated the sliding glass doors with a nod of his chin and crooked his fingers inward—he wanted her to come outside.

Natalia shook her head.

Oh no...*nope*...she needed...she needed a cup of coffee.

She fumbled through the cupboard, desperate to find a mug, anything to remain distracted.

Natalia, come outside. He spoke in her mind, and she shivered.

"You can do this, Talia," she whispered beneath her breath. "Just go outside and say good morning, then come right back inside and finish making coffee. Easy peasy."

He was just a man.

Well, he was just a vampire...

Just a flawless, gorgeous, overwhelmingly intimidating, masculine, half-naked vampire who thought she belonged to him.

But yeah...

She could do this.

It was no big deal.

Raising her chin and lifting her shoulders, she strolled gracefully to the patio doors and misjudged the width by about six inches. She slammed into the aluminum door frame with the bone of her right hip and immediately reached for the tie on her robe, trying to play it off by fumbling with the fabric. She retied the knot and shuffled quickly to the left, out of the reach of the dangerous aluminum, her head still held high. *Oh, Lord,* she muttered inwardly, concentrating far too hard on just making it out the door.

The corner of his mouth quirked up in a sexy, devious smile, and she wanted to throw something at him—but she had nothing in her hands.

This wasn't cute or funny.

The situation was dire.

Very serious.

Their lives—her life—had just been upended.

"How did you sleep," he asked, and there had to be an extra ounce of grit and vibrato in that sin-laced voice.

Natalia stared at the ground. "Very well...surprisingly. And you?"

He cocked one shoulder in a lackadaisical shrug. "I slept okay."

She nodded.

"How are you feeling this morning?" he asked her next, and her eyes went straight to...his crotch.

She gasped at her own impropriety—*what the hell was she doing?*—and she took a couple of clumsy steps back. Oh lord, it wasn't that she was curious...like, sexually... She would never come on to a man so directly. It was just...well, perhaps she had just been trying to avoid his face and maybe, just maybe, she'd wanted to make sure he wasn't...aroused.

Aroused?

Natalia, get a grip!

She placed one hand over her heart and the other over her throat. "I...I'm feeling kind of overwhelmed."

He studied her then, those stunning crystal-blue orbs boring into her dark brown irises, before appraising her expression, her stance, and her body language...before settling back against the railing and crossing his arms lazily over his middle. "Over-whelmed?" he repeated.

Natalia's mouth was very dry.

She needed that cup of coffee.

"I...I just think I'm hungry." Oh, heaven; had she just said *hungry?*

Santos' penetrating gaze swept down to her throat, and his pupils zeroed in on her jugular.

She felt her larynx constrict. "I meant...thirsty. I think I'm very, very thirsty."

He appraised her thoughtfully for the span of several heartbeats, and then he extended his hand. "Come here."

She eyed the patio doors, the railing, and finally, the space between them, every cell in her body wanting to take off running. Just why, she couldn't articulate if she had to. "I'm fine," she murmured.

"Natalia, what's going on? Have we not made further inroads than this? You know me, at least a little. You know who I am. Why the sudden fear?"

God bless her—and if the angels were truly merciful, they would just strike her dead—but her eyes went back to his crotch, *again*. There was just so much...going on there. Well, not like *things* were moving...or changing...but there was just way too much...*stuff*...packed in those gym shorts, and it was seriously making her nervous. Mortified, she dropped her head into her hands and covered her face with her fingers.

She was a bona fide idiot.

"Hey..." His voice was soft and sultry—and directly in her ear. Somehow, Santos had glided forward, though she had never heard him move. "Natalia girl..." He tunneled one hand in her hair, and slowly lowered her wrists with the other.

She peeked up at him through descending lashes, and he held her gaze, unerringly.

She started to jolt, to pull backward, and he slid his hand down from her hair to the small of her back, holding her steadily in place. "It's okay," he murmured. "You can look at me."

She blanched, felt her face grow flushed, but he didn't seem to notice.

He just stood there, his eyes locked to hers, anchoring her in place with his hand.

Her gaze drifted up from his eyes to his perfectly shaped

brows, and she reached out with a tentative finger to trace the symmetrical outline.

He didn't move a muscle: He was so quiet, so steady, so easy…

She drew back her finger and angled her head to the side, momentarily shying away.

He just waited…

And she regarded him again, this time studying his timeless features; the sharp, dynamic angles of his cheekbones and the straight, solid ridge of his nose. And then her eyes dropped down to his lips—those tantalizing, firm, almost pouty lips—she had never seen anything like them. Her breath quickened as she reached out once more to trace the contours of his mouth, before swiftly withdrawing her hand, closing her eyes, and retreating back into awkward silence.

He took her hand in his, slowly raised it to his mouth, and pressed a kiss into the center of her palm. "You know what I find most surprising?" he asked, waiting until she reopened her eyes.

She shook her head shyly and bit her bottom lip.

His expression warmed. "The fact that you are the single most beautiful woman I have ever laid eyes on, and unquestionably, the most alluring, yet you find my presence…my body… intimidating." Following the lead she had already set, he traced her slender shoulders, outlined her narrow collarbone, and trailed a soft, gentle finger along the swell of her breasts, causing her satin robe to fall open. "Rest assured, Natalia, I am the one who is at your mercy."

Natalia gasped.

She swept a nervous hand into her hair and tucked a thick grouping of long, dark locks behind her ear. "I'm like a fish out of water." She spoke so softly it was nearly inaudible.

"You are like a precious, uncut diamond, still ensconced inside a magnificent mountain: sharp, yet stunning; dazzling, yet pure; dangerous, yet so very resplendent," he said, caressing her cheek with his hand, and then he slowly bent down to kiss her, stopping just short of touching his lips to hers.

She shivered, waiting, as he hovered above her, but to her surprise, he did not close the distance between them. He simply lingered...tantalized...settled into the magnetic connection. And in that moment, his breath mingled with hers like the scent of fresh snow on a pine-topped mountain—crisp, cool, and inviting —and his soul transcended her hesitation.

Natalia rose up to her toes, braced both palms on his shoulders, and pressed her lips to his.

And that's when Santos took over.

* * *

Natalia Giovanni was a walking paradox.

Bold, yet shy.

Hungry, yet reluctant.

Deeply desirous of sensual contact, yet wholly terrified of intimacy.

And the way she stared at Santos had set his blood on fire...

But he had to be careful.

Oh, so careful...

Scooping her into his arms, he carried her off the terrace, through the living room, and down the hall, back to his master bedroom. Their first time would not be carnal and wild, outside on the open deck, or hurried in any way.

Laying her gently atop his mattress, he felt both her fear and her hesitation: the way the hairs stood up on the back of her neck, and her arms coated with goose bumps.

But he also felt her longing.

And he wanted her to feel his presence, the full measure of his masculine desire, the security of his arms and his body wrapped around her, so he didn't hesitate to blanket her feminine curves with his rock-hard frame, or to settle his hips up against hers.

She squirmed just a bit, nervous and uneasy, but then she settled quietly beneath him.

Careful to keep the brunt of his weight off her slender figure, he began to caress her in non-intrusive places: along the length of her neck, down the curves of her shoulders, under her arms, and beside her breasts...down the length of her body.

She arched into his touch, and he lowered his mouth to taste her.

First her lips, then her jaw, then the hollow beneath her ears.

He dragged his fangs, ever so lightly, along her jugular, and he felt her hips swivel beneath him. He groaned because he couldn't help it, and then he captured her mouth once again, this time tasting her lips, her tongue, and her curiosity, before deepening the contact with more passion.

When Natalia pulled back, Santos moved his attention to her forehead, her eyelids, her jawline. When she turned toward him, he took her mouth again, dancing between pleasing and tasting. When she initiated exploration, seeking his tongue with hers, he knew she was coming awake beneath him, and he nipped her bottom lip with his canines and swirled his tongue in the blood, allowing his primal being to savor the taste of his *destiny*.

She was panting now and beginning to squirm in earnest.

He brought his wrist to his mouth, scored it with the tips of his fangs, and held it just above her parted lips, allowing the crimson elixir to drip into her mouth like wine. A few droplets stained her bottom lip, and despite all her previous reservations, her tongue darted out to taste it. When a soft, feminine purr rose in her elegant throat and her stomach clenched beneath his, Santos knew that he had her.

His hands went to her breasts: claiming, kneading, massaging.

He circled and teased her nipples—at first, through the satin —until he felt the peaks respond to his touch and stiffen. Drawing back to remove her robe—to slide the straps of her night-gown off her shoulders—he suppressed a shudder at the sight of her soft, full, perfect breasts.

Dear   celestial   gods;   she   was   utterly...and unequivocally...flawless.

He bent to taste each of the tantalizing offerings, spending more time than a male had a right to, teasing her into near inco-herence.

She breathed his name, and it was like a prayer: a beautiful, spiritual offering.

"I want you, Natalia," Santos rasped. "Your body...your mind...your essence. I want to bury my body deep inside yours and take you with me to heaven. Will you come with me, angel?" He slid his hand down her waist, over her hips, and into the alcove between her pelvis and her thigh. Her head fell back against the downy pillow, her trembling lips parted in wonder, and her dark, glorious hair fanned out around her like a celestial halo.

She looked like an angelic goddess with a crown made of deep brown, gossamer silk.

Santos grinded his groin against her, allowing her to feel the full length and girth of his masculine desire—his hunger, his arousal, and his need—wanting her to grow familiar with his throbbing erection.

She stiffened just a bit.

Froze for a couple of seconds.

And then her thighs drew back, and she cradled him in the nexus of her body.

He moaned in pleasure, rotating his hips again...and again... and again, against her.

"Santos..." Her voice was raw and breathy.

He drew back, just far enough to slowly undress her—to remove the rest of her robe and her nightgown—and then he dipped down to taste every inch of feminine flesh, the moment he exposed it: tantalizing...teasing...exploring, through her panties.

Oh gods, they were delicate, red, and lacy.

He almost snarled, but he repressed it.

Rather, he slid his tongue beneath the lace as he removed it: tracing every contour, claiming every silhouette, and exploring every centimeter of exquisite definition, until his lips finally settled on the heat at her core, and he began to suckle in earnest.

Natalia writhed and whimpered.

She buried her hands in his hair and jackknifed off the bed, and Santos knew he had her invitation.

Slipping out of his gym shorts, he locked his mind with hers, redirecting her pain receptors to filter through his synapses instead. And then he didn't give her time to overthink it or worry. He buried the full length of his erection deep into her center and held his body above hers as she adjusted and finally shuddered in pleasure...pain...and satisfaction.

The corners of her eyes filled with tears, but she wasn't experiencing any discomfort.

If anything, Santos was the one catching his breath as Natalia's stretching, burning, and invasion channeled through his quivering body.

A few tentative moments.

Relaxing into the union.

Allowing her body to receive his penetration.

And she began to rock against him.

He released the mental hold on her sensations and began to thrust in earnest: slow and steady, then rhythmic and firm, until he was finally driving with abandon.

Time stood still, their union seeming to last for a lifetime, until at last, they reached a climax together, and she clung to his shoulders and cried out in ecstasy.

Gently lowering his mass to settle on top of her, he kissed her forehead, her nose, and then her lips before he withdrew his body, rolled to his side, and cradled his *destiny* close to his heart.

Natalia was weeping.

And Santos had to take a moment to process the intensity of her emotion...

Closing his eyes, he dipped into her mind—he had to be sure he hadn't hurt her: not her body, not her spirit, and not their burgeoning connection. He had to know she wasn't crying out of regret...but it was nothing like that.

Natalia was crying because she had finally let go...

Of all her fear, her self-control, and her endless isolation.

She was crying because it had finally hit her...

For the first time in her life, she was free.

For the first time in her life, she was no longer alone.

CHAPTER TWENTY-SEVEN

K eitaro Silivasi stared at Marquis as the Ancient Master Warrior paced along the expansive front porch.

Zayda was still sitting on the front stoop, looking shocked, terrified, and completely lost.

Nathaniel and Nachari were each leaning against the log-pine railing, restless but keeping a lid on their emotions. And Kagen; he was fit to be tied. The Ancient Master Healer was having a very hard time accepting the fact that, at least initially, Keitaro would have to go it alone, embark on the mission without any backup, but Xavier's instructions, via a text on Keitaro's phone, had been explicitly clear:

When the clock strikes midnight (Sunday becoming Monday), meet me alone at the original cobblestone well. You will find a single harness affixed to a single rope. Lower Zayda into the structure. Arielle will already be in the water, waiting. When Zayda slips out of the harness, Arielle will take her place—you may draw her up at exactly 12:05 AM. Don't try anything stupid. We have manufactured a temporary, makeshift entrance, deep inside the well, a provisional portal to Mhier. If you don't come alone (and a werewolf can smell a vampire several miles away), you will never see Arielle again. If you try to hold on to Zayda, you will never see Arielle again. If you, or any other warrior, approach the well before midnight, you will never see Arielle again. Ms. Nightsong-Silivasi has not been harmed, but she will be sufficiently trussed in diamond-embedded restraints, so don't count on her assisting in her own escape. This is a one-time offer, a one-time exchange. As badly as I want to bring my daughter home, I am willing to let her perish: I doubt you feel the same about Kagen's mate. Midnight. The old abandoned well. Come alone—just you and Zayda.

Keitaro knew the exact location Xavier had referred to, a section of forest outside of Dark Moon Vale, and thus, absent of energetic wolf traps: When the Vampyr had first come to the new continent, following their banishment from Romania—and long before the house of Jadon was well-established in the Dark Moon valley—they had been drawn to the Rocky Mountains due to their uncanny similarity to the Transylvanian Alps. Along with their lives, families, and treasured belongings, they had brought many human servants in tow—after all, they had needed a reliable food source, and as it turned out, many of these families would remain loyal for generations. In establishing a small human colony around 791 BC, deep in what was now the Roosevelt National Forest, they had built a cobblestone well for their wards, and the old, abandoned structure was still standing in its original location—to this date, it was still filled with water.

How Xavier had known about the colony or the well, Keitaro had no idea. But then again, the lycans were an ancient race, a timeless species, and they had likely existed in Mhier long before the Vampyr came to North America. And they had hunted vampires since the species' inception. It wasn't unreasonable that they knew about the well.

Nonetheless, Kagen was infuriated. He objected to the entire plan on the grounds that the vampires had no leverage, Xavier was certainly planning to double-cross them, and it was *his* mate whose life was at stake.

But what could the vampires do?

They couldn't exactly call Xavier in Mhier and insist that he craft a more amenable proposal: The time to get a leg up on the werewolf was *before* he took Arielle, not after.

In a very real sense, Xavier was holding all the cards because, as he had pointed out, he was willing to let his daughter perish, whereas the Silivasis were desperate to get Arielle back. And they had thought of virtually every contingency: Hiding Marquis, Nathaniel, or Kagen nearby was an absolute *no-go*. Xavier would smell the additional vampires. Having Napolean Mondragon send his essence into the well—the fearsome male could travel through space and time, appearing anywhere in physical form in an instant—was also dead on arrival. The piece about the makeshift portal was far too risky and volatile. If the lycans could also travel through space and time, appear inside the well, or exit it just as swiftly, then the moment the king materialized, Arielle could be gone. Keitaro had no doubt he could best the lycan general in one-to-one combat, but it didn't sound like he would get that chance. Xavier had made no mention as to where he, himself, would be during the five-minute window.

Again, they would all be mere heartbeats away from an open portal...

And while Nachari had offered to use magic—or the panther —it still didn't nullify the risks.

According to the Master Wizard, discovering how to open a portal to Mhier had taken around four weeks, before, when Keitaro's sons had entered the forbidden world in a journey to bring their sire home. The boys had been lucky; the entrance had since been destroyed; and the magic had been recalibrated—there was no guarantee that the vampires could ever do it again, and they most certainly could not approach the well to scope things out, prior to midnight.

The whole damn thing was infuriating.

As it stood, there was little Kagen could do to retrieve his beloved *destiny*, other than to wait on Keitaro and trust a filthy lycan to keep his unreliable word.

"He's not going to keep his promise," Kagen spat, repeating the same point for the umpteenth time. "The moment we lower Zayda into that well, he'll take both women back into Mhier."

Nachari regarded his older brother circumspectly, the wizard's deep green eyes filling with shadows of concern. "There is a very good chance of that, Kagen, but I don't believe he'll do so. I honestly don't."

Marquis grunted and glared at Nachari sideways. "Is this some wizardly intuition, some sort of divine premonition, or are you just pontificating out of your ass?"

Okay, Keitaro thought, *that was entirely uncalled for, but Marquis is riding a razor's edge.* Despite his surly ways, he loved his brothers, and his copper-haired sister-in-law had indelibly captured his heart. Marquis would die for Arielle in a minute…

Nachari seemed wholly unaffected. "Brother," he said in a calm, even voice, "I truly believe that all Xavier wants this time is his daughter. Think about it, if they take Arielle back through the portal, they know we will never give up. We will never stop trying. We will never stop looking. We will never stop attempting to discover and open another door to their world." He shrugged his broad, powerful shoulders and took a deep, steadying breath. "Look, it may be true that they've sealed the gateway so securely, we may never find or open it again. But there has to be just a fissure of doubt—we did it before; perhaps we can do it again. I don't think they would want to take that chance, knowing we could bring Napolean with us next time and annihilate their entire race. Why dangle a red cape in front of a house of bulls? I think Xavier just wants Zayda."

Zayda hugged her arms to her chest, shuddering at Nachari's words, and Keitaro strolled to the stoop to place a reassuring hand on her shoulder. "Zayda..." He spoke her name softly. "Don't be alarmed. We will figure something—"

"No," she interrupted, standing up abruptly. "You don't know if you will figure something out. Please, don't give me false hope. Don't make promises none of you can keep." She sighed in frustration, her shoulders curling inward, and her lovely, mystical eyes seemed interminably sad. "Look, Keitaro, you have done so much for me already—I really do mean what I said: You can't let Arielle go. You can't risk Kagen's *destiny*, not for me, not with Xavier. It just isn't an even trade."

Keitaro's heart constricted in his chest. "Zayda, no one here is comparing your worth to Arielle's."

Marquis Silivasi turned his back, and Keitaro knew he was biting back a calloused retort. *Son*, he spoke telepathically. *Do not. The female is already terrified enough.*

Marquis grunted so that all could hear, but he answered his father on the private, family bandwidth: *I know that you are invested in this female, and I know that you wish to see her unharmed. But we are vampires, one and all, and blood is thicker than water. Blood is life. Blood is honor. It is everything we hold dear. If we can save Zayda, we must, but none of us will trade Kagen's mate, the daughter of your heart—and now of your blood —for a half-human, half-Lycan girl. The very prospect is unthinkable.*

The fact that Nathaniel, Nachari, and Kagen remained silent told Keitaro all he needed to know—his sons would go to war for Zayda; they would go to war to honor and serve their father; but their loyalty between the females was squarely with Arielle. He nodded and crossed his arms over his chest. So be it. He had raised the boys to put family first, to be loyal to one another unto death.

"Zayda," he spoke aloud, "you are right; we cannot make any absolute promises. This thing we're about to do is full of untold risks, but you do remember the plan, correct? You do know that it could work out?"

The slight, wild-haired female nodded slowly, displaying all the courage her frail frame could muster. "Yes, I remember," she whispered. And then she raised her chin. "I can swim. Very well. Like a fish. So, the moment I am lowered to the bottom of the well, the moment I see Miss Arielle, I am to dive down into the water and swim toward the earth...keep going...keep swimming... keep diving as deep as I can go."

"Yes," Keitaro said. "From what Nachari explained about the portal my sons once opened—the energetic nature of the previous door—it would be difficult for any opening to encompass the entirety of the well. It may not function as easily under water; and Xavier will only have a fraction of time. You are half-human, so I can read your thoughts. You must signal me in your mind the moment you see Arielle—and prior to midnight, I will also ingest your blood so I can track you anywhere in that well. Marquis and Nathaniel will be hiding underground, albeit several miles away. Nonetheless, they can tunnel very quickly to the bottom of the well and pull you out from beneath the earth's clay.

"Nachari will be as close as possible in the form of a panther, and Kagen won't be far away from the wizard, should any other lycans show up. Indeed, Napolean Mondragon, our venerable king, will be tuned in and waiting, following events...ready to travel through space and time in an instant. If Xavier doesn't come alone, all bets are off." He paused to collect his thoughts and to say a silent prayer—they would need one. "I swear on my honor as a warrior in the house of Jadon, we will do all in our power to keep you here in Dark Moon Vale, to return in the morning with both you and Arielle."

Zayda smiled weakly, trying to appear as brave as she could, and all four of Keitaro's sons regarded her with compassion, if not a hint of pity...as well as respect.

"I can traverse three miles underground in sixty seconds, Zayda," Nathaniel said in a soothing yet authoritative voice.

"And I can keep you breathing with magic," Nachari offered. "Even under water. Even underground. Do not forget the technique we practiced—you can trust me to remain in control."

"It will not take my father another five minutes to draw Arielle up from the well," Marquis added. "If she's in that harness, he'll have her in less than five seconds. The moment you dive down into the water, we will be on our way to retrieve you."

Kagen was hard-pressed to say anything reassuring to Zayda —or anyone else. He was far too concerned about his mate. Just the same, he made a valiant effort to join his brothers and at least honor the girl's bravery. "If there was anything else we could do for you, Zayda, I hope you know that we would..." His voice trailed off as he considered the ominous statement and made a piteous attempt to repair it. "If nothing else, please know: We appreciate your bravery and your willingness to give up your freedom, more than words can express."

Okay, so that probably wasn't helpful, Keitaro thought.

In fact, that definitely wasn't helpful.

At all.

But all things considered, Keitaro understood—his son was doing the best that he could.

Zayda linked her hands in front of her and twiddled her thumbs like a little girl, looking wretchedly vulnerable and hopelessly lost. She batted her impossibly long lashes, trying to hide the tears that were gathering in her luminous, silver-blue eyes. And then true to her open, often unrestrained nature, she blurted, "If this is to be my last night in Dark Moon Vale, my last night of freedom—or maybe even my last night alive—perhaps your father will have pity on me and take me to his bed."

Both Nachari and Kagen visibly recoiled: the former barking a harsh, feline cough; the latter covering his mouth with his hand in a failed attempt to hide his disgust.

Nathaniel just stood there with his mouth hanging open.

"What the hell!" Marquis bellowed, staring angrily at Keitaro. "Fifty freakin' faces of Zayda! *Dad?*" He posed the last word as an incredulous question. "You wouldn't...*you haven't*...what the actual—"

"Marquis!" Keitaro held up his hand. "Warrior...*son*...stop! Now." He shook his head sternly before turning to face the guileless female. "Zayda, that's not appropriate, and either way, it's a private conversation." He pressed a finger to his lips as if silencing a child, and then he turned his attention back to his sons. "We meet back here tonight at eleven. Until then, ask the celestial gods for their assistance...and their mercy. Ask Lord Auriga, The Charioteer, to watch over his daughter, Arielle."

CHAPTER TWENTY-EIGHT

Braden Bratianu stepped out onto the front porch of Nachari and Deanna's brownstone. "Hey, Red," he greeted Kristina Riley-Silivasi.

She held up a slender, well-manicured hand in protest. "Stop. Just don't."

Braden frowned. *Stop? Just don't?*

Kristina didn't want him to say...*hello?*

She ran an anxious hand through her curly red locks, the bracelet Braden had given her about a month ago—a sleek platinum band peppered with onyx and ruby gemstones, jewels he had crafted with his own two hands—catching the noonday light of the sun and shimmering. "Is she still here?"

Braden sighed. Ah, so that was it. "Of course." He tried to keep his tone neutral, if not indifferent.

Kristina nodded curtly, then crossed her hands over her chest in a blatantly defensive posture. "And have you figured out why?"

"Why what?" Braden scrunched up his nose.

"Seriously?" Kristina asked. "Never mind." She turned on

her heel and started to stomp off the porch, heading in the direction of her pink Corvette.

"Whoa," Braden called after her, taking two generous steps
forward, grabbing her just above the elbow, and spinning her
around to face him. Now that he'd grown several more inches,
she barely came to his shoulders, yet it didn't make her any less
intimidating. Kristina was a hot-headed spitfire with a mind and a
will of her own, and she could pack a whole lot of attitude into
that feisty little body. Braden released her elbow and held up
both hands in an ingratiating, submissive gesture. "I thought you
didn't think of me...*like that*," he teased, trying to make the situation more playful. "Last I checked, you still thought of me as a
youngster." He smirked, feeling a bit too self-satisfied. "So why do
you care if Gwen is still here?"

Her hands shot to her feminine hips, and he immediately
regretted the question. "Do you think this is funny?" she
snapped.

"Uh, no," he murmured.

"Do you think you're cute?" she posited.

He cocked both eyebrows. "Kind of." He smirked. "Little
bit?" He smiled. "Especially when my hair is laying back...just
so." He brushed his hand over and around his ear, following the
fall of his chestnut-brown locks.

She frowned, and he instantly felt guilty.

After all, their situation was a bit sensitive and confusing...

It was a long story, but many years ago, at the age of twenty-
one, Kristina Riley had been brought into the house of Jadon by
accident: She had been a homeless runaway when Kagen Silivasi
had saved her from a Dark One, given her a job as a waitress at
the Dark Moon Casino, and brought her in on the truth of the
Vampyr. Many years later, the Dark Lords had played a terrible
trick on the red-headed female—well, they had played a terrible
trick on Marquis as well—manipulating the Ancient Master

Warrior's Blood Moon to make it look as if Kristina was the vampire's *destiny*. Under the black magic protection of a tainted omen, orchestrated by the Dark Lord Ocard, Marquis had converted Kristina to their species rather brutally. And only after Braden and Nachari had unraveled the spell and uncovered the plot had the truth come out just in time: Ciopori Demir, an original princess from the time of Prince Jadon and Prince Jaegar, was Marquis's true *destiny*, and Kristina was more or less a casualty of a manipulated Blood Curse. The Silivasis had basically adopted her, and she would forever be a part of the house of Jadon.

Braden's story, on the other hand, was wholly different, but just as convoluted.

He was the only vampire in the house of Jadon who hadn't been born to a vampire sire, a natural descendant of the original curse. He had been *made* by his stepfather, Dario Bratianu, under the protection of the celestial god Pegasus. Again, a really long story. Suffice to say, Braden's mother had been married to an abusive human, Braden's biological father, before she'd been claimed by Dario, and the gods had allowed the male to convert Braden, due to Lily's trace celestial blood—all the *destinies* had it. Once Nachari learned that Braden was exempt from the Curse— it had been cast upon the direct blood lineage of the original males, the sons of the sons...and their sons...forever—the king had made the call: Braden and Kristina were to one day be mated. For all the king knew, they could even produce female offspring. And so, the cat-and-mouse, chase-and-retreat, wait-for-Braden-to-grow-to-adulthood dance had begun between them.

And it wasn't easy on either one.

Still, Braden was more than a little surprised that Kristina had reacted so strongly to Gwen's presence in the brownstone: She almost seemed jealous of the human captive he'd brought back from The Fortress.

He took a deep breath and relaxed his shoulders, deciding to take another tact. "I'm sorry, Red. I guess it's not funny. But no, I still have no idea why I felt so compelled to bring her back to Nachari's brownstone, to keep her close to the Vampyr and the house of Jadon." He tilted his head to the side, presumably looking as confounded as he felt. "It's just...it's just...I swear; there's something deeper going on, something almost paranormal about her ending up with Luca Giovanni, crossing paths with the warriors...surviving the slaughter in the northern quadrant. There's something running through her that also runs through the heart of the house of Jadon. I dunno. Like a synchronized pulse. Don't know how else to put it, Red."

Kristina pursed her lips and averted her eyes, her hands tightening on her hips. "You sure it isn't all that pretty blonde hair, or maybe it's those sexy green eyes—or just *maybe*"—she drew out the word—"it's that cute, curvaceous body that's making your *pulse* speed up? Maybe you took one look at her while she was huddled and naked in the ductwork, and something far more basic than the house of Jadon thrummed in your veins."

Braden laughed aloud—he couldn't help it. "Kristina..."

She slapped his well-defined bicep and shuffled back a few inches. "Don't mock me, Braden. It's a legitimate question."

His cheeks warmed, and his mood brightened. "*Red...*"

She scoffed.

"You like me, don't you?"

"You're obnoxious."

"Maybe," he drawled, keenly aware of the deep, masculine brogue creeping into his voice. "But you still drove all the way out here to see me...to question me." Without consciously thinking about it, he stepped into her personal space and used his much broader, more muscular shoulders to herd her like a sheep: to turn her around, back her up, and corner her against the bricks on the brownstone. It wasn't an intentional maneuver; it was just that every week—every day—his vampiric instincts grew stronger, including those subtle, dominant, alpha inclinations that came so naturally to his species.

She rolled her eyes, appearing more than just a little bit flustered.

He reached for her wrists, admiring the fall of the bracelet; gently raised them above her head; and pinned them against the building. Then he bent to her mouth and hovered about an inch and a half above her heart-shaped lips. "Gwen is still terrified," he whispered. "She's confused, defiant, and she basically hates all of us. Not even Deanna, with her pure heart and easy nature, has managed to get through to her. You want the truth? The situation sucks. The female has already been terrorized, and here we are, still holding her hostage..." He shook his head, revealing his inner conflict. "No, I'm not objectifying the poor, terrified human, or keeping her here because I think she's attractive." His gaze swept over Kristina's eyelids, her cheekbones, and the pouty contours of her upturned mouth. "Besides, my veins and my pulse are attuned to a very different...frequency." He nipped her bottom lip, swirled his tongue over the bite, and then pulled back, released her wrists, and smiled.

She just stood there.

Mouth draping open and panting.

"Would you like to come inside?" he asked, sidestepping toward the door.

Kristina blinked three times. "You know what?" she said, her voice a bit hoarse and breathy. "Everyone in the house of Jadon thinks you're so innocent, naïve, and compliant, but I know better —you're wicked, Braden Bratianu. They don't see that evil, sinful nature, but I do."

He leaned against the doorframe, crossed his foot over his ankle, and extended a lazy, roguish hand in her direction. "*Kristina*...are you coming inside or what?"

CHAPTER TWENTY-NINE

S antos Olaru strolled noiselessly over the uneven terrain in the central valley, clutching the soft, feminine hand that was placed so trustingly within his own. He gave it a familiar, comforting squeeze and glanced askance at his *destiny*. "Beautiful, isn't it?" he said, referring to the lush, green wild grass and tall Douglas firs that flanked the Dark Moon Stables. Off to the right, a cluster of quaking aspens rustled in the breeze.

Natalia smiled.

She looked content.

At least, as content as anyone could be in her strange new circumstances.

Somehow, giving herself to Santos, making love to him earlier that morning—not once, but twice—had solidified something between them. It had given her permission to hold onto his hand, to walk next to him in silence, without any emotional resistance... to allow him to show her the valley and her new home, without so much fear.

Grateful that Ramsey and Saxson had seen to this small but

important detail ahead of time, Santos tried to hide his excitement.

"It is lovely," she said, taking a deep, cleansing breath of breezy mountain air. "So this...these stables are yet another business run by the house of Jadon?"

"Yes," Santos replied. "It's part of the house of Jadon's tourism industry. At least half of the stables are used for commerce." He pointed at a gorgeous set of log buildings in the distance, in front of a meandering creek. "Those stables over there—they're private. The king keeps his horse, as well as his sons' horses, in those stalls. Many vampires do. But this one—" He gestured toward a larger group of buildings. "This one is simply part of our industry: trail rides, private rentals, and the like. The whole of the equestrian range is run by a human named Kevin Parker. He lives about four or five acres behind the private stables with his wife, Lou Ann. Their family has been loyal to our house for generations."

Natalia released Santos' hand long enough to press her thumb and forefinger to her forehead, while she appeared to adjust her newly enhanced vampiric vision to see into the distance. "And you said Nachari Silivasi, one of the Master Wizards, often breaks new horses?"

Santos chuckled aloud. "It would seem Nachari has a penchant for all things *Mustang*, whether cars or animals." A ray of sunlight shined into Natalia's eyes, and a glimmer of honey-brown alighted in those dark, mocha depths, causing his heart to constrict in his chest. By all the gods, Natalia was supermodel gorgeous, only she had a quiet confidence, a stately, almost regal bearing that accentuated her beauty like a golden crown. She was simply sublime.

And smart as a whip.

She remembered every single detail he'd told her—her mind was like a steel trap.

She hesitated for only a moment before reaching out to reclaim his hand, and he folded her beneath his arm, wanting her close to his heart.

They walked in companionable silence past the first set of stables toward the house of Jadon's private facilities, and then he reached for the rustic handle on a large, cross-beamed door. "Come," he entreated. "I think you will really like this." He led her down the central hall, past a half-dozen glorious horses, including Prince Phoenix's beloved Percheron, to the last stall on the right. It was meticulously clean, incredibly roomy, and flooded with fresh air and sunlight.

Natalia stopped dead in her tracks; her impeccable features came alive with joy; and both hands shot to her cheeks. "Midnight!" she exclaimed, padding confidently toward the stable's railing.

The proud stallion tossed his head back, whinnied a bit, and pranced in place. Then he ambled in her direction.

She climbed two rails, leaned over the bannister, and stroked his glistening mane. "When did you do this? How did you do this?" Her smile lit up her eyes. "When did you possibly find the time?"

Santos tilted his head from side to side in a humble admission: "Ramsey...Saxson...I had some help."

Natalia inhaled a deep, excited breath and practically giggled as she released it. "Thank you, Santos," she said, sincerely. "I really don't know what to say."

He sidled up behind her, just as he had done that morning in the barn at the Giovanni compound. Only this time, she didn't stiffen in response to his presence. Rather, she leaned into his warmth and slowly turned around. Tentatively cupping his cheeks in her hands—they were just about eye to eye now—she stared into his seeking gaze, then briefly lowered her lids. "What am I going to do with you?" she whispered, blinking her eyes back open and studying each of his features in turn.

"Keep me," he rasped, curling his fingers over both her wrists. He turned his head to the side to press a kiss into the palm of her hand. "Keep me, continue to trust me, and give me a son."

She drew back reflexively, lowering her arms. "The Curse..." she murmured absently.

"No," he argued. "A blessing. The final hurdle before we make our union permanent. Well..." He shrugged one shoulder. "Well, that, and our mating and naming ceremony—but those are just formalities. The child secures my life, my immortality, and seals us together forever. Will you conceive a son for me, Natalia?"

She blinked her eyes three times, then glanced nervously around the stables. "Santos!" She visibly shivered. "Here? You want us to...do that...here?"

He smirked, certain that his eyes reflected his amusement. "Well, that's not a very fair question: I want us to do *that* everywhere." He grasped her by the waist, lifted her effortlessly off the beam she was standing on, and planted her perfect derriere on the top rail, moving his hands to the top of her thighs. "But it isn't necessary to do anything again...right now...in order to command your pregnancy." He pressed one hand to her lower belly, and his amused grin grew more devious. "There is still enough of me, right here."

She gasped, blushed, and turned her head to the side, biting her lower lip to conceal a nervous smile. "Santos..." she repeated.

"What?" he answered slyly.

She snickered. "Is it really that easy?"

He cocked his brows.

She rolled her eyes. "I meant the pregnancy. Is it really that easy to command one?"

He nodded. "It's very easy. Dangerously easy, really. It's why males in the house of Jadon have to be so careful."

This time, she cocked her brows. "Oh," she said sternly. "So then, you were not a virgin when we met?"

He chuckled: slow, deep, and languorous. "I was a virgin to true, timeless beauty," he said. "I was a virgin to your—"

"Shut up," she snipped. "Do I really look that gullible?"

He curled his lips over his teeth, trying to restrain his laughter.

"I am going to want places, names, and stories. All of them, Santos."

He blanched, his humor quickly vanishing. "Natalia..." He sighed. "I have lived a very, *very* long time."

She cocked her brows in censure. "Well then, you may as well get started. We only have twenty-six more days—twenty-four, if you count the necessity of a pregnancy. Twenty-three if you want a buffer of time." Although she'd tried to sound playful, there was an obvious and deep gravity in her voice.

Ah, Santos thought, *then she's thought about little else...*

Of course...

He was about to address the subject head-on, in a much more serious manner, when she lowered her chin toward her chest, pressed her forehead to his, and shivered. "Santos..." She whispered his name like a prayer.

"Angel?"

She sighed. *There is no part of this that isn't overwhelming... terrifying.* She spoke in his mind, and his respect for her deepened. Why wasn't he surprised that she had picked up on telepathic communication so effortlessly? He somehow knew that she was using it to speak words that were too difficult...too intimate...to say out loud. *The thought of uprooting my life, choosing a husband—or having one chosen for me...* She paused. *A mate. I can't even wrap my mind around it. And the Curse...the babies...*

the sacrifice required of your kind...of our kind... Her telepathic voice trailed off.

We don't have to act now...today, Santos responded in kind. *I was just—*

"Shh." She made the sound audibly. "You don't want me to lose my courage," she murmured. "I don't want to lose my courage."

He waited, listening intently.

"Yes, Santos. The answer to all of it is yes."

He held his breath, tuning into Natalia's heartbeat, the way it beat in time with his. "Are you sure, *cara mia?*" he asked her.

She chortled a nervous laugh then. "Of course not. That's a pretty tall order. But in terms of my life and everything that has happened until now? I've never been more...hopeful...of anything. That, I'm very sure of."

He smiled, albeit wanly. Then he pressed the pads of his middle three fingers to her lower belly and allowed his intention to flow through the gesture.

Just like that, she must have felt a flutter because she jumped in place and her mouth fell open. "Is it done?" she asked, her voice laced with both apprehension and wonder.

"It is done," he answered, and then he held her close while she processed that statement.

Finally, when it seemed as if time might stand still forever, the two of them locked in each other's arms—locked in a fate and a purpose that was grander than either of them—he drew back and caressed her jaw. She shuddered lightly at his touch, and it was all the encouragement he needed to kiss her.

Lightly at first.

Both corners of her mouth.

And then with the fullness of his passion, savoring her awe-inspiring lips.

She moaned softly and leaned into the kiss, offering the tip of her tongue for the vampire's exploration, and he felt his body instantly harden. Caressing her waist, then the underside of her breasts, his thumbs swept forward to tease her nipples—and that's when he felt a heavy, domineering nudge.

Midnight had loped his head over the banister, tossed his muzzle at Santos' chest, and pushed the vampire away from Natalia, nuzzling her head with his chin.

Natalia broke out in unrestrained laughter, the tension in the stables immediately evaporating. "Apparently, my horse does not want you to take advantage of a pregnant woman," she teased, still laughing.

Santos stared fixedly at the territorial animal, a trait he understood quite well as a vampire. "I can see that," he mused, regarding the proud black stallion with a newfound appreciation. "Perhaps Nachari can find a suitable wild mare to move into Midnight's stall, so he has somewhere else to focus his attention." The thought was immediately met with a heavy heart as Santos considered Nachari, Keitaro, and all the Silivasis...

They were dealing with an incredibly grave matter themselves.

A matter of the utmost importance to the house of Jadon, the king, and the sentinels.

Had Santos not been involved in his own critical Blood Moon, he would likely be at Napolean's manse right now, discussing and monitoring events with his brothers and their fearsome leader...waiting on pins and needles to see how Arielle's kidnapping—and Zayda's exchange—turned out.

He said a silent prayer before banishing the heavy thoughts from his mind.

The female in front of him was his foremost priority.

Especially now that she was forty-eight hours away from having his child.

Since he wasn't wearing a watch, he closed his eyes, tuned

into the rotation of the sun, and calibrated the celestial orbit with Natalia's native biorhythms. Satisfied that he had recorded the exact moment of conception—two o'clock on Sunday afternoon—he logged the information in his memory: The twins would be born at the same time on Tuesday.

"Can I take you home?" he asked his *destiny*. "I'd rather not manage any part of your pregnancy here in the Dark Moon Stables. Besides," he added, "there is much we still need to talk about."

Natalia wrapped a loving arm around Midnight's neck, patted the horse on the crest, above his mane, and shimmied off the bannister. Biting her bottom lip and blushing—she was clearly feeling both shy and playful—she crooked her finger at Santos, strolled to the end of the hall, and ducked around the corner, waiting for the vampire to follow.

It didn't take any extra encouragement.

Santos immediately followed his *destiny*.

Backing her way into an unoccupied stall filled with hay and several saddle blankets, Natalia lowered herself onto a haybale, pointed at the pile of blankets, and giggled. "You can take me home soon, Mr. Olaru; but first, you have to finish what you started."

CHAPTER THIRTY

The Old Cobblestone Well ~ Midnight

Zayda Patrone stared blankly, fixedly, at the harness and the thick cord of rope as Keitaro Silivasi tightened the belt, secured each loop, and tugged on each fastener to test its strength. The rope was anchored into the ground by a metal stake. Apparently, Xavier had thrust it deep between two flat stones atop the outside of the well, an easy enough feat for a werewolf, and Keitaro had assured Zayda that the stake was also secure.

She blinked several times, trying to slip into one of her old compartments, those cold, empty mental rooms, without windows or doors, that she had spent so much of her life moving in and out of. Despite the Silivasis' careful plan, she knew she had to be ready for anything.

Ready to be taken by her father.

Ready to emerge from the well into the land of the Lycan.

And though she would have never shared her deepest fears or doubts with Keitaro, she had already reasoned it out: Perhaps there would be less torture this time. Xavier would view her as his own flesh and blood—and although he would undoubtedly give her away to some male, perhaps there wouldn't be so many. Perhaps the abuse wouldn't be quite as brutal...or often.

Her mind split again.

That compartment was much too dangerous...

And so her consciousness meandered to the next open room —fairy tales, wishes, and daydreams. *Ah*, how she wished she had her biological father's powers, that she could shift into a werewolf and tear his bloody throat out, but such dreams were not to be.

Keitaro's strong, sure hands snapped her out of her musings— he was helping her straddle the upper wall of the well. "Zayda," he whispered, his eyes glued to hers. "Are you ready? Do you remember everything we talked about?" He didn't say anything more specific, lest Xavier was close by, listening. Who knew if the werewolf was hovering inside the well, suspended on the edges of a half-open portal, or tucked behind a tree or a rock in the nearby woods, safely out of the reach of a wolf trap.

Zayda shuddered before nodding. "Yes." She remembered. She needed to unfasten the harness and dive into the well; swim as fast as she could, deep into the earth; then hold her breath until Marquis and Nathaniel showed up.

She remembered.

Keitaro pressed a chaste kiss to her forehead, and she almost wished he hadn't—she needed to remain as numb as she could. "Be strong," he uttered, and her throat constricted. He placed a small silver flashlight into the palm of her hand, flipped it on, and rotated her leg until both feet were pointed toward the bottom of the well. And then, without preamble or further gestures—she knew he would not say goodbye—he began to lower her into the cobblestone structure, gracefully working the rope hand over hand.

* * *

The black panther stirred restlessly on the branch of a giant willow tree, several miles away from the old cobblestone well, the Master Wizard inside its nimble body, burrowed deep inside his father's mind: Nachari Silivasi could hear what Keitaro heard; he could see what Keitaro saw; and with such an open and unencumbered connection, he could feel what Keitaro felt.

His father was wound as tight as a drum, all his senses seeking outward. He was acutely aware of the time—every single second that ticked by—as he lowered Zayda Patrone into the well. And as Keitaro was perusing Zayda's thoughts, Nachari had access to both.

Zayda's mind was like an ancient Egyptian pyramid: a series of bleak, underground tunnels, meandering in every direction, each channel closed off from the world of the living. And just like an ancient mummy, she saw her descent into the well as a passageway to another world. Zayda did not expect to make it back. She was preparing herself for an afterlife, an existence far away from Dark Moon Vale.

No matter.

Nachari could not get caught up in Zayda's terror.

He had to stay focused on the well...and his magick.

He rolled his haunches to release some stress and watched as Zayda watched—as his father watched through her—the darkening of the cobblestones as the female descended, deeper and deeper, into the belly of the well.

At last, the beam from the flashlight cast light upon the water, and Zayda caught her first glimpse of Arielle Nightsong. *I see her*, Zayda signaled telepathically, just as she had been instructed to do, but the heads-up had not been necessary. Keitaro and Nachari could see her too.

Thank the gods and goddesses!

The wizard and the Ancient Master Warrior breathed a sigh of relief in unison as Arielle's damp copper hair reflected off the dim beam of light, and oddly enough, Zayda made an immediate internal comparison: She contrasted her thick amber braid to Arielle's' loose copper strands and wondered which woman's hair Keitaro found more attractive.

Nachari blinked the nonsense away.

Zayda's thoughts were truly scattered.

And truth be told: They would likely become progressively disjointed...increasingly inappropriate...as the exchange grew nearer.

He withdrew from her cognitive musings and anchored, instead, to the sole thread connected to the girl's five senses: what she was seeing, smelling, touching, hearing, and tasting. Despite her dim awareness of her preternatural half, she was a lycan after all, and her senses were extremely heightened.

Arielle was breathing evenly.

She was clearly scared, as evidenced by the spike of adrenaline coursing through her veins, but Kagen's mate was a warrior. She was no stranger to battle or conflict—and she wouldn't panic easily.

Keitaro, on the other hand, was growing increasingly restless.

His anger was rising, his muscles were bunching, and his eyelids were literally twitching as he lowered Zayda those last few inches and gazed down into the well...zeroing in on the water with his preternatural vision.

The women remained deathly quiet.

The entire night grew still.

Other than the sound of rustling water brushing against ancient stones and the hoot of an owl in a distant treetop, not a single utterance could be heard.

To her credit, Zayda unbuckled the harness quickly and slipped gracefully into the ice-cold water, but perhaps to her detriment, she didn't dive down—she stayed, instead, to help Arielle, securing her into the harness.

And that's when Xavier Matista's malevolent voice rang out, as if from inside a dark, ghostly chasm: "You lying bastard," he spat. "There's another vampire inside this well!"

The panther reared back in shock, trying to make sense of the werewolf's words.

It wasn't true!

He zeroed in on Marquis and Nathaniel's positions: Both warriors were still miles away, burrowed deep underground, and waiting, prepared to tunnel to the bottom of the well.

And as for Kagen...

Nachari reached for the Ancient Master Healer's essence and found him about half an acre north of the willow tree, crouched impatiently behind a large round boulder, nearly desperate with rage and wracked with worry, focused entirely on his mate, Arielle.

What the hell was Xavier talking about?

There wasn't any time to figure it out—

A pop, a sizzle, and a bright, rainbow-colored prism flashed at the waterline, deep inside the well, and Nachari knew the lycan had opened the portal.

The panther bounded down from the tree, landed on his feet as a vampire, and thrust both palms forward in the direction of the well, sending a blast of mystical power across the surface of the water while chanting a powerful holding spell, the gist of which was *stay put, stay put, stay put!*

It wouldn't keep the portal from opening—or closing—but it would buy the Silivasis a couple of seconds.

Without hesitation, Kagen materialized at the top of the well and yanked on the rope with a fury, flipping his *destiny* out of the cobblestone depths like a fisherman retrieving a fly cast. He caught her as she jettisoned out of the water, even as Keitaro Silivasi dove past her, equally desperate to get to Zayda, who was finally swimming downward as she'd been instructed.

Zayda dove down...down...down into the dark musty pool, kicking her feet like a wild woman, and all the while, Marquis and Nathaniel bored through the earth with their oscillating bodies, speeding toward the bottom of the structure like two supernatural drill bits, determined to meet up with Zayda.

And Xavier Matista—he was a male on a mission.

He lunged from the portal, both desperate and feral, streaming like a water snake after Zayda and grasping wildly at her ankles with his claws.

One grasp.

One clutch.

It would only take a moment—just a tentative hold—and Xavier could snatch her back through the portal.

CHAPTER THIRTY-ONE

The water was so incredibly cold.

Zayda felt the frigid bite all the way down to her bones.

What the hell had just happened?

She pursed her lips together as a glob of slimy green moss—or was that algae?—brushed across her eyes, her nose, and threatened to enter her mouth. She wanted to gag, but she had to keep kicking, keep swimming, keep tunneling down with her arms as propellers. She had to keep holding her breath so Nachari could regulate her breathing.

Was the wizard paying attention, or was he engaged in some battle, along with his father...or his brothers...along with Kagen?

No, she decided, stunned at how cloudy, dense, and murky the water was becoming. Bits of debris—floating, swirling, expanding—were everywhere around her, and she was *this close* to panicking.

"You lying bastard," Xavier had snarled. "There's another vampire inside this well!"

What the heck was he talking about?

Other than Arielle—

Her thoughts made a sharp right turn.

She didn't know anything about being half Lycan, being born to a species of inbred vampire-hunters, but she knew what it felt like to have an overpowering instinct, a *knowing* so deep in her gut that she couldn't deny it. And her biological sire had been right—the entire well reeked with the essence of vampire. Not Keitaro at the top of the well. Not Arielle, trussed and helpless in the water, but overwhelming, overpowering...*vampire*!

Someone must have tugged on Arielle's rope, because she was only half strapped inside the harness when she shot upward like a rocket, and it had looked like Keitaro had dived into the well. *Where is he now?* Zayda thought, swimming even deeper.

Her throat constricted in an effort not to reach for air, and she had to redouble her efforts.

Nachari had made her practice. Earlier. Back at Keitaro's homestead. He had laid her in a clawfoot bathtub, beneath the water, to show her what it felt like to let her breathing go, to just relax her throat and give the function over to the Master Wizard. It was strange not to draw breath, but it wasn't painful like she'd imagined. More like...it felt a bit like sleeping, being unconscious, not thinking or trying, just expecting the air to always be there. Most of all, he'd wanted her to understand that she could not take in any water.

That as long as she didn't panic, her lungs would keep functioning without her assistance.

A sharp tug!

A piercing pain.

As fingers, or knives—*no, claws!*—scraped her ankle, and blood began to pool in the already filthy water. *Oh gods, oh gods, oh gods!* Xavier was at the bottom of the well, right behind her.

She kicked backward for all she was worth; she couldn't let Xavier catch her.

He scrambled for her feet again, and she spun around, rotating in the water so she could kick upward and stomp at his face.

His pale amber irises were wild, bloodshot, and bulging—the lycan was seized with panic.

He needed to breathe, just like her, and there was a frenzied desperation in every inhuman contortion of his features. His entire massive body was trembling. Oh gods, he was ready to flash through the portal, and he was desperate to take Zayda with him.

"No!" she shouted, or at least she tried. Her mouth filled up with water, and she strained to push it out. But Xavier was coming at her like a battering ram now, grasping for any part of her body he could sink his claws into. She gasped, and more water flowed into her lungs—it felt like fire, piercing needles, a chemical assault on her chest. Terror-stricken and desperate for breath, she kicked with both feet in unison, snapping Xavier's head back and spinning around in a panic. She spiraled downward, even farther—swimming, choking, gulping more water—desperate to reach the bottom of the well.

The entire earth was quaking, rocking, trembling...

Where were Marquis and Nathaniel?

The pain in her chest was unbearable. The sensation of being trapped, being smothered—being harmed—was beyond any torture she'd ever known as she lost her fight against air-versus-water and succumbed to the agony in her lungs.

She couldn't kick, and she couldn't swim, not another desperate stroke.

She just wanted the suffering to end.

Please, God...

Someone...anyone...have mercy.

The water churned in violent waves all above her, and she knew something brutal was happening, but her mind was too far gone. She glanced absently over her shoulder, but she couldn't make sense of the turbulent images. Just the same, the water turned crimson with blood, and that's when three things happened at once: Marquis Silivasi shot up through the murky pit of the well, Nathaniel Silivasi right behind him; Keitaro's chiseled, handsome features came into view, and he was clutching Xavier's decapitated head like a bowling ball in his fist; and Zayda's lungs folded inward, collapsing, and the entire well went black.

* * *

Time passed slowly.

Peacefully.

Maybe not at all.

As Zayda watched the scene unfold from a safe, painless distance.

Marquis grasped her body by both shoulders and shot up toward the mouth of the well; Keitaro released Xavier's head, leaving it to sink in the water, and followed on Marquis' heels.

Nathaniel took up the rear.

He collected the sinking head and Xavier's floating torso, and began to kick more leisurely toward the surface.

Silly Silivasis; didn't they understand?

Zayda no longer inhabited that body.

She had no further use of it, and she didn't want it back.

She drifted backward, her arms spread out to each side, and breathed the deepest, cleanest, purest breath she had ever taken. The weight of a thousand lifetimes lifted from her shoulders, and the dark, murky water in the well turned bright, luminescent, and whiter than fresh snowfall.

She could stay in this place forever.

Voices echoed in the faraway distance...

"Lay her down!" Keitaro's commanding brogue.

"Step back! I need to get the water out." Kagen Silivasi.

"What the hell happened at the bottom of that well?" Marquis' unmistakable bark.

"I couldn't keep moving the oxygen—not after she swallowed so much water." Poor Master Wizard—he was really very kind.

"Be gentle," Arielle Nightsong-Silivasi...

Zayda tuned it all out.

On some deep, detached level, Zayda knew they would continue to work to revive her, but on a much more spectral plane, she also knew it would be of no use. She wasn't going back —no way, no how, *not ever*—not to that broken body, that violated corpse, that life that had always been one of torment.

She turned her full face to the welcoming light and began to swim gracefully toward it.

And that's when two elegant, fluid hands pressed against her shoulders.

"No." An enchanting, feminine voice like an angel. "Go back."

Zayda started and shook her head. She did not want to go back—she wanted to go forward! She wanted to swim into that golden halo...or...or was that a golden fall of luxuriant blonde hair?

No.

No!

NO!

"Shh, be at ease," the angel said. And then she reached out with that gentle, slender hand and slid it inside Zayda's chest, right over the cavity of her long-ago damaged, broken heart. When the angel drew it back, she held a mass in her fist—a dark, inky, blood-red mass, filled with briars and thistles and jagged thorns. She blew on the mass and it floated away, disappearing into the depths of the well.

And then the beautiful light—the elegant angel—began to fade into the distance.

"Come back!" Zayda called. "Please, don't leave me." She wanted to stay in that unnatural peace, with that unearthly beautiful angel, with that sublime...serenity...forever.

Serenity...serenity...serenity.

She wanted to keep that serenity...

But no, not serenity. The word floated just outside of her reach—and then it drifted down and settled like a soft golden feather on her consciousness.

No.

Not serenity...

Serena.

CHAPTER THIRTY-TWO

Keitaro Silivasi was absolutely frantic.

He had followed Xavier's instructions to the letter, and still the general had betrayed him: "You lying bastard; there's another vampire inside this well!"

That was total, unconscionable bullshit!

Kagen had flashed into view at the top of the well and tugged on Arielle's rope like the secrets to the universe were on the other end of the line and he had three seconds to retrieve them or perish.

Keitaro hadn't waited around to receive the daughter of his heart, not when the female he had sworn to protect was being pursued by her wicked biological father—not when Zayda might drown...

He had dived into the well and started swimming.

Down...down...down.

Scenting, smelling, *feeling* everything.

And then he had seen her, swimming and struggling: kicking at Xavier, trying to keep her feet and her ankles free from the lycan's clutches, and gulping too much water.

The well was like a murky blender: mud, filthy debris, and algae churning everywhere.

Keitaro's rage had virtually exploded.

Channeling all the supernatural strength he possessed into his right hand and his bicep, Keitaro dove forward, slammed his fist into Xavier's back, and shattered the lycanthrope's vertebrae. He dug his claws into Xavier's shoulders and wrenched the bastard backward, sinking his fangs deep into the general's neck. And then he tore, back and forth, like a rabid animal—biting, snarling, twisting his head, spitting out mouthfuls of flesh—until all that was left was the stem of Xavier's cervical spine.

Keitaro wrapped both fists around the discs and snapped them!

Then he tore the monster's head from his shoulders, clutched it in his hand, and began to swim toward Zayda...

Dear gods, no!

She wasn't breathing.

Her body was floating—*weightless and lifeless*—in the blood-drenched water.

* * *

"Can you hear me? Zayda!" It was Kagen's voice, and she blinked her eyes open, two or three times.

She sputtered, she coughed, and she spit out several gulps of water. Then her eyes latched onto the male who was kneeling beside the healer, his brows furrowed with concern as he clutched Zayda's hand: Keitaro could not have looked more handsome—or more protective—in the pale, glistening moonlight. "I can hear you," she croaked to Kagen, and a collective gasp of relief filled the air.

Focusing her full attention on the hero who had rescued her from her life in The Fortress, the one who had taken her home for no other reason than to nurse her back to health and give her a chance to live as a whole—and free—living being, she squeezed Keitaro's hand and felt her heart swell with gratitude.

Gratitude...and something far more precious.

Peace.

There were no longer any broken chambers, no longer any split, separate compartments for Zayda to wander in and out of. Her mind no longer felt fractured, but more than that, she finally understood: Keitaro Silivasi was not a brutal, self-absorbed male who could have—or ever would have—used her body. He had not taken her home to one day seek his own selfish pleasure at Zayda's expense. And he would *never* have given in to her broken, desperate advances because his heart was filled with something so pure. So real. So untainted...

This man had known serenity for most of his life.

This man had been loved by Serena.

And the couple's unselfish, celestial love still lived on beyond the grave.

All at once, Zayda understood exactly what Serena Silivasi wanted: Cherish him. Love him. Be his friend. Offer laughter and companionship...and hope. Let time heal—as time always does—and just walk through the world beside him, as long as he will allow...

Zayda could do that.

Zayda would do that.

Sometimes broken souls came together for no other reason than to heal one another, and if more was meant, it would gently unfold. Zayda would revere the gift she'd been given because Keitaro was one in a million.

"I'm here," she said softly, this time to Keitaro. Then one by one she met the seeking gazes of Keitaro's beloved sons. "Thank you," she choked out to all, yet no one specific.

It was the best she could do under the circumstances.

There were truly no words to express the depths of her newfound awareness...her gratitude...or her love.

CHAPTER THIRTY-THREE

Natalia Giovanni struggled to prop herself up on the
three fluffy pillows beneath her head so she could
have a better view out the panoramic, wall-length
windows in Santos' master bedroom. She wanted to see the lake
more clearly, to draw strength from its peaceful blue-gray waters.
She dug her heels into the mattress and shoved, trying to scoot
her heavy body—and enormous belly—backward, but she barely
budged an inch.

Santos smiled wanly. "Can I help?"

The sentinel had been at her side for the last forty-seven
hours, ever since the conception had taken hold, seeing to
Natalia's comfort, blocking any pain, doing all he could think of
to ease her mind and make her more comfortable. He had
patiently walked her through what was to come: the details of the
birth, how vampires were born, what to expect when the dark
twin emerged, and what was required of the sentinel with regard
to the sacrifice. The fact that he planned to do that part alone.

They had talked about their lives up until this point: Natalia growing up in the Giovanni compound and Santos growing up in Dark Moon Vale; Natalia being educated in private schools, with private tutors; and Santos attending the Romanian University to become a Master Warrior. They had talked about Natalia's required duty to Luca's operation, however seedy, and Santos' sworn duty to Napolean Mondragon, his agonizing induction into the house of Jadon—his initiation into the elite guard of sentinels—when he had knelt before the king and fought to remain conscious as the monarch carved the letters HOJ into the warrior's heart with a burning stylus.

Natalia had shared some of her fondest memories—although, admittedly, there were few—of the stable man who had taught her how to ride horses when she was just a girl; her best friend Mandy in second grade, the friend who never saw her as Luca's daughter or cared that she lived in such a strange, corrupt place; and of course, her personal maid, Sylvia, who was far more of a friend than an employee: a wise counselor and a loyal companion.

Santos had promised to do all he could to reunite Natalia with Sylvia, make sure the short, petite spitfire remained in his *destiny's* life...make sure Sylvia's family and her loved ones were extremely well cared for. He had understood what the maid's loyalty and kindness had meant to Natalia, and he had been grateful that someone had been there to at least fill in one of the glaring gaps in Natalia's upbringing.

He had also reciprocated by sharing some stories and memories of his own: He had some pretty tall tales about growing up with Ramsey and Saxson, the trouble they had gotten into as children, the antics the twins had played. While some of the tales were hilarious, others were terrifying and grueling. It was a wonder that any of them had survived to adulthood, yet it was crystal clear that Santos had something Natalia had never known:

a true, unbreakable, ever-present sense of family and community. The bonds were unbreakable, and the roots ran deeper than those of an ancient tree, planted beside a river.

He had also described his immediate circle of colleagues, his closest friends: Julien Lacusta, the tracker; Saber Alexiares, a male born to the house of Jadon but stolen by the house of Jaegar, who had finally returned to his rightful place; and of course, the venerable king.

Last, but not least, the two had shared something perhaps more intimate than their blossoming physical relationship: They had shared the memories—and the loss—of their mothers. Natalia had recalled her Tanzanian mother's exquisite, gentle beauty and her rich, vibrant culture, the fact that she had been a loving, reliable harbor in a truly stormy life. And Santos had described Ruth Jensen-Olaru as charming, witty, and tough as nails, something that hadn't surprised Natalia one bit. The fact that Magdalene Laiseri had fallen in love with a handsome billionaire from Italy and later followed him to the United States, only to lose her life in such a violent manner—some sort of drug deal or arms deal gone wrong—had not been lost on the compassionate sentinel. His mother had also fallen in love with a handsome stranger, a vampire, albeit ordained by an ancient curse, and her life had been cut short at the hands of vampire-hunters, not by bullets, but by a wooden stake.

The two would always have their grief in common.

They would always share the loss of both parents, albeit by different means.

And to that end, Santos had made Natalia another important promise: When she was ready...if she was ever ready...they would have a private memorial service for Luca Giovanni.

For her father...

Somehow Santos just understood: The male may have been a

monster, but she had loved him as a little girl. She would still need closure and a means to process such a far-reaching, soul-shattering loss. She would need to grieve both the father he was... and the father he had never been.

"Angel?" Santos' silky, loving—and yes, weary—voice sliced through the silence, pulling her back from her reverie. "Can I help?"

She huffed, considering the now lumpy pillows behind her, and tried to weigh whether it was worth it: moving her massive belly, exerting any more energy or strength. It had to be getting close to 2:00 PM. "What time is it?" she whispered, still undecided if she really wanted to move at all.

Santos chuckled softly. "One fifty-five, my love. Here, let me do it for you." He rose from his perch in the wing-backed chair, slipped one palm beneath her lower back, and raised her effortlessly off the haphazard pillows. "I think these have shifted a dozen times." He fluffed each one with his free hand, repositioned all three, then tugged her backward, ever so gently, and lowered her onto the new configuration. "Better?" he asked.

She glanced out the window, gazed at the lake, and sighed. *Yeah, that was a whole lot better.* "Thank you."

He nodded, then took her hand in his and sank back into the chair. Rubbing the bridge of his nose, he asked, "So, are we decided then—we agree on the name?"

The subject made Natalia smile. "I think it's absolutely perfect."

"You sure it won't be upsetting or uncomfortable, hearing your mother's maiden name, again and again?"

Natalia shook her head. "Laiseri Andrei Olaru." She tried the combination on her tongue: her mother's maiden name, Santos' middle name, and Olaru, forever in the place of Giovanni. "Laiseri," she repeated again, and the more she spoke the word aloud, the more the "S" rolled off her tongue like a "Z." She figured it would be no time at all before they were shortening the child's name to Zeri, but that would work just as well—he would have his own identity and his father's namesake, as well as a precious piece of Natalia's culture. So be it. It was perfect. "I'm sure," she said softly.

Just then, a cacophony of noise filled the peaceful lake house: the front door unlocking and opening; two deep male voices echoing in the foyer; and two softer feminine lilts accompanying the males. "Saxson and Kiera," Santos explained. "Ramsey and Tiffany."

Natalia's eyes grew wide, and she glanced down at her belly—oh, gods; was this how she was going to meet her new family? Well, at least formally—Saxson and Ramsey had already seen and protected Natalia that night in the Morrison meadow when Oskar had tried to assault her, and even before then, she had seen their photographs online, the night of the New Year's Eve party at the Dark Moon Casino.

"No worries, Natalia girl," Santos reassured her, seeming to understand her angst. "They understand what's happening. Don't forget; both *destinies* have already been through it—and they're only here to help." Sensing her continued unease, he explained a bit further: "Tiffany picked up a bassinette, some clothes, diapers, and a bunch of other necessities—the gods only know what—and Kiera came, as well, to help you watch the baby while I attend to the necessary sacrifice. As always, Ramsey and Saxson are here to get my back. They're here to help with the dark twin and to watch over you, their mates, and Laiseri while I'm gone."

Natalia gulped, trying to take it all in.

So this was really...actually...happening?

The Curse playing out: the birth of two twins—one light and one soulless.

She and Santos were really having a baby, and this bizarre, inexplicable miracle was happening...now.

"Santos," she groaned, her voice sounding strained. "I think... I think." She glanced down at her belly, which was rising and falling like a restless wave in an incoming tide. "I think something's happening."

A hulk of an Adonis with vivid hazel eyes and dark blond, chin-length hair shimmered into the bedroom and stood by the bed like a guardian angel, both fearsome and protective. He was careful to avoid eye contact and remained respectfully quiet while Santos stood up, inched closer to Natalia, and nodded in affirmation. "Ramsey," he said by way of greeting.

The massive warrior inclined his head.

"It's time, angel. Are you ready?" Santos asked.

Natalia's eyes shot back and forth between the two brothers, and then she struggled to catch her breath. If Santos didn't call these babies out of her soon, they might just stage a jail break. Yeah, it was definitely time. "I think so," she muttered weakly.

Santos squeezed her hand. "You're ready," he reassured her. "Are you sure you want to remain awake...and aware...the entire time? You would not rather look away?"

Natalia shook her head.

Between her father, his associates, and his henchmen, she had seen the many faces of evil all her life, and she knew the damage a sociopathic, unredeemable monster could wreak on countless souls over many years, let alone over an eternal lifetime. She felt she was strong enough to see the dark infant and to never look back with regret.

Regret was living alongside the face of evil and not freeing oneself from its clutches.

"I'm sure," she insisted.

* * *

Santos Olaru released Natalia's hand; waited as his *destiny* steeled her courage and steadied her breathing; then placed his full, focused attention on her undulating girth, tuning into the energy of his children, both entities writhing in a bid for freedom from her enormous belly. He took a deep breath as well to calm his nerves, and then he began to gather the restless kinetic energy into a condensed stream of light. Two beating hearts thrummed in his consciousness as he began to murmur an ancient prayer, spoken in the primordial language of the Vampyr.

He called his sons from the confining cavity, commanding them to materialize before their father, and several bright prisms of light filled the lake house like a dozen shimmering rainbows, each undulating into a central arc above Natalia's belly, while casting a glorious misty halo around the mattress.

A steady, hypnotic pulse filled the room, thrumming in even, mesmerizing waves of sound, and Santos drew the energy toward his center. "That's it," he murmured, tugging on each pulse with the whole of his intention.

Sparkles, like gold dust, began to gather and swirl at the tips of the sentinel's fingers.

A funnel formed at the center of his open palms.

And just like that, the first of the two infants crystallized into physical matter, his soft, bare bottom nestling into his sire's left hand.

Santos pressed the babe to his chest, cradling his son with large, splayed fingers.

Laiseri Andrei Olaru.

He had his father's crystal-blue eyes, only with dark chocolate pupils; his mother's perfect nose, with a well-formed little ball at the tip; and Natalia's exquisite hair, complete with dark waves and silky, brilliant texture. Santos ran his thumb over the soft, downy tresses, his heart filling with wonder, and the child remained completely serene and still.

Without wasting another second, Santos handed the babe to Ramsey and stretched both palms over his *destiny's* belly, maintaining absolute silence in the bedroom. To her credit, Natalia followed Santos' lead. Although her eyes darted back and forth between her mate and their newborn infant, fortunately—and to Santos' great relief—she was intuitive enough not to interrupt the delicate process.

The golden sparkles of dust, those that had recently illuminated the vampire's fingertips, became an opaque, ominous vapor. The funnel became a murky cloud. And instead of the child's bottom nestling into his father's palm, a pair of sharp, jagged fangs latched onto Santos' hand.

The warrior didn't flinch.

Rather, he supported the dark twin's stomach with his other hand, placing it firmly beneath the infant's belly. A long, drawn-out hiss filled the room, and it was akin to fingernails scraping against a chalkboard.

Natalia gasped.

And Tiffany Matthews-Olaru shimmered into the bedroom as if on cue.

She had a soft yellow cashmere blanket held in one hand, and she immediately swaddled Laiseri, transferring the child from Ramsey's arms to his mother's without uttering a single word. She then placed her body between Santos, the dark twin, and Natalia, shielding the latter from the dark twin's antics.

Ramsey stepped forward and pried the baby's fangs free from Santos' flesh. He stroked the infant's jugular twice, using two firm fingers, and the hissing came to a halt.

"Take him to the living room," Santos said to Ramsey. "I'll be there in a minute."

There was nothing more that needed to be said—there was no salvation for the child born of darkness, a malignant entity formed from a curse and born without a soul. No matter what the child might look like, act like, or seem like, he was evil—pure and simple—undiluted iniquity disguised in human flesh.

The Curse brooked no arguments.

And it made no exceptions.

Once again, Santos had to give his *destiny* enormous credit: She didn't ask Tiffany to move; she didn't ask Santos to show her the dark soul; she didn't cry out or get confused. Rather, she turned her full attention on the cooing, swaddled babe, and greeted him with kisses and caresses.

"He's amazing," she finally whispered, the awe in her voice transforming the disturbing moment. "Santos, he has your eyes." Then she turned her attention to Tiffany Olaru and smiled with both relief and gratitude. "Thank you. I'm Natalia."

The smart, beautiful blonde reached out to touch the baby's hand and slid her pinky inside his tight, reflexive grip. "Congratulations," she said softly. "I'm Tiffany, but you can call me Tiff or even sister." She crooked her thumb toward the space where Ramsey had been standing. "I would say I'm the huge one's ball and chain, but the way I see it, he belongs to me—not the other way around." She winked conspiratorially, and Natalia laughed.

"Well, thank you just the same."

This time Tiffany spoke more resolutely. "You're welcome, Natalia." She removed her finger from Laiseri's hand and stepped away from the bed. "I'll be just outside the bedroom door, along with Saxson and Keira. Call out if you need anything, no matter how small." She turned on her heel and strolled out of the room as gracefully and unobtrusively as she had entered.

Santos approached the bed, sat down beside his mate—and his child—and placed a gentle hand on Natalia's forehead. "You did very well, *cara mia.*"

She studied him in earnest. "I can't believe...I just can't

believe it." She stared down at the baby and choked back a sob. "I can't believe this is real, Santos. A week ago, I had nothing, and now...*look*." She shut her eyes to conceal two crystal teardrops, and Santos pressed a tender kiss against her lips.

"It's only the beginning, my love," he whispered, even as he knew that *love*—deep, abiding, soul-level love—would continue to grow in time. Yes, the gods had already seen to an inherent, unbreakable bond, sealing the couple's spirits together the moment they were born, but eternity would offer them the chance to confirm that covenant and expand their connection— and he couldn't imagine any other woman he would rather grow into deep, abiding love with. "I do have to go, Natalia, but I'll be back within the hour. Are you—"

His speech stopped abruptly as Natalia sat up, swung her feet over the side of the bed, and laid the baby gently against a thick, fluffy pillow, watching for a moment to make sure his tiny body was stable.

"What are you doing?" Santos asked, as Natalia shimmied out of the loose, oversized nightgown, reached for a light, cotton tank top, which was crumpled on the nearby nightstand, slipped it over her head, and stood up, testing the strength and mobility of her post-pregnancy body. Unlike human gestations, a female vampire's torso retracted very quickly. Natalia was already small enough to slip back into her clothes.

"Watch Laiseri," she said, indicating the baby with her chin. "I don't think he can roll over or bury his face in that pillow, but he isn't human, so I don't really know. Just sit with him for a second while I get dressed."

Ah, Santos thought.

Of course, that makes sense...

Natalia didn't want to be half dressed, clothed in a way-too-roomy nightgown that was sure to slide off her shoulders when she interacted with her new in-laws. Whether the others joined her in the bedroom or she took Laiseri out to them, she would want to maintain a modicum of decency and decorum. He watched as she slipped into the bathroom and re-emerged about thirty seconds later, wearing a soft pair of cotton sweatpants and a matching duo of comfortable sneakers. "I'm ready," she said bluntly.

Santos smiled. By all the gods, she was so damn gorgeous, even after the last forty-eight hours. "It won't take me long," he reiterated. "I'll be back before you know it."

"It won't take *us* long," she corrected.

Santos cocked his brows. "Excuse me?"

She raised her eyebrows to mimic his expression and mirror his confusion, but she didn't speak a word.

"No," he said firmly, finally catching on. "You're not going with."

She pursed her lips and tilted her head. "Yes, Santos, I am."

He shook his head slowly...dubiously. "Natalia..."

"Santos."

"Seriously, I don't think you understand what this involves. It's not something you should ever see or have stored in your memory. It's not something I wish for you to endure."

Her features softened then, and her stunning mocha eyes deepened with compassion. Nonetheless, she held her ground. "Ah, but is there a law against it? Does your king forbid it? Are females not allowed in the Chamber of Sacrifice and Atonement?"

Santos drew back, surprised by her question. "Uh, no...I mean, of course, they're allowed. You're allowed. It's just—that's not the way we do it."

She pointed at his chest and then aimed the same forefinger at her own, repeating the process, back and forth, two times. "By *we*, do you mean you and I?"

His tongue snaked out to wet his lips, and he glanced over his shoulder to check on the baby. Laiseri was sleeping so peacefully, it was almost as if he knew his parents had something to work out, and he was giving them a quiet moment to do so. "Okay. I see where you're going with this, sweetie, and I appreciate it. *I do.* But it's—"

"But what?"

"Natalia, a rift between worlds will open up. There's an actual ancient altar inside the chamber, and the Blood itself, in all its malevolence, will be there. The dark child will be taken... removed...swept up. It's—"

"It's what?" she interrupted, defiantly. "So much worse than living six or seven miles away from The Fortress, from human slavery and sexual brutality? It's worse than what Oskar did to me in that meadow? It's worse than being my father's property, just an attractive armpiece to fool and appease the community? It's above my what? My comprehension...my pay grade...my ability to withstand as a woman? It's something you must endure; it's a memory you will always carry—for me, and for Laiseri—but it's not something you will allow me to endure beside you?" She placed her hands on her hips, not in anger, but in emphasis. "Are we in this together or not, Sentinel2000?"

Santos sighed in frustration. "ArabianNight500," he murmured, realizing that *this* was the side of Natalia he was dealing with in this moment: the clever, strong-willed woman who could dig in her heels and keep them firmly planted, without budging.

She seemed to read his thoughts, or maybe it was just his expression. "And how did that work for you before? When you tried to stay three steps ahead of me in cyberspace? When you tried to break into my computer? When you insisted on taking—and keeping—the lead? Santos..." Her voice grew deathly serious. "I know that this has been hard for me, and I know that many aspects of this strange new world are frightening. And I even know that your every inborn instinct is to protect me, but I can't go back to the life you just took me from. I can't go back to being an armpiece, to existing in the shadows, to obeying without question or an opinion. I won't go back to it, Santos. And I would rather face the devil himself beside you than to wait in your room...*in our room*...like a sheltered bird inside another gilded cage. I am twenty-five years old, and I've just discovered intimacy. I no longer wish to exist on the sidelines, and don't get me wrong—I know this is a horrific duty, and I know that it will not be pleasant—but either you see me as worthy of supporting you too, of loving you too, or you only wish to possess me...like Luca." She paused long enough to let the statement linger. "Which is it, Santos?"

He glanced out the window for a moment, staring at the lake, even as his heart constricted. "Natalia...*cara mia*," he finally murmured, turning his gaze back to his *destiny*, "is that honestly what you think of me? That I'm anything at all like your father?"

She shook her head emphatically. "No, it's not what I think of you, warrior. And that's why this is so important. Let me go with you, Santos. Let us face *all of this curse* together. I need to know my new life is going to be different. I need to know that you trust and believe in me. And honestly, I *want* to be beside you."

Santos held his breath for the space of several heartbeats, turning Natalia's words over in his head and weighing several internal arguments. He really did not want her to enter that chamber and encounter such a dark, supernatural entity, but he also understood the life she had lived—the absolute and unrelenting isolation—the way Luca had always marginalized her existence.

And he also knew that his *destiny* was strong.

Natalia Giovanni was a fighter.

A female chosen by the celestial gods to stand beside a vampire sentinel.

"Okay," he whispered. "In this, I'll relent." He wanted to make it clear that there would be events, there would be issues, especially within his official capacity as a mercenary for the house of Jadon, that he simply could not...would not...allow his *destiny* to get mixed up in. He was not a human male. He was Vampyr. And he would shield and protect her, even at risk of her disappointment or anger.

But only when it was absolutely necessary.

He checked Laiseri one last time, reassured that the baby was still sleeping, and then he rose from his perch on the bed, closed the distance between them, and wrapped his arms around her, enfolding her tightly against his chest. "I do love you, Natalia," he whispered into her hair, "and that love will only grow in time." He pressed a tender kiss against the crown of her head and reveled in the warmth of her presence, the light of her being. "Since we're going to drive, rather than transport, I'm going to ask Ramsey to come with us. I don't want you handling the dark twin."

Natalia slipped her arms around Santos' waist and laid her head against his heart. "Santos?" she murmured. "I have a confession."

He nuzzled her closer. "What is it, angel?"

"I love you, too," she whispered. "Truth is, I have loved you for a very long time. Even before I saw your picture at that New Year's Eve party—you know, the photograph of you and your brothers at the Dark Moon Casino, the one you quickly removed?" She laughed softly. "I fantasized about you long before then. Why do you think I sought out your avatar on iChat Platinum? Point is: I think I have always loved you."

Santos shut his eyes and meditated on Natalia's words, allowing them to sink deep inside his consciousness...to wrap around his immortal soul.

Truly the gods were more than generous.

They were more than benevolent and more than omniscient. They were wise, infinitely kind, and worthy of veneration.

And Santos would be forever grateful that they had chosen Natalia Giovanni, ArabianNight500, to walk in this world beside him.

CHAPTER THIRTY-FOUR

One week later

Keitaro and Zayda walked hand in hand along the long, winding trail that led to Santos' hidden lake on their way to the sentinel's sunset mating and naming ceremony. They had driven three-quarters of the way before leaving Keitaro's forged-copper Nissan Armada Mountain Patrol parked behind the Dark Moon Academy and setting out on foot to enjoy the crisp, clean air and the spectacular views.

Zayda's hand felt comfortable nestled inside Keitaro's palm: warm, trusting, and companionable. There was nothing romantic or inappropriate about it, no reason for Keitaro to worry that he might be sending the wrong type of signals. In fact, that was just the thing of it—Zayda's signals were no longer crossed. Her circuits were no longer...broken.

Ever since that night at the old cobblestone well, Zayda Patrone had been different: calmer, rational, reasoned. She had let down her defensive guard, relinquished her unseemly advances, and settled into her own skin like she was finally comfortable wearing it. Zayda had actually made Keitaro feel at ease with their association. While she was still *childlike*—her uninhibited laughter; her playful, impulsive nature; her wide-eyed wonder at the world all around her—she was no longer *childish* at times. Rather, she had approached Keitaro as an equal, hoping to be a friend as well as his ward.

The Ancient Master Warrior still didn't know what to make of it, only that she had gone into that well broken, damaged, and terrified, and she had come out purged, strong, and resilient. At first, he wasn't sure if he could trust it—the subtle yet powerful transformation in her personality—but day in and day out, one conversation after another, Zayda had proven that the change seemed lasting. The healing was real.

"I can't believe she invited me to the ceremony," she said softly. "I can't believe she invited *us*."

Keitaro glanced at his companion sideways with amusement. "It would seem that *Princess Natalia* is very eager to meet you. She can't wait to see you after all these years." Again, two weeks ago, Keitaro would have had to tiptoe around such a sensitive subject—Zayda's childhood and growing up in The Fortress—but now they could speak openly about difficult subjects.

Zayda rolled her stunning, mythical eyes at the reference to Natalia Giovanni as a princess. "Yeah," she acknowledged, "she really was like a legend to me, and I guess my mind invented a fairy tale to make it all more...digestible." She shook her head. "And in that story, it would seem Prince Oskar was not a knight in shining armor after all, but a really evil villain. Oskar Vadovsky was a Dark One." She shivered, and Keitaro squeezed her hand for reassurance. "Vampires...werewolves...Dark Ones," she murmured absently, apparently taking inventory of her strange new world. And then shrugging her slender shoulders to dismiss the heaviness of such reveries, she pivoted back to the initial conversation. "I'm just surprised that Natalia remembered me after all these years."

At this, Keitaro smiled warmly. "I'm not," he said. "You're not so forgettable, Zayda."

She flashed an appreciative grin and then they rounded a bend in the trail, and the beautiful crystal lake came into view. Zayda stopped dead in her tracks, her eyes shooting to the crowded pier. "Dear gods," she whispered, her arms dotting with goose bumps. "There's so many of them."

Keitaro released her hand, slid his arm around her shoulder, and ran his palm up and down her skin, as if he could smooth out the prickles with his fingers. "You remember Santos, right? The male with the black-and-blond hair? That's Natalia's mate...her husband." He pointed in the distance. "The warrior standing to Santos' right is his brother, Ramsey Olaru. The woman beside him is Tiffany, Ramsey's *destiny*, and she's holding their son, Roman."

Zayda nodded slowly, her lips mouthing each name as if she were trying to commit it to memory.

"The guy on Santos' left is his other brother, Saxson—Saxson and Ramsey are twins. The female is Saxson's mate, Keira, and their child is Legend." He waited while Zayda absorbed the information.

"And that terrifying gladiator, the one with the mahogany hair and the overwhelming presence?" she asked.

"Ah," Keitaro said. "That's Julien Lacusta, the valley's tracker. He works very closely with the king and the sentinels. His mate isn't here, possibly because he's not direct family, and these are very close-knit ceremonies. It isn't unusual to only see one's brothers and their mates, unless there's an equivalent familial connection."

Zayda paused for a couple of seconds, considering Keitaro's words. "Then Natalia thinks of me as her family?"

Keitaro shrugged. "She must, or we wouldn't be here. In a way, it makes sense..."

Zayda tilted her head to the side, processing the vampire's words, and then she drew in a deep breath for courage. "And the other one..." Her voice trailed off to a whisper. "Good Lord, Keitaro, he's absolutely petrifying. I don't know if I can go near him. He's...he looks like...from what you've described, he looks like he's from the house of Jaegar!"

Keitaro barked a good-natured laugh. "That's Saber Alexi-ares, and I assure you—he's one of us, one of Napolean's sentinels. As long as you're on the right side of the house of Jadon, you have nothing to fear from Saber."

She took a cautious step back. "The king." She swayed in place. "At the tip of the pier."

Keitaro braced the small of her back with one hand to steady her. "Yes. That's Napolean Mondragon—he's here to officiate the ceremony. I assure you, he's harmless as well." He paused to rethink those words. "Okay, so *harmless* and *Napolean* don't belong in the same sentence, but I assure you, he is no threat to you."

Zayda gulped, trying to settle her nerves. "Well..." She rubbed a sweaty palm against her dress. "And to think, I used to believe the guards in The Fortress were the most dangerous and menacing men I'd ever seen. They look like harmless children compared to these beings." She shook her head in wonder. "Your race is unbelievable...kind of horrifying, really."

Keitaro laughed out loud again before considering his next words carefully. "So is yours, Zayda. Formidable, I mean. The lycanthrope. Don't forget, your race hunts ours by instinct."

Zayda turned to face him. "Keitaro, you don't think—" She licked her bottom lip in a curiously wolverine gesture without even realizing it. "The sentinels—are they going to have a problem with me being here? With my species? Will they fear that I might do something...instinctual?"

Keitaro shook his head in earnest. "No, Zayda. I think they're going to be aware of you, and I think they will have a guarded respect for your nature. But believe me when I tell you: The sentinels don't fear much of anything—or anyone—no matter what race one comes from. They serve our king for a reason."

At this, Zayda shuddered.

"Too strong?" Keitaro asked.

She hesitated. "Maybe just too real." She started to reach out for his hand, once again, then immediately pulled it back. Natalia Giovanni was walking up the path, heading in their direction, and she looked like a supermodel in her strapless summer dress: a light, golden antique cotton, with three simple bows stitched across the front, and three billowing layers, falling to mid-thigh, displaying long, shapely legs. Zayda's eyes zeroed in on the proud cast of Natalia's shoulders, then her level chin, and possibly, her easy gait—Keitaro could not be sure—before traveling naturally to the hem of the dress: The back fell a little longer than the front, perhaps to mid-calf, and the material rippled as Natalia walked, sweeping against her smooth, bronzed skin in rhythmic waves.

Zayda's hand shot self-consciously to her thick lion's mane of wild amber locks, and Keitaro wondered for a moment: Did she have any idea just how beautiful she really was? "Zayda, you look lovely," he whispered, so only she could hear.

She briefly shut her eyes, her features softening with appreciation. "Thank you, Keitaro," she said, and the sincerity in her voice was both thick and earnest.

"Zayda?" Natalia called, as she approached within five or six feet.

Zayda took a tentative step forward. "Miss Giovanni."

Natalia shook her head. "No," she argued. "Mrs. Olaru, but please, call me Natalia."

"Natalia," Zayda repeated, shuffling a couple more inches forward.

Both women stopped about three feet apart. Their eyes met and their gazes locked, a lifetime of emotion passing between them. "Your eyes," Natalia whispered, "they're mesmerizing." As if she were viewing a priceless artifact behind a locked glass panel, Natalia studied the much shorter girl with an open show of reverence. "I've never forgotten them...or you," she murmured, and her own deep-brown orbs filled with tears. She fought valiantly to keep those tears at bay, but in the end, she couldn't hope to restrain them. She extended her arm, her graceful hand trembling, and waited for Zayda to take it. "I'm so sorry," she blurted, beginning to sob. "I'm so, *so* sorry, Zayda."

Zayda placed her palm in Natalia's open hand and swiftly closed the distance between them. "There was nothing you could do," she said, her voice sounding hushed and regretful.

Natalia's elegant, proud shoulders folded inward, and she began to tremble as she wept. "Oh, Zayda, if you only knew... there simply are no words...no way to tell you. In some ways, I was as much a prisoner as you were, but don't get me wrong"— she withdrew her hand and held it up in protest—"I don't mean to make a comparison—there's nothing to compare. What happened to you was unimaginable...unconscionable. My family...my father...that horrific fortress. Oh god, can you ever forgive me?"

Zayda didn't hesitate to respond, only her reply was wordless.

She wrapped her willowy arms around Natalia's equally delicate shoulders and pulled the trembling woman into a full embrace. "I'm glad you got out, too, Natalia," she whispered in her ear, and Keitaro had to turn away for a moment—the exchange was too intimate to witness.

He thought he heard Natalia whisper something next...

Something about mercenaries...something about obedience...

something about doing the only thing she knew how to keep Zayda and the other women alive—something about wondering if that choice, too, had been the ultimate privileged cruelty.

And at that point, Keitaro turned down his hearing and tuned the conversation out.

The Ancient Master Warrior didn't know how much Santos had shared with Natalia up until now: whether or not the sentinel was waiting for the perfect moment—for the naming and mating ceremony to be over—before telling his *destiny* about the fate of her father and Luca's goons. Needless to say, Julien Lacusta had made quick work of tracking his quarry, following the night of the raid on the Giovanni compound, and Luca Giovanni, as well as his right-hand man, Domenico, were no longer above ground.

The same held true for the four heartless mercenaries, men who had hidden safely in other countries, ready, willing, and able to slaughter dozens of innocent women at a moment's notice. It had taken the tracker a bit more effort to sniff the hired killers out, but money always left a trail.

Before he had passed away, Luca's deceased lawyer, Max Brazilian, had deposited the five million dollars each in four separate offshore accounts, and Luca's private ledgers had revealed the secreted banks and countries. Julien had started with the actual banks, and he had not needed Santos to hack into their records, not when he could compel the current managers to dig up whatever information he wanted. Going back over the time period in question, he had devised a list of all the banks' customers, those who opened or held such large accounts, and then, one by one, the tracker had paid each man on the list a visit.

A quick delve into their minds.

A quick scan of their memories.

And Luca's infamous henchmen had finally been revealed.

Had it been time consuming? Sure, a little bit. Laborious?

Absolutely. But Julien Lacusta was a vampire, and he could travel as fast and as far as he wanted. In the end, the world was better off without the miscreants, and since any loose ends in Natalia's life were now HOJ business, Julien had put the entire matter to rest.

For good.

The tracker had spared no lives.

Speaking of Julien, Santos, and the house of Jadon, Keitaro thought, *the warriors on the pier have got to be growing restless.* No sooner had the thought crossed his mind than Santos Olaru began to meander in Natalia's direction; his gaze shot up the hill to the females; and his large, imposing shoulders began to twitch with nervous energy.

Yep, the sentinel was getting worried.

And if Keitaro didn't call him off in the next two seconds, he was going to transport from the pier, materialize in the middle of the two women, and interrupt a very sensitive, important conversation.

Keitaro waved his hand and shook his head, trying to make eye contact with the anxious vampire. *Give them a few more minutes, warrior,* he spoke telepathically on a private line. *They have quite a few...threads...to unravel. This conversation has been a long time in coming.*

Santos nodded half-heartedly, but he didn't look reassured.

Just then, Keitaro heard Natalia say something about mercenaries...something about her father...and something far too vile to repeat about The Reaper, and Keitaro knew that Santos had told her everything.

And now, Zayda was also aware of the truth.

A light flashed in Zayda's eyes: Whether it was understanding, relief, or a spark of righteous indignation—the girl finally had some justice, albeit indirectly—Keitaro couldn't tell. But she was half Lycan after all, and now, all her enemies, including Xavier

Matista, were dead. There had to be some freedom, if not innate satisfaction, in knowing that truth.

"I'm only sorry I wasn't there myself to slit their throats," Zayda murmured in an icy voice.

Alrighty then, Keitaro thought. *Question answered.*

He shrugged. The female was different—she was wiser, more discerning, more even-natured—she wasn't impotent or dead. And she wouldn't be half human, or even sentient for that matter, if she felt any other way.

Natalia's throat visibly constricted as she swallowed what appeared to be mixed emotions and expressed her understanding to Zayda.

Lowlife or not, Keitaro thought, *Luca Giovanni had been Natalia's father.* And that's when Keitaro knew he needed to take his leave. The final layers in this tangled web were too convoluted for a third party's intrusion. The women would get through this together, and perhaps over time, the history, the memories, and the process of grieving—accepting and making peace with all that had happened—would be less of a burden, now that it was shared.

Perhaps Zayda and Natalia could help heal each other.

In truth, the world they now lived in was just as brutal and unforgiving—vampires suffered no enemies and took no prisoners —but Zayda and Natalia's futures were ripe with hope, potential, and protection, more than either woman had ever known.

Content in this knowledge, Keitaro Silivasi shimmered out of view, allowing the females to conclude their reunion in private.

CHAPTER THIRTY-FIVE

Now that Natalia and Zayda had joined the assembly on the pier, their emotions seeming to be more settled and an obvious bond forming between them, Santos breathed a sigh of relief.

He hated to see his mate upset, but Natalia had waited a lifetime to come face-to-face with Zayda—the little girl with the faery-princess eyes—and despite their candid, open conversation, Zayda would likely never know how her ghost had haunted Santos' *destiny* all those years or the power of the threat Luca had held over his daughter's head: the thought that a simple act of disobedience could lead to Zayda's death as well as all the other women's executions.

Santos felt a primal growl collect in his throat, and he swallowed the feral impulse, regarding Julien Lacusta instead—the tracker had handled the business. It was time to let that piece go. Luca Giovanni would never terrorize another woman, let alone his daughter, Natalia...

The woman Santos loved.

Santos blinked to dismiss the thought and turned his full

attention on his stunning *destiny*: Truly, Natalia looked as if she had stepped out of the pages of a fairy tale, herself, in that simple but elegant dress. And those smooth, bare shoulders; that regal, delicate collarbone; that long, shapely neck...

Santos needed to control his thoughts.

Later, he told himself.

There would be lots of time for that...later.

He smiled warmly as Natalia's eyes met his, and following the couple's cue, Napolean Mondragon cleared his throat, standing just a bit taller from the apex of the pier. "It is with great joy that I greet you this day, my brother, my sentinel, a fellow descendant of Jadon, a Master Warrior, mate to the daughter of Delphinus, father to this newborn son of Canes Venatici—the hunting dog who makes his home beside Ursa Major," the monarch began in a melodious tone. "What name have you chosen for this male?" His intense, penetrating onyx eyes, with their haunting silver slashes, fixed on the babe in Ramsey's arms. While Santos was the eldest of the three Olaru brothers, Ramsey was next in line, being born just five minutes before Saxson, and that made it his duty to hold the child for the ceremony.

His heart swelling with pride, Santos said, "Should it please you, my Lord, and find favor with the celestial gods, the son of Canes Venatici is to be named Laiseri Andrei Olaru." Despite his previous calm and his obvious joy, Santos' handmade Brioni suit suddenly felt a size too tight. He had wanted to look handsome for Natalia, but now he wished he had worn something a little more loose-fitting—say, a T-shirt or a tank top—the darn thing was strangling his throat!

Stressful much? Saxson purred in his mind, chuckling lightly beside him.

Very funny, Santos replied. *This damn tie feels like a hangman's noose.*

You could always strip naked, Saxson teased, *get to know the king a whole lot better, although I'm not sure Napolean would appreciate it.*

The gibe did the trick, and Santos relaxed, watching as Napolean reached out to take the baby from Ramsey's arms, and Natalia followed the king's every move, watching the monarch like a hawk, her dark, mesmerizing eyes instinctively going to Laiseri's head and neck, and the exchange of hands beneath the child's torso. She was making sure they were supporting him properly.

Santos' throat constricted, and he made a mental note to reassure his *destiny* later, to let her know that vampires did not break easily. Even if they dropped Zeri, he'd probably be okay, and even if something broke, they could probably fix it. Short of draining his blood, beheading him, removing his heart, or incinerating his body, the kid was going to be just fine.

Wow. Saxson dipped into his mind again. *Is that what you plan to tell her? Newsflash, brother: way too much information. Piece of fatherly advice? Don't use the words 'blood,' 'drop,' 'break,' or 'beheading' in conjunction with your child unless you would like to be incinerated by Natalia.*

At this, Santos snarled. *Get out of my head, Saxson.*

Ramsey grunted. *You're projecting, warrior. Take a breath. Chill out. And Saxson's right—you may as well prepare to put that kid in a car seat, add bumper pads to his crib, and get your ass chewed off if you don't cradle his neck every second that you hold him. Makes no damn sense, but there it is.*

Santos frowned for a moment. *Good thing our women didn't see how we grew up.*

No doubt, Ramsey grunted.

And this caught Napolean's attention. The fearsome king leveled a stern, heated gaze at all three warriors, ostensibly reminding them of the seriousness of the ceremony, and all three formidable vampires averted their eyes like children.

Both Julien and Saber chuckled in the background.

"Now then," Napolean said, strengthening his voice and regarding Santos directly. "The name pleases me, warrior, and there is no objection from the celestial beings?"

Have they really ever objected? Saber asked on the collective sentinel bandwidth, from his place behind Saxson.

"Saber," Napolean bellowed out loud, and the one affectionately called *dragon* smirked.

All humor left the pier as the sovereign king bent his head, his fangs began to elongate, and Natalia audibly gasped.

"It's okay, my love," Santos reassured her, placing a firm hand on her lower back.

"Be careful," she whispered to Napolean, and the ancient king smiled, the visage of those ivory fangs flashing in the waning sunlight possibly making things worse.

Santos caressed Natalia's back as the king pierced the child's wrist vertically along his radial artery and drank slowly from his vein.

Natalia swayed to her right, and Santos caught her, setting her back upright. "Breathe, *cara mia*," he whispered in her ear. "Everything is fine." Laiseri squirmed a bit, but he didn't cry out, and this seemed to satisfy his mother. She smoothed the skirt of her tri-layered dress, straightened her back, and raised her chin, all at once filling Santos' heart with warmth.

Napolean sealed the wound with venom and held the child away from his body so he could look into Laiseri's eyes. "Welcome to the house of Jadon, Laiseri Andrei Olaru. May your life be filled with peace, triumph, and purpose. May your path always be blessed."

He gave the child back to Ramsey, who pressed an unusually tender kiss on the baby's forehead. "Welcome to our family, Laiseri Andrei Olaru, and to the house of Jadon. May your life be filled with peace, triumph, and purpose. May your path always be blessed."

Saxson took the baby next and repeated the refrain before passing him to Tiffany, who then passed him to Kiera.

Julien, Saber, and Keitaro went next, while Zayda watched on with fondness and appreciation—she was not a member of the house of Jadon, but she certainly seemed right at home, and she could not have looked happier for Natalia, which raised her estimation in Santos' eyes.

Once Laiseri had been greeted by everyone, he was given back to his father, who held him against his heart and pulled Natalia beneath his arm.

Napolean addressed the couple directly. "By the laws which govern the house of Jadon, I accept your union as the divine will of the gods and hereby sanction your mating. Natalia Antoinette Giovanni-Olaru, do you come now of your own free will to enter the house of Jadon?"

Natalia's dark, mocha eyes beamed with hope and love, the honey-brown sparkles woven into their depths alighting with true sincerity. "I do."

"Hold out your wrist," Santos instructed, and Natalia didn't hesitate to do so.

She neither cringed nor whimpered as Napolean raised her arm to his mouth, bent to pierce her vein, and shrouded his fangs with his long, silver-and raven-black locks.

She closed her eyes as he drank, which made Santos feel a bit...funny...but he wasn't about to challenge his king, ask if he might be taking a little too long. Once again, Saber Alexiares snickered in the background, and Santos knew the other vampires were catching his territorial vibe. He took a long, deep, calming breath and waited for the monarch to finish.

Finally, he thought, as Napolean pulled away, sealed the

puncture wounds, and smiled at the couple—at the family—like nothing uncomfortable had just happened.

Natalia seemed fine and completely unaware of Santos' momentary discomfort. At least her eyelids were open, and she hadn't moaned aloud—that would have been pretty incendiary.

Napolean regarded Santos thoughtfully. "You good?"

Santos bit his bottom lip, then forced a respectful nod. "Never better, milord."

Napolean laughed softly. "Very well." He held up both hands, congratulated the couple, and just like that, the ceremony was over.

Santos' shoulders relaxed, and he loosened his tie, even as Zayda crowded forward and asked if she could hold the baby.

Santos thought he said yes.

He thought he passed Laiseri over gently...carefully...but the entire moment was a blur.

He was too absorbed in thoughts of his *destiny* to pay attention to any of the guests. A soft ray of sunlight was streaming from behind a fluffy white cloud, even as the golden orb began to dip beneath the mountain skyline, giving way to dusk, and the golden glitter shimmered off the hidden lake like a celestial nimbus, radiating around the couple and the pier. And in that moment, it was all so crystal clear: how well Santos and Natalia were truly suited...

Yes, her beauty was astounding, and his attraction to his mate ran bone deep—*blood deep*—but that was only the tip of the iceberg. Natalia Antoinette had an overdeveloped left brain; it was evident in her quick wit, her problem-solving, her computer prowess, and her expert hacking. Yet that day he had found her in the barn with Midnight, she had sought solitude in nature and repose from the bustle of life. By comparison, Santos was also considered a genius in the house of Jadon, a guru with electronics and technology, yet he chose to live beside a hidden crystal lake—he needed the isolation and the tranquility.

Serenity aside, and at the end of the day, Santos was still a sentinel in the house of Jadon: a mercenary, a hunter, and a hired killer who would protect the Vampyr and his king with his life. He did what needed to be done in a brutal world filled with vampires, lycans, and formidable human enemies.

That could have made him unapproachable.

It could have made a life with him seem daunting or overwhelming...

But Natalia Giovanni was no stranger to violence, conflict, or martial duty—she wasn't a shrinking violet, and she wouldn't shy away from darkness or brutality.

She had accompanied Santos to the dark twin's sacrifice.

And she had been stoic, strong, and infinitely supportive.

Yes, the celestial gods had truly gotten this one right.

And Santos Olaru would be forever grateful...

He turned to his *destiny*, ArabianNight500, enfolded her in his arms, and whispered harshly in her ear, "Do you have any idea how much I want you? How badly I need you? How deeply I love you, *vita mia?*"

Not *my dear*.

Not *my heart*.

He called her *my life*...

She laid her head on his chest, pressed her ear to his heart, and sighed in utter contentment. "Sentinel2000," she whispered, "I waited for you for a lifetime."

EPILOGUE

Gwendolyn Hamilton hugged her knees to her chest as she perched on the large, uneven boulder and watched the team of vampires—*yes, vampires!*—continue to inspect the old cobblestone well. Her captors were an unlikely crew: Braden Bratianu, the tall, muscular, good-looking hero who had rescued her from The Fortress; Kristina Silivasi, Braden's girlfriend or companion—Gwen wasn't quite sure what the redhead was to Braden, other than extremely possessive over every inch of his hard-cut body; Deanna Dubois, who was a stunning beauty with a generous spirit to match; and Deanna's mate, Nachari Silivasi, who honestly defied common words.

Nachari was extraordinary.

The kind of gorgeous that stole a woman's breath, made her lose her words and stutter, and caused her heart to skip a beat every time he spared her a glance.

Yeah, he was that damn beautiful...

And, in truth, all of them had been nothing but kind, generous, and accommodating to Gwen since the moment they had taken her in at the brownstone. Kristina had bought a host of new clothes and shoes for her "boyfriend's" house-guest; Braden and Nachari had bent over backward to make Gwen feel at home; and Deanna had gone so far as to redecorate one of the luxurious guest rooms just to suit Gwen's personal taste—as if the panoramic mountain views from the private balcony, and the deluxe adjoining bathroom, with its decadent rain-shower and hammered-copper clawfoot tub, were not enough already. Gwen was living in the lap of luxury, and she was being treated like a queen. It was almost enough to make her forget her predicament...

Almost.

Not quite.

One simple truth remained: Gwen was still being held captive, against her will.

Nearly seven weeks ago, Gwen had been abducted from a ski resort and taken to a brutal fortress to be sold as a high-end prostitute and used as a human slave. Fortunately, she had been rescued thirty-two days later, but her rescuers had been a horde of vampires.

Vampires!

Immortal, blood-sucking creatures of the night.

Not only were they real, but they were living in Dark Moon Vale, and for some inexplicable reason, they refused to let her go. Yes, they were treating her kindly, and yes, they expressed regret for having to keep her "a little bit longer"—whatever that meant—but from all Gwen had learned and overheard, they could erase her memories of the entire event, fill in the time-gap with something far more pleasant, and deposit her safely, back at home in Denver, where she could get on with her life and her post-graduate plans.

She could go back to her friends—they had to be worried sick.

She could reunite with her parents, and lord knew, she

missed Mark and Mary Hamilton more than words could express.

Yet and still, here she was, her rear end planted on a rough, dirty rock, watching a group of ungodly beautiful creatures circle around a well like it contained the secrets to the very universe in its depths. Braden was taking samples from the stones and the water. The wizard, Nachari, was doing heaven-knows-what with his fingertips and some creepy spells, and the women—Deanna and Kristina—kept asking questions about invisible doors, portals, and the interior of the structure reeking with the smell of vampires, according to some girl named Zayda. And much to Gwen's chagrin, there was a whole lot of talk about something that sounded a lot like...*werewolves*.

No.

Just no.

Gwen refused to let her mind entertain the thought—she had more than enough supernatural freakishness to process as it stood. She was not going to entertain the thought of werewolves.

Just then, Nachari Silivasi placed his fingertips on a pale, wheat-colored stone that sat atop the well, and began tracing the dark gray mortar all around it. He had done this a dozen times already, outlining stone after stone—but this time, he absently glanced over his shoulder at Gwen, and the stone began to sizzle: The wheat-colored rock turned molten red; an electric charge filled the mountain air; and a high-pitched whir vibrated through the canyon.

The vampire drew back his hand.

He stared fixedly at his fingertips.

And then he blew what appeared to be icy shards over the singed flesh in order to cool it.

He touched the stone again.

Nothing happened.

He let his hand fall to his side, and he glanced once more at Gwen—

Nothing happened.

He placed two fingers on the rock, locked his gaze with Gwen's, and *pop, sizzle, flash!*

Flames, electricity, another buzzing sound.

He withdrew his hand with a quickness—his fingertips were literally on fire, but he didn't bother to put it out.

"Shit," Gwen murmured, standing up on the rock. *What the hell was happening?*

"Gwen," Nachari said in that smooth, cocky tenor. "Come here for a minute."

Gwen shook her head so briskly her ears began to ring.

He pitched his voice an octave lower. "Gwendolyn, come to me."

Deanna and Kristina backed away from the well, even as Braden drew closer, and Gwen's feet, defying her better judgment and willpower, began to inch their way down from the boulder. "No," she spoke out loud, trying to regain control over her body. "Stop, stop, stop!" She dropped onto her butt and scooted down from the rock. "Stop it, Nachari!" she shouted, realizing he was using some sort of compulsion.

His amazing forest-green eyes softened. "Shh. It's okay. Come. Take my hand." He extended the limb that wasn't burning.

"I'd rather not," Gwen squeaked, her voice betraying her terror. Up until this point, the vampires had never exerted their power over her, and Gwen didn't like it one bit. Nachari crooked his fingers, and her feet kept right on shuffling. "Please, Nachari. That well freaks me out."

"It's just energy," Braden offered, trying to smooth over the situation. "What'd you get your degree in, again? Integrative Physiology? So you took a whole lot of science, right? Think of it this way: Nachari's just doing a controlled experiment, but neither one of us is going to let anything hurt you."

Gwen felt her face flush and grow pale, as if all the blood was draining out of it. "His fucking hand is on fire," she argued. "And he doesn't seem to give a shit."

Nachari smiled, and despite her fear, her heart went pitter-patter. "I'm blocking the nerve impulses right now—can't feel a thing. Trust me, Gwen; it'll only take a moment."

Gwen's eyes shot nervously from Nachari to Deanna, from Deanna to Kristina, and from Kristina back to the wizard. They were all as surprised as she was—no one knew what the hell was happening with this well. Against her better judgment—and well, because she had no real choice in the matter—she slowly padded her way to Nachari and reluctantly took his free hand.

He held hers gently.

He rotated the trunk of his body toward the well.

And he placed the full palm of his burning limb on top of the stone in question.

There was an eerie moment of silence...stillness...hushed anticipation.

And then a neon bolt of lightning lit up the heavens, followed by a thunderous explosion, an echo so enormous it shook the stones loose from the cylinder before crackling outward in waves across the valley.

Another bolt of lightning shot up from the well—*not down from the heavens*—and the pure electrostatic discharge radiated outward in a horizontal circle, wave after wave of lethal energy coursing sideways through the air like a burning scythe chopping wheat from a field.

Nachari threw Gwen to the ground, dived beyond her body, and leveled Deanna and Kristina before the wave could hit them. Braden lunged on top of Gwen's back and shielded her body with his heavy torso. The once high-pitched whir became a piercing, deafening drone—a never-ending, cascading echo across the valley—as the group hovered beneath the fire line waiting for the sudden mystical storm to pass.

"Build a holding cell, Braden!" Nachari shouted from the other end of the well. "Draw carbon from the living organisms around you and bond each atom covalently to four other atoms." Even as he spoke, his hands were working furiously, and a thin, sparkling dome was beginning to form over the vampire and the two other women.

Braden arched his back, pushed up on his biceps, and raised his body a few inches off Gwen to call out to the Master Wizard. "A holding cell or a restraining cell? You want me to construct it out of *diamonds*? Nachari, that'll neutralize our power! It'll leave us completely defenseless!"

"I've already called out to Marquis. When the storm is over, he'll come and unlock the barriers; but yes, you need a multiple layered cell, constructed from the strongest element possible. Build it to contain and restrain—nothing in, nothing out. Braden, the only energy surge I've ever seen like this was from Napolean Mondragon, when he was harnessing the freakin' sun. This storm is being created by a vampire, and whoever he is, he's drawing from my power—he's a thousand times stronger than you or I. If you don't build that cell, you and Gwen will die."

* * *

Thump-thump.

Thump-thump.

Thump-thump.

The vampire's arcane heart beat in his chest at a steady, even rhythm just as it had done for decades...centuries...millennia.

He was aware of no one.

He was aware of nothing.

He had not been aware for over twenty-eight hundred years...

At least not until now—not until he felt a subtle prick of magic piercing his blood-starved organ: the sensation of familiar power; the taint of another wizard; the pulse of a singular woman's heartbeat.

Destiny...destiny...destiny.

His *destiny?*

The word was as odd as it was unfamiliar, yet it rang inside his ears.

And then something—someone—connected the circuits: her eyes, his power, a stone from the well.

All fell silent, yet again.

Then another connection, stronger still: *her eyes, his power, a stone from the well!*

Fabian's eyes blinked open, only to find darkness above, below, and all around. All the world was dark and dank; water and mud; earth and clay. The circuit closed once more, and this time, it was teeming with electricity, sorcery, and power: an undiluted pool; an unrestricted chain; a pure, untainted channel to the source that fed his heart...and awakened his timeless soul.

That wizard.

And that girl.

Thump-thump; thump-thump; thump-thump—his heart sprang to life, and he let out a thunderous roar, releasing a millennium of anguish, confusion, and famine! He was starving all the way to his core, the hunger gnawing, bone-deep. His muscles spasmed in agony, and his skull began to throb.

Blood.

He needed blood.

He needed *her blood*, and he needed it now.

And then his power flowed back into him like water breaking through an ageless dam, and he sent the full breadth of it lambasting forward, exploding through the grave...the mud...the sand...

The well.

Fabian Antonescu, the most infamous wizard to have ever been born to the union of a celestial god and a human mate, was lying at the bottom of a simple archaic well.

He was...

He was...

He was no longer in Romania, leading the convoy of warriors, a secret group of mercenaries, through the Transylvania Alps. He was no longer holed up in the southern Carpathian Mountains, hiding Ciopori and Vanya from their bloodthirsty brother, Prince Jaegar. He was no longer changing, suffering, wishing for his final death, along with his loyal followers, as claws and fangs and power beyond imagining assailed them...changed them...made them into something else.

And he was no longer in that rotting ship, being tossed about at sea.

He was...

He was in North America, awaiting Prince Jadon's return.

No!

He was lying beneath a well.

Starving.

Ah, yes...yes...*yes!*

He was Vampyr.

His hunger overcame him, and he called to the four cardinal winds. He tunneled one hand into the dirt and extended his grimy fingers, reaching for that wizard's power, the one who had spoken to the stone, and he suckled on the magick like a newborn babe, growing stronger, more determined...more alive.

He threw back his wild hair and embraced the elements all around him, gave vent to his feral nature, and became the untamed storm, lashing out in all directions. And then he exploded from the belly of the well, emerged into waning sunlight, and recoiled from the unbearable glare of the light.

Where was she?

That woman...

His woman!

The one who would feed him her blood?

He scanned his surroundings like a stalking predator, sinking down onto his haunches as he prowled.

Domes.

There were two carefully constructed domes...

Carbon.

Intricate bonds.

Powerful, magical weaving...

He tossed his head back and laughed.

Flicking his wrist in the direction of the nearest conical structure, he sent an explosion of diamonds scattering across the mountain, then reached inside the collapsing rubble and snatched the female by her arm. Her legs kicking and dangling beneath her, he drew her to his mouth, sank his fangs deep into her convulsing throat, and groaned in exquisite pleasure.

Ah, yes...

Blood.

Release.

Destiny.

Still drinking to his heart's content, he wrapped a firm, unyielding arm around the female's waist and dove back into the well.

COMING NEXT: BLOOD ECHO
Book #11 in the Blood Curse Series

BOOKS IN THE BLOOD CURSE SERIES

Blood Genesis (prequel)
Blood Destiny
Blood Awakening
Blood Possession
Blood Shadows
Blood Redemption
Blood Father
Blood Vengeance
Blood Ecstasy
Blood Betrayal
Christmas In Dark Moon Vale
Blood Web
Blood Echo ~ Coming Soon

ALSO BY TESSA DAWN

DRAGONS REALM SAGA

Dragons Realm ∼ Book 1

Dragons Reign ∼ Book 2

PANTHEON OF DRAGONS

Zanaikeyros ∼ Son of Dragons (Book 1)

Axeviathon ∼ Son of Dragons (Book 2): Coming Soon

NIGHTWALKER SERIES

Daywalker ∼ The Beginning (A New Adult Short Story)

JOIN THE AUTHOR'S MAILING LIST

If you would like to receive a direct email notification each time
Tessa releases a new book, please join the author's mailing
list at...

www.tessadawn.com

A SNEAK PEEK FROM ZANAIKEYROS

SON OF DRAGONS

(Book #1 – Pantheon of Dragons Series)

He continued to take the stairs, two at a time, until he had passed her without incident, and then he suddenly stopped in midstride and spun around to face her.

She sensed it more than she saw it.

She could literally *feel* his domineering presence behind her, and despite her immediate impulse to *run*, she turned to face him instead.

The stranger tilted his head to the side and emitted some strange, feral sound. It was almost like a snarl, and Jordan's heart began to race. They locked eyes a second time, and she almost let out a yelp: He was glaring at her now, like she had stolen his first-born child, his dark, sculpted brows creased into a frown.

She unwittingly took a step back, clutched the rail, once again, for stability, and stifled a terrified gasp. Determined to appear calm, she stuffed her free hand into her pocket, hunched her shoulders in some instinctive, submissive gesture, and slowly backed away, feeling carefully for each stair beneath her.

He took a casual step toward her, and she almost bolted.

He halted, almost as if he dared not frighten her any further, and then he did the oddest, most animalistic thing: He inhaled deeply, sniffed the air, and he *groaned.*

Whether it was a groan of annoyance, impatience, or anger, Jordan had no idea, but that was the final straw—she had no intention of sticking around to find out.

Releasing the rail, she spun around in a whirl, leaped the four remaining stairs—almost twisting her ankle—and took off running for her car, all the while digging frantically for her keys as she ran. She could hear the stranger's footsteps behind her, and she cringed at the stupidity of her choice. *Why hadn't she screamed or tried to push past him? Headed back in the direction of the mall, to the safety of other people?*

Rounding the corner of the parking garage, she eyed her forest-green, metallic BMW, only five spaces away, and rotated her key-fob in her hand, pressing the *unlock* button over and over, just to be sure it opened. She glanced over her shoulder to judge the distance between herself and the stranger, and gasped, her feet skidding to a sudden halt.

He wasn't there.

Even though she could have sworn she'd heard his footsteps just moments ago, the man was no longer behind her.

She pressed her hand to her heart and fought to catch her breath, feeling a curious mixture of both relief and embarrassment. She scanned the garage in all four directions, making sure she hadn't overlooked his presence, that he wasn't hiding behind a nearby post or a vehicle, and then she started once again for her car.

Angry tears filled her eyes as she finally reached her BMW, yanked on the door handle, and bent to climb inside.

"*Stop.*" An *invisible* hand snatched her by the arm, slammed her door shut behind her, and pressed her back against the driver's-side panel. And then, just like that, the stranger was standing, once again, in front of her.

What the hell!?

ABOUT THE AUTHOR

Tessa Dawn grew up in Colorado, where she developed a deep affinity for the Rocky Mountains. After graduating with a degree in psychology, she worked for several years in criminal justice and mental health before returning to get her master's degree in nonprofit management.

Tessa began writing as a child and composed her first full-length novel at the age of eleven. By the time she graduated high school, she had a banker's box full of short stories and novels. Since then, she has published works as diverse as poetry, greeting cards, workbooks for kids with autism, and academic curricula. Her Dark Fantasy/Gothic Romance novels represent her long-desired return to her creative-writing roots and her passionate flair for storytelling.

Tessa currently splits her time between the Colorado suburbs and mountains with her husband, two children, and "one very crazy cat." She hopes to one day move to the country, where she can own horses and what she considers "the most beautiful creature ever created"—a German shepherd.

Writing is her bliss.